*Dark*LIGHT

BOOK 1 OF THE DARK LIGHT SERIES

S.L. JENNINGS

Dark Light

For friends that always pick you up
when you fall
And catapult you when you want to
fly.

And for my Forever.
xoxo

MARCH 23RD

Oh, what a difference a year makes.

A year ago, I was the embodiment of a reckless nineteen year old girl, hell-bent on drinking my way through community college until I couldn't function and not giving a damn how it made me look. A year ago, I was madly in love with my best friend, Jared, but couldn't find the courage to tell him. A year ago, the only family I knew of was Chris and Donna, my adopted parents since the day I was born. A year ago, I was content with mediocrity and my love life was non-existent–exactly what I thought it should be.

A year ago, I was human. At least I thought I was.

It's easy to take something as conventional as your humanity for granted when it isn't threatened. And being that I had no idea what life would be like without mine, I lived it up like there was no tomorrow. Now I have an eternity of tomorrows, and the last twenty years seem more like a fairy tale than my less than remarkable adolescent life. Because *my* life–the life that was predetermined for me, the life that so many have died for–is anything but ordinary.

The upside to my newly evolved existence?

Dorian.

Normally, hauntingly gorgeous and intimidating strangers would have me running for the hills. But there is something so inexplicably magnetic and all-around erotic about Dorian that I can't stay away. I want him; I crave him. And as hard as I try to fight it, I need him. But the million dollar question is *Why*? Why would any somewhat sane, shrewd young woman deem it necessary to completely throw herself at a man she's only known for a week?

And why would she show up to his freakin' hotel room at damn near 1 in the morning, unannounced and tipsy, just to see if he is alone and not banging the hot raven-haired beauty that followed him around tonight like a lost puppy?

Even as I step off the elevator and make my way down the hall to his suite, my stomach snarled with apprehension, the questions go unanswered, yet I don't turn away. I have to know.

What he is . . . enthralls me. Captivates me. Utterly disarms and beguiles me. And if I hadn't felt his soft, warm lips on mine, had never tasted the delectable sweetness of his tongue or his tingling, moan-inducing caress, I probably wouldn't be here, ready to strip away my clothes and inhibitions. I would have wised up and gone back home with Morgan. I probably would have even drunk dialed Jared and professed my undying love for him.

But it's too late; I have felt all those things. I know what it feels like to be under Dorian's spell. Because that is exactly what I am. And right now, I am about 2 seconds from learning the truth about him, eagerly hoping to unveil the mystery behind the man.

ONE

MARCH 15TH

Twenty is purgatory.

Not quite old enough to legally drink but too old to get away with being young and stupid without serious repercussions. I've never been the birthday celebrating type, usually opting to commemorate the day with Señor Tequila and a few of his heady friends. But this particular birthday, marking my 20 inconsequential years on this earth, in short, blows. Just another reminder of how I have no clue what I want to do when I grow up and will probably waste away as an overqualified, bitchy sales clerk at the mall. *Which isn't a far stretch from what I am now.*

Twenty years old. Twenty-*freakin'*-years old. Time to get my shit together.

"Here we go," I mutter as I pull myself out of bed and trudge into the bathroom to shower. I really, really would rather stay in bed and sleep through this day. There's nothing to celebrate. Pity party for one, please!

The only thing I have to look forward to is a night out with my best friend, Morgan, which never fails to disappoint. Morgan is my polar opposite in every way–tall, thin, and desirable to every member of the male species, straight and gay alike. She used to be a dancer and has the body and poise to prove it. With her baby smooth mocha skin, exotic Haitian features, and designer clothes, Morgan is the epitome of an 'It Girl.' Style is her religion; she lives and breathes all things fierce and fabulous.

Before our night of drinks and dancing, no doubt sponsored by some poor, clueless sap enraptured by Morgan's charms, I have to attend my annual birthday dinner with my parents. They, too, are my opposites but that's because they're my adopted parents and are about as patient and good natured as it gets. It's pretty evident that Chris and Donna are not my birth parents. The most obvious factor is that they're Caucasian and I'm . . . *Unknown*. How's *that* for an identity crisis? I never knew my birth parents and there is virtually zero information on them anywhere. Chris and Donna have tried to fill in the blanks but since I've been with them pretty much since birth, they are my real parents. And you can't miss what you've never had.

I turn the faucet on and wait for the hot water to kick in before flicking on the shower. Once the steam begins to billow out from behind the shower curtain, I ease myself in and let the water wash away my weariness. I could stay in here for hours but I've got class this morning and can't afford to be late again. Just a couple more months and I'll have my useless Associates degree. *Then what?* A 10% raise from minimum wage? I shake the question out of my head to avoid further frustration at my indecisiveness and finish showering.

After selecting a pair of jeans, a fitted t-shirt and some athletic shoes, I opt to keep my long, wavy hair down in observance of my special day. I usually flat iron it to tame the volume and loose curls but the clock is telling me it's not happening today. I apply some mascara, a little loose powder & lipgloss. I'm not really high-maintenance but I *am* a girl after all.

"Good morning, Gabi!" my mom squeals from the kitchen as she pours some pancake batter onto the griddle. She's beaming, her blue eyes sparkling with pride and affection. Her blonde hair is cut into a chin length bob, courtesy of Morgan, and she's wearing yoga pants and an athletic top. Donna teaches yoga and Pilates at a local gym so to say she is in shape is an understatement. She's got a killer physique but doesn't plague us with gym-rat propaganda or deprive us of our favorite foods, Thank God. I just regret that I'm usually too dreadfully hungover on the weekends to attend any of her classes.

"Geez, thanks, Mom," I feign embarrassment as I grab the fresh fruit smoothie that Donna makes for me daily. It's her one healthy contribution to my diet that I'll accept because I actually like them. She can keep those funky teas and wheat grass crap though. *Ick.*

"So the big 2-0, eh, Kiddo? Any special plans?" my dad asks from behind this morning's Colorado Springs Gazette.

Chris's sandy brown hair is meticulously styled and he's sharply dressed in his usual suit and tie. Being a Senior Engineering Project Manager at Lockheed Martin, he definitely looks the part: handsome, well-groomed and to outsiders, intimidatingly commanding. But to me, he's the big softie that used to make blanket forts with me as a kid and cry at every one of my grade school play performances, even if I was just a tree.

"Other than slumming it with you two?" I smile. "Not really. Probably go out later with Morgan."

"Sounds like fun, what time should I be ready?" he chuckles, winking a brown eye at me.

Not many people get to see this side of Chris. Being retired Air Force and a former boxer in his youth, people are usually quite intimidated by him. The same has been said about me, which has secretly made me wonder if he and I could really share the same bloodline.

"Looks like another brutal attack, honey," Chris says impassively. Donna gives him a sideways glance and then shakes her head solemnly. "You girls better be careful tonight. And take your Mace," he peers at me from over the paper.

That was more for Donna's reassurance. Chris has trained me in hand to hand combat since I was old enough walk and he knows I can handle myself against any assailant. I've proven myself enough times in fights growing up, whether it was the typical mean girl or some ass-grabbing douchebag.

"Sure, dad," I say digging into my birthday pancakes and bacon.

Classes are the same tedious, humdrum ramblings of useless information. Many of the students are buzzing about the latest 'Ice pick Murder' and there are even rumors of the campus closing until further notice. A third young girl was found dead from what seems to be thin stab wounds around the neck and chest. It's as if the psycho was purposely aiming for the jugular. A shiver runs down my spine and I glance around me as I read quietly in the atrium between classes.

"Happy Birthday, Beautiful," a deep, velvety voice murmurs.

I look up to find my good friend, Jared, beaming down at me. We've been close since high school and I've always been drawn to his laid back demeanor and sincerity. Being over 6 feet tall, with sparkling emerald eyes and a hard, muscular body, Jared is clearly more than a catch. His humble, good natured attitude makes him that much more attractive. He could have gone off to any college of his choosing to play soccer but when his mom was diagnosed with breast cancer 3 years ago, he opted to stay local. He is just an all-around good guy and one of the few people I genuinely love.

Jared sits then pulls a little box out of his backpack and hands it to me tentatively. I'm tempted to stow it and open it at another time when I'm more equipped to handle my vulnerability but I don't want to offend him. I open the box and inside lays a little silver picture frame, enclosing a photo of Jared and me in the 9th grade. I was new and quickly made enemies among the popular girls who felt threatened by me and Jared willingly took me under his wing. The picture was taken outside of my house, when Jared picked me up (chauffeured by his older brother, James) for the Fall Formal. I wore a dark plum dress, my long, dark curls cascading down my back. My Dulce de Leche complexion looked clear and radiant though I was visibly anxious standing next to a dapper young Jared in my department store frock. Even then, Jared was handsome: chestnut hair, bright smile and glittering green eyes.

"Oh Jared . . . I love it," I choke, my voice trembling. *Do not cry . . . You better not freakin' cry!*

He really is one of my oldest, dearest friends. And while I may have admired his good looks in secret, our friendship is exceedingly more important than any romantic possibilities. I quell the foreign thoughts and clear my throat in an over-exaggerated manner.

"Glad you like it. So, um, any plans for tonight?" The static in the air from the tender moment swirls and sticks to us like humidity and I'm thankful for the changed subject.

"Dinner with the folks, drinks downtown . . . You game?"

"Hell yeah!" he exclaims and we fall back into being normal.

Dinner is at an upscale steakhouse in downtown Colorado Springs and Chris spares no expense. It's dimly lit, plush and I get a whiff of mouthwatering meats, leather and big spenders as we are greeted by the prim and polished hostess. I immediately regret simply upgrading my shirt and replacing my white tennis shoes with plain black heels. From what I can see, most of the women are donned in cocktail dresses in rich, lush fabrics with the killer heels to match. Morgan would not be pleased with me if she could see me now.

"This is a special occasion, how about some wine, Kiddo?" Chris asks once we are seated. He isn't overly strict and knows that I enjoy the occasional drink (or 2 or 3 or 8), but he's never offered alcohol outside the privacy of our home.

"Sure, dad," I reply, shyly, as if I'm 12 again, sneaking a taste of cheap, water-downed beer.

Chris orders a delicious, full-bodied bottle of red that I'm sure is substantially pricier than the $5 grocery store libations that I'm used to. It's the perfect combination of sweet and tart and feels like silk in my mouth. I let my eyes close and feel the smooth liquid slide down my throat. When they reopen, I notice that I am being watched by a set of sad grey eyes. When I return her gaze, the young beautiful woman at a nearby table returns her attention to her mundane house salad. Her date, a much older and rounder gentleman, digs into his Porterhouse in ecstasy, his mock napkin bib catching droplets of grease and steak sauce. I instantly feel sorry for her; she's so slender, her pale skin clings to her protruding bones like glass wrapped in silk. It's evident that her waifish figure is no accident as she looks at her partner's saturated fat-laden plate in longing. Like Jared says, *'Homegirl needs a sandwich.'* I smile at our little inside joke, thankful that though I wouldn't consider myself skinny, I'm fit, strong, and comfortable in my own skin. Nope, I'm not a salad-eating chick.

"So Gabriella, any more thoughts about your plans after graduation?" Donna inquires, breaking me from my reverie. She is simply asking me; not nagging like most parents would when questioning their child about the future. Chris and Donna have never done that. They've always taught me to live for today because tomorrow is not promised. Now looking back at my underwhelming list of achievements, I'm wondering if they were too laid back.

"Not sure yet, still considering the military. I just don't think I can do another 2 years of college without having some sort of real passion for something. Plus I'd love to travel and see the world," I reply as our waiter places luscious entrees of steak and lobster before us.

"Just let me know and I'll go see the recruiter with you, Gabi," Chris chimes in before digging in with enthusiasm.

Colorado Springs is a true military town. Housing Peterson AFB, Schriever AFB, the Air Force Academy and Fort Carson, just about every person in town has some connection to the military. For that reason, the city is bustling with the arrival of new people and businesses.

"Honey, your dad and I have a little something we'd like to give you to help you celebrate your big day," Donna says towards the end of our sumptuous meal, her gentle eyes gleaming with pride.

She hands me a yellow envelope and an elaborately decorated gift bag. I open the card and 3 crisp 100 dollar bills spill out onto the white tablecloth. I look up in surprise; surely dinner is more than enough. Chris and Donna smile warmly, yet there's a hint of something else. Sadness maybe? They urge me to open my gift and I store the card in my bag to read later to avoid a public outburst of tears. Inside the adorned bag lies a beautiful Coach bag and matching wallet. I squeal with glee and jump out of my seat to hug them. Just as I pull away from their loving embrace, I hear the familiar mantra of the Happy Birthday song. *Oh no!* I cringe but my parents are so happy I can't bear to groan in annoyance. I graciously accept my decadent piece of chocolate cake and blow out the candle, genuinely thankful for the overwhelming amount of love that surrounds me.

Once back at home, I scurry to my room to prepare for my night out. Dinner has lasted longer than expected with the copious amounts of food and wine and I know Morgan will be here soon. Right on cue, the doorbell rings. Donna answers the door and I hear the click clack of Morgan's Louboutins approach my bedroom.

"Happy Birthday, Bitch!" she squeals holding up a bottle of Moet from her designer bag.

Only Morgan could look this stunning coming straight from her part time job at a high end salon. She's wearing a tight one shoulder coral mini dress and dangerously high heels. Her hair of the month, a long sleek jet black ponytail, sweeps her backside with each exaggerated movement. She's also brought a rolling carry-on that houses an array of beauty arsenal, all ensuring that I'll get the Morgan Pierre makeover magic treatment. She takes one look at the sleek black pants and flouncy black top I've laid out and cringes with disgust.

"Oh hell no, Gabs. This will not do you justice after I'm done with you. Here." She fishes out something from her carry-on bag and tosses it to me. It's a sexy black lace dress from one of Morgan's favorite stores, meaning it is way out of my modest price range. "It's yours," she smiles, showing off her magnificent, gleaming white teeth.

I get a glimpse of the attached price tag, realizing that it's about three times more than I've ever paid for a dress. "Morgan, I can't accept this! It's too much!"

"You can and you will. And you will rock the hell out of it! Now let's get you ready so we can go turn some heads," she says sitting me down and getting to work.

When Morgan is done creating her masterpiece, I almost don't recognize myself. My creamy skin looks flawless and my gleaming hazel eyes are accented by shimmering kohl. My lips are perfectly pouty and glossed and my onyx hair cascades in soft ringlets down my back. I smile my approval and Morgan hands me a glass of the champagne that she's expertly popped without alarming my parents. We toast to my birthday and her hard work and then head out to conquer the night.

We step into the lounge bar, surpassing the line of waiting customers huddled together trying to keep warm in the frigid night air. It's March so the temperature is still quite low, plummeting as soon as the sun sets. Of course, Morgan knows the doorman and he lets us right in. We bound up to the hostess station where we are escorted to a VIP table behind a red velvet rope. When Morgan goes out, she goes *all* out! Chilled champagne and glasses are stationed at the little table centered between plush leather couches. The lounge is draped in rich jewel tones and emanates a sexy Middle Eastern vibe. The lighting is a dim rose tint and I instantly sway my hips to the sensual tunes bumping from the speakers. The place oozes eroticism and I love it. I try hard not to look overly impressed and dazzled but can't wipe the stupid grin off my face. Already feeling the warm effects from the champagne, I let my steely façade roll down and replace it with a carefree smile. *This is my night.*

"Morgan, you sure know how to show a girl a good time! Who else are we expecting?" I ask noting the number of glasses at our table.

Right on cue, Jared, his older brother James, and their friend Miguel stroll up. After a barrage of Happy Birthday wishes and hugs, we toast to my official initiation into my twenties. I can't help but beam as Jared clinks his glass with mine, his green eyes twinkling under the disco lights. I honestly couldn't imagine celebrating this occasion with anyone else.

Over the next few hours we dance, laugh and drink to our

hearts' content. Between the champagne and tequila shots, my head is swimming and my inhibitions have taken a dive along with my already questionable morals.

I'm rocking my hips to Katy Perry's "E.T." when I catch the most magnificent eyes I've ever seen from across the room, instantly stopping me in my tracks. They are ridiculously light under long dark eyelashes. His gaze is unyielding, intimidating and almost startling. It's as if everyone in the club is suddenly frozen in time and he and I are the only two unaltered. I am so entranced by his glower that I hold my breath for what seems like several minutes. Someone taps me and I break free of his hypnotic daze. Only then do I have the privilege to marvel at the rest of him. Dangerously dark hair styled in chaotic perfection halos the most beautiful face, man or woman, I have ever seen. I can see his taut, muscular build even under the long sleeve black shirt and jeans. He isn't unusually tall yet I can easily see him above the mass of partygoers. Deep set, unbelievably light eyes, full lips, alabaster skin . . . I swear that I'm gazing upon an angel. *Holy shit!* And he's staring at *me*!

"Oh my God, do you know that guy?" Morgan asks me, following my gawking hazel eyes.

"Um, no," I reply, trying to sound impassive.

"Are you sure? Because you two have been eye fucking for the past 10 minutes," she chuckles, a hint of suspicion in her voice. She downs a Patron shot like a pro.

"Seriously, I've never seen him before," I insist, blushing scarlet. I glance back at him and he's still staring, unmoving. The contrast of his statue-still body with the rest of the rowdy partygoers is strange to say the least. It's downright unnerving.

"Mmm hmm, sure, Gabs," she taunts. And just like that she waves him over. My jaw hits the floor and I don't know whether to run or launch Morgan across the bar. *Dammit!*

The beautifully daunting stranger strides toward us, never breaking eye contact, not even so much as pausing to maneuver through the crowd. It's as if people are automatically parting like the

Red Sea. In what seems like seconds, the stranger is standing before us, staring down at me as I sink into the plush couch, secretly wishing it would swallow me whole and save me from the blow of rejection that is sure to ensue.

"Hi, um, I'm Morgan and this is my, uh, friend, Gabriella," Morgan stammers nervously. *Perfectly poised Morgan?* Nervous? Even she must feel the menacing vibes rolling off him. But I don't feel scared. I'm . . . intrigued. Maybe even a bit aroused.

"Nice to meet you," he nods in her direction, returning his unbreakable glare to me. "Gabriella," he states thoughtfully, enunciating each syllable. His voice is like warm honey, delicious and sickly sweet.

I sit up and meet his gaze. I don't back down from anyone, even incredibly scary yet gorgeous men in clubs. I give him my best 'hard ass' guise and nod at him rigidly. He regards my stance curiously and furrows his brow, a smile playing on his succulent lips. The change in his expression sends a jolt of electricity between my legs, something I haven't felt in many moons. I gasp at my body's uncontrolled impulse and he parts his lips fractionally, silently murmuring something. *What the hell?*

His face softens and his tense shoulders relax. Only then do I realize that the energetic buzz in our section has ceased and all eyes and ears are on our mystery guest, though he doesn't seem to notice. He is maddeningly confident and impassive, as if no one else exists. And at this moment, no one does. His mere presence consumes the small space and I swear the air has become unusually dense upon his arrival. He literally takes my breath away.

"I am Dorian," he states smoothly to no one in particular. *Mmmm, Dorian.* Even his name melts on the tongue like butter.

"Well, Dorian, please sit with us. Would you like some champagne?" Morgan sputters hastily, trying to regain her infamous Man-eater stance. She pours him a glass without waiting for a reply and holds it up to him. He carefully takes the glass from her and gracefully sits in the space between the two of us.

With Dorian in such close proximity, I am almost positive my heart will beat out of my chest and land in a goopy mess on the dance floor. I refuse to look directly at him for fear that I may freeze under those intense eyes, that I've now realized are ice blue. It is the lightest blue I have ever seen. I gulp down my remaining bubbly and smile meekly at him.

"So Dorian, what brings you out tonight? Special occasion?" Morgan questions. Dorian doesn't answer. He just continues to gaze at me intensely, so she continues. "Hey, it's actually Gabs' birthday!" My eyes widen as I literally try to spurt fire from them at her. In an instant, Dorian's eyes darken, a storm brewing behind the shroud of azure.

"Is that right?" he replies dryly with a hint of boredom. What the hell is his problem?

"Yeah, uh, she just turned 20," Morgan blurts out when I don't take the bait and offer any information.

Dorian shifts his body towards mine. He is so bold and sure of himself, it's weirdly turning me on, and I hate it! I breathe in his intoxicating scent, praying the rise and fall of my chest don't betray me. His unyielding gaze completely unnerves me yet I can't tear my eyes from him. I know I should; everything about him is screaming sex and danger. The combination of the two mixed with my weakness for bad boys could very well be my kryptonite.

"Well, Happy Birthday, Gabriella," he breathes.

Dorian brazenly takes my hand in his and strokes it gently, leaving a trail of icy tingles where his long fingers meet my skin, causing an involuntary gasp to fall from my wanting lips. He then brings it up to his face and lets his dazzling blue eyes close as he inhales the inside of my palm deeply. When they reopen, his pupils dilate and flash momentarily, his eyes becoming so light that they appear almost white for a split second. *What the . . . ?* He then lets his full lips brush the back of it, again causing the warmth between my thighs to quiver. Then in one swift movement, he's on his feet again.

His touch is . . . odd, to say the least. *Beguiling.* The intense tingling sensation almost stings my hand but it's strangely pleasurable. I'm panting, unable to form an intelligible response, and realize that I haven't said anything to him at all! He bows his head slightly and then retreats to the exit, disappearing from my sight, leaving me a panting, blubbering mess.

"What the hell was that about?" Jared asks suddenly sitting next to me. I didn't even notice the movement. "Mr. Stanger Danger looked like a serious mental case. One of your friends, I assume, Morgan?" he jibes.

"No, but I damn sure wouldn't mind if he was! Damn! He was sexy as hell!" she shrieks. "He only had eyes for Gabs here though," she winks at me.

"Well, dude looks like an ultimate creeper. I get a bad feeling about him. Hey, maybe he's the Ice pick Murderer! Gabs, you better watch out!" Jared jokes, though I don't return his playfulness.

I try to enjoy the rest of my birthday celebration though my heart is just not in it. I can't stop thinking about . . . *him.* Dorian. I've only just met him yet he has already claimed space in my slightly inebriated mind. The way he touched me was unlike anything I have ever experienced. And though the gesture was modest, chaste even, I feel as if he has exposed me–stripped me bare and naked with just a simple touch. I know I should be disturbed by my muddled feelings but I am anything but. I'm fascinated; downright intrigued.

After calling it a night and I am finally in the confines of my messy bedroom, I have to convince myself that I didn't just imagine it all. I touch my hand to my face; it just barely still tingles and I savor it, reminding myself that I was face to face with the most beautiful creature alive. I giggle dizzily and flop back onto my full size bed, landing on a box that crushes under my weight. How did I not see this? It isn't wrapped but has just a simple red ribbon tied around it. Tucked under the ribbon, is a handwritten note from my mom, Donna. I force myself to sober up to read it.

Gabi,

Now that you are old enough to understand, we feel you should have this. Read it. Form your own opinions and do what you think is right. We understand that you may have questions and your father and I will do everything we can to answer them. We know that you can handle anything; you are so strong and resilient. We sincerely hope that you don't hate us for keeping this from you all these years but you have to understand . . . this was a very time sensitive matter. It's difficult for us to explain to you so please, just read before you make any hasty decisions and I hope you can forgive us for our concealment.

We will love you always, no matter what you decide.
Mom

Hmmm, ok. That's strange, to say the least. I snap the red ribbon, suddenly feeling solemn and eager to know what information could lie inside. I hold my breath as I remove the crushed top of the box and exhale when I see the brown, leather bound book. Feeling silly at my angst, I open up the aged book, revealing a letter written to me on the first page. Anxiety again floods the pit of my stomach and I focus on the faded words scrawled on the yellowing page.

My Dearest Gabriella,

If you are reading this, you have reached your 20th birthday. I am so happy for you yet so incredibly sorry that I cannot be there to commemorate this day with you. I can only imagine how bright and beautiful you are. I want you to know that you were born out of immense love. Love so deep that it is worth dying for. You were born to be an incredible force. I know it may not seem like it now, but you will change the course for countless lives in the near future. Because of this, my child, it is important for you to know exactly what great responsibility this entails. In these pages, you will find the story of your past and your present. Only then can you write the story of your future. You are more valuable than you could ever know, believe me my sweet child. And giving birth to you has been my greatest honor. I love you so much. Thank you for choosing me.

Love always in this life and the next,
Natalia

What. The. Fuck.
It's from my birth mother.

My heart races at a dangerously rapid pace as I try to digest the words I have just read on the aged paper. *What?* All this time, not knowing who I was and the answers were here all along? So many times I felt lost, alone and abandoned and my parents could have eased that pain. They watched me fight my way through school after school and then come home and empty my tears onto my pillow. I don't even know my nationality, for Christ's sake!

Suddenly I'm furious to the point where I'm clenching my jaw until it hurts. I look down at my shaking hands as I let the book tumble onto the comforter. Instinctively, I stroke the area that was just kissed by the elusive Dorian and a shiver runs up my spine. I try to shake the feelings of anger and take my mom's–well Donna's– advice and read. There's got to be a good reason why they kept this from me for the past 20 years. At least there'd better be. Reluctantly, I pick up the journal and flip to the second page, afraid yet eager for answers.

I know you must have many questions and may feel as if I have abandoned you. My dear, please know that as I write these words, my heart aches with the knowledge that I cannot be with you in this life. You are everything to me, my heart and soul, and I will sacrifice all that I am to protect you.

In order for you to understand exactly what this sacrifice entails, let me start from the beginning . . .

You were born into an ancient lineage of Light Enchanters. We are Sorcerers. We have been known by many names—good witches, wizards, etc.—but we prefer Enchanters to separate us from other types of soothsayers. Our magic is one of the oldest and purest forms ever known and one of the most secretive. Do not be confused with modern society's perception of magic. Our power lives within us and cannot be acquired through chants, pentagrams, and potions.

WHOA. My head is spinning and my stomach curdles with nausea. The saliva in my mouth feels thick, my skin clammy and hot. I bolt for the bathroom outside my door and make it just in time to heave my dinner and drinks into the commode. Slinking onto the floor, I rest my sweaty forehead onto the cool porcelain of the bathtub. None of this makes sense. I expected my birth mother to be some reckless teenager, maybe even a drug addict. *That* I could wrap my head around. But she's some kind of Sorceress? How is that even possible? I immediately imagine pointy hats, long flowing robes and flying broomsticks. *Get the fuck outta here.*

As if the night could get any more ridiculous, I break out into hyena-like laughter, cackling until large salty tears run down my face. I'm not sure who would play such an evil trick but I'm sure I'm getting Punk'd. I wouldn't be surprised if Ashton jumped out from behind my shower curtain right now.

Once the wave of nausea subsides, I pick myself up, brush my teeth and wash off my smeared makeup before retreating back to my bedroom. Realizing I'm still dressed in the lace mini dress, I peel it off and slip on an old pair of sweats and a tank top then casually pick up the book as if it were some Clearance Bin cheesy romance novel.

I have nothing to fear. I don't feel supernatural. And there's never been anything magical about my life, that's for damn sure.

I've never been good at anything. Ever. Wouldn't I exude some kind of extraordinary ability in sports or be able to move things with my mind or something? This is surely some hoax or I'm a whole lot drunker than I thought. I open up the book, determined to prove myself right.

I know this a great deal to take in and you may doubt the validity of my words, so let me begin by telling you about the history of our people. From the beginning of time, the struggle between good and evil has always been prevalent. The fighting was brutal and innumerable lives were lost. Both sides, we Light Enchanters and those we call Dark Ones, or Warlocks, were in imminent threat of becoming extinct. Though we are immortal, we can be killed or frozen in time by magic. See, while most people roam the Earth unaware and unseeing of the truth, we were created to help, heal and spread Light. I'm sure that even in your society, there are stories of amazing people who accomplish extraordinary things, things that can't be explained by science or logic. Each of those remarkable people had the spark in them, whether they knew it or not.

But there were some so hungry and consumed with power that they broke away, deciding that they could command their destiny. It was much easier to use magic to gain riches and power than live humbly and do good works. In the process of combating their greed, we, too, became consumed with the taste of vengeance. So we were scattered and forced into hiding by the Divine Power. We formed our own social orders and cultures. The Dark Ones used their magic to gain affluence and authority, even in the human world. You would be horrified to know how many Warlocks possess significant status in government and religious branches. They have the ability to control the thoughts and emotions of mortals and use it freely. They are also known to be incredibly alluring, desirable and beautiful to human eyes.

Our people, the Enchanters of Light, feel more comfortable in nature. It speaks to us and gives us energy. We choose to blend in with human society by seeking humble roles that do not draw attention to us and our abilities. Many of us settle into positions as teachers, counselors and doctors, though some have been assigned in positions of power in your world. We place ourselves in situations where our gifts would be most useful. The modern day miracles you may learn about on television or read about in newspapers are actually the works of the Light.

My role as an Enchantress is a hunter. Our ancestors have been hunters since the birth of our kind. What we hunt are not animals, per say, but those who choose to do our kind harm. We hunt the Dark. We, too, can appear to be desirable and attractive to humans, but most importantly, we are fashioned to appear that way to the Dark. They find us, the hunters, irresistible and cannot control their urge to be near us. That is how we lure them. Then kill them. We are also incredibly strong, fast, and skilled in weaponry.

However, war and hatred has diluted not only our powers but also our resolve. I was incredibly gifted and determined as a hunter. The taste of Warlock blood completely consumed me and I wanted nothing more than to see them dissipate. Dark Hunters are nomadic so I lived an isolated life, scouring the earth alone in search of the next kill.

Of course, the Dark Ones have their own force of hunters. They are called the Shadow. The Shadow are more than just assassins; they are the law enforcement for the Dark. They, too, were in fear of exposure that could end their manipulation of humans. They had their tricks: changing their distinct appearance, downplaying their beauty, hypnotizing unsuspecting humans to do whatever they please. The defenseless mortals around them had no free-will, and were fashioned as slaves, playthings for the Dark.

While the Warlocks have a much more structured and intricate regime, we do have rules that must be followed to conceal our identity. Those who choose to disobey those rules are punished . . . harshly. The rules are engrained in us from birth.

1. Do no harm to the innocent.

2. Conceal the identity of the Light. And all other supernatural beings.

3. Never consort with the Dark. Ever.

This brings me to OUR story. The story of the creation of my precious daughter, sent to us to save our kind from hatred, greed, and evil. And the story of my demise; the reason I was put to death and forced to abandon you.

I unconsciously let the book fall from my fingers and take a deep breath. If this is a sick joke, someone has gone an awfully long way to create such an elaborate story. But part of me knows that this is no ruse. Though every fiber within me is hoping, praying for it to be fictitious. I can't be some . . . Enchanter. Or is it Enchantress? *Oh my God*, why am I even entertaining this garbage?

I clench my fists until the skin over my knuckles is stretched white and translucent. I will not succumb to such idiocy and read another damn word. Picking up the journal, I turn it over in my hands before throwing it against my bedroom wall. It takes out a couple old stuffed animals before landing open-faced on the floor with a thud. There's no way this could be real! There's no such thing as magic! No such thing as Warlocks and Enchanters, and Sorcery! *This shit is utterly ridiculous!*

And as if my anger and confusion conjured up some sleeping force within me, I began to feel the heat from my discontentment. I can feel it oozing from my pores, radiating in a fog around me. *What the . . . ?* I hold my arm out in front of me and I swear there is a reddish orange mist hovering over my skin, twirling and writhing before my eyes. It's like the feelings of doubt and turmoil are seeping right out of me into the vapor. My intoxicated haze has dissipated and I am completely abstemious. I feel so subdued, gazing into this auburn fog in awe. Seconds tick by but it feels like hours. Absolutely mystified.

My resolve falters for just a fraction of a millisecond and the mist is gone. It has disintegrated just as fast as it manifested, as if it were . . . *magic*. I'm alone again with my uncertainty and anger. But I'm also left with something else: A new found determination to find out exactly who I am and where I came from.

They say in order to know where you're going, you need to know where you've been. Is that why I've been so undecided about just about EVERYTHING? School, career, even my feelings for Jared? I walk over to retrieve the rumpled book on the floor before running my fingers over the worn cover and placing it gently on my comforter.

In these pages lie my past, and hopefully a glimpse into my future. Am I willing to take a leap of faith and believe that these supernatural beings really could exist? And as asinine as it sounds, could I actually be one too? Could there really be a secret, underground world full of magic and mayhem?

So many questions bombard my mind and there's only one way I can find the answers I seek. I have to keep reading. And whatever I may find, I have to accept it. Because this is me. This is *my* story.

THREE

The morning light greets me with warm kisses of sunshine. I chuckle at the irony and rub my tired eyes. It feels too early but my alarm clock tells me it's close to noon. I spent the better part of the early morning hours reading through my mother's book until I fell asleep, sometime around 4am. I had gotten close to the end, reading about my birth mother, Natalia, and her conquests as a bad ass Dark Hunter, hunter of the enemy race of Warlocks that had tormented her kind, our kind, for years. I smile at the read memory, wishing I could've met her. Anyone that could single handedly lure and annihilate an evil adversary is pretty freaking awesome in my book.

Wait a minute. So am I accepting this tale of fantasy and myth? Can I actually believe in this stuff? Do I really even have a choice? Nothing in my life has made sense and finally I have just an inkling of hope that I just didn't fall from the sky or come down in the mouth of a stork. I have to hold onto to something but can I really instill my trust in a fairytale?

Thankful for no classes on Fridays, I stretch and trudge out of bed, and prepare to face my next challenge: my mom, Donna. She's got some serious explaining to do and I've got a shitload of questions. She had to have known all along about where I came from. Why didn't she tell me? She must suspect that I'm in here, confused, hurt and angry with her and my dad. I have half a mind to stall and torture her with my silence. But that passive aggressive crap has never been my style. I put my big girl panties on and head to the kitchen where I know she'll be and decide to face this head on. My birth mother, Natalia, wasn't a punk, and neither am I. I guess the apple doesn't fall too far from the tree in that respect.

I make my way down the hall, passing my dad's empty study.

He won't be home until later tonight and I'm interested to get his take on my sudden revelation. He always seemed so up front with me, never treating me like a child and letting me make my own decisions. However in this case, information was withheld so I couldn't form an opinion. I frown in disappointment.

The kitchen is immaculately clean, as is the rest of the house, aside from my room, of course. Donna is at the sink, washing the blender she used to make my smoothie, which is sitting on the breakfast table. Suddenly our morning ritual seems tainted–a lie, like my entire life. I sit down and wait for her to acknowledge my presence. Seems like I'm not the only one who's stalling.

"Good morning, sweetheart," my mom greets me sullenly as she dries her perfectly manicured hands on a dish towel. She grabs her cup of tea and sits down across from me, eyeing me thoughtfully. Maybe she's expecting me to flip out and yell at her. Maybe I should. She fingers her blonde bob in expectation of my response.

"Morning, Mom." No matter what, this woman is still my mother. She raised me and deserves my respect.

Donna instantly relaxes and gives me a rueful half-smile. "So . . . I'm sure you have questions. Let me start by saying that we never meant to keep secrets from you. You have to understand. We had to wait for the right time," she explains. She takes a sip of her tea, opening the platform to me.

"*The right time?* How could you determine that? I've been lost my whole life, not knowing where I fit in! And you could've rectified that! And you wait all this time to tell me I'm some kind of supernatural *freak*?!" I feel my blood starting to boil and remember the mystical auburn glow. I instantly will myself to calm down in fear that it will happen again and scare the living shit out of my mom. "Look, I don't know what to think about all this. I don't even know if it's real. I'm just confused."

"Well, let's start slowly. How much have you read?" she asks.

"A lot," I answer. "But not all of it. I got to the part where, um, my mom, I mean, Natalia finds out that the Shadow are after her.

She goes into hiding in the woods, trying to prepare herself. You know, um uh, restoring her power. Getting stronger," I say, clearly uneasy just uttering the words out loud. This seriously sounds like a load of bull but if I want to get some answers, I have to speak up. I take a large slug of my smoothie to wash away the reluctance.

Donna takes a deep breath. I can tell she's nervous. "Ok, so what do you want to know?"

"Did you know my mother?" I ask meekly. I feel bad, referring to Natalia as my mother but that's what she is. Or was.

"Yes. Natalia was a great friend." Donna takes a deep breath and looks me in the eye. "She saved my life."

"How?" I asked. Ok, I didn't see that coming. I couldn't imagine Donna ever being in any danger. She seems so . . . *safe.*

"I am what people would refer to as Wiccan. What little power I do have, I was not born with. It is more of a spiritual connection to nature. I don't practice it much now because I wanted to keep it from you. I needed to. I couldn't draw any undue attention to you," she explains.

"Wait, what? So what . . . you're a witch or something?" *What the hell?* Have I been walking around blind for the past 20 years? What else have they kept from me?

"No, we don't like to say witch. It's more of a religion." She sips her tea and looks at me. I nod for her to continue. "I was alone one night, in the woods, practicing a spell. A Dark One approached me. I had no idea who or what he was, but he was gorgeous and alluring. I was mesmerized, almost hypnotized by him. I'll never forget his cold, menacing eyes. Sometimes they still haunt me at night."

Donna visibly shivers, clutching her teacup tightly in her petite hands. "I don't remember much of what happened but the next thing I knew, I was waking up on a wet pile of leaves with Natalia crouched over me. She told me that I was momentarily entranced by the Dark One and his will was to kill me and gain my tiny measure of power. That's what they do, you know."

"What do you mean?"

"They spellbind those who hold magic and suck out their power. Killing their prey is what makes them stronger, more powerful. Plus . . . other benefits." She shivers again. "The one who attacked me must've simply been bored to waste time on my miniscule magic. I was a mere flea to his power."

Donna stares down at her teacup with trepidation. I can tell the memory still unsettles her and I reach over to give her a reassuring pat on the hand to encourage her to continue.

"Natalia stopped him as I was just seconds from dying. Then she healed me. She could've left me there to die in order to avoid revealing what she was but she didn't. She was good. I owe her everything. " I can hear the emotion in my mother's wavering voice. I can tell she cared for her deeply and it makes me wish that I could've known my mother in that way.

"So she saved you. What happened to the guy? The Warlock who tried to kill you?" I ask. I'm on the edge of my seat but I already know the answer to my question.

Donna's eyes darken, her breathing becoming shallow. "She killed him."

This must still bother her after all these years. *What did he do to her?* But I don't dare ask for details, not after seeing how much the recollection of the attack still affects her. Whatever it was, it must've been horribly brutal. I've never seen Donna this shaken.

"Then what? You all stayed in touch? Became friends?" I want to steer the conversation away from the bleak remembrance.

"Yes, we did," Donna perks into a smile, looking up as if she's recalling a memory. "Since I already had the sight, the belief and acceptance of supernatural powers beyond me, my third eye was wide open since Natalia used so much of her own magic to heal me. Things became crystal clear. Everywhere I'd go, I could *see* power! So I could tell who had a little something extra." She winks at me.

"The Dark and the Light, disguised in plain sight as ordinary people–I could *see* them. It was amazing and frightening at the same time. All this time, thinking I was interacting with regular people, I was in the presence of great power. Power that could have killed us all in seconds."

She looks down and shakes her head. When she returns her gaze to me, compassion and solemnity are in her eyes. "You have no idea how much is out there. It's so overwhelming, I couldn't take away your childhood with knowledge of all of that. If you feel confused now, imagine how you'd digest that as a little girl. You would have never been free from worry and fear. And of course, you could potentially expose the secrets that so many have died for. They would have locked you in a mental institution. Or worse." *Worse?*

"So my mother, Natalia, she helped you. And in turn, you took me in?" I want to understand how and why Natalia had to die. And why she chose Donna and Chris to protect and care for me. "And what about Dad?"

Donna's eyes grow wide with question and apprehension. She's looking everywhere but at me. "Um, what do you mean?" she stammers.

"You know, Chris. My dad," I say a bit more condescendingly than I intend. "Did he know her too?"

"Oh, yes, Chris," she exhales, a hint of relief in her voice. I take note of it and file it away for later. "He knew her. She is the one who assured me that his heart is pure. She said he was a natural protector and would never let anyone harm those that he loves. I was so untrusting and wary of people after the attack. Chris showed me how to live again."

There's love in her eyes. I am relieved at the sentiment because I know that I was accepted into a real family, one built of real love. Not a constructed ruse to imitate a normal household for my sake.

"Are there many more like me?" I ask. I gulp down the rest of my now room temperature smoothie. *Ick!*

"There are supernatural beings all around us, but no . . . No one quite like you," she smiles. Typical moms, always thinking their kid is special.

"Why don't I have any magical powers? Aren't I part . . . Enchantress?" The word sounds ridiculous out loud.

"You don't but you will. Immense power. I don't know what kind though."

Immense power? I am momentarily floored. I can't imagine having power over anyone or anything! I can't even control my mediocre GPA, my hopeless love life or my crappy job. Which unfortunately, I have to be at in less than an hour. I'm not ready to end this conversation, not while my mom is being so forthcoming. How can I possibly work, knowing that there are mythological creatures roaming around? Now I can understand my parents' apprehension at telling me sooner.

After a hot, soothing shower to wash the stench of club smoke out of my hair, I take a long look at myself in the vanity mirror. I don't look magical. And there's nothing enchanting about me. Almond-shaped hazel eyes stare back at me, puzzled, searching for answers.

What am I?

I exhale loudly and commence to combing out my long dark locks. I'm more confused about my identity than ever.

I retreat to my room to pick out my outfit. One of the many downfalls of working at a generic retail clothing store is wearing their merchandise like walking, talking billboards. Luckily I get a pretty sizeable discount and most of the clothes are bearable. I slip on a pair of jeans, a tee, and flats. *Time to blend in with the common mortals!*

Work is as dull and mundane as ever. I fetch sizes and ring up purchases in my usual robotic, yet painstakingly polite manner. By 7pm, I am in desperate need of a coffee and trot down to Starbucks during my break.

Sitting down in a comfy chair with my favorite latte and a muffin, I pick up a magazine that someone has left behind. It's a racy women's magazine, the cover boasting the 'Top 12 Oral Tricks That Will Make Your Man Melt.' I roll my eyes and reluctantly open it up, trying to distract my mind from the day's revelations.

After a few minutes of mindless distraction, I suddenly get a feeling of unease. A shiver runs down my spine and the thin hair on my arms stand at attention. A gust of cold air sweeps through the shop, causing me to tremble involuntarily. And my hand . . . it's tingling again. Tiny prickles like a thousand miniature icicles assault the same spot where the most beautiful lips embraced it less than 24 hours ago. I put the magazine down and go to grab my warm coffee in hopes to dispel the sudden chill. Only then do I realize that I am being watched by a familiar, mesmerizing pair of ice blue eyes.

Dorian.

FOUR

He's sitting across the small shop in a large leather chair, just a few yards away. *Holy shit!* What the hell is he doing here? As if my shocked expression was an unspoken invitation, he stands gracefully and strolls over to my table, standing directly across from me. I realize I've been holding my breath since I spotted him and will myself to let it out slowly. This man will not unravel me again!

"Gabriella," his silky baritone croons, looking down at my dumbfounded expression. "How lovely to see you again." He is perfectly pleasant yet he seems indifferent.

I haven't muttered a single word to this man, in fear that my speech would be incomprehensible. He's even more gorgeous now that I see him in the light, noticing that his skin tone is more olive than alabaster. His eyes literally glitter behind long dark lashes and his black hair is perfectly disheveled. Oh, what I wouldn't give to run my fingers through his locks, to his shoulders, down his taut back . . . *Chill out, Gabs!* Enough of being star-struck; it's time to redeem myself from the night before.

I gather my resolve and muster every ounce of confidence within me. "Hello, Dorian," I say coolly. There, that wasn't so bad. "Please, sit."

"She speaks," he whispers, smiling.

Great, *of course* he noticed. But I don't have time to dwell on his perception; I am rendered utterly senseless at the sight of his stunning smile. He holds it for just a beat as he takes the opposing chair then he's back to mystery and pleasantries.

"I was hoping I would see you again."

"Why?" I ask a bit too hastily, my voice sounding unnaturally high. I take a sip of my warm brew in an attempt to swallow my giddiness.

"I'm new here. You seem like a friendly face. Those are so very rare these days," he replies without missing a beat. Even the most innocent of explanations sound like sexual innuendos falling from his lips, bathed in his deep voice.

His explanation would be feeble, and frankly, creepy from any other guy but all I feel is the warm flush of my cheeks and a deep ache from below. I look down to recover and mentally chastise myself for being so easily roused.

"Do I?" I ask looking up at him through my long lashes. What the hell has gotten into me? I don't play coy very well.

"Oh yes, most definitely. Very friendly," he enunciates seductively.

Ok, enough of this BS! I'm a melting pile of slush over here. "Ok, Dorian, let's be honest. You don't know me from Eve. Why are you really here?" I ask, satisfied with myself. I can tell my candor has caught him off guard and his eyebrows rise in surprise.

"I simply want to get to know you better. You seem fascinating," he recovers evenly.

"I am anything but fascinating. I can assure you that." Well . . . that *used* to be true.

"I seriously doubt that, Gabriella. Would you happen to have time to meet me later tonight? Maybe for a drink?" Ugh! There's that smile again. He's laying it on thick, and I'm lapping it up like a kitten to milk.

I will myself to play it cool as I mull over his question. "Possibly," I answer, secretly ecstatic at the thought of having more time with this enigmatic stranger. *Yes! Say yes!* I scream from within. "Ok, sure. I guess I can do that. But you have to promise me one thing."

"Anything," he breathes, sending my hormones into overdrive.

"Cut the shit. I'm not some giggling schoolgirl and I don't take kindly to games. So save the googly eyes and phone sex voice." And with that, I stand and throw my trash into a nearby bin, and stride boldly out of the café. "And I get off at 9:30," I say over my shoulder as I make my dramatic exit.

Hell yes! I squeal to myself. I literally dig my fingernails into my hand to keep from turning around to read his expression.

At 9:20, I retreat to the stockroom bathroom to primp for my date. I'm way more excited and nervous than I'll admit to myself. I fish my small makeup pouch from my new tote and commence to applying fresh coats of powder, mascara and lipgloss. I expertly line my eyes, courtesy of Morgan's tutorial, and finger-comb my waves. Waving goodbye to my co-workers, I take a deep breath before exiting out through the employee entrance.

I step out and see random store workers but no sign of Dorian. *Humph*, for someone so adamant to get to know me, you would think he'd be on time. I glance at my watch; 9:30 on the dot. I try to stifle my disappointment and resolve to head to my car and go home if he doesn't show up in a few minutes. I'm not a spoiled princess but I'll be damned if I wait around outside in the cold for some guy I don't even know, even if he is ridiculously gorgeous and alluring.

Then it hits me . . . I didn't even tell Dorian where to meet me! I was so overwhelmed by his mere presence that once again, I turned into the bumbling village idiot, totally ignorant of conventional civilities and dialogue. *Good going, Gabs.*

Begrudgingly, I start to fish my keys out of my purse, and panic when I don't see them. I pat my jacket pockets and come up empty. I peer into my purse again and find them in one of the many pockets. Whew! I sigh with relief and grasp them to my chest. Deciding that I might as well call it a night, I step towards my car and nearly walk right into a broad chest shrouded in a dark leather jacket.

"Gabriella," he breathes, his smooth voice bathing my name in warm butter.

"You came," I stammer, struggling to gain my composure under his penetrating gaze. I clear my throat and square my shoulders. "You're late."

"No, I don't think so," he says confidently.

Arrogant douche. I look down at my watch, prepared to prove his tardiness despite my own oversight, and it reads 9:29. Crap, looks like my battery has died. I shrug off my misstep.

"Ok, then, where to?" I try hard to seem unaffected by my slip and our near collision. The thought of actually touching him excites me more than it should.

"Why don't you choose? I'm sure you know the area better than I do," he replies. I can tell he's trying to seem casual, putting his intensity on the back burner for now. I smirk with triumph.

We walk down to the nearby sports lounge in the mall complex. There are plenty of witnesses here just in case Dorian turns out to be an ax murderer and I just don't trust myself with him in a quiet, more intimate setting. Psycho or not, I may just let him have his way with me.

"What would you like to drink?" he asks, politely as we settle into a booth.

"Um, just a Coke, please," I reply.

He raises an eyebrow at me. "Is that what you really want? Please, order whatever you like." He sounds a bit offended as if I'm insinuating that he can't afford it.

"Well, I'd really like a beer but you know there's this little thing called a legal drinking age. Just turned 20, remember?" I smirk.

Right on cue, the buxom blonde waitress strolls over to ask us what we'd like to drink. She instantly flinches once Dorian looks up at her to order our round of beer. All she can do is nod in response and retreat to the bar to fetch our beverages. She doesn't even ask for ID, and I know I look young for my age. She's obviously flustered, and I chalk it up to his captivating glacial stare and smoldering good looks. But when she returns with the beer, I catch a hint of fear in her stance. She looks down, attempting to avoid eye contact, her small mouth fixed into a tight, rigid line. Her hands wring her small black apron until her knuckles are white. Suspicion nags at the back of my head.

"Um, an ex of yours?" I ask once the waitress is out of earshot. I casually wave my hand in her direction. Dorian tears his eyes from mine and momentarily glances at her. She almost cringes under his gaze.

"No, I've never seen her before in my life," he shrugs. I'm not going to argue with him. He has no reason to tell me anything; we're practically strangers. I let the subject drop to avoid humiliation.

"So, Dorian, what is it that you want to know about me?" I ask, and then take a long sip from my beer. Ah! Refreshing.

"Everything," he replies in a feathery breath. Then he smirks with nonchalance, no doubt toying with me by ignoring my earlier demand. "But I'll start with your hobbies."

"Ummm. I actually don't have any, really." It's the truth, sadly.

"No hobbies? So there's nothing you enjoy doing?" Dorian seems intrigued. He tilts his head to one side as if he's trying to figure out the secrets hiding behind my hazel eyes.

"Well, when the weather is nice, I like to be outdoors. You know, just soakin' up the rays. I like to hike I guess, though I'm no hardcore hiker with gear and stuff. Other than that, there's just not much to me," I chuckle, nervously. I know how unintelligent I must sound but being this close to Dorian, close enough to smell the captivating scent of his cologne, makes me anxious to say the least. "What about you?" Anything to steer the conversation from me.

"Oh, you know, the usual. Reading, sports, movies, music," he prattles. "So when you aren't out hiking, what are you usually doing?" He's really not going to let me off the hook.

"I'm a college sophomore by day and a lowly, underpaid retail clerk by night," I joke. "And when you aren't seducing young women in clubs and hanging out in coffee shops all day, what do you do?" I hope he's not put off by my playfulness.

"Seducing young women in clubs? Who are these women you speak of?" he grins back at me. Whew. Intimidatingly gorgeous and a sense of humor? Pinch me.

"Oh, you haven't counted all those pairs of panties that every chick in that club was throwing at you last night? Or did you lose count?" I snicker. Dorian returns my crass remark with a bemused expression, his brow furrowing for just a moment. "I'm kidding! Really. What do you do?" Maybe I shouldn't scare him off with my vulgar behavior just yet.

"Hmmm," he smiles slyly. "I'm in Law. But I'm taking a little break. Thinking about a career change."

"Law, huh? So like a lawyer? Impressive." Let's just add brilliant to his list of attributes. "How old are you anyway?"

Dorian looks deep into my eyes with such intensity I can feel the electricity radiating from them. The sparks sizzle through my veins, making a direct path to the pit of my stomach. It feels as if I've swallowed a handful of Pop Rocks. Then the sensation sinks down South, turning from a fizzle to an aching throb. I catch myself before I reflexively put my hands between my legs to coax my raging desire. I squeeze my thighs together alternatively.

"Twenty five," Dorian says. His lips twitch before spreading into a cunning smile.

"Huh?" I'm dumbfounded.

"You asked my age. I am 25," he replies. *Snap out of it, Gabs!* My face is red hot with shame. Somehow I think he knows my dirty little secret.

"Oh yeah," I recover. "That's really young to be so accomplished." I take a long swig of beer. "So tell me, Dorian, what brings you to Colorado Springs? Business or pleasure?"

Dorian licks his succulent lips and the dam breaks in my Victoria Secrets. "A little bit of both."

For the next hour, we engage in easy conversation, offering everything from our favorite movies to our favorite books. It's seamless, though I find myself getting lost in his eyes every few minutes. He acts as if he doesn't notice and we press on about childhood memories and first crushes. I am just thankful he's eased up on torturing me with his sex-drenched gaze. Maybe he noticed that I was turning into a pile of unintelligible mush and grew tired of trying to decipher my confused ramblings. Dorian is oddly . . . normal, despite his extraordinary good looks.

We skim through our family life vaguely, neither one of us wanting to give too much away about our personal lives. He has one brother and I simply tell him I was adopted with no other siblings. I've been so caught up in our relaxed exchange that I totally forgot to check in. Crap, Chris and Donna will be worried since I didn't come home right after work and didn't call to inform them otherwise. They probably think I went off the deep end with the sudden turn of events in the past 24 hours.

"Oh crap, Dorian, I gotta go," looking at the time on my cell phone since my watch is out of commission. I also notice a text and 2 missed calls but ignore them for now and shove my cell back into my purse. My time is ending with Dorian and I'm ashamed to admit that I'm sincerely disappointed.

"Can I give you a ride home? I wouldn't want to get you into trouble."

I politely decline then Dorian motions towards the bar, signaling for the check. The blonde waitress reluctantly strolls over and drops the small black folder without saying a word. After Dorian stuffs a few bills into the small leather black folder we make our way outside. I notice that my car is the only one left in the empty side entrance lot of the mall.

"Maybe I should be asking *you* if you need a ride. Where's your car?"

"Oh, it's around the other side of the mall," Dorian replies with his usual nonchalance.

Noting the extreme drop in temperature, a cold shiver crawls up my spine as we step out into the frigid night air. I pull my jacket around me, hoping to dispel the chill. "Let me drive you to it," I say between slightly chattering teeth.

"That won't be necessary. I can walk; it's not that far," he declines.

"I insist. Really. Don't you know there's a killer on the loose?" I say, waving him over to my Honda.

For a split second, Dorian grimaces as if the thought of a sadistic murderer physically pains him. He exhales nervously and reluctantly agrees. I'm grateful because I really didn't want to stand out here and argue with him in the cold. Then I wonder why Dorian was so hesitant to accept my offer. Was he lying about owning a car? Or could he be embarrassed of it? I reprimand myself for being so pushy and try to plaster on a reassuring smile as we ride around the backside of the building.

"It's right over there," he mumbles, pointing toward a department store. He really does seem nervous and a pang of sympathy grips my chest. I can spot a shadow of a car but I can't make out what type it is. I tell myself it wouldn't matter anyway.

I pull up alongside the silhouette and my jaw literally drops. I can see the sleek, dark frame of a luxurious sports car twinkling under the moonlight and am instantly flooded with guilt mixed with embarrassment at my mental misstep. It's a Mercedes-Benz SL 65 AMG, a car I recognize from one of the exclusive car shows Morgan has dragged me to, or as she calls it, 'Sponsor Hunting'. As if his looks weren't already so impressive, now he has to wow me with his exotic, expensive car? Mild humiliation washes over me as I take in my own 5 year old, trusty Honda Civic. Of course, he'd have a gorgeous car. It wouldn't make sense for him to own anything otherwise.

"Nice car," I stammer. "Black Series?" I only remember the model because it was one of my favorites, being that it is elegant and sexy without being too over the top. I try hard not to seem star-struck.

"Yeah," he mutters with a shrug. Oh geez, is this his play at modesty? I roll my eyes in the darkness.

"So will I see you again?" my mouth asks before my head can stop me. *So much for playing it cool!*

Dorian's mouth turns up on one side, the movement of his lips nearly causing me to gasp aloud. "Do you want to see me again?" he asks, his silky voice sounding even more sensual in the shroud of night.

"Yes," I answer too quickly, growing angry with my mouth for yet another betrayal. I hold my breath in anticipation and to keep from saying anything more to humiliate myself.

"Then you shall."

Dorian leans over just an inch, his alluring azure eyes finding mine, holding my gaze. With just a dim streetlamp illuminating his face, he looks so . . . dangerously delicious. I want him. And the realization of how deep that hunger aches within me disturbs me. I can feel the heat radiating between my thighs, the pit of my stomach quivering in expectation. I blink rapidly, breaking our reverie and force myself to focus on something, *anything*, other than his beauty. Or his body. A body that I want pressed against mine, limbs and tongues twisted and tangled, our flesh contortioned into X-rated abstract art . . .

Ugh! What the hell is wrong with me? I've got to get out of his proximity.

"I better get home," I stammer. I need to get away from him yet I don't want him to leave. I feel like my erratic emotions are being completely ruled by my hormones.

"Yes," he breathes.

Dorian takes another long, torturous look, causing my body to squirm one last time before he reaches for the car door handle. *No, don't go!* I want to scream, but for the first time, my mouth checks in with my brain and stays shut. Dorian clicks open the door and steps out gracefully. He fishes out a key and hits a button, chirping the gorgeous car to life. After a sexy smirk in my direction, he folds his muscular frame in with precision and revs it up. Then he's gone.

I gather my bearings, totally baffled at what just went down. I barely know this guy yet I'm imagining having sex with him? And not just any sex at that. I'm talking lip-biting, toe-curling, back-scratching, no holds barred sex. I'm no virgin, but the thought of intimacy with Dorian not only excites me, but scares me. Scares me because I want him so damn badly. I've never wanted anyone more, and so quickly at that. Dorian feels like a designer drug; I know I'm not supposed to do it but I want to anyway. And for that reason alone, I know I should stay away. *But will I?*

In an attempt to regain some sense of composure, I reach into my purse and fish out my cell phone to check my messages before driving home. It's a text from Morgan asking if I'm still alive and hopefully not too hungover, and the missed calls are from my parents.

Parents.

Just a day ago, that had a completely different meaning. If someone asked me who my parents were, Chris and Donna were the only names that popped into my head. Not Natalia and some mystery baby daddy. And since there was such an overwhelming lack of evidence that my birth parents even existed, I just assumed they were dead and even started telling people that. Now all of my unanswered questions have created new unanswered questions, leaving me more confused and frustrated as ever.

But at least there's Dorian.

His unexpected arrival into my once drab existence has definitely been a bright spot. Something different, mystifying, for a change. And after years of pining after a guy who only saw me as his BFF, Dorian's interest in me is more than welcomed.

An inkling of movement out the corner of my eye shakes me from my musings. I quickly turn my head to look in the direction of a group of tall bushes lining the side of the department store brick wall. I don't detect anything strange so I look down at my phone, beginning my *"I'm ok"* text to Morgan. But before I can hit send, I sense movement again. Only this time, when I look, I can clearly see the bushes quivering, as if something, or someone, is in them. *Just a raccoon*, I tell myself but I can't truly believe my own theory. I throw my phone back into my purse but when I look up again to put my car in Drive, I see that the bushes are no longer shaking. Instead there is a shadowy figure standing in front of them, not 30 yards away from me. It's too dark and too far away to tell if it's a man or a woman but I can tell that whoever it is, they are glaring directly in my direction.

Before I can reach the steering wheel, the figure is moving towards me. *FAST*. In an unnatural, ghostly way, it's closing the distance between us in an extraordinarily rapid pace. *What the hell?* Is it *floating* towards me? Like frames from a horrifying strip of film, the figure advances towards me in flashes of ethereal light, each mutated frame more distorted than the last. In the split second it takes to pry my terrified eyes from the approaching shadow, I gather my bearings and hit the gas, the tires screeching against the pavement. Whatever that was, it was unlike anything I'd ever seen. Yet something about it was oddly, horrifyingly familiar.

I pull up to my house in record time, thanking God for no red traffic lights or police cars in my path. What the hell was that? Before stepping out onto the driveway, I check around and behind me, ensuring that the coast is clear. Then I book it down the stone path and up the three stairs to our front door. I feel slightly foolish as I close and lock the door behind me and sink to the floor, suddenly exhausted with fright.

"Hey, Kiddo, is that you?" Chris calls from his study. Crap. He's waited up for me. I pick myself up off the floor and kick off my shoes.

"Yeah, Dad, sorry I'm late," I call out, reluctantly making my way down the hall to him, passing numerous family and school photos hung on the walls. A hallway of memories. It all seems like someone else's memories now.

Chris is at his large oak desk, only the light from his computer illuminating his handsome face. He looks tired and I know I've worried him with my tardiness. He looks up at me and grins, little lines crinkling at his brown eyes. I know all is forgiven. He seems melancholy and a pang of regret squeezes my chest.

"Went out after work?" he asks. I can tell he's dancing around the real issue. The issue of my biological mother and his part in the concealment of her existence.

"Something like that," I shrug.

He probably thinks I stayed out because I wanted to stall our conversation, and he's partly right. We stare in silence, neither of us knowing how to broach the subject. On one hand, I want to know more about my mother, the Light, and this new world of magic that I've been thrust into by birth. How does Chris fit into all this? Is he supernatural too? How does he feel about all this Hocus Pocus, being the straight-laced, no-nonsense guy that he is? Only one way to find out.

"So you knew my birth mother," I say. It's not a question but it's the only way I know how to get the ball rolling.

"Yes," he replies curtly. Ok, this is going to be like pulling teeth. I make myself comfortable and plop down in the chair across from his desk.

"Did you know what she was? Right away?"

"No, not right away. As your mother, I mean Donna, and I became more serious, it was brought to my attention." Chris drums his fingers against the arm of his chair anxiously.

"And how did you feel about that?"

Chris pinches the bridge of his nose between his thumb and forefinger, contemplating the answer. Then he rubs his weary eyes. I brace myself for the worst; he must've hated being coerced into all this.

"How did I feel?" He looks up at the ceiling and then returns his earnest gaze to me. "Your birth mother gave me the opportunity to meet the love of my life. And then furthermore, I was given the honor to love and protect the most beautiful, curly-haired little baby girl I had ever seen." His solemn expression morphs into a heartwarming smile and my apprehension melts away.

My new knowledge of my birth mother must be incredibly hard for them. Maybe they're afraid of losing my love. And with the discovery of a birth mom, comes the discovery of a birth dad. In all my confusion, I had hardly considered their feelings. They must be just as scared as I am.

Instead of launching into the interrogation I had rehearsed in my head, I get up and walk over to Chris and wrap my arms around his broad shoulders, giving him a heartfelt squeeze. He's been my dad my whole life and I honestly could not imagine anyone else replacing him, blood or not. I can feel him instantly relax and before either one of us becomes emotional, I release him from my embrace.

"Goodnight, Dad," I grin. He answers with a smile of his own and I turn on my heel as I notice his watery brown eyes. I'm not emotionally strong enough to see him unraveled.

I retreat to my disheveled bedroom and flop noisily on my bed, exhaling the day's events. Donna's Wiccan revelation, Dorian showing up at my job, having drinks with him after work, the eerie parking lot phantom . . . it's been a helluva day. That was no crazed homeless person in the bushes outside the department store. Whatever it was moved in a way unlike anything I've ever seen. It was ghostlike. Alien, even. The thought chills me to my core and I shiver uncontrollably. Seeking comfort, I look at my mother's book, resting on my nightstand. Surely whatever attempting to accost me tonight would be something she would know about.

Before I can flip to that page where I left off, my cell phone perks to life, indicating a text message.

Unknown, 11:46 PM

– Are you ok?

I usually ignore all unknown phone calls but an unknown text? Who would have my cell phone number? I know I haven't given it out lately. I think about hitting Delete but my curiosity gets the best of me.

– Who is this?

— Dorian.

Damn. Amazing how one name can hold so much weight and instantly make my heart jump into my throat. A big, goofy ass grin spreads across my face. Wait, how did he get my number? *Stalker alert!* Maybe Jared is right. Maybe Dorian really is a creeper. A ridiculously sexy, alluring, gorgeous creeper that I wouldn't mind being accosted by in a dark alley.

— Yes, why? How did you get my number?

— That is not important. You are safe?

Okay, now he's freaking me out. Why would he think otherwise? He was long gone by the time that freaky apparition-like figure came out of the bushes. Right? I quickly text *"I'm good"* and plug my phone up to its charger, putting it on silent.

As much as I'd like to chat with Dorian, I can't shake the unnerving feeling that something is wrong. Whatever was out there tonight was out to get me, I'm sure of it. Not only that, there was something strangely familiar about it, though it was obviously otherworldly. Why didn't I ever notice these things before? Never in my 20 years have I ever seen something nearly glide across a parking lot, not to mention with such incredible speed. It was mostly blurred, though I could visibly make out its eyes. Deep, vacant, icy eyes, fixed on me with violent intensity.

I shudder and pick up the book, finding where I left off the night before. I indulge myself in Natalia's account of her days living underground, preparing herself for her encounter with the Shadow. She was smart; it was two against one and she knew they'd have a chance to overpower her. Her plan was to have them come to her, on her grounds. No one knew the forests better than the Light, especially Dark Hunters. The Shadow would be disoriented, sitting ducks for her to take out at will. I was enraptured in her account and couldn't wait for her to strike, putting a permanent end to her vile pursuers. My mom: bad ass, strong and cunning. She was the epitome of everything that I've ever wanted to be.

I anticipate the Shadow's arrival as I perch high upon the trees. I can sense them; hear their voices echo through the still night air. I crouch silently in expectance of their approach. Though it is dark, I can see them perfectly. I can see the tops of their dark, glossy hair and dark suits. I've heard of these two. They have a reputation for being exceptionally brutal and proficient assassins. No Enchanter or Dark Hunter has ever lived to tell their tales of carnage. They are, of course, gloriously handsome but their beauty is a lie; an accumulation of stolen souls and siphoned magic. They kill without mercy and supply their constant need for more magic to refuel. The thought infuriates me and I thirst for the vengeance of the countless lives taken to feed their greed for power.

I wait for my chance to strike yet when I prepare to leap down, something stops me short. A force, beckoning me, calling to me. I look down only to lock eyes with an endless pool of pale blue irises. He doesn't look angry or vicious; he looks intrigued, curious even. Virtually silent, I leap down and face him. His looks are striking, unlike anyone I've ever seen. I know the Dark uses hypnotism on their prey but being a Light Enchantress, I am impervious to their charms. He doesn't flinch, nor make an aggressive move. We just stare in silence, mere yards apart. It seems like we've been eyeing each other for hours. We are foreign to the other. Alien. I've never actually been this close or this peaceful with a Dark One, not to mention the Shadow, being the pack of ruthless savages their reputation boasts. But this one is different. Peaceful. Resigned.

The other Dark One calls out from a far distance, speaking in their native tongue, asking if he has found anything. Many Light Enchanters do not understand their language, but I have been versed in it as part of my training. A moment passes, and he responds, informing him that there is nothing. His eyes never leave mine. They are searching for something in desperation. And then just like that, he turns and flits towards his partner. And they're gone.

I've never forgotten that night. Not only did my life change but the entire existence of our kind was forever altered. This was the first night I laid eyes on your father.

My father. My father was a Dark One. An assassin of the Shadow. My father was a cruel, callous Warlock who killed innocents for their magic. He manipulated people's minds to gain wealth and power. He frequently pursued Dark Hunters, like my mother, and took pleasure in their suffering. My father was the enemy. My father was the embodiment of evil.

FIVE

"*Another young woman was found dead last night in what looks to be the latest victim in the Ice pick Murder case. Twenty-one year old Casey Klein, a student at Colorado Technical University, was found brutally stabbed in her vehicle outside of her dormitory. No witnesses have come forward and the killer is still at large. If you have any information, please call the . . . ,*" the polished brunette anchorwoman reports from the small television in our kitchen. My parents and I listen intently, worry and disgust etched in our faces.

"It's getting worse," Donna mumbles from the stove, tending to her scrambled egg whites.

"I know," Chris replies, solemnly.

"Can't something be done? Innocent girls can't keep dying!" Donna shrieks, nearly dropping the spatula.

I look up from my own breakfast. "What's going on?" I can tell they know more about the situation than they've let on. Chris and Donna exchange a strained glance.

Chris sighs with reluctance and looks at me intently. "Gabi, honey, the girls' deaths are no random act. They are being murdered by the Dark." He gulps and waits for my reaction. This is the first time he's admitted their existence to me.

"Why?" is all I can choke out.

My dad pinches the bridge of his nose before exhaling. He looks to me with weary, apologetic eyes. "Because they are looking for you."

My blood runs cold, everything around me completely muted. I'm numb. All sense of sight and sound has been stripped away from me. The rhythm of my rapidly pounding heartbeat resonates in my head. Just its steady drumming reminds me that I am still here, still breathing. Not drowning in my own wretched trepidation. Someone is after me and they've left a trail of tortured, mangled girls. Whoever is out there looking for me wants my blood. They want to do to me what they've done to these poor innocent girls. Maybe even more.

"Gabriella, do you understand what I'm saying?" Chris asks, raising his voice a bit to get my attention.

"Huh?" My brain has obviously turned to mush.

Donna sits down next to me and gently places her small hand on my shoulder. "They can't find you. They can't pick up your scent or sense what's in you. I've made sure of that." She tries to smile reassuringly, but it's strained.

"How?" I croak.

Donna points to the wild berry smoothie sitting above my plate of cheese omelet and bacon. "The smoothies I make for you daily are a concoction of herbs that dull your scent. It's harder for them to feel your power." Reflexively, I reach over a take a large laborious swallow. I place the glass down with a shaky hand.

"So the smoothies keep whoever is out there from finding me but innocent girls will continue to die?" This doesn't sit well with me at all. Dozens of women will be killed just so I can be saved? For what? How is my life any more important than theirs?

"It's more complicated than that, sweetie. If we could, of course, we would do something. But it's impossible to force complete strangers to ingest anything without telling them why and risk exposure. We would be slaughtered on the spot for that." Donna pauses to let her words sink in so I understand the severity of the situation. They were sworn to secrecy to protect all of our lives. "Even if we did tell someone, no one would ever believe us. Our job is to protect you and that's what we're doing."

I shake my head, trying to conjure my senses. This is all ludicrous. How can any of this be possible?

"Why are they being stabbed around the throat?" I ask, trying to bring some logic to the conversation.

"To make it appear to be a vampire attack," Chris replies.

Oh, hell no! "Wait a minute!" I yelp incredulously. "Did you just say . . . ? Vampires are real? You have got to be kidding me!" I don't know whether to be frightened or hysterical. Or a mixture of both.

"Do you really want to know?" he asks with a raised eyebrow.

I mull it over for a beat before shaking my head vehemently. "No, I don't." Let's limit these revelations of the existence of mythical creatures to once a year. "So the Dark have sent someone to kill me. Why?"

"You are the first of your kind," my dad replies. He resumes eating his eggs as if we are discussing the weather. "No one knows what you'll become once you ascend. You could have power that surpasses anything they could have ever imagined and annihilate all of them. At least that's what many of the Light are hoping for, anyway."

"Ascend? Like get my power? When? And how do they know I'll even have any? I don't feel like I do." I look down at my now cold breakfast and pick up a piece of bacon to nibble. I don't even taste it. I just have to keep myself busy before I have a nervous breakdown.

"When you turn 21. There is no doubt that you'll be powerful, considering who your parents were," says Donna. The reminder of my wicked Warlock bio dad causes a shiver to run down my spine. "However, no one knows what type of magic you'll have."

"You mean no one knows if I'll be good or evil," I whisper.

"We know you're anything but evil, sweetie. And you could very well put an end to all of the fighting. Your mother, Natalia, had hoped for that. She wanted there to be peace among the Light and the Dark and wanted you to be that bridge. But it had never been done before. Ever. People fear what they don't understand." Donna places her hand over mine in reassurance.

"But does anyone even have a clue what I'll become? What if I'm some crazed psychopath or something? Can't I just opt out of this ascension?"

"It doesn't work that way, honey. You are what you are. And that is a very special, very unique young woman," says Donna. For someone who has no idea what will happen in another 12 months, she's oddly optimistic. That's even if I make it to my 21st birthday being that there's someone trying to kill me. *Oh yeah, that.*

"For now, just focus on keeping yourself safe and out of harm's way," adds my dad as if he can read my anxiety. "The herbs will work on concealing your identity. Just be smart and no risky behavior, okay, Kiddo?"

"Right," I reply flatly. Demented Warlock out to kill me. *No big deal.* They must be pretty damn confident in Donna's concoction. "I've gotta get ready for work."

I rise and walk over to the trash to scrape my leftover food, and then place my dish into the sink. Once I've retreated to my room, I mindlessly get my clothes ready for work, deciding on soft cowl-neck cream sweater, fitted jeans, and brown riding boots. It's dressier than my usual jeans and t-shirt work attire but I need a pick me up after the news of my potential attacker. I put in some stud earrings and leave my long tresses down in soft waves. I smile at myself in the mirror and think *I feel pretty.* Not that I think I'm ugly. Just not very glamorous, especially next to Morgan. *Morgan!* I pick up my cell phone and call her, knowing she'll be agitated with my brief text last night. Did I even get a chance to send it?

Shoot, her voicemail. "Hey, Morg, sorry bout last night. Crazy shit. But I do have something quite interesting to report!" Not only do my cheeks heat at the thought of Dorian, but my heart instantly beats into overtime. "Heading to work now. Call me later?"

I grab my purse and my favorite brown leather jacket just in case it's cold after I get off. Before stepping outside, I check to make sure there's no one out there waiting for me. It's a beautiful day, the warm sunlight kissing my cheeks with Vitamin D. I smile up at the sky and my trepidation instantly vanishes. One of the perks of Colorado's high altitude is the sun always feels closer and brighter.

There's a chill in the air but I'm comfortable in my light sweater. I pop in my favorite John Mayer cd and blast it all the way to Chapel Hills mall. It's going to be a good day, I can feel it. I've at least earned it.

No matter how hard I try, I just can't get motivated at work. I want to be out enjoying this beautiful Saturday just like everyone else, not wasting away selling overpriced denim to bratty teenagers with Daddy's credit card. As I'm retrieving about 10 articles of clothing that some pesky kid has tried on and left in the dressing room, I feel my cell vibrate in my back pocket, indicating a text message. I begin to rehang the apparel on their appropriate racks then pull out my phone once I'm masked by the shroud of the jeans display. I suspect it's Morgan but to my surprise it's Dorian. My heart beats furiously and my breathing becomes ragged as if I've just run the length of the entire mall complex.

Dorian, 1:17 PM

— *I want to see you.*

God, it's amazing the feelings this man can evoke with just a sentence. I think about delaying my response in an attempt to not seem too eager, but to hell with playing coy.

— I'm working :(

There. If he really wants to see me, maybe he'll suggest meeting up later after work like the night before. At least that's what I'm hoping.

"Hey, Gabi, there you are!"

Holy shit! My disturbingly cheerful supervisor pops up out of nowhere and scares the crap out of me, causing me to drop my phone and the pair of jeans draped over my arm. "Oh my God, Felicia, you scared me!" I clutch my chest in a cheesy soap opera fashion and scramble to pick up my phone and the jeans. "What's up?"

"Oops! Sorry!" she smiles. This bitch is way too perky. It's like she's hooked up to a caffeine IV. "Hey, I am so, so, so sorry to do this but I've got to start cutting back a little on shifts. I think something is going on with the company but we'll just keep that hush, hush!" She winks over exaggeratedly. "Would you be too upset if I let you go home early today?" She gives her best puppy dog look and even goes as far as jutting her bottom lip out. *Gag.*

"Sure!" Now it's my turn to be cheery. Has wishful thinking finally paid off?

"Awesome! You're the best, Gabi! And I promise it won't just be you feeling the cutback on hours. It'll be spread out, myself included." She's doing that damn sad face again but I don't even care enough to be annoyed.

"No problem, send me home anytime," I cheese like a lunatic. Her chirpy disposition must be rubbing off on me. That and the fact that my plans for the day have just took a turn for the better. I hurriedly fold the jeans and shove them on their reserved shelf and head back to the stockroom, vigorously texting on the way.

To Dorian, 1:28 PM

  — Plans just changed. I'm off :)

Geez, I've got to quit with these damn emoticons. I get a reply just seconds later and am nearly jumping with glee. Dorian has got me wide open and I haven't even known him a mere 48 hours.

  — *I'm at Starbucks. Come see me.*

Though it's a demand, and I don't take kindly to demands from any man, I am only too eager to race down to the coffee shop in record time. I stop at our employee restroom to finger comb my hair and reapply my lipgloss before grabbing my things and waving goodbye to my coworkers without a second glance. *So long, Suckas!*

As I approach Starbucks, I slow my pace and take a few deep breaths, trying to get my head in a more level, nonchalant space. But no matter how cool I try to appear, it all evaporates as soon as I see him sitting at the very same table we sat at the day before. I pause for a beat and have to consciously remind myself how to walk. *Left foot, right foot, left foot, right foot.* I shakily approach the table and just stare. The man is simply gorgeous, clothed in a black V-neck t-shirt, jeans and a black leather jacket. He gazes back at me in a sultry, lustful way. I can't tell if he's laying on the sex or if that's his usual look but I'm buying it. *All of it.*

"So we meet again," he smiles crookedly. His ice blue eyes flash momentarily and my knees almost buckle underneath me. He waves toward the opposite seat. "Please, sit."

I do as I'm told, again, with controlled movements, careful not to seem too compliant. That's when I allow myself to tear my eyes away from him long enough to notice that he has two disposable coffee cups in front of him. He pushes one towards me.

"I hope you don't mind," he says.

I take a tiny sip of the steaming liquid and let it quench my parched mouth. It's a cinnamon latte, my favorite! How did he know? "Thank you," is all I can choke out in surprise.

"So it seems we have the whole day to enjoy each other. What shall we do?" He takes a sip of his own drink and looks up at me seductively through his thick eyelashes. They are ridiculously long and lush, giving any *Covergirl* model a run for her money. Contrasted with his unbelievably light eyes, the combination is downright dazzling.

"Hmmm," I ponder. Then I have an idea that will score me some alone time with him and offer an opportunity for us to enjoy the sunshine. "Ever been to Garden of the Gods?"

"Can't say that I have. But I'm always up for an adventure." Dorian cocks his head to one side as if he's contemplating something. The gesture makes him look incredibly sexy.

"Well, I don't know about an adventure but it is one of my favorite places," I smile sheepishly.

Revealing a personal detail about me, especially something as intimate as one of my favorite hideaways, makes me feel bashful, childlike even. I really do care about his opinion of me. It's more than just the physical attraction; I want him to know me.

"Then I'm sure it will soon be one of my favorites as well." Dorian then stands, grabs both our coffee cups and I follow suit. "Come on. I'll drive," he winks.

The ride in the sleek, black Mercedes is invigorating and I'm pleasantly surprised at how much I'm enjoying it, having never been much of a car enthusiast. Dorian is an impeccable driver and he makes it seem so effortless. We cruise down Academy Boulevard, Robin Thicke crooning sweet, soothing melodies from the state of the art sound system. He's singing about being all tied up and urging his lover to rescue him, pleading his need for her. It's provocative and I instantly find myself swaying to the beat. I glance over at Dorian to find him smirking at my little performance.

"Like the music?" he asks when I catch his gaze behind the dark lenses of his designer shades.

"I do. So you listen to a lot of music like this?" Perfect time to squeeze out some information.

"My tastes are eclectic. I listen to whatever moves me," he responds.

"Humph. Me too, I guess," I reflect. I do like to mix it up a bit.

"The power that a musician holds is truly fascinating. To touch the masses, relaying their pain, anger, joy, lust . . . through song . . . ," he stares ahead lost in his own train of thought. I look intently at him, hanging on to his every word. He seems so passionate, so full of conviction. "The true artist is one who can evoke those raw emotions in their audience, bring them to their knees, and convey their message to them in a foreign tongue. Or without words at all. That type of power is immeasurable."

I'm totally consumed by Dorian's outpouring of emotion. It's so unexpected and unbelievably alluring. Like maybe there is more behind the incredible looks and sex appeal. As if he can sense my suspicions, he turns to flash me a heart-stopping smile.

"Seems like you know a bit about the music business," I comment, desperately trying to recover from the sight of it.

"A little," he smirks, and we go back to enjoying the tunes and sensual static of our close proximity.

When we arrive at the park of bizarre red rock formations, I feel a surge of energy. I'm excited even though I've been a dozen times. The possibility of spending time with Dorian and sharing this place with him is exhilarating and part of me really wants to impress him. We walk down to the first display of rock and marvel at nature's splendor.

I take a moment to reflect on all I've learned since my birthday, just a meager 2 days ago. What if the red boulders weren't fashioned this way simply by nature? What if this was the work of a supernatural being? What if the rocks were erected as a result of an intense battle between opposing forces?

"Weird, huh?" I turn to Dorian to gauge his reaction.

"Peculiar, yes, but beautiful." He grins down at me and I notice he's removed his shades, giving me full access to his magnificent irises, safeguarded by long, black lashes. I blush and hurriedly turn away to hide the flush of my cheeks.

We walk through the park in content silence, stopping every so often to admire the red sandstone. It totally boggles me how I can be so comfortable with Dorian, a complete contradiction to my usual distrusting nature. Being in his presence feels oddly right, as if we were somehow meant to be in this moment together.

"So you like to come here. Why?" he asks after a while.

"I don't know," I say with a shrug. "I guess I've always enjoyed being outdoors if the weather is nice, of course. And I find the stones to be intriguing. Like, how on Earth did they end up like that? An act of God? Or something else entirely that we could never imagine? Nature is fascinating that way." I look up and Dorian is studying me intently. Being that he's at least 5 inches taller than my five feet four inch frame, I tilt my head upwards to meet his gaze.

"I find *you* fascinating," he breathes. An unnamed emotion washes over his face and his expression is unreadable. It's as if he's trying to relay something to me but is unsure if he should.

"Sorry to disappoint you but like I told you before, I am far from it," I reply. My eyes drop to the ground, my own words wounding me because it's true. "I've never been fascinating or interesting. I am so unbelievably ordinary, it's a surprise that you haven't gotten bored with me yet." I pick up my head and mask my discontent with a rueful smile. No need to let my pessimism ruin the mood.

We stroll upon one of my favorite sandstone formations. "Kissing camels," I say when we stop to admire it. The red rocks have created the impression of two camels facing each other engaged in a charming lip-lock. The sight makes me grin involuntarily. When I look to Dorian to gauge his reaction, he is looking down at me, much closer than I anticipate. I am momentarily startled at his close proximity, and can feel an intense heat surge through my veins at the prospect of contact.

Dorian looks at me with hooded eyes and licks his lips. The sight of the pinkness of his tongue spikes my breathing and my own lips part reflexively from the excitement. As if I have given him some carnal signal, he slowly, deliberately bends his head down and places his soft, full lips on mine. They are strong and dominating yet as supple and light as satin. My mouth parts wider, welcoming his tongue to explore further. The sensation from his touch is electric and the familiar tingling that I experienced on our first encounter returns with a vengeance. From the pout of my lips down my neck, through my breasts and down in my belly, it's spreading like wildfire. It meets its desired destination with ferocity and my pleasure counters the inexplicable prickling with its own throbbing. I've never felt anything like this; it's simply amazing. It can only be best described as when hot and cold collide. *Fire and ice.*

Lost in my body's own symphony of sensation, I hardly notice the extent this kiss has deepened. Our bodies are pressed against each other as if we have melded into one. Dorian's hand is knotted in my hair, firmly massaging my scalp, while the other is on my lower back, pulling me closer still. My own hands roam his soft, tousled black hair and broad hard shoulders. I know we must be making a spectacle of ourselves but we're oblivious. At least I am. Tongues intertwined in a slow, seductive dance, exploring, tasting, teasing. It could go on forever and I still could not get enough of Dorian's succulent flavor. He tastes refreshing and cool like an ice cold drink on a hot summer's day. Yet the current our bodies emit is pure fire and heat. The mixture is intoxicating and addicting.

Approaching voices break our trance and we simultaneously pull away. I'm panting and flustered, looking up at Dorian in wonder. He looks oddly calm and collected, smug even, as if he knows he's unraveled me. Shit, he knows he's got me under his spell. But there's no turning back now. I can't even begin to walk away from him, not after what just transpired between us. He's the only thing that even remotely makes sense right now. His presence these last few days has given me the comfort and happiness that I so desperately crave-that I so desperately *need*-to keep sane. Even if his only purpose in my life is to provide me with mind-numbing passion, I'd happily accept it with open arms. *And open legs.*

"That was . . . Interesting," I say, breaking the tense silence between us.

"The stones are interesting," he replies, licking his lips. He closes his eyes for a long moment, as if he's savoring the memory of our mingled tongues. "You are absolutely delectable."

Suddenly, a horrifying clap of thunder roars overhead and I notice that the skies are dangerously dark. Just seconds before we were basking in the warm sunlight without a cloud in the sky. I am baffled but I know we should find shelter to avoid getting drenched. A violent storm is approaching and lightning strikes in the Springs are a known threat.

"We should head back," I remark as a bright flash of electricity lights the dark sky. A loud rumble quickly follows, indicating that the lightening is close. Dorian looks up and frowns at the heavens then nods, grasping my hand and ushering me back towards the parking lot. We make it back just as the torrential rain begins.

"Did you want to go home? Or would you mind spending a little more time with me?" Dorian asks as he fires up the Mercedes. He looks devastatingly sexy, with his jet black hair slick and speckled with rain. I'm tempted to lean over and lick the raindrops from his face, expecting them to taste as sweet as his lips.

"I don't mind," is all I say. Inside I'm jumping for joy since I expected our date to end because of the weather. I use all my willpower to keep the goofy grin off my face.

"There's a little place I want to take you," he says. And with that we are back on the road.

Robin Thicke is still playing and he's singing a smooth ballad about being dangerous. Though his words warn his lady love to stay away and to avoid falling in love, his sugary sweet melody doesn't match his threat of imminent danger. It's alluring and inviting. You don't want to turn away; you want more and more no matter the risk. I recall Dorian's account of the power of music and my brow furrows. He was onto something.

"Would you rather listen to something else?" Dorian asks suddenly and the song switches abruptly. It's Coldplay's "Paradise."

"Well, no but you've already changed it," I reply.

"Oh? I thought I saw a frown on your face. Maybe you took the song as a warning." He flashes a devilishly sexy smile. I squirm against the leather upholstery.

A warning? Oh shit. Has he realized that being around me could be perilous to him? Of course. How could I have been so stupid? I've got a sadistic Warlock out for my blood and here I am, ready to spread my legs and do the forbidden dance with an innocent, though totally gorgeous and mysterious, man that I hardly know. Yes. That song was a warning. For him.

"No, this song is fine. You can let it play." I turn my head to look out the window at the beating rain, wishing it could wash away my shame. And my fear.

We pull up to a little bistro that could best be described as quaint. It's beautifully decorated with fresh flower arrangements, magnificent framed artwork and several displays of wine. It's a warm welcome from the relentless rainfall. Our friendly hostess smiles at us sweetly and leads us to a quiet table for two, noticeably separate from the other diners. I eye the display case of fresh-baked pastries and cakes on the way and my mouth instantly waters. I am famished and glad that Dorian thought to come here. I quickly open the menu once we're seated and scan their selections.

"Hungry?" Dorian smiles, peering over his own menu.

"Starved," I say sheepishly. And not just for food. "So what's good here?"

"I've only been here once and everything I had was fantastic. Do you like seafood?" Dorian puts down his menu and folds his hands on the table in front of him.

"I love it," I reply.

"Good. Their mussels and clams are excellent," he remarks.

Just as I've decided what to order, our server approaches us, a tall, thin brunette with a bright smile, a notable change from our waitress from the sports bar. She is pretty in a girl next door kind of way and has kind eyes.

"Bonjour, mademoiselle, monsieur," she greets each of us with a bow of her head. Dorian returns her friendly acknowledgment and answers back in flawless French. I fail at hiding my shock after the waitress leaves.

"Whoa. You speak French?" I ask, clearly impressed.

Dorian answers with a sheepish half-smile and a shrug of his shoulders. "Yes. Among other languages."

I note his nonchalance with a raised eyebrow and a shrug of my own. We make small talk until our server returns with glasses of wine and a large bottle of sparkling water. I take a swig of the cool, crisp rose wine and an involuntary '*Mmmm*' escapes my lips.

Seeing as it is still pretty early in the day, I opt for a Muffeletta sandwich while Dorian orders a Nicoise salad. The waitress smiles at us both and leaves to put in our food orders, returning moments later with a large platter of clams and mussels in a white wine sauce. They look and smell amazing. Dorian must've ordered these in his perfect French along with the wine.

"Dig in," he offers and he scoops a few shells onto each of our plates.

He was right; the seafood is exceptional. We lose ourselves in the delicious shellfish and giggle as sauce dribbles down our chins. It's remarkable how down to earth and easygoing Dorian is. Though I am taken aback by his startling good looks, he has a way of making me feel totally at ease with him, something I've only experienced with Jared. I feel this inner draw to him, as if I can tell him anything. Like I can already trust him wholeheartedly.

"So what do you plan to do after you receive your degree in May?" Dorian asks.

"Really, I have no idea," I reply, finishing the last mussel on my appetizer plate.

"No plans to head to a 4 year university to get your Bachelor's?"

"That would be the most logical thing but I really don't have the desire to. Then again, I definitely don't want to be a sales clerk for much longer." I put my napkin down and sigh. "To tell you the truth, I have no idea what I want to do with my life."

"Really? What's your major?" he asks.

My mouth twists into an uncomfortable grimace. "Undecided." *About just about everything, that is.*

"Well, what are you passionate about?" Hmmm, good question.

"Honestly?" I give him a fake smile to mask my shame. "Nothing. I've never been great at anything in school. Never was a cheerleader or even an athlete. The only thing I really excelled at was martial arts but that was some years ago." Dorian looks at me quizzically. "Oh yeah, I was known for being a bit of a bad ass," I snicker, nervously.

My rough and tumble ways are probably a direct opposite, if not insult, to Dorian's cool and polished demeanor. Even with his bad boy good looks, I can tell he comes from a refined background. Might as well lay all the cards on the table now.

"You? Really?" He eyes assess the length of my body, causing me to squirm.

"Yeah," I shrug sheepishly. "I never was one of those girls that wanted to be a princess or a ballerina. A while ago, I really wanted to enlist in the Marine Corps. Then ultimately, try to join the CIA. But it was just a crazy dream." I chuckle nervously, shaking my head at my absurdity.

"It's just . . . I never wanted to be some dainty damsel in distress. I never wanted to be rescued. I've never been *that* girl. I wanted to be the one kickin' ass and taking names. I wanted to be the hero, you know." I can't believe I'm divulging such an outlandish idea to him but something about Dorian puts me oddly at ease. Like I've known him for years. I had never told anyone my career goals, not even Jared.

Dorian licks his lips before they spread into a sexy half smile. "I can understand that. Pretty damn sexy if you ask me." Our server suddenly appears to collect our dirty dishes and hurriedly rushes away, no doubt feeling the sexual static between us. I take a long sip of wine to wash down my anxiety. I'm thankful when Dorian signals to our server for a refill.

"Well, that was a long time ago. I promise I'm a good girl now," I say, giving him my best naughty smirk.

"Pity," he retorts, his eyes flashing arctic blue. "That could've been fun. But I'm sure you've still got some bad girl in you. At least, that's what I'm hoping." He leans in closer and I can almost feel the coolness of his breath. I hold my own breath in expectation.

"Excusez-moi," the polite waitress nervously interrupts with our meals. She sets them in front of us and asks if there is anything else we need. Dorian and I both answer with a shake of our heads and she scampers towards her other patrons.

I look down at my huge sandwich and my eyes grow wide. There's no way I'll be able to finish this. Dorian's perfectly dressed salad seems more practical. "Please tell me you'll take half of this," I chuckle. It looks as if our orders have gotten switched around.

Noting the irony, Dorian snickers and says, "I'll tell you what. Only if you share some of this with me."

"Deal!" I reply and begin to portion him more than half of the mountain of delicate meats, cheeses and olive salad.

We enjoy our meal with easy chatter and chuckles, enjoying the delicious cuisine and refreshing wine. I find myself giggling at every joke and hanging onto every word that passes Dorian's lips, which are pretty damn hard to take my eyes off of. I imagine tasting those lips again, nibbling them, feeling them against my skin, between my thighs . . .

"I hope you've left room for dessert," Dorian remarks breaking me from my sinful thoughts.

"Dessert?!" I exclaim. "I can hardly breathe!"

"Oh come on, this place is actually best known for their desserts. Award-winning, I hear." Right on cue our server scoops up our empty plates and places a dessert menu on the table. I can see why they're known for their sweets; it's as long as their regular menu.

We agree to go with the Fresh Fruit Tart, as long as I promise to try the Triple Chocolate Mousse Cake with him another time. It gives me hope and warms my heart that there could actually be a future for us. Then the looming remembrance of my murderous stalker rips that hope in two. The thought causes me to shiver and I give him a sorrowful tight-lipped grin. He looks at me with a question in his eyes but before he can ask me what's wrong, our server returns with our dessert. The bright berries and flaky butter pastry look like a page out of Food & Wine magazine.

"We won't need this," Dorian says to our waitress, handing her one of the two small forks she brought with the tart. She looks puzzled and a bit embarrassed, as do I, but takes the fork and scurries away, leaving behind a pregnant pause.

Dorian takes the remaining fork and cuts into the tart, scooping up a bit of crust, custard and a fresh raspberry. He holds it in front of my lips, his eyes urging me to take a taste. I open my mouth slowly and Dorian eases the fork inside, sliding the creamy treat onto my tongue. I close my eyes as I savor the sweet silky custard, the rich crumbly crust, and the tartness of the berry. It's divine. I open my eyes to meet Dorian's smoldering hooded gaze. I lick my lips in response and smile slyly.

"Ok, your turn," I say, taking the fork from him. I ration a small portion and slowly, deliberately feed Dorian the bite. He keeps his eyes on me the entire time, his stare intensifying as he gently chews. It's enough to make me ache below and I secretly wish it was me he was consuming.

We continue on this way for the remainder of the tart and a glass of dessert wine when the familiar sound of a cell phone vibration interrupts us. It's Dorian's. He looks at the number, frowns and hits Ignore, stuffing the phone back into his jacket pocket. It makes me uneasy though I know I have no right to ask him who it is and why he didn't answer.

Dorian's demeanor shifts instantly and darkness creeps onto his face. The lighthearted, tender moments that we shared today are a distant memory. It's as if I am looking at a stranger. The man who pressed his soft lips against mine in an impassioned, frenzied lip-lock is no longer present. The hidden darkness displayed on his caller ID has taken him away from me.

"Well, I better get home. It's getting late," I say after an uncomfortable beat. That's right, better to end things on my terms before he dismisses me. My cold, guarded front is back with the intrusion of his.

"Yeah, that's probably best," he mutters and signals the waitress for the check.

When I offer to pay for my share, he waves me off without a word and pulls out his wallet. I sit in silence, fingering a loose thread on my sweater. Suddenly, I feel a warm finger on my chin gently pull my face up. Dorian is leaning over the table and his eyes connect with mine. He smiles kindly and I notice that he looks older, solemn. Remorse washes over him and I instantly soften. Once he notices that I've relaxed a bit, he exhales with relief. He then stands to his feet and holds his hand out to help me up. I oblige, and we make our way out into the cool evening air, hand in hand.

"I have to go out of town," Dorian says somberly as we make our way back up to the northern part of town. When I don't ask him where or why, he continues. "A family issue. I'd love to see you when I return. Do you have any plans for Friday?" There's an apology in his voice. For what?

I think to make him sweat a little and don't answer right away. "Ummm, I don't think I have anything planned." Who am I kidding? *Of course*, I'm free! I can't even pretend to be a tease. "Sure. I think I can swing that."

I look over and notice Dorian smirking in the shroud of darkness as he pulls up next to my car in the employee lot. There are many cars scattered around, being that it is only early evening. It seems wrong to call it a night so early on a Saturday, but Dorian seems urgent to get home.

"Where do you live, Dorian?"

"I'm staying at The Broadmoor for now," he says a bit embarrassed. I nod my head, wondering why he'd feel embarrassed about staying at the most posh, luxurious hotel in town. Could he be one of those rebellious trust fund kids, ashamed of their inherited wealth? "Have you ever stayed there?"

"Can't say I have. But I've heard it's pretty swanky. That's over by Cheyenne Mountain, right?"

"Yes, it is. And you? Where do you live?" he asks.

I think about my next answer carefully. "With my parents still. But Morgan and I are planning to get an apartment this summer." No use in giving away too much information. As much as I want to, can I trust Dorian? With more than just my body, that is.

Dorian leans closer and my heartbeat quickens. "Thank you, Gabriella, for a wonderful evening," he breathes. I reflexively inch closer to him.

"Anytime," I smirk. I wish I could come up with something clever or sexy, but I go with the truth.

We sit staring at each other as our desire heats the small contained space. Dorian moves in a bit more and I gladly match his distance. We are so close, our breath mingling between open, inviting lips. Dorian nuzzles the bridge of his nose against mine and the contact is electric. I giggle at the gesture and he swiftly swallows it with his mouth, igniting the fire down between my thighs. I moan submissively and surrender to his curious tongue. Dorian relishes the admission; it only encourages him to deepen the kiss, cradling my face in his large hands and grabbing a handful of my tresses. I'm completely lost in him and want him to take this kiss further still. *I want him.* I've known this man for all of 10 minutes and I already want to feel him inside of me. And if his kiss is any indication of his sexual ability, I won't be disappointed.

The aggravating double *Ding!* from my cell phone intrudes on our intimacy and I curse it under my breath. Dorian and I gaze at each other, still high on each other's flavor and craving more. But the moment has passed; the magic has dissipated and we are back in the here and now.

"I better go," I say, wishing Dorian would beg me not to. He looks slightly dismayed but doesn't respond so I gather my coat and purse.

"Friday," he says as I reach for the door handle.

"Friday," I smile. I open the door and swing my legs out of the car as gracefully as I can. I turn to Dorian just before I rise. "Dorian, what is your last name?" The question has been gnawing at me all day. It's only right; I have locked lips with him twice already. *Score one for college sluts!*

Dorian looks at me, his expression searching yet somewhat tortured as if he would really rather not tell me. Resignation washes over him.

"Skotos," he replies, accenting the word in a foreign tongue. It sounds European; Greek maybe. That would explain Dorian's exotic good looks.

"Well, goodnight Dorian Skotos," I say, careful to pronounce it correctly, and with that I gently close the car door and make my way to mine. Dorian waits until I am safely inside my Honda before pulling off. I quickly start it up and pull away before risking a repeat of the night before.

Six

"Where the hell have you been?" Morgan shrieks from my phone. I'm lying on my bed, flicking mindlessly through the channels on my bedroom TV.

"I've been around. I called you earlier . . . Didn't you get my message?" I decide on some train wreck reality housewives show.

"Uh, yeah, and I've called you back at least a dozen times since then!" She's still fired up, no doubt being overly dramatic as always.

"No you didn't. I only got one missed call and I called you back as soon as I got back home!" Now, I'm getting annoyed.

"Gabs, I swear it. I've been calling you all day. Even went by the mall to see you at work and your boss said you'd left early." She sounds worried so I remove the phone from my ear and take another look at it. Nope, only one missed call.

"Humph, guess my phone is on the fritz. Sorry. What's up, girl?"

"I was just worried. And you said you have something juicy to share!" I can hear the familiar clinking of her oversized earring on the receiver.

"Well, kinda," I reply sheepishly. "I've been seeing Dorian."

"Dorian? Dorian who?" I hear her rustling through what sounds like her makeup bag. "Wait! Not the guy from the club? *That* Dorian?!" she exclaims.

"Yes, *that* Dorian," is all I can say before she yips a combination of praise and expletives.

"*Oh. My. God.* Gabs, that is awesome! Whew! So I guess he's not as creepy as he appeared to be on Thursday, huh?"

"No, not as creepy. Though I must say he is quite intense. Not to mention intimidatingly sexy. I straight up lose my head around him,"

I admit. *And I would love to lose my panties as well.*

"Well if anyone can handle him, it's you. I'm just so happy for you! So you've gone on a date with him? How was it? Did you guys hook up? Oooh, you dirty ho!" she squeals excitedly.

"Well, actually we've been on two dates. And what do you mean by '*hook up*'? Did we have sex? Hell no! I just met the guy." But do I want to? *Hell yes!* Morgan doesn't need to know all that though.

"But you like him, right? Two dates in two days is pretty major for you, Miss No Dude Will Ever Be Good Enough . . . other than Jared, that is," she snickers.

"I never said that! Just no guys are really worth getting serious with. And what do you mean, *other than Jared*?" Oh crap. Am I that transparent? I've never disclosed how I felt about Jared.

"*Mmmm hmmm*, you might be able to fool everyone else, but I know my girl. Seems like Dorian might change all that though. Look at you . . . already flaking on your friends for him!" I know she's joking but I can't help but feel some irritation. I've never been that type of girl. "Anyway, are you getting ready?"

"Ready? For what?"

"Uh, do you not know what today is? It's St. Patrick's Day! You know we're all going to O'Malley's tonight!" she says is disbelief.

Shit! I totally forgot. And I really, really don't feel like going. Not to mention, I still haven't lived down last year's fiasco.

"Awww, Morg, can't I pass this year? I'm really tired." I whine.

"Hell no, you cannot! It's a tradition! And you had enough energy to play kissy face with Mr. Hot Ass. You are going, Gabriella Winters!" she shouts. Ugh, Morgan can be a total pain in my ass when she wants to be.

"Fine! Fine! But I am not driving! If I have to go, I will be getting insanely wasted and will probably embarrass you . . . Again." I lie. There's no way I can risk being banned from one of the only bars in town that hardly ever cards, making it a legendary college coed hotspot.

"That's cool, Jared offered to DD. We'll be by to get you at 10." And with that, Morgan hangs up. I look at the clock and decide I can squeeze in a nap and still have time to get ready. Only Morgan needs three hours of preparation for a night out. Besides, it's St. Patty's Day. As long as you wear green, you're good.

It's 9:45, I've slept too long and I'm scrambling to get ready. I'm showered, half-dressed, and hopping around with a flat iron sizzling in my hair when my cell perks to life.

"On our way, Gabs! Are you ready?" Jared shouts over loud music and laughter. I can hear Morgan in the background; she's already started the party.

"Ummm, I will be. I still have a few minutes, right?" I stammer. I've got on my top but only pink lacey panties clothe my bottom. Not to mention, I haven't even touched my face. I look a hot damn mess.

"Yeah, I'm swinging by to get Miguel then we'll come and get you. Damn, girl, feels like I haven't seen you in forever." Jared's voice sounds husky, full of emotion. Is he ok? It's only been a couple days.

"Well, I'll be ready and waiting."

Thirteen minutes later, I am dressed in tight black jeans, a dark green low cut top and heeled boots. My hair is bone straight down my back and my makeup is flawless. *Pretty damn good*, if I do say so myself.

"Wow. You look great, Gabs," Jared says, gathering my frame into a bear hug. He's always been affectionate, but something else is in his embrace. His hands grip my skin, gently caressing the surface. It's weird, but I'd be lying if I didn't admit that it felt good. I've been longing for his touch for years.

"You too," I squeak against his solid chest, only the thin fabric of his polo shirt separating my mouth from his nipple. I breathe in his freshness. As always, he smells of Irish Spring soap, fitting for this occasion. He releases me from his grip, holding me at arms-length to observe my body. I do the same and note that he's wearing a green striped polo, blue jeans and fresh white Nikes. His chestnut locks have been freshly trimmed and his green eyes twinkle brighter than ever. It feels like I haven't seen him in months, though it's been a mere two days.

Honk! Honk! Morgan lays on the car horn, relaying her impatience and scaring the crap out of Jared and me.

"Come on! Let's go!" she hollers from the front seat. I can see she's donned in hunter sequins, way too dressy for O'Malley's but you can't tell her that. I grab my purse and coat and we make our way down the driveway, ready for pitchers of green beer, loud music and a few laughs to make me forget missing Dorian for the next six days. And that there's a vicious killer tracking me.

O'Malley's is in full swing when we arrive, and it doesn't disappoint. Rock music blares through the speakers, and there's a beer pong tournament underway. It's an endless river of green and many of the college girls are determined to wear as little of it, or anything else for that matter, as possible.

We find a table and settle in before it gets too crowded and becomes standing room only. Jared, James, and Miguel bound up to the bar to order pitchers of beer while Morgan and I scope out the scene. Mostly coeds from the numerous colleges and universities in town fill the bar and many are obviously on the hunt to find someone to occupy their bed tonight. We get a few glances from random men but no one has the chance to approach us before our handsome entourage returns with drinks.

And handsome they are. Jared is a tall wall of hard muscle in his fitted polo. I love how the fabric stretches over his mountainous biceps, accentuating his impressive build. Soccer and weight training has really done his body good. James is a bit taller than his baby brother but not as built. Being a competitive swimmer, he's in impeccable shape but a bit on the thin side for my tastes. He shares the same green eyes and auburn locks as Jared though he wears them shorter. Miguel is shorter than the two yet stocky and built like a football player, his sport of choice. His bronze skin, almond eyes and dark, glossy tresses make him desirable to most of the female population, but he's always just been Jared's friend in my eyes.

The guys pour us mugs of beer and we all toast to an awesome St. Patty's Day. Jared sips his free soda, compliments of the bar, since he's been appointed the designated driver for the evening. Hours later, after a couple drinking games and shots, we're all feeling jovial and festive and I've hardly thought about Dorian, my evil pursuer, or much else for that matter. Jared and I have retreated back to the table after a game of darts and are sharing a basket of curly fries. Miguel and James have entered the beer pong tournament are doing pretty well. Morgan is entertaining a nearby table of frat boys and they are eating out of the palm of her hand. Thanks to her, I haven't had to pay for a drink all night.

"Gabs! Come join us!" she calls over to us. The guys are holding up their drinks as if to air-toast with me. I hold up my glass of water in return and shake my head. Time to sober up. No need to have a repeat of last year. Morgan shrugs and goes back to mesmerizing the guys with her charms.

"Sure you don't want to go over there and help her out?" Jared smiles and pops a curly fry into his mouth.

"Oh, she needs no help from me. Besides, frat boys aren't my thing," I say, slowly swirling my fry into the ketchup.

"Well, what is your thing?" Jared says in a low, raspy voice that causes me to meet his eyes. There's desire in them, and it instantly makes me look back down at my now soggy fry with flushed cheeks.

"Ummm, I can't really say," I say thoughtfully. "I like athletes. Physically fit guys. Nice eyes." I say, gazing into his glittering greens. It's the truth but I know I could be opening up a can of worms that I'm not prepared to deal with right now. *Or am I?*

Before Jared can address my remark, a very drunk, very scantily clad girl falls into his lap. The term *slore* comes to mind.

"*Heeeyyyyy*, Jared! Remember me?" she slurs. She's thin, tan and blonde, wearing a UCCS t-shirt that she's fashioned into a mid-drift top, too short cut off jean shorts and cowboy boots. She's beautiful and indicative of the type of girls Jared usually dates.

"Uh, yeah. Summer, right?" Jared stammers. A blush of crimson bathes his cheeks.

"Yup! How are you?" She squeezes him hard, letting her hands roam his boulder-like shoulders. I feel my blood boil.

"I'm good. Hey, this is my friend Gabriella," he motions towards me, stealthily trying to wriggle from her grasp. Summer glances in my direction, and flashes an insincere smile. I reciprocate with a fake grin and a roll of my eyes when she returns her attention to Jared.

"So hey, how about you buy me a drink? And then maybe me and you can get outta here." She tries to whisper that last sentence but fails miserably. Jared's eyes grow wide with horror and he looks to me for aide. I nearly spit out my mouthful of water and try to stifle my laughter. The poor girl is oblivious to our humorous exchange at her expense.

"Actually I'm here with my friends. I'm the DD tonight so I can't leave them," he replies, speaking slowly so his gentle rejection sinks into her dim-lit brain. If there's one thing I can't stand it is a loose girl who can't control her liquor. Or her morals, for that matter.

"Oh, I'm sure they can manage without you. Gail here looks nice and sturdy," she chuckles at her tasteless joke.

"It's Gabriella," I state loud and clear, giving her a stern glare. "*Dumb ass*," I mutter under my breath.

"Oh, whatever," she waves me off. "Anyway, let them catch a cab. My roommate won't be back tonight and I was hoping we could finish what we started," she says, fingering her blonde locks and biting her bottom lip in an attempt to appear seductive.

I look away before I gag and catch Morgan's eyes on us, shaking her head as if to tell me to let it go. Her frat boys have followed her stare so I plaster on a grin and shrug to indicate that there's no worry. I start to get up and walk away, noting that Jared is whispering something to her that he obviously doesn't want me to hear, but before I can get up, all hell breaks loose.

"Fine then! You must be fucking gay! No wonder you'd rather hang with this ugly bitch!" she screams, attempting to slap Jared before he catches her arm.

Okay, now this chick has pissed me off. Before she can spew another vile word, I palm her face and shove her backwards onto the floor. Her flailing arms take out another table's beer and it lands all over her, drenching her bleach blonde hair. The bar erupts in laughter and cheers but I know I better get out of here before I'm thrown out. Wouldn't be the first time.

"Hey, Gabs wait up!" Jared calls from behind me. The chilly air instantly cools my hot temper.

"You didn't have to come out here. I can wait 'til you guys are ready to leave." Alone. In the pitch black night. With someone from the Dark after me.

"No, I'll wait with you. I just told the guys and Morgan we'd be in the car." He grabs my hand and we stroll quietly to his old Nissan. Once inside, Jared flicks on the heat and puts in a CD. It's one I know well, John Mayer's Continuum. I close my eyes and let John soothe my troubles.

"What am I gonna do when I can't see you every day? Sure you don't want to transfer to UCCS with me in the fall?" he smiles his boyish grin, leaning on the arm rest separating us.

"And have to fight off drunken blondes every night? No thank you!" We chuckle at the prospect of me defending Jared's honor.

"You know, you wouldn't have to, if you came. You wouldn't have to fight off anyone for me," he says seriously. *Whoa*, what happened to our lighthearted banter?

"Well, once you start playing soccer, it'll be so hard to juggle that, your studies, your love life and hanging out with me. One of them would have to give." I look at the car ceiling, unable to bring myself to gaze into his emerald eyes.

"That's where you're wrong. You and my love life would be synonymous." His voice is full of raw emotion and the sentiment startles me. I turn my head to gauge his expression. He isn't joking. "You know, when my mom got sick, you were there every step of the way. I shared things with you that I've never told anyone. You've always been my best friend. And I love you for that," he adds. *Love?* Oh God.

I search for the right words and give him a sincere smile. "You know how I feel about you. We've been through so much together," is all I can come up with. There's so much I've wanted to say to him all these years, yet articulate thought fails me now.

He nods his head. "Yeah, I know. I couldn't do that to you. I couldn't jump into something with you and not make you my priority. With all of our family stuff going on, it wouldn't have been fair to you."

Oh shit. He knows how I've felt all these years? What am I, an open book? I feel my cheeks heat in the darkness.

"Well it's not like you've been celibate all this time," I mumble. It's true. As noble as it is that he's been helping to care for his mom, it's not like it's halted his dating life.

"Those girls were nothing to me!" he says vehemently. "They were just something to do, something to get my mind off my mom dying in front of me and not being able to do anything about it." His words stop me up short and I instantly regret my prior comment.

"Sorry," I mutter, embarrassed at my lack of tact.

"Now that she's doing better, I can stop worrying so much. I can start my life. I want to start it with you, Gabs."

I can't believe what he's saying. It's all I've wanted to hear for years. So why am I just sitting here in disbelief? Why am I not telling him I want that too?

"Jared. I don't know. I mean, how?" Geez, is that the best I can do? What is it with me losing my wits around gorgeous men?

Then it hits me. *Dorian*. He's the game changer.

"You don't have to answer me now, but I want you to know how I feel. It would be easy. There's nothing we don't already know about each other," he breathes, looking at me intently.

Well, that *used* to be true. Would Jared still feel this way if he knew about my new secret life? Would he think I was a freak? He wouldn't be that far off.

As if reading my forlorn thoughts, Jared reaches to stroke my cheek with the back of his hand, pulling my eyes to his. His touch is so soft and inviting and I instinctively nuzzle into it. My hazel eyes turn to warm caramel as I gaze into his dazzling greens. His face slowly inches closer to mine as his large hand cups my chin. He's all I've ever wanted to for so long, and soon I will feel his lips on mine, something I've dreamt about since I was a girl.

The familiar *click clack* of stiletto heels stops Jared's lips a mere centimeter from mine. I hear Morgan laughing with Miguel and James about how the drunken college slut, Summer, was crying on some poor sap's shoulder. They tumble into the back seat with a clatter all obviously very intoxicated.

"*Damn!* The windows are all fogged up! What have you two been doing?" Morgan snickers. She's encouraged by a chorus of *'Ooooohs'* from Miguel and James, and they erupt into cackles as Jared turns beet red.

We stop at a local Denny's for breakfast, packed to capacity with green-clad partygoers. We are lead to a booth only meant for 4 people so Morgan, Jared and I all cram into one side. Morgan is by the wall, I'm in the middle and Jared sits on the end so he can at least stretch his long legs. Feeling the warmth of his body touching mine, my arm brushing against his, thighs bonding under the cover of the table, makes my heart sputter. I breathe in and out deliberately, trying to regain control of my faculties. We make small talk about Morgan's new frat boy conquests, the beer pong tournament that Miguel and James lost in the fourth round, and of course, my tussle with Little Miss Hot Shorts.

"Yeah, man, sorry about that," James says to his younger brother. "If I would've known Summer was a total nut, I would've never introduced you two. I thought you guys hit it off?"

Oh ok, that makes sense. James attends UCCS along with Miguel. Jared must've met Summer while visiting the campus. She said something about her and Jared finishing what they started. What did she mean by that? The thought makes me cringe.

Jared shakes his head at his brother. "That chick was all kinds of crazy. Next time, don't bother. I'm not interested in meeting anyone else."

His head turns towards me just a fraction of an inch and I look down at my menu, even though we've already ordered. Thankfully, our waitress returns with our breakfast platters and everyone's mouths are too stuffed with pancakes, eggs, French toast, bacon and sausage to discuss the matter any further.

"I really want you to think about what I said," Jared says under the lamp of my front porch. "I meant it," he smiles crookedly, peering down at me. He again caresses my cheek and my heart picks up the pace. He cups both sides of my face pulling it slowly up to meet his. My head is dizzy, full of questions and uncertainty.

This is it. Once our lips touch, we can't go back. He'll never be my good old buddy Jared again. Can I live with that?

Blaaaarrggggg!

Holy shit! Once again, we are interrupted, this time by James throwing up his breakfast on the concrete, half his body dangling out of the open rear door. Jared and I both flinch in disgust at his violent heaving and I hurriedly unlock the door and run inside to retrieve a bottle of water and a trash bag just in case James gets sick on their way home. We awkwardly bid each other goodnight and I lock up. Once in my room, I kick off my boots and clothes and flop on the bed. I pull my cell phone out of my purse, where it's been stashed all night, and see I've received 3 text messages, all from Dorian.

Dorian, 9:07 PM

– *Thank you for spending time with me today. I will think of you while I am away.*

Hmmm, he must've sent that while I was taking my nap.

Dorian, 10:36 PM

– *Please be careful tonight.*

Ok, that's beyond strange. How would he know I wasn't at home in flannel PJs and bunny slippers? What would make him assume I was doing something that would put me in danger?

Dorian, 12:48 AM

– *Let me know when you're in safely. I look forward to Friday.*

The time shows that it's almost 3 AM, way too late to call him now so I make a mental note to give him a call in the morning. The day has been so long and full, I just can't muster the strength to talk to him now anyway. I quickly wash my face, brush my teeth and climb into bed with just my bra and panties, too beat to even bother with pajamas.

I'm woken way too early by a knock on my bedroom door. I peek at my alarm clock and read that it's 8 AM *What the hell?*

"Honey, we need you to come out here please, as soon as possible," my dad raps on the door again. The tone of his voice instantly wakens me and I scramble out of bed, only to realize that I'm almost naked. I pull on a pair of sweats and a t-shirt and pop into the bathroom to brush my teeth and wipe away the remaining raccoon eyes from last night's mascara. When I bound down the hall, I am jolted by the sight of two police officers. *Whoa.*

"Ms. Winters, I am Detective Perkins, this is my partner, Detective Cole," he motions towards a brown haired lady with a no-nonsense look on her plain face. Looks like she was woken up too early as well and isn't happy about it. "We need to ask you a few questions." Detective Perkins is a brown-skinned, robust man with a thinning hairline. His forehead is shiny with fresh sweat thought it is quite cool this early in the morning.

I motion for everyone to sit. My parents opt to stand together behind the recliner I choose to take. "Ok, what kind of questions?" I ask. I really am puzzled and I'm sure my face looks the part.

"Do you know this woman?" Perkins holds out a picture and I take it in my hands.

"No, I don't know her, but I met her briefly last night." It's the drunken slore from the bar, Summer. *Crap.*

"And you had an altercation with her?" Detective Cole interjects. Her voice matches her face—flat and emotionless.

"I wouldn't call it that. She was drunk, yelling obscenities at my friend, Jared, and me. She even took a swing." I leave out that the swing was meant for Jared. "I pushed her and then left the bar."

"And your friend? What did he do?" Cole asks. She seems bored.

"Nothing. He left with me. We waited in the car until our friends were ready to go," I answer.

"And his name is?" Perkins asks, a pen and pad in his hand.

"Jared Johnson," I answer skeptically.

I look up at my parents and read their grave, worried faces. I must've really done it this time. Summer probably has some rich daddy who is threatening to sue the pants off us. *Shit.*

"Look, Summer was aggressive towards us. There's a whole bar of people who saw what went down. Is she really trying to press charges over a little shove?" I sigh and shake my head.

"Ms. Winters, Summer Carlisle isn't pressing charges," Perkins says, looking at me seriously. "Summer's body was found early this morning."

Shit just got real.

$\mathscr{S}$EVEN

"What do you mean, '*her body was found*'? What happened to her?" I ask, flabbergasted. I instantly regret my spiteful musings.

"It means that she's dead. More specifically murdered," Cole says dryly. She leans forward and rests her elbows on her knees, for dramatic effect, I'm guessing. "Now being that you admit to assaulting her, all fingers point to you. Tell me, Gabriella, why did you want Ms. Carlisle dead?"

Is this woman for real? Someone has obviously been watching too many episodes of Law & Order. *Simmer down, Detective Dramatic.*

"What? Look, there's no way I killed Summer. I had no reason to. She got out of hand at the bar. Yes, I pushed her, but that's it," I retort, fervently.

"No one's accusing you of murder, Gabriella." Perkins gives his partner an irritated glance. "But I do need to ask of your whereabouts last night approximately between 1 and 3 AM About what time did you leave the bar?"

"Well, after I got into it with Summer, I left and waited outside with my friend. Then we headed to Denny's around midnight, I guess, maybe a little later. I got home after 2 or so," I recall.

"And can anyone vouch for that?" Perkins asks.

"Yes, Jared Johnson, of course. And my friends Morgan, James, and Miguel. Wait!" I jump up and sprint to my room, returning just seconds later with a small slip of paper. "Here's my receipt from Denny's. I paid with my debit card." I shove the piece of paper in Perkins' face, pointing at the time stamp. It reads 1:52 AM

"This should check out." Perkins nods, noting the time. He picks up his notepad. "And your friends? I'm going to need their names."

"Sure. Jared and James Johnson. Morgan Pierre. And Miguel Espinoza."

"And we'll need to know where to find them," Cole snaps.

I look at Cole squarely. "At their homes," I say with a cynical smirk.

"Their addresses," she adds, brusquely. She's shooting daggers at me with her hard, muddy brown eyes.

"You're the detective. Investigate!" I say incredulously. "Hell, you found me easily enough." I give Cole a cold stare of my own. I hear my mom gasp in disbelief at my outburst and I turn back to my parents and mouth '*What?*' with shrugged shoulders. I return my attention to a now furious Cole, and Perkins, a smile playing on his full lips as he scribbles down the names of my friends.

"Thank you for your time," Perkins says, rising. He shakes each of our hands. Cole jumps up and makes a beeline for the front door without a word. *Rude ass.* "Here's my card. Call me if you hear anything and we'll be in touch if we have further questions."

"No problem, Detective. Oh, Detective Perkins? Can I ask how she died?" I add, wondering if my suspicions are true.

Perkins looks back at his partner who is rolling her eyes, waiting impatiently with her hands on her hips. He hesitates for a beat. "Puncture wounds to the jugular, it seems, but we're still waiting on the autopsy report."

Chris shakes his head grimly and Donna grasps her chest with horror. I'm frozen in my seat, unable to process this horrible revelation. Finally, I meet Perkins' eyes and nod my understanding. He looks solemn and exhausted as he walks to the door, as if he's been working to catch the killer day and night. Little does he know that the assailant he's searching for cannot be confined by handcuffs and a jail cell.

"Why don't we go ahead and have breakfast," my mom says after the police leave. She tries to usher me to the kitchen but I stop in my tracks.

"No. I'm going back to bed." I turn on my heel and head back to my bedroom. I have no intention of sleeping but I definitely can't eat after what has just transpired. I think to call my friends to warn them about the police but decide against it. I don't want it to seem like we were plotting anything just in case they check our phone records. I really want to talk to Dorian, but I'm not sure if he's on a plane or if he's even awake. I decide to try a text message.

To Dorian, 8:31 AM

– Hey, sorry I didn't call you back. Hope you have a safe trip. I'm looking forward to Friday, too ;)

No need to alarm him with my troubles. What would he do about it anyway? And would he even care?
Ding! Ding!

– *I'll be thinking of you until then.*

It's amazing what that man can do with a simple text message. I just wish it were enough to make me forget all that's troubling me. Whoever is out there longing to kill me is getting closer. Could they have been at the bar too? I scan the familiar faces in my head, wondering if anything was suspicious or out of place. Nothing sticks out to me. Even if the Dark were there, what could I have done to save myself? Or save my friends? I'm powerless against any supernatural adversaries at least until I turn 21. *Then what?* Do I wave around a twig and say '*Abracadabra*'? Will I trade in my little Honda for a broomstick?

I look over at my mom's book, sitting on my nightstand. So many unanswered questions and it seems to be the only thing, other than Chris and Donna, that sheds some light on my newfound destiny. I reach over to pick it up, and then recline comfortably on a mound of pillows. After flipping through the pages for a few moments, I come to the part where I left off. Oh right, my mother, the great Dark Hunter, comes face to face with the sadistic Shadow, and instead of slaying them, she decides to procreate with one. *Way to stay strong, Mom!*

I read on for the next hour or so about Natalia's confusion at her choice to let the Shadow live. It was the first time she had ever been so close to one of them without it ending in bloodshed. She was curious. For nights, she had dreams about the mysterious Warlock; his cold, blue eyes burning into hers, his unfathomable, tortured expression, his compliant stance. She didn't understand why he lied to his partner about seeing her. Did he think she couldn't take them and took pity on her? It angered her to think that they saw her as a weaker adversary. She didn't need rescuing. And for her choice to let them live, she was angry at herself. She was trained to fight her enemies and was exceptionally efficient at it. What was so different about him? It baffled her how she could allow herself to become influenced by the Dark One. He surely must've used powerful hypnotism to persuade her to let him live.

I had no explanation for how the Dark One escaped with his head. I had trained and planned for their arrival, leaving a trail of clues that would lead them straight to me. Then once they were separated, searching for me, I would pluck them off with ease. But seeing that man, the Dark One, startled me. He had awoken something inside me that I didn't even know existed. I hated to admit that it was desire. I wanted the Dark One. And I hated myself for feeling that way because I knew that we could never be. He despised me and would surely suck the life right out of me if given the chance. I buried myself in training for our next encounter. They would not

escape me again.

My poor mother, tortured by her carnal desires. Guess we share that trait. I read on about Natalia's growing affections for the Dark One, and her self-loathing for not being able to shake the foreign feelings. She wanted to hate him, just like the rest of them. But in her dreams, she never killed him. He never killed her. Her dreams were full of passion. Lust. *Love.*

I tracked the Shadow for thousands of miles, more determined than ever to bring them to their demise. Maybe even a bit reckless. I felt that if he was dead, my irrational feelings would die with him. Plus if anyone from the Light ever found out how I felt . . . . No good could come from it. He had to die.

On one particularly cold night, I catch their scent towards an old abandoned factory site. I stealthily approach the area, making virtually no noise in my pursuit. The scent grows stronger. They're here. I can feel them. Everything inside me is telling me to turn back, it's surely a trap. It's just too easy. Something isn't right. But I have to do this; I have to get it over with. It's the only way I can get him out of my system and retain my sanity.

As if they could hear my internal struggle, the two from the Shadow ambush me, materializing out of thin air. They have paralyzed me with their magic, no doubt for easier slaughtering. They are both there, both viciously beautiful. I struggle unsuccessfully against their strong combined currents. They step into my line of vision, giving me a clear view of the object of my desire. I give up the hopeless fight as I lock eyes with him. I will die with his magnificent face being the last thing I see.

His partner murmurs something in their native language. He's telling him to 'Do It.' I close my eyes and wait for my demise peacefully. Minutes pass but death never comes. My eyes flicker open and I see that he has dropped his hold on me, releasing me from my temporary paralysis. His partner stands in disbelief, shouting at him but he's talking too fast for me to understand. They begin to argue and I have to ask myself why I haven't taken this opportunity to kill them both while they're distracted. But I know I can't. I won't. He spared my life once again. I have to find out why.

His name is Alexander. I eventually know him affectionately as Alex. He is the most gorgeous man I have ever seen. But beyond that, he is different from anything I have ever learned about the Dark. He is kind, decent, and compassionate. And he has the ability to LOVE, something we, the Light, have been taught is impossible for them. We are told that they are nothing more than cold, hard shells. Devoid of humanity. But Alex is so full of life and passion. This caused me to question everything I was ever taught.

I know Alex has killed many times. His conscience had grown weary with the constant carnage. He wanted it all to end. The day in the woods, he had been hoping I would kill him. Put him out of his misery. For hundreds of years, he led a contrived life. He wanted to settle down, have a family one day. That is virtually unheard of for the elite Shadow. They have their pick of throngs of women, both supernatural and human. Alex had quenched his thirst for lustful flesh decades ago. He wanted something more. And he thought that I could help him.

The first time Alex appeared to me, I nearly killed him. He was not defensive. He let me attack him until I realized he had not come to harm me. He wanted to learn about love and family. He was interested as to what we, the Light, thought about the Dark. Of course, he suspected that we view them all as murderous, unfeeling villains. We met in secret for many nights like this, talking about our lives, and how we wanted more. I only knew how to be a Dark

Hunter, to track and kill the enemies of the Light without mercy. Alex had been recruited into the Shadow when he was very young. His exceptional tracking and fighting skills had served him well and he easily moved up through the ranks. Plus he was known for being dreadfully brutal and torturous. Possessing those qualities will eventually weigh you down with guilt and regret.

Soon the time we spent together grew from sheer curiosity to something more. Much more. We would find ourselves longing for the other's company, sneaking away from responsibilities, lying to our own loved ones so we could be together. We tried to fight the overwhelming emotions. We even walked away from our relationship several times, concluding that it could never work between us. We would surely be put to death for our association. In the end, love won out over our fear. We could not simply turn away from what we had.

But as you may know, nothing worth fighting for comes easy. Alex's partner had grown suspicious of his constant disappearances and odd behavior. One night, he followed him and found us together. He was outraged; they had been like brothers for over a century and Alex had kept a staggering secret from him. At first, his instinct was to kill us. He would have been doing us a kindness, to say the least. If he told what he had found, we would have been ripped apart, limb from limb. But Alex pleaded with him, explaining his feelings for me . . . . And the child that grew within my womb. Your father's partner was utterly disgusted, and turned away from Alex. We thought for sure he had gone to alert the Dark of our transgressions. We waited for death together, cherishing our last moments in this life. But his partner returned alone. He vowed to help us and protect us. He did not fully understand but his devotion to Alex was unshakable. So he concealed our secret the best he could.

As the saying goes, everything done in the Dark must come to Light. As my belly grew, rumors began to fly amongst our kind. It wasn't hard for them to find that I had consorted with a Dark One. Word traveled back to the Dark and Alex was immediately taken from me. I was beyond devastated. I knew that he would not survive this. The Dark are merciless and his death was imminent. His friend was also punished harshly for his treason. I will be forever thankful for his allegiance.

As for me, the Light felt they would show me a bit of mercy by giving me a choice. I could live but my unborn baby would be killed as soon as I gave birth. Should I choose to keep you alive, I would pay the ultimate price. Death.

I chose the latter.

I close the journal gently and set it on my nightstand. Then I allow myself to do something that I've tried to avoid at every cost. Something any normal person would've done days ago.

I cry.

EIGHT

My head is aching when I waken to the bright sunlight streaming through the blinds. I must've cried myself into exhaustion and fallen asleep. I squint against the intensity and clumsily reach for my cell phone. *Shit.* 12:07. I have to be at work at 1 PM I sluggishly roll out of bed and trudge to the bathroom, thankful that my parents are nowhere in sight. Once in the shower, I let the hot water soothe my ragged body. The last few days have been eventful to say the least, and I haven't allowed myself to process it all. I haven't let myself feel, in fear that once I accept these emotions, allow these fears to come to life, they would take over. I can't have that.

I shut the water off, vaguely wishing I could turn off my emotions just as easily. Just a flip of a switch or a turn of a knob and all feeling would cease. All crippling pain and frustration would just dissolve. I could go back to blissful ignorance and forget everything that I am, and what I was birthed to be.

Work is more of the same. I just don't have it in me to deal with obnoxious teens and volunteer to stock a new shipment of tops. It is mindless work and I welcome the change from manufactured smiles and false courtesy. Now more than ever do I feel the need to make a decision about my future so I'm not stuck in this dead end job forever. A vibration in my back pocket indicates that I have a text message, breaking me from my forlorn thoughts.

From Jared, 4:56 PM

— *Cops were here. U ok?*

So I guess Cole actually put her detective skills to use. *Useless trollop*, I snicker to myself.

— Yeah, I'm good. At work.

— *Ok. What I said last night . . . I meant it.*

I smile at the tender memory and instantly perk up. Life is too short to wallow in self-pity. At least my life is. And here I have this amazing, totally gorgeous, kind, generous guy that genuinely likes me. He's all I've ever wanted for years and now he wants me too! Why shouldn't I take him up on his offer? Why do I even need to think about this? Jared could have any girl he wants yet he desires me. He wants to start a life together, he said so himself. I could be completely happy with him. It'd be the best of both worlds–best friends and lovers. A true fairytale ending. *Yes!* This could work!

But can it? *Really?*

Could we really build a future together based on a lie? I could never conceal what I truly am–half Light, half Dark. Both good and evil. And how would he feel about me having supernatural powers? He'd think I was a freak, like most of the population, surely. Could I hurt him accidentally? Could I hurt others?

The thought that I could be a potential danger to society stops me up short and I let the shirt I'm holding tumble to the ground. I don't have anyone to help me in this, no one to guide me after I ascend. I won't know how to use my powers. My mom said so herself–I am the first of my kind. Nothing my birth mother could write in a journal could prepare me for what to expect in 12 months. *She* didn't even know. She was just hopeful that I would be something great. What if mixing the two forces is harmful to me? What if that much power *kills* me?

In all my mental turmoil, I have lost track of time and before I know it, it's time to go home. I pack up the rest of the merchandise, grab my stuff and leave to drive the five minutes to Briargate.

"Just in time for dinner, Kiddo," Chris says as I enter the

kitchen. He's setting the table.

"Cool, it smells good," I remark washing my hands at the sink. "Need any help?"

"Um, could you check the dinner rolls, honey?" my mom asks, placing a bowl of tossed salad on the table. I grab a potholder and pull the bread out of the oven. By the time I turn with the bread basket, it's time to eat our feast of honey baked ham, mashed potatoes, roasted brussel sprouts, fresh green salad, and buttery baked rolls. Sunday dinner: a reminder that no matter what, we're still a family.

"So the cops went by Jared's house," I say, scooping out some potatoes onto my plate.

"And everything ok there?" Chris asks with a raised eyebrow, as he slices his ham.

I nod as I chew and swallow. "Yeah. Like I said, we had nothing to do with Summer's death. Dad, when I tell you this girl was wasted . . . She was making a fool of herself. She tried to get Jared to go home with her but when he refused, she got irate. Tried to slap him and called us all kinds of names. I swear I just gave her a good shove. Just to get her to back off." I pop a whole brussel sprout in my mouth. Chris nods, indicating that he believes me. Between him training me to box at the gym, 10 years of Karate instruction, and my overall distaste for dumb, slutty girls, he knows I could've seriously hurt the girl if I wanted to. The push was a warning shot.

"That poor girl," Donna mumbles. "I wonder if she knew whoever it was that hurt her." She looks somber, as if her own horrid memory of her attack has come back to haunt her.

"Well, I did overhear Morgan saying that she was crying on some guy's shoulder afterwards." A light bulb blinks to life in my head. "Maybe if Morgan could remember what he looked like, we could find out if he's the Warlock that's been killing all these girls." I reach for my soda and take a sip. "And trying to kill me."

"Honey, even if it is him, do you realize how easy it would be for him to change his appearance?" She's been stabbing the same piece of lettuce with her fork for several minutes. "And to think, he was that close to you."

"Well, let's just hope he is too cocky to even think he needed to. Like you said, we are miniscule to them. They feel as if they are gods among mere mortals. Why waste magic on a bunch of dumb kids and risk a few wrinkles?" I chuckle at first but then dread washes over me, my eyes widening in horror.

"What?" Chris asks, alarmed at my sudden mood change. He looks around as if expecting an intruder and his fists clench tightly.

"How old will I be?" I mutter, my glossy eyes fixed on nothing in particular.

"What do you mean?" Donna asks, though I know she knows what I'm talking about. She puts her hand over mine.

"For the rest of my life? How old will I be forever?" I can't even look at them.

"It all depends. If you use magic, it ages you. But you can draw from nature to replenish your powers and your youth. That takes longer than . . . you know. But you will be fine, I know you–"

"No!" I shriek, cutting her off. "You know what I mean! How old will I be? Tell me!" My outburst startles her and she looks to Chris for guidance.

"Twenty-one," he answers somberly.

The only sounds Chris and Donna hear next are the scraping of my chair and the slamming of my bedroom door.

For the next few days, I bury myself in schoolwork and my job at the mall. It's hard to believe that just a week ago my biggest worry was getting to class on time. Now I've got my impending ascension in an unknown world of magic, an evil murderous stalker, the possible accusation of murder, and Jared's proposition.

Oh, Jared. No matter how many times I try to rationalize it, I can't put him at risk. He is so innocent. So ridiculously genuine and good. Subjecting him to this life that is still a mystery to even me is unfair. I would never forgive myself if something happened to him. I know he's waiting on an answer from me but I just can't find the words to explain it to him. Guess I'll have to go with the semi-truth.

"So I've really put some thought into what we talked about the other night," I say as we're sitting in the atrium on campus. It's Thursday and both of us have been in a weird space since our talk. Time to get it over with so we can go back to being normal. I miss my friend. "Right now, where my life is at, there are just too many uncertainties. But the one thing I am completely certain about is you. You are more important to me than you will ever know. Sometimes seeing you here is the only reason I wake up to come to class at all!" I chuckle nervously.

"I feel the same way," he breathes, taking my hand into his, making me more than a little uncomfortable in such a public place. I don't have the heart to yank it away.

"I need to be my very best for you. I can't weigh you down with my indecisiveness and personal struggles. You deserve someone who's got her shit together. I wish I could be that for you, God knows I do. But I'm not. And I have no idea if I'll ever get it right," I say looking down. My heart constricts in anticipation of his reaction.

"So what are you saying?" Jared asks flatly. I look up at him with fresh tears brimming my hazel eyes and he immediately softens, stroking my hand. Of course, he would be consoling me when I'm the one rejecting him. *He is too damn good for me!*

"Gabriella, I don't want you to be anything else for me than what you already are. You could never weigh me down. Ever. Let me help you through your problems like you helped me through mine."

"I can't," I choke, shaking my head. "I can't do that to you. Not now. I can't lose you and I'm afraid that if we move forward and things go wrong, I will. We'll never be this way again, and I need your friendship." One fat salty tear escapes the rim of my eyes and rolls down my cheek. Jared reads the pain etched in my face and nods. Acceptance washes over him and I exhale with relief. I don't think I could have said another word without completely losing it.

"You won't lose me. I'm not going anywhere," he smiles. He leans over and kisses my forehead gently and the warmth of his lips instantly soothes me. He feels me relax under his touch and gives my hand a reassuring pat. "Now I think you owe me lunch today after breaking my heart," he jokes, clutching his chest dramatically. I erupt with giggles, and it's the first honest laughter I've had in days. I feel an enormous weight lifted off my shoulders.

"No problem, whatever you want!" I say, wiping my tear-streaked face with the back of my hand. I could use a bite to eat as well seeing as I haven't had much of an appetite lately.

"Well, in that case, I'll take a burger and fries. Oh, and one of those big cookies for dessert! To ease my pain, of course." His eyes light up like a child. His glee is infectious and I smile brightly at him.

"You got it," I say with a wink and head to the snack bar.

Later that night after my shift at the store, I decide it's time to pick up the book again. I had been avoiding it like the plague, not feeling strong enough to deal with any more disappointing revelations. Confronting my feelings for Jared has given me a newfound confidence. It's time. I have to read on about my mother's sacrifice to save my life.

As I write these words to you, my precious child, I await your birth, which could be any day now. I know I am not there to prepare you for what is to come once you ascend and I know this platform is not sufficient enough to teach you all you need to know. But I sincerely hope it sheds some Light on the many questions I so desperately wish I was there to answer in person.

Children of the Light, and the Dark, are born with their power. However, it is limited until ascension which happens between puberty and adulthood, about 18 years of age. Yours will be delayed. Part of the deal I made with my kind was that you will be spelled, unable to ascend until your 21st birthday. This is to ensure that you are mature enough to conceal the identity of the Light. Since you will be raised by mortals, it had to be done to guarantee that you did not harm them or anyone else. The Light has agreed to let you live in peace so they will not be able to interfere with your upbringing. They also cannot protect you, at least until you ascend into the Light.

Before ascension, you must choose. The Light or the Dark. Your power will be different from both; however you must pledge your allegiance to one and only one. Please, my love, this is imperative. I do not want you to find the same fate as me. Once you have made a definite decision and are completely certain of it, you will ascend and all the wonders of the world will open up to you. You will see things you didn't see before. You will feel things you never felt before. Your own kind will appear before you, even though mortals may not see them. You will gain incredible speed and strength. It will all be overwhelming at first but Donna and Chris will help you with the adjustment.

So I have to choose? The obvious choice would be the Light. But why the hell would I want to belong to an alliance that murdered my mother? They knew I existed yet chose not to help me because I wasn't one of them? I thought the Light was all about helping and healing. Where were they all these years? And now that it is common knowledge that someone wants to kill me, where are they now?

I know you may have floundered for most of your life, and have felt unexceptional, to say the least. That is for your protection. You were spelled to appear unsuspecting, making it easier to hide you from those that wish to do you harm. From the Dark. They know you were allowed to live but they cannot find you. Donna will make sure your scent is dulled and there are other defensive tactics in place. My darling, I know it is cruel to subject you to a life of mediocrity when you are so phenomenal. However, you were not created to merely be an exceptional human. You were made to be an extraordinary force of Light.

Defensive tactics? Ok, that makes sense. Explains why I've been allowed to live in peace and lead a mediocre life. I sigh in frustration and shake my head. So my entire existence has been constructed, molded so I could never succeed at anything. Never the prom queen, never the superstar athlete, never the student council president or even the straight-A student. I've been *Nobody.* Can I honestly say that up until this point that I know who I am? And now at 20 years of age, I am supposed to *magically* grow into the person I was destined to be. Humph.

The most important thing you must remember is that the magic is in you. Forget everything you may have seen in movies or fairytale books. You will not need potions or spells. YOU are the magic. Your body is but a vessel for the amazing force that is within you. The Light you hold is the brightest, most magnificent that there ever was and with this Light, you will do great things. You alone, have the power to end centuries of wars and suffering between the Dark and the Light. You will bridge the gap, bringing peace and prosperity for all who follow you. And those who choose not to . . . you have the ability to annihilate with ease. I was weak, my dear. You will not be.

Well, let me just forget about any plans I had for the rest of *my* life, because it seems my mother has it all mapped out for me. What if I don't want to bring peace among the Dark and the Light? It's not my fight; I don't know anything about it. Come to think of it, I don't want any part of this! If I have to ascend, fine. But I can then choose to lead a normal life and blend in with everyone else. The Light and the Dark have been doing it all this time, and so will I. I can do this. I will not be used as a pawn in a war that I have nothing to do with. The Light has failed to intervene and now innocent girls are dying. Why should I fight on their behalf?

I close my mother's journal and put it back on the nightstand. That's enough reading for today. Right on cue, my cell phone rings. My heart jumps in hopes that it's Dorian but the caller ID indicates it's Morgan.

"Hey, Bitch, what are you doing?"

"Homework," I lie. "What about you?"

"Leaving work. So listen, I got these tickets for an exclusive salon opening tomorrow night. I want you to come with," she says. I can hear her climbing into her candy apple red Mustang and revving it to life. The racy sounds of Rihanna blast through the sound system, causing me to hold the phone away from my ear until she's turned it down.

"I don't know, Morgan. You know that's not really my scene," I say apprehensively. Usually these things are full of schmoozing and boozing. I'm not one to turn down free drinks and food but I'm just not in the mood to deal with the fake and phony.

"Aw, come on, Gabs! I got the tickets from a really sweet client of mine and it will be a really great networking opportunity for me, being that I'll be a licensed beautician in less than a month! She told me the salon will be amazing. And she'd even hook me up with an introduction!" she squeals. She really does sound excited.

"I thought you were staying at Posh once you got your license? They offered you a chair and everything, right?" Morgan is only officially a shampoo girl there since she's still unlicensed, but the owner has been nice enough to let her actually cut and style to get some experience. Morgan already has quite a client base and it'd be stupid to leave.

"I know, and that's still the plan. But I want to see what's out there. This new salon only caters to the big spenders and VIPs. Even the grand opening is invite-only. My client is close with the owner and gave me tickets. She said she really thinks I have the talent to land a position there. This is the type of opportunity that veteran stylists dream about. Working in a place like that would really contribute to my future goals. Please Gabs! Pretty please!" Oh God, Morgan and her spoiled princess ways. But I love her and can never say no.

"Ok, ok. What time?" I ask, exasperated. If I don't say yes now, I'll have to endure an hour of her begging and whining.

"Great! I'll pick you up at 8! And please, Gabs, wear something hot. I would dress you myself but I have to work. Love ya, babe!"

And with that, she hangs up. That's Morgan for you. Quick and to the point.

It then dawns on me that I've already made plans with Dorian for tomorrow. *Shit!* If I cancel on Morgan, she'll be pissed, plus it is a good opportunity for her. I quickly text Dorian.

To Dorian, 9:04 PM

— What time did you want to meet tomorrow?

Oh, please say early in the day. I really don't want to cancel our date. It's the only thing I've been looking forward to all week! *Ding! Ding!*

— *Noon ok for you?*

Whew, disaster averted.

— Noon is perfect :)

Damn me and those emoticons. But something about Dorian just makes me feel so flighty and giggly, I can't help it. He's so unexpected but oddly right on time. With all the crazy twists and turns my life has taken over the past week, he is a welcomed distraction. Hard to believe I only met him seven days ago. The chemistry we share is uncanny, unlike anything I've ever had with anyone else. Sure, there have been guys before. Even a couple guys I thought I could really like. But none of them measured up to Jared so they were more of a consolation prize. But now there's Dorian. And frankly, there's no comparison.

Dorian is an enigma that I want to decipher. I want to get to know him but I relish the mystery. I like the excitement of not knowing everything about him, and I want to take that journey of discovery. I want to know his likes, his dislikes. I want to know his fantasies. I want to *be* his fantasy. And as improbable as that may be, I'm willing to take the risk in trying. *Why?* Because I have nothing else to lose. I could be struck down by the Dark tomorrow and the last thing I want to die with is regrets. And if I do survive the next year, I'll be 21 forever. Time to start living for today.

I flick off my light and try to drift off to sleep, excited to meet the daylight and see Dorian again. Friday can't come soon enough.

Nine

It's too early when I wake up but I don't mind at all as I leap out of bed. Today is going to be a good day, I can feel it. The sun is shining brightly, impervious by the threat of rain clouds. I stretch my limbs and head to the kitchen for breakfast. I'm not surprised at all when I see my mom there whipping up some oatmeal and my ritual smoothie.

"Good morning, Mom!" I beam. She looks at me with disbelief in her eyes.

"Good morning, sweetie," she says cautiously. My good mood must be the calm before the storm judging by the sour face I had been wearing for the past few days. I give her a reassuring smile.

"Looks like a beautiful day," I note. For some reason, my mood is always enhanced when the sun is shining. It had been rainy and gloomy all week, and I had the disposition to match.

"Yes it does," she remarks, setting my glass in front of me. I get up to grab some cereal and milk and join her for breakfast.

"So, I read some more of my mother's, I mean Natalia's, journal last night," I say, taking a spoonful of Frosted Flakes into my mouth.

"Oh?" she asks, with a raised eyebrow. She takes a sip from her mug of tea.

"Yeah. It was about different things. Mainly my ascension." Donna nods but doesn't respond so I continue. "Is it really true that I was made to be unremarkable on purpose?"

Donna puts her cup down gently on the breakfast table and gazes at me lovingly. "Sweetheart, you are anything but unremarkable. You're a wonderful young lady."

"But you know what I mean," I say, a bit exasperated. Sometimes I just want to say *'Cut the crap and tell me the truth!'* but that would be rude. Seriously though, I really wish she'd quit trying to dance around the truth. It's making me dizzy. "Was I spelled so it'd be easier for me to blend in?"

"Yes. It had to be done. If your true self was revealed, the Dark would have come for you a long time ago." She resumes picking at her oatmeal, which looks extremely unappetizing to me.

"And there are other things? To keep me safe?"

"Yes. The smoothies, of course." She points to the glass and I take a large gulp in response. "There are wards around the house also. No one that wishes to harm you can get through." Humph, that's pretty smart. But what about when I leave the house? "You have a protection spell around you as well," my mom says, answering my unspoken question. "Unfortunately, it's superficial but it's served you well thus far."

I don't have the heart to tell her about my ghostly assailant that night in the parking lot. I don't want to worry her and it hasn't happened since. Could I have been seeing things?

"Before I ascend, I have to choose. How?" I ask. Do I have to sign some paperwork or pledge my allegiance in blood? It all seems very sketchy.

"You just choose. In your heart. You have to be completely decisive though. You can't waver."

Hmmm, but how will . . . *whoever* know? I think Natalia called it the Divine Power. I get a shiver up my spine.

"She wants me to choose the Light." I look down at my empty bowl. "Natalia," I clarify.

"Yes. It's the logical choice," my mom says. "She thought you could bring the Light and Dark together. Though she despised the Dark. After what they did to your father."

"Why bring them together? If she hates them so much?" I just don't understand why she'd want any dealings with the murderous Dark Ones.

"To bring peace. The Light did not have the influence and resources that the Dark had. The Dark have status, wealth. You on the side of the Light would even the playing field, so to speak." Donna can't hide her annoyance at the thought.

"You don't agree," I remark.

My mom thinks about her answer carefully before shaking her head. "I don't. The Dark will never succumb to the Light. They are extremely powerful. It will only bring more violence. Violence I don't want you a part of."

Donna wants to protect me, like a real mother does. Her love for me is genuine. Natalia may have loved me but she didn't know me. She had no time invested in my future, though that wasn't entirely her fault. As much as it pains me to admit, she had her own agenda.

"Will it hurt?" I whisper. It's a trivial question and I am almost embarrassed at my concern. I've got a pretty high threshold for pain, but all things supernatural, quite frankly, scares the shit out of me.

Donna smiles her warm, loving smile. "I don't think so, honey. It might be a bit of a jolt, but from what I've heard, it doesn't hurt." *Whew*, thank God for that! Or is it the Divine Power? Or are they the same? God is the only divine power I've ever known of.

I put my bowl and spoon in the sink and give my mom a quick peck on the cheek before heading back to my room. She is genuinely worried for me and I hate to see her troubled. At least she knows I am handling this as well as can be expected. That's one less worry.

It's only 9 AM, too early to start getting ready so I decide to go to the garage to hit the heavy bag. I slip on the pink 12 oz. gloves Chris bought me and begin to pound into the hard sack. It sways and rocks from the assault and I unleash a flood of blows, letting my mind drift to the myriad of concerns plaguing my mind.

My life is no longer mine. I was only brought into this world to save a race of Light Enchanters from conflicts with the Dark. Yet, they are nowhere to be found in my time of need. Do I really need them? I've actually done pretty well, considering I was set up to fail. If it weren't for the spell cast on me to be insignificant, would I have been a great human? Would Jared have fallen for me years ago? Would I have gone off to a prestigious university? So many unanswered questions and no reset button to go back and do it all again now that I know the truth. But had I known, I would have possibly let it cripple me. I probably would have turned out even more screwed up than I am now.

Before my tired arms break me from reverie, I am dripping sweat and exhausted. I maneuver my gloves off and toss them on the small work bench. I'm not going to let this crap ruin my day. The sun is shining and I get to see Dorian. *Live in the moment*. Maybe that should be my new mantra.

After taking a long hot shower and washing my hair, I step out into a steam filled bathroom. I take another 45 minutes to blow dry and straighten my long tresses until they are bone straight. I smile at the result in the mirror. Dorian has only seen me with curls and I think I look older and more sophisticated when it's straight. After much deliberation, I decide on my favorite pair of tight jeans, a royal blue top and flat boots. The blue looks great against my milky skin and the boots are comfortable enough for walking yet dressy enough for a restaurant, since I have no clue what we're doing. I'm carefully applying my eyeliner when I get a text message.

From Dorian, 11:16 PM

– *Where would you like to meet?*

Hmmm, good question. I've been so wrapped up in getting ready, I didn't even think about that.

– You can come to my house if you want.

Donna has gone to the gym for one of her classes and Chris won't be home until later this evening. I'm not quite ready to introduce Dorian to them yet and I don't know how he'd feel about meeting the parents.

– Can you meet me at Jamba Juice off Woodmen Rd.?

Humph. Just as I suspected. Maybe I should've told him I'm home alone but no use in making a big deal out of it.

– Sounds good. See you in a bit.

I finish applying my makeup and triple check my outfit in the mirror. I don't want to appear too eager but I want to look nice, which I think I've pulled off. After grabbing my jacket, I'm out the door. I put on some Maroon 5 and let Adam Levine fondle me with his sinful voice all the way to Woodmen Commons.

Dorian is sitting at a small table when I arrive, looking every bit as strikingly gorgeous and sexy as I remember. He looks up at me with hunger in his eyes and I nearly freeze where I stand. Thankfully, he's dressed in jeans and a thin, form-fitting charcoal sweater so I don't feel underdressed. The sweater hugs his physique in a way that should be outlawed; it should be a crime to look that damn good.

"Gabriella. I've missed you," he breathes when I approach. His eyes scan the length of my body, flashing with approval with a hint of desire. I start to sit but he rises before I can. He extends his hand and I slowly take it, confused as to why we're here. "Come," he says, leading me out the glass doors.

"So I'm assuming we're not here for juice," I snicker. Ok, maybe I am a little hurt that he didn't want to come to my house, but I know that it's premature for such a step. I'm just having an irrational '*girl*' moment.

"No, we don't need any juice. I have everything we need," he states casually, choosing to ignore my snide tongue. He opens the passenger car door for me and I climb in as gracefully as I can.

"So where are we going?" I smile, showing him that I'm in good spirits, despite our greeting.

He pulls the Mercedes out of the parking lot and into the flow of traffic. "You'll see."

I instantly recognize Memorial Park as we approach and a wide smile spreads across my face. It's one of my favorite places to hang out in the summer, and this sunny day has brought out a crowd of families, pets, and skateboarders, though there's still a chill in the air.

"I thought we could have a picnic," Dorian says. He opens his car door, and goes to the back to retrieve something from the trunk. Before I can collect my purse and sweater, he's already at my door, holding it open so I may step out. Such a gentleman. He's holding a large wicker basket and a blanket. I feel like I'm in a corny chick flick but my heart swells at the sentiment.

We walk down to a secluded grassy area, away from the prying eyes of teenagers and senior citizens. Dorian spreads the blanket out on the grass in one swift flail. After we sit, he begins to remove a feast from the basket. He's thought of everything! Piles of delicate Italian meats, cheeses, a warm sliced baguette, fresh strawberries and grapes, stuffed olives, and wine. Everything looks mouthwatering and I'm thankful once again that Dorian has thought of food. He must know the way to my heart.

I distribute a bit of each delicacy onto small paper plates while Dorian pours the wine. It feels . . . nice. *Normal.* Like what real couples do. I smile at the romantic prospect, as ridiculous as it may seem.

"What?" Dorian asks, handing me my disposable glass.

I smile and shake my head. "It's nothing, really."

Dorian gives me a knowing look, challenging me to speak my mind. I never back down from a challenge. "I was just thinking how nice this is. Like something you'd see in a movie. It feels good." I know the blush on my cheeks could rival the red, juicy strawberry I bite into.

"Yes, it does feel good," he says thoughtfully. It sounds more like a question though. "You've never come here for a picnic before?"

"No, not quite like this," I respond then break into a tirade of chuckles. "Honestly, most guys I've dated would consider a soggy hot dog from the cart and a warm Coke a picnic!"

Dorian laughs along with me. He gives me a long scan of his eyes and I squirm under his sensual gaze. "Your hair. You changed it."

"Just straightened it. Why, you don't like it?"

"It's nice. But I like the other way too. Any way you wear it is beautiful, Gabriella. *You're* beautiful." I blush my gratitude and return my attention to my drink, taking a hearty sip.

We enjoy the sounds of nature and distant children's laughter with our lunch. It's all delicious and we nearly finish it all between flirty chatter. When we have had our fill, we lay side by side on the blanket, soaking in the sun's warm rays.

"Dorian, how did you know I was out last Saturday?" I had almost forgotten to ask him being how I'm so easily distracted in his presence. It seems like all thoughts not pertaining to my carnal urges for him escape me whenever we're together.

"I wasn't sure. But it *was* St. Patrick's Day, and you *are* a college student. I remember when I was a wild college kid."

"Well, that wasn't that long ago." You'd think he was 60 years old, the way he's recalling the memory. "Where did you go to college anyway?"

"Overseas." He offers no more information and I figure it's because he knows I wouldn't know where it is anyway. Oddly, I am pacified by his vagueness. Where did my usual skepticism go?

Dorian rolls over onto his side, propping himself up on his elbow, gazing down at me with lust dripping from his angelic blue eyes. I turn my head towards him, revealing the fiery desire I also emanate. This is it. What I've been waiting for this entire week. As if reading my wicked thoughts, he bends down to place a soft kiss on my wanting lips. It's enough to flood my body with a barrage of tingles, and when he pulls his face away from mine, I can't hide my disappointment. I want more. *So much more.*

"You don't know what you're doing to me," I utter, between gasps. I've lost all sense of censorship and modesty. I just want him and I couldn't care less how it makes me look.

"Then tell me," he breathes. His breath is cool and sweet, and I want to taste it once again.

"I'd rather show you."

And with that, I grab a soft handful of his black, silky locks, and pull his lips down to mine. God, my body needs this. The feel of his mouth breathes life back into me after such an emotional few days. I invite his nimble tongue into my mouth and savor the wine and strawberries all over again. It tastes even better mixed with his luscious flavor. I let my hands explore his soft hair, the back of his neck, the solid ripples of his shoulders. But before I can let my hands wander south, Dorian rolls his body on top of mine, totally imprisoning my frame with his. My excitement rises as I feel his hardening length against my thigh, and I gasp. The darkened look on his face tells me that he's taking back control, and I gladly relinquish it.

Dorian exhales noisily into the base of my neck. "*Mmmm.* You have no idea what I want to do to you." His soft lips brush a trail from my collarbone to my chin. "And I've got you out here all alone. Undisturbed. To do with you as I please," he whispers into my throat.

I'm on fire. With the length of his rock hard body pressed against mine, I know he can feel the intensely rapid pace of my heart. His hip is inserted between my legs, my own thigh pinned beneath the impressive makings of his erection. Impulsively, I flex my hips upward to welcome him into my heat.

"Then do it," I breathe, panting desperately. The dramatic rise and fall of my chest makes my erect nipples that much more noticeable through the thin fabric of my shirt and I'm thankful when Dorian takes notice. He smiles wickedly and licks his delicious lips, and my body begs to feel the dampness of his tongue on my flesh.

"Oh, I fully intend to. But not here. Not now."

He places a gentle kiss on my right nipple then slowly nuzzles his nose against it, causing it to ache under the restriction of my bra and top. He then moves to my left breast and repeats his delightful torment. An involuntary moan escapes my lips and his hand finds my mouth, as if he's encouraging me to succumb to my carnal responses. He caresses each lip with the soft tips of his fingers. I want them in my mouth. I want *him* in my mouth.

"I want to take my time with you. Torture you slowly. I'm going to savor every second of your undoing," he coos, kissing and sucking his way back up to my mouth.

Oh. My. God! How do I even begin to respond to that? I mutter a mixture of moans and unintelligible babble before Dorian swallows them in a deep, fervent kiss. His soft tongue mingles with mine in a slow, deliberate dance, his lips locking onto mine, fitting so perfectly like two missing pieces of a puzzle. I surrender to his sensual assault and my arms fall back into the grass, unable to grab hold of anything, especially my willpower. I feel him all over me. His hand is knotted in my hair, cradling my head and guiding me to his rhythm. His other cups the backside of my thigh, just right where it meets the base of my ass. He palms its softness and squeezes, kneading it as he lifts me higher into the hard thickness imprisoned in his jeans. His entire body envelopes and consumes me, yet I yearn to be closer still. I'm slowly dying, and only he can put me out of my misery.

Dorian sucks then nibbles my bottom lip just before breaking the kiss all too soon to my dissatisfaction. He reads the disappointment on my face, and appears seemingly amused at my eagerness. "Soon," he promises before lifting himself off of me and standing. He is unruffled and back to his meticulous, controlled self. I, on the other hand, must look every bit as hot and bothered on the outside as I am on the inside. He extends his hand to help me up and I am on my feet in one swift, effortless movement. I smooth my rumpled clothing while Dorian picks a leaf out of my hair. Somehow we had shimmied right off of the blanket.

I want to ask him when he plans to ease my sexual frustration being that he is the source of my body's unease, but he extends his hand to me, indicating that he wants me to place mine in his. I do so, and relish the tender gesture, something I've always shied away from, especially in public. He smiles sweetly and it's hard to believe that this is the same man who spoke of slowly torturing me with his sex just minutes ago. The same man who I all but begged to fuck me deaf, dumb and blind in a public park in the middle of the day. And now we're walking, holding hands, smiling like lunatics, engaging in trivial chitchat, like normal couples do. And I like it, because I like Dorian. Really, *really* like him. But would Dorian return those feelings if he knew who and what I am? Could anyone? Will I ever be able to have a normal relationship? Lead a normal life?

The corruption of my thoughts stops me up short and Dorian turns to read my troubled gaze. "What?" he asks puzzled.

I shake the inner ramblings from my head and resume strolling, plastering a fake grin on my face to save our lighthearted exchange. "Oh, nothing. Just wondering what you're going to do about the basket and blanket," I lie.

Dorian knows I'm withholding my true feelings. His baby blues scan my own eyes, searching for the truth. He frowns for a fraction of a second and gives my hand a gentle, reassuring squeeze.

Before I can dwell on his charming gesture, a startling discovery grabs my attention. A light blue, cloudlike haze surrounds Dorian's entire frame. It's ethereal, angelic.

"*Holy shit!* Ok, the sky must be ridiculously blue or I'm seeing things! What the–" The rushed words are out of my mouth before I can even stop myself and from the wide-eyed, shocked expression on Dorian's face, I know I sound like a total nut-job. *Dammit, my eyes are playing tricks on me again!*

Dorian quickly drops my hand, no doubt recoiling from my odd outburst, and then the blue puff abruptly dissipates. He gazes at me with a perplexed yet sexy eyebrow and I silently curse myself,

Natalia, Alexander, and all things unexplainable and paranormal.

"Wow, I think the air is really thin today. And then the wine . . . I'm probably just a little dizzy," I explain, solemnly, hanging my head in embarrassment. Why the hell did I have to ruin this moment?

Dorian lifts my chin to meet his eyes with a single finger, causing me to forget my momentary misstep and I lose myself in his hypnotizing stare. It instantly warms me from the inside out and I'm at ease. All is forgotten and forgiven in his deep pools of gleaming azure. He grabs my hand again, intertwining our fingers like old lovers, and we set back off on our walk. But I can tell he's a bit more rigid, more guarded, because of my strange conduct and I painfully receive my answer.

No. I absolutely cannot have a normal relationship.

"I have to get you home," Dorian mumbles as we stroll back towards the blanket. I want to ask him why but I am too embarrassed to question him. Though my body often gives me away, I am careful not to seem too eager. I give him a quizzical look. He continues, "I have an engagement this evening. Hence the reason we are not back at my hotel room right now." He gives me a wicked wink.

Dorian knows I want him badly and I know I should be more modest about it but what's the use? We are both adults and I honestly can't say if I'll make it from one day to the next. *Live in the moment*, I think to myself. And even if I wanted to resist my innate attraction to him, could I? Whenever he is near, whenever he touches me, all apprehension and doubt simply melts away. It's like Dorian is purposely keeping me out of my own head, making it so I can't question my body's craving for him. But why? And most importantly, *how*?

"I want you to hear this," Dorian says as we ride back towards Woodmen Commons where my car is parked. He presses an unseen button and a drum beat interludes the sounds of electric guitar and a soft, mellow male voice. The music gradually grows, becoming hauntingly beautiful, enchanting even. I listen to the words; listen to the man's melodic struggle. Empathy washes over me. It's a tortured plea of honesty, lust, pain and deceit.

"Who is this?" I ask turning to face Dorian.

"The Foreign Exchange. The song is called '*Authenticity*.' Do you like it?" He turns his head to gauge my reaction.

"I do. Very much."

There's a message in the evocative melody–something that Dorian is trying to convey to me. He's on the cusp of disclosure, still teetering between admission and obscurity. Though I feel his mystery contributes to the allure, I can't help but wonder what it is Dorian is hiding from me. And do I truly have a right to press him further? Everything is still so new, yet even if it weren't, I would never, ever tell him who I really am. What I really am. I could never fit the mold of a vibrant, carefree young woman. I could never truly give him all of me. And for that simple fact, I cannot demand all of him, no matter what my heart aches for.

TEN

"So an engagement, huh? Business, pleasure, or both?" I jibe, though the honest part of me is genuinely curious. We sit in his car in the Jamba Juice parking lot, neither of us ready to say goodbye just yet.

"Oh, definitely business. The only pleasure I'm interested in is yours," he smirks. I blush instantly though I'm a bit skeptical. It's Friday evening; what kind of business would he need to tend to? Dinner with a client? He did say he was looking to change careers.

"Well, sorry to disappoint you but I have plans as well." There. Let him try *that* on for size.

Dorian responds with a raised eyebrow and a sexy smirk. "Oh, do you? Business, pleasure, or both?"

"Ummm, pleasure. Definitely pleasure," I quip.

Dorian moves in to quickly close the space between us. His eyes are dancing with fury and passion. He looks pissed. *Really* pissed. I begin to recoil when he grabs the back of my head feverishly, harshly gripping my tresses and plants his lips on mine with such intensity it frightens me. My first instinct is to fight him and I forcefully shove my fisted palms against his hard chest. But as he pries open my mouth with his tongue and it begins to massage mine, sucking me hard into his mouth, I relax and accept his brutal tongue lashing. I've been naughty and I want to be punished. Just as I begin to reciprocate and my hands find his face, he pulls back hastily, leaving me breathless and wanting more. So. Much. More.

"Well, I do hope you'll think of me when you are engaged in your pleasure." He flashes a devilish grin. He knows exactly what he's doing to me! *Cocky ass.*

I try to escape the car with what's left of my dignity and bid him goodnight. Dorian waits until I'm safely in my vehicle before speeding off hastily. The temperature has dropped dramatically so I shrug into my worn leather jacket and flip on the heat. My body heat mixed with my labored breathing causes the windows to obscure with fog, and I hit the defrost button. But before it has the chance to clear the condensation, I notice that someone has taken their finger and written something on my windshield. Surly, just some punk kids playing around; it probably says '*Wash me*,' which would be an appropriate request. But at a second glance, I realize that this is no juvenile prank and the message is meant specifically for me.

ALIGN WITH THE DARK OR DIE

Oh. My. God. I look frantically around me. This can't be happening. Someone is out there watching me! They know who I am! I shakily lock my doors and check behind my seat. All clear. Though the Defrost has begun to work and the words are dissipating, I hurriedly wipe it with my sleeve to erase it from my sight.

It wipes away clean.

Fear knots my stomach and I feel as if the wind has been knocked right out of me. If someone had marked this on the outside of my car, it would not have simply disappeared. This was written on the inside of my windshield. Someone was in my car. The Dark was here, waiting for me. I can't breathe; I can't move. My head is shouting for me to go, get the hell out of there, but it's as if I've been placed in cement. *Snap out of it, Gabs! This is not the time to break!* the voice inside me screams, shaking me from my trance. I've got to get home, where I'm safe from whatever evil awaits me tonight. With a renewed tenacity, I put the car in Drive and race home to safety.

"Morgan, I don't know if I can make it tonight," I say over the phone, once in the shelter of my bedroom.

"Oh hell no, you are not backing out now! This could really be my big break! I need you, Gabs!" she whispers into the receiver. She is still at work.

"But . . . I . . . uh," I stammer. *Crap*, I should've come up with a story before I called. My nerves are still too shot.

"Seriously, you can't back out. I'll owe you big, I promise," she pleads.

I sigh heavily. "Ok, I'll go," I reply exasperated. There's no other way to get around it. It's not like I can tell her the truth.

"Great!" she squeals. "Remember, dress to impress!" And again, she hangs up.

I still have a couple hours to burn before I have to get ready so I pull out Natalia's journal and flip towards the end, realizing I only have a few more pages to read. I'm just not motivated enough to deal with whatever new tidbits about my enchanted life she has yet to share. I place it back on my nightstand.

"Hey sweetie," my mom greets me, as I step into the family room. My parents are watching television, looking every bit as normal as they did before my twentieth birthday. You would think they didn't even know they were harboring a half Dark, half Light immortal.

"Hey guys, what's up," I say flopping down on the soft carpet, folding my legs.

"Just hanging out. Haven't seen much of you, Kiddo," my dad remarks. It's his way of checking up on me.

"Yeah, I've been busy. Work, school, you know," I respond. I want to get to the point. "Can I ask you guys a question?"

"Sure, sweetie. Anything," Donna says. Chris turns down the volume and awaits my query.

"I know we said that someone is . . . looking for me. But would the Dark want me to become one of them, maybe? Like, would they want me to, um, ascend into the Dark?" It sounds ridiculous as I'm saying it but I've got to get some insight into the horrifying message left on my windshield.

Donna nods her head gravely. "I suppose they would. It makes more sense than killing you. You'd be a great asset to them."

"But you understand how dangerous that is, right?" Chris chimes in. He's hoping, praying I'm not considering it. "They will just use you and your power to gain more influence."

"Is that any different from what the Light wants to do with me?" I ask incredulously. "I mean, I don't want to be a part of either one. It seems like each side has their own agenda. I'm just a weapon to be obtained for their own selfish reasons."

"I suppose you're right," Chris says thoughtfully. "I guess I just see the Light as the lesser of two evils. But you will have to choose for yourself."

"Do I?" I ask, looking at them both intently. "Why do I have to choose? What happens if I don't?" Chris and Donna look at each other, confused and speechless.

Finally Donna shrugs. "I can't say. It's not something that's ever been done before. Natalia just assumed that you would choose the Light. You know how I feel about that." Chris looks at her questioningly. She must have not shared all her reservations about my ascension with him, which would be a first. They always seem so in sync.

I nod, understanding what she's trying to convey. It's just as I suspected; I am of more use to the Dark alive than dead. They want me just as much as the Light does, and that message was them officially throwing their hat into the ring, though their scare tactics prove to be more disturbing than inspiring.

"I have to get ready. I'm going to a new salon opening with Morgan tonight. Have to get all dolled up," I say, trying to feign lightheartedness.

The truth is, I'm scared shitless. I've never been this afraid to walk out of my home before. But I can't be a prisoner. I can't hide here without alarming my parents. And the last thing I need is for them to start asking questions. I've never, ever ran from a fight before and I'm not about to start now. I just pray that one side, either the Light or the Dark, wants to keep me alive enough to intervene if a supernatural threat comes my way. It'd only be right, being that they're both vying for my allegiance.

"Ok, honey. Will you be having dinner with us? It's just about ready," my mom says, hopefully. Our family dinners are becoming more few and far between. I have got to make more of an effort to cherish these moments.

"I'll grab something really quickly. Morgan wants me to look my best so I need all the time I can get!" I chuckle.

"You are perfect just the way you are," my dad says. His face is serious, grim even. I flash him a toothy smile to show him that I'm ok, though my insides are snarled with fear and apprehension.

I retreat to my room, and put on some music to drown out the anxiety echoing in my head. I pull out one of the few sexy, chic dresses I own: a black long-sleeve slinky mini dress with a drastic dip in the back. It's quite provocative and Morgan would approve. I head to the shower to primp myself from head to toe, making sure my skin is silky smooth to the touch. I decide to wash my hair again, since I had a roll in the grass with Dorian. Plus I want to wash the smell of fear off of me completely. After a thorough blow dry, I pull out my curling iron and commence to fashioning dangling ringlets. I then pin my long tresses to one side with a decorative silver hair clip. Perfect! Makeup is my usual routine, with some extra shimmery dark eye shadow and a bit more eyeliner and mascara. I give my cheeks a brief sweep of peach blush and smack on a pinkish-nude lipgloss. I nod to myself in the mirror; I think I did Morgan proud.

I am slipping on my tight black dress and a pair of shimmery black almond-toe platform pumps when I hear the doorbell. Before I can hobble to greet her, Morgan is bounding down the hallway and delving into my room with excitement.

"I can't wait for tonight! If I get hired, do you know what that means? It means that we can get a crazy nice bachelorette pad!" Morgan's delight is infectious and I sincerely am thrilled for her. If anyone could land a job at an exclusive salon, it's Morgan. Her talent speaks for itself and she emanates style.

"Well, fix me up if you need to. I know you want me to make an impression, even if I am just your wing-woman," I wink.

"No, Gabs, you look great! You really do," she nods, motioning for me to turn around. "Ok, I see you, girl! You are workin' that dress!" We both giggle with glee, and I truly feel pretty next to Morgan and her 5ft 9in frame draped in a body-hugging peplum dress and red bottom pumps. I can't believe she actually goes to work wearing things like this, heels and all, standing 8 hours or more. The girl has got a gift.

"Well, my dear, I believe there's a salon owner to be wowed. Shall we go?" I ask, extending my elbow so Morgan can link her arm in mine. She loops it in and we head downtown in Morgan's red Mustang.

"So I have to tell you something," Morgan says, as we head southwest. She turns her music down; uh oh, it must be serious. I brace myself for the worst. "So last night, I went to UCCS for some little gathering they were having. I don't know—some kegger and one of my classmates took me. I so would have called you but after I spoke to you and you agreed to come with me tonight, I didn't want to push my luck. Plus it was last minute," she explains.

"It's fine, Morg," I reassure her. She always feels bad about excluding me, though I keep telling her I don't mind.

"Ok, so of course, I saw James and Miguel there. Everyone is having a good time, drinking, and somehow . . . I slept with Miguel." The look on her face is a mix of shame and anticipation.

"Morgan! Are you serious? How?" I ask incredulously. It isn't like Morgan to hop into bed with a guy just for the hell of it. Especially a lowly college kid.

"I know, I know! It just sort of happened. One minute we're playing quarters, and the next minute, we're in his room bumping uglies!" We both erupt with laughter at her analogy.

"So . . . how was it?" I ask, once our giggles have ceased.

Morgan looks at me with wide eyes. "Fan-fucking-tastic."

My expression mirrors hers. "Really? *Miguel?* Who would've

thought?"

"Girl, tell me about it. I had no idea he was a pipe layer on the side. Dude had *me* speaking Spanish by the end of the night!" And with that we have another laugh and turn the music back up.

Luxury vehicles line the parking area reserved for the grand opening of Luxe. The simple yet chic marquee gleams in the dark night, while a banner hangs below it, stating that it's the Grand Opening. We park around the corner, foregoing the valet parking, as to not draw undue attention to ourselves just in case someone from Posh is spying. However, all eyes are surely on Morgan's svelte frame as we approach the door, handing our tickets to a young woman dressed in all black, which seems to be the color scheme for the evening. Her asymmetrical cut is sleek and severe and her makeup is dark and smoky with bright red lips. She seems friendly enough though I detect a hint of envy as she spies Morgan's couture. I tightly grin a warning when she brings her eyes to me.

Luxe is chic and modern, being that it isn't over the top with ostentatious décor. However, the twinkling chandeliers, marble countertops, and plush black leather couches scream opulence. Even the stylists' chairs at each work station look more lush and comfortable than what most people have in their homes. The color scheme is simple: white, black and steel grey. It's clean and almost sterile looking but it's tranquil. Luxe exudes serenity–a woman's ultimate haven.

Morgan and I snag champagne glasses from one of the many servers circulating with drinks and hors d'oeuvres. Shrimp ceviche in shot glasses, mini crab cake sliders, bacon wrapped scallops, chicken satay with peanut sauce, caramelized onion crostini, lobster stuffed mushrooms, mini Beef Wellingtons, various canapés, dessert shooters, and cake pops–I am in seventh heaven! There's even a raw oyster bar along with a sushi station with a chef making fresh maki and sashimi. The spread alone makes me glad I decided to come along and I secretly hope my stomach isn't protruding in my form-fitting dress. Party guests mingle and network over cocktails, aged scotch, wine and, of course, champagne. I stand in the background, nodding, sipping, and grazing as Morgan works the room with ease and grace.

"Morgan!" a silky soprano rings out from across the spacious room.

We both turn our heads to see a tall, buxom young woman in a black body-hugging bandage dress and sparkling red Louboutins covered with gold spikes making her way towards us. Her long dark hair is layered and highlighted with auburn streaks, and her makeup looks as if it's been airbrushed. She's flawless. She smiles brightly as she approaches and I notice her eyes are gorgeously blue, like clear waters off a tropical island. Her body is ridiculous–curvaceous yet toned. I feel like a pervert admiring her so intently so I plaster on my own smile, and step back a bit to get out of the way.

"Aurora! You're here!" Morgan squeals. They embrace and Aurora air kisses each of Morgan's cheeks.

"Aurora this is my best friend Gabriella. Gabs, Aurora is the client I was telling you about. The one who hooked us up with the tickets." I smile genuinely at Aurora and extend my hand to her. Aurora meets it with her own perfectly manicured hand and a slight jolt shoots through me from my fingertips crawling up my arm, causing me to retract. Aurora's expression grows dark just a fraction but she recovers, though she's looking at me quizzically.

"Oh, sorry, must be the static," I shrug uncomfortably.

"Yes, must be," Aurora replies, still gazing at me questioningly. She plasters on a rigid smile and looks back to Morgan. I feel like an idiot.

"I am so glad you came. The owner is here and like I said, I know him personally," she gushes. "He's more of an investor, but he has a good amount of influence on the hiring."

Morgan's eyes grow wide with delight. "Ooooh, really? That would be amazing. I mean, look at this place! It's gorgeous!" I can tell Morgan is feeling buzzed from the champagne. I make a mental note to keep her away; she's our ride home.

"Come on, I think I spot him over there." Aurora points towards the rear of the salon, which is a lot larger inside than it appears from the outside. "Wait until you meet him; he is drop dead gorgeous. And between us girls, let's just say our relationship goes a little beyond professional. I really think he's the one!" she winks.

We weave through the crowd towards the back where there are several doors leading to different spa treatments. I think there's even a room for Botox and other procedures since the pamphlet we received boasted their on-sight doctor.

As we saunter further, the crowd becomes less of the hip and fashionable, and more mature and formal. I instantly feel uncomfortable in my backless dress and begin to tell Morgan that I'll meet her by the bar when I get a glimpse of the breathtakingly handsome man dressed in an all-black tailored suit. His dress shirt, also black, is unbuttoned at the top, provocatively revealing the ridged curves of his throat leading to a well chiseled chest. He excuses himself from his stale conversation with a stuffy older gentleman and flashes a seductively crooked smile upon our approach. My heart races furiously as he takes in the three young women standing before him, gazing at us with an air of arrogance mixed with bad boy allure.

It's Dorian.

ELEVEN

Aurora approaches Dorian with familiarity, beaming at him adoringly. "Dorian Skotos, this is Morgan Pierre, hair stylist extraordinaire." She gently puts her hands on Morgan's shoulders, as if she's presenting her as a sacred offering to him. Morgan looks shocked and is rendered speechless. "And this is her friend . . . .I'm sorry, honey, what was your name again?"

"Gabriella," Dorian breathes, heatedly. It looks as if I've been momentarily frozen by his icy gaze that hasn't left me since we approached him.

"Yes, that's right. You two know each other?" Aurora asks, struck with disbelief. How could someone like *him* know someone like *me*? Her eyes dart rapidly between Dorian and I.

"We've met, yes," I answer her snidely. I get what she was trying to say and I don't appreciate it.

"Yes, Dorian, I mean, Mr. Skotos showed up at the same club we were at for Gabs' birthday," Morgan replies. I'm grateful that she doesn't mention that he and I have been seeing each other since. I don't need Dorian to think I have loose lips and I sure as hell don't need Aurora in my business. If there's one thing Morgan is, it's trustworthy.

"Is that right? Well now that we're all acquainted, I was just telling Dorian the other day about how great of a beautician Morgan is." Aurora gracefully slides next to Dorian, resting her petite hand on his forearm. They know each other better than I initially assumed. The image of me breaking each one of those pretty little fingers of hers flashes in my mind.

"Oh thank you, Aurora, you are too kind," Morgan says stiffly. This situation has clearly made her uncomfortable and she's put her business face on.

"Well, it's true! And for you to be so young and already so talented; just imagine the clientele she could bring to Luxe. And she already has quite a following at the place she is at now." Aurora is laying it on pretty thick, and while everything she is saying is true, I don't like her talking about Morgan as if she really knows her.

"Is that right? I do think a fresh, young perspective would be useful at this type of salon," Dorian replies thoughtfully. I want to slink into the background, somehow blend in with the rest of the crowd, when Dorian turns his attention to me. "So what do you think, Gabriella? Do you think our more mature clientele would appreciate Morgan's youthful appeal?" A smile plays at his lips.

I square my shoulders and look Dorian in his bright blue mesmerizing eyes. "I believe they would. Most women are in search of the Fountain of Youth, shelling out thousands on plastic surgery and temporary fixes to appear younger. Why not find out firsthand what fresh new styles are in? Morgan is a trendsetter; whatever is popular now, she was wearing it.last season. I think she would be so much more than a beautician in your salon. She would be a style icon." I look at Morgan proudly and she's nearly gushing with gratitude. Dorian nods, letting my words sink in.

"Exactly! Well put, Gabriella. You really know your stuff. What industry are you in?" Aurora questions, eyeing me slyly. She inches closer to Dorian, no doubt, to rouse me.

"Retail," I state dryly.

"Oh?" Aurora says, amused. "A buyer at Macy's?" I can see what she's trying to do, and I will not be her fool.

"A sales clerk," I proclaim as if I've just told her I own my own boutique showcasing lavish couture.

"Oh." Aurora remarks, smugly. "Well if you ladies will excuse us, I need to introduce Dorian to some very important potential clients. Morgan, I'll see you next week!" And again, she gives her double air kisses. "And it was good meeting you, Gabriella. I'm sure we'll see each other again soon."

I'm sure we will, bitch. "You too, Aurora," is all I can muster without sounding totally fake. *Just a slore in designer shoes*, I tell myself, secretly wishing she'd trip over her fiercely gorgeous heels.

Aurora tries to tug Dorian's arm in a different direction but he is completely unmovable. "Later, Aurora. I need to have a word with Gabriella. In private." His words are gentle yet commanding. Morgan motions to me that she'll be towards the front, where she's spotted some friends, and I nod. Aurora can't hide the sour look on her face, and I swear she's seething as Dorian ushers me into a back office. It's simple: white walls, a desk and a black leather swivel chair. He shuts the door behind us and then sits on the edge of the desk.

"So this is your pleasure?" he asks with intense hooded eyes. He licks his lips, causing my blood to heat and pool deep between my legs.

"Well, it's not really business, now is it?" I smile, hoping to mask my unease. Being alone with Dorian in such a confined space makes me hyperaware of how bad I want him.

"I suppose not. For me it is, as you can see." He rolls his eyes and waves his hand at the grandiose party on the other side of the door. "But with you here, dressed like that, all I can think of is pleasure."

I blush and pretend to ignore his flattery. "I didn't know you own a salon. I thought you said you were in law?"

"I'm just an investor. The opportunity fell into my lap and I felt it could be lucrative. A good way to plant some roots here."

"Is that what you want to do? Plant some roots?" I can't help the excitement building inside of me.

"Thinking about it," he says nonchalantly. He switches gears, his eyes becoming pools of Aquamarine, surging into mine. "You look incredible tonight. Your back . . . the sight of it does something to me."

"Does it?" I ask, innocently. I walk slowly towards him, eyeing him seductively. He's not the only one who can play this game. Just as we are mere inches from each other, I stop, drinking in his aroused, eager expression.

Dorian strokes my exposed back with the tips of his fingers, sending shockwaves up and down my spine. I gasp from the contact, resisting the urge to beg him for more. He brings his face down to my neck, letting his lips brush my earlobe. "Gabriella, I would love to bend you over this desk right now and pull your dress up past your thighs and over your ass," he murmurs, sex dripping from his soft lips.

"That sounds good to me," I breathe, turning my head a fraction. "What's stopping you?" Never in my life have I been this bold and eager with a man but Dorian has awakened the sleeping sex giant within me. If my days are numbered, I want to at least die happy.

"Oh, I would do it. But I know Aurora will come looking for me and I don't want to be disturbed when I . . . ruin you." *Ruin me?* It sounds so threatening and violent. I love it.

"Aurora." *Ugh.* Even the sound of her name irritates me. "You two know each other well." It's not a question, it's an observation.

"Yes," is all he offers, looking me sternly in the eye. I don't dare to ask him how well though the question is eating me alive.

"She says you might be the one." Ok, spilling the beans from our brief girl chat is not my style but Aurora is no friend of mine. I have no loyalty to her.

Dorian shakes his head and chuckles. "That girl and her imagination." I want to ask him at least how they know each other, but I'm not ready to show him that I actually care. Just ready to jump into his bed. *No big deal.*

Dorian extends his hand to me and when I place mine in his grasp, he brings it up to his lips and leaves a lingering kiss on my knuckle. His eyes never leave mine, just like the first night we met. It feels like such a distant memory, considering all the twists my life has taken since then.

"Well, you better get back to your party," I say, pulling away from his trance. Once again, I don't want to give him the chance to dismiss me. Even though all I want to do is stay here with him all night.

"No, I'm going home. They can party all they want to. I'll get the bill in the morning," he replies indifferently.

Dorian escorts me back into the swarm of people, saying his polite farewells as I stand by his side meekly. I feel like I'm intruding so I bid him goodnight, for the second time today, and set off to find Morgan. Before I can put ten feet between us, I hear the familiar sound of Aurora's soprano voice, greeting him back with enthusiasm. It takes every ounce of my self-control not to turn back around and slap her silly.

"There you are!" Morgan exclaims when she spots me. I try to replace my vexed expression with a friendly grin.

"Here I am," I respond.

She's surrounded by a group of dramatically adorned men with outrageous hair styles. Bright, shimmery colors bathe their eyelids and their lips are perfectly pouty with various hues of lipstick. Ah yes, Morgan loves gay men, and gay men love Morgan. I smile brightly at all of them as they greet me with a chorus of '*Oooohs*' and '*Ahhhhs*' at my daring dress. A couple of them are new stylists at the salon and they are overjoyed at the prospect of Morgan joining their team. Their humor and goodhearted nature instantly perk me up from my Aurora-funk.

"Did you see Mr. Tall, Dark and Handsome back there?" one of the men asks. His name is Carlos and he has brightly colored feathers embellishing his fire engine red faux hawk. "*Giiirl*, when I found out he owned this place, I said '*Hell yes! Where do I sign?*' Papi had me wide open. I was ready to work for free just so I can look at that ass!" We all erupt with laughter, and I secretly sympathize with Carlos. Yes, Dorian definitely has that affect.

"But that one little chick can't keep her damn hands off him. She was here all last week, while we're trying to set up, chasing after him. *Oooh*, and she's a mean little bitch too. Don't let that pretty face fool you," his friend, Jackson, chimes in. He's tall and svelte and could easily be a male model with his long platinum blonde locks and tan skin.

The guys engage in raucous banter about their run-ins with Aurora while Morgan and I listen intently, exchanging the occasional glance and nod. We're taking it all in, trying to find out what's really going on with Dorian and Aurora.

"Well, I say we drink this free champagne, eat this free food and really get this party started!" their other buddy exclaims. His name is Xavier but he would rather people call him X. His hair is a bit more tamed–short, full and chocolate brown–being that he works in the governor's office. But he makes up for it with vivid colored eye makeup that's fashioned into a peacock. It looks like a true work of art and I'm in awe.

We all grab glasses of champagne and raise them in celebration. Soon after, the smooth sounds of jazz change to booming bass-lines and drumbeats and the real fun begins. We dance, eat, drink, and laugh until our sides hurt. Still, all I can think about is Dorian and if Aurora is occupying his bed tonight.

It's nearly midnight and I am tipsy, feeling the fuzzy effects of champagne and Patron. Carlos and his friends know how to have a good time and we all promise to go out to Denver for a real night on the town soon. Morgan ushers me to her Mustang though I'm more than capable of making it there on my own. She's worried about taking me home in fear that my parents may catch me stumbling in the house so I construct a text, informing them that I'm staying at her house. Her parents are more lenient with their little princess.

We head North, passing nightclubs and bars, bustling with music and laughter. I roll down the window and let the frigid air sober me up while Jay-Z pumps through the sound system spinning an evocative tale of his past and present, dreams and realities, life and death. I urge the hypnotic drumbeats to carry me to another place devoid of all my trivial qualms about my hopeless love life but my intoxicated mind refuses to abandon the nagging questions.

"Wait. Take me to the Broadmoor," I command suddenly.

Morgan is looking at me warily, probably thinking that I've had way too much to drink. "Seriously, Morg. I need to go to the Broadmoor."

She gives me a pointed look, pursing her full, glossed lips. "What's at the Broadmoor?"

I look at my best friend, conviction in my eyes. "Dorian."

Without another word, Morgan makes a U-turn at the next light.

We pull up to the grand resort and simultaneously gasp at its splendor. It's beyond gorgeous. And with spotlights illuminating the vast estate, it looks more like a modern-day castle than a hotel.

"So do you know what room he's staying in?" Morgan asks.

"No," I respond, sheepishly.

"Then how do you expect to get to his room? Hotels like these just don't give away room information. People pay for discretion, Gabs." Morgan obviously has had more experience with this stuff than I have.

I look in the back seat and grab the gift bags we received from the salon opening, emptying the swag into our purses. I open a nude lipgloss and give my pout a fresh, glimmering coat. Morgan grabs a comb and begins to work her magic, releasing my ringlets from the hair clip and letting them cascade down my back. She gives me a fresh sweep of blush and hands me her jacket. I shrug it on and after a second glance to ensure I'm presentable, I grab the empty gift bags, my purse and step out of the Mustang.

"Thanks, Morgan. You're the best," I smile sweetly.

"Yeah, yeah, I know. Now go get your man."

I stroll through the entrance and enter the majestic lobby, careful not to look too awestruck at its brilliance. I bound gracefully to the reception desk to be greeted by a young man with freckles and fiery red hair.

"Hello, I am Mrs. Skotos. I've just flown here to surprise my husband for his birthday and I can't seem to remember his room number," I say confidently, showing him the gift bags.

"Yes, of course, Mrs. Skotos. Um, no luggage we can help you with?" He's clearly testing me.

I eye him suggestively. "Well, it's not the kind of visit that requires much clothing, dear."

Freckles' face turns as red as his hair as he looks down to tap on his computer. "Mr. Skotos is in the Lakeside building, ma'am." He gives me the room number and begins to spout off directions and I thank him for his assistance.

I begin the trek to the neighboring building, nervously aware that it is pitch black and deathly quiet out, though the path is sufficiently lit with lamp posts and garden lights. I jump at every creak and pull Morgan's jacket tightly around me. Suddenly I'm freezing and begin to walk briskly despite my five inch heels to the Lakeside building to safety. A friendly doorman opens the glass doors, welcoming me into the warmth. I thank him before stuffing the empty gift bags into a nearby trashcan then saunter into the elevator.

Ok, this is it. I can't leave now; I have to know. Either Dorian is up there alone or he's with Aurora. Or maybe someone else? Oh God, what if he's sound asleep and is upset that I've woken him? What if he isn't even there and simply lied at the party to escape? He didn't invite me over so he obviously didn't want me here. I really didn't think this through. Damn me and my impulsiveness! Damn that liquid courage! I can't call Morgan to come back and I don't have enough cash on me to call a cab. *Shit!*

The *Ding!* from the elevator breaks me from my agonized reverie and the doors slide open, indicating that just a few steps and a set of double doors separate me from the truth about Dorian. I walk tentatively towards the doors that signify his suite, holding my breath every step of the way. I exhale noisily as I reach my destination, feeling dizzy from the lack of oxygen mixed with champagne. Time to face my fears. I will my shaky hand to make a fist and raise it to the door. *Here goes nothing.* I quickly rap three times and take a precautionary step back. Soft footsteps pad towards the door seconds later, and then a rustling sound follows. Maybe a belt buckle? *Oh no, this isn't good.*

Dorian opens the door, shirtless, his abs a rippling stone path towards the unbuttoned dress slacks that hang from the severely sexy V of his hip muscles. They're draped so low that it's evident that he isn't wearing any underwear. I take in a sharp breath at the sight of him nearly naked. He's even more gorgeous than I could have ever dreamed. I then take in his disheveled, half-dressed appearance, the look on his face a combination of shock and alarm. I've caught him off guard and it doesn't look like my unexpected appearance is a welcomed surprise. His icy irises glare at me, freezing me where I stand.

I can't turn back now.

TWELVE

Before I can say a word, Dorian grabs my arm and yanks me into his suite as if I'm weightless. He pushes me up against the wall and buries his tongue inside my mouth with great ferocity. My coat falls from my shoulders, allowing his hands to roam my body, exploring the dips and rises of my delicate curves. Reaching to my backside, he palms its roundness and slowly massages, matching the rhythm of our intertwined tongues. I feel the hardness of his middle, grinding into my belly button and I gasp against his lips.

Dorian's hands slowly move up my bare back, over my shoulders and down to my aching breasts. I am ever so grateful when his fingers begin to flick and fondle my nipples through the tight fabric of my dress. I let a moan escape through our fused mouths and Dorian devours it, muffling my cry of pleasure. He lets a hand travel south, easing between my thighs, searching for my heat. I'm on fire– a white hot flame of scorching ecstasy. The gap between my legs is humid with expectation. Dorian pushes my damp lace panties aside and slides a finger across my clitoris with slow, relentless torment. My knees buckle at the contact, and he continues his torture–back and forth, back and forth–until my muffled moans can no longer be contained. Just when I think his assault has ended, he slides the finger inside of me, feeling my walls throb and contract around him. A chorus of whimpers and expletives quickly follows.

Dorian takes his other hand and wraps it around my lower back, lifting me off my feet effortlessly. I reflexively wrap my legs around him, kicking my heels off and letting them tumble to the ground. Astonishingly, his long, agile finger is still nestled inside of me and we are still engaged in our feverish lip-lock. My fingers are tangled in his tousled hair, elbows resting on his shoulders to support the slow grind against his finger. He inserts another, and I cry out a garbled plea, begging him not to stop.

Dorian easily carries me to what I assume is a bedroom. He sets me on the edge of the bed, and I whimper as his lips and fingers abandon me. He slowly places them in his mouth one by one, sucking away my sweetness while watching me intently. I stare back at him in awe; *Holy fuck*, I want him.

"Now that you've come all this way to see me, what will you do with me?" he asks in a low, raspy voice. It's the first words he's uttered since my arrival yet we have already said so much. I know the taste of my pleasure has affected him. He wants this just as bad as I do.

I look directly in front of me at his unbuttoned slacks dangling off the cut of his hip muscles. Slowly, I pull the zipper down, holding my breath in anticipation as his pants fall around his ankles, liberating his generous erection. I am nearly floored at the size of him, a mixture of apprehension and excitement overcoming me. I lick my lips reflexively while gazing up at him through my dark eyelashes. He gasps in surprise at my boldness. I turn my attention back to his splendor wondering for a split second if I can really do this; I've never given oral before but I want to so bad in this moment. I shake the doubt from my mind and submit to my carnal urges, taking the swollen head of him in my mouth.

I gently swirl the tip with my tongue, savoring the trickles of sweetness that escape as a result. His flavor is delectable, and with eagerness I try to take all of him in my mouth. Dorian's head rolls back and a barrage of deep, hoarse moans escape him. I continue to bathe him with my tongue, sucking slowly and tightly up and down. I let my tongue explore every inch of his ridged shaft, tracing each vein, swirling it from base to head. He's losing control; I can feel his legs quiver. He grows longer, thicker in my mouth and I know the end is near for him. I pick up the pace, craving to taste him once more when he pulls away, leaving my wanting mouth.

"No, not yet," Dorian smiles down at me, still panting.

He leans down to pull my dress down over my shoulders, slowly stripping it from my body until it is on the floor. I sit before him, bare-nippled, wearing only a lacey black thong. I want to wrap my arms around myself to shield my breasts but the look of admiration in his eyes urges me not to. He advances inch by inch, placing his knee between my legs to scoot me up farther on the bed. When my entire body is flat on the adorned satin comforter, he gently peels my panties off, admiring the view once again.

"So beautiful," he murmurs, his fingertips grazing the skin over my ribcage ever so gently.

Dorian hovers over me, locking his penetrating azure gaze on me. Our bodies do not touch yet I feel a powerful sensation run through me. Prickly yet pleasurable, just like the feeling I got the first night that Dorian's lips brushed my hand. The feeling grows stronger, turning from a prickle to a pulsation, coursing in my veins, kissing every nerve ending in my body. I'm gasping, unable to hold on anymore. The satin comforter rumples and stretches under my desperate grip. Dorian's eyes never leave mine, and I am unable to blink and break his hypnotic stare. I want to scream, want to thrash from this sweet agony but I am totally paralyzed in his captivity. And just as I feel as if I can take no more, the pulsing centralizes, leaving my limbs, crawling to a path leading to my sex. It is so overwhelming, so intense, and I call out to God, the Divine Power, and Dorian. He still doesn't touch me, still doesn't save me as I drown in a pool of pleasure.

Before I can catch my breath and slow my pounding heart, Dorian spreads my legs wider, exposing the waterfall of my release. And in one swift movement, he thrusts himself inside of me, filling me to capacity. We gasp in unison. The feeling is so . . . *perfect*. So right. I'm in disbelief at how good he feels inside my warmth. Dorian begins to slowly grind, stirring himself within my walls. I can feel every inch of him, and from the look on his strained face, he can feel all of me. His torture is unhurried, deliberate. He wants to make this last and I never want it to end.

"*Shit*, you feel good," he breathes into the base of my neck. His teeth graze my throat and I shudder from his touch.

Soft moans leave my lips, joining Dorian's low sighs in a harmonious song of hedonism. The tempo increases with each stroke, and soon it is a tune of sharp cries and deep, throaty groans. I feel it growing inside of me, and my whimpers evolve into agonized yelps with his increasing length. It's painful yet oh so pleasurable and the combination brings me to my brink. My flame is now a wildfire and only he can extinguish it. I feel it; feel it building inside me, climbing higher and higher. Dorian's expression is a mixture of strain and defeat. He can't stop himself. He needs this too; he needs to surrender himself to our carnality.

In one deep thrust, he relinquishes his resolve, his fingers digging into the sides of my backside as he pushes himself deeper still. The feeling of his eruption causes me to submit to mine as well, and I cry out his name as our rivers unite into a deep, endless ocean.

"You looked upset," I reflect. We are both lying on top of the comforter, finding our breaths, covered in a glistening sheen of sweat.

"I was shocked. Didn't expect you to come here," Dorian says, lightly panting. We stare at the ceiling, both gloriously spent.

"Neither did I."

I exhale and allow myself to look at him. He looks scrumptious; even with disheveled hair and sweat on his brow, he's still the most beautiful man I've ever seen. I know he can feel my eyes on him but he doesn't turn towards me. He looks thoughtful. *Oh no*, I hope he doesn't regret what just transpired between us. I know I don't.

"You wield powerful magic," he says, barely above a whisper.

The fuck? Does he . . . ? No. He can't possibly know. I laugh off his remark nervously. I can't even wrap my head around it. I know it's just a figure of speech but it hits too close to home.

"I could say the same thing about you."

Dorian abruptly turns his head and looks at me with a hint of alarm. I smile to ease the rising tension and he returns my grin. He eases up on his elbow and plants a tender kiss on my lips. Just the gentle contact stirs something within me. I want this. I don't want to be some Enchantress. I don't want to be the Light's savior from the Dark. I just want this. This man in front of me, naked and utterly gorgeous, I want *him.*

"I'm glad you came," he says.

"I didn't know what I was doing until I was already here. And I wasn't sure what I would find. At the party, seeing you with Aurora . . . I had to know what was between you two." My words are strained but I'm being honest. Our intimate exchange has made me vulnerable, something I don't make a habit of showing.

"So you thought you'd show up here and find out for yourself? What'd you think; that you'd catch us in the act?" He's smiling but there's an edge to his voice. And I'm painfully aware that he hasn't denied that they have something going on.

Don't ruin this, I tell myself. *Live in the moment.*

"Maybe. Or maybe I just wanted to see you. Either way, I don't regret coming," I say. I take my finger and twirl it in a loose lock of hair on his forehead. It's so soft and still damp with sweat.

"No regrets," he remarks. "You never know when your days are numbered."

"You can say that again." Once again, he is right on point.

"Enough talking." And before I can utter an objection, Dorian leans down to conjoin his mouth with mine, his hand hungrily cupping my breast, and I forget that Aurora even exists.

THIRTEEN

The gods of hot one night stands, salacious sleepovers and embarrassing morning afters are certainly smiling down on me today!

Not only did I get to wake up to the most beautiful creature ever made after not one but two raucous sex sessions, but one of the gifts from the Luxe swag bag is a Walk of Shame Kit. *Score!*

I open the little canister after tiptoeing to the bathroom before Dorian wakes. I initially was planning to just finger brush my teeth but included is a little toothbrush with toothpaste. I think about showering but that would be too obvious. Plus he might want to do that together and go for Round 3. After a quick brush, a fluff of my wild after-sex hair, and a little dab of nude lip gloss, I sneak back out and get under the covers. A nude Dorian is sleeping peacefully on his stomach and it's all I can do not to lean over and place a kiss gently on his perfect face.

"You didn't have to do that," he mutters, eyelids still closed. *Shit!* Busted.

"Do what?" I whisper innocently.

"I know you're a real woman. No one wakes up with minty fresh breath and glossed lips." He finally opens his sleepy eyes and gives me a crooked grin.

"Well, then why do *you* look so good?" And Lord knows he does. His tousled black locks are the only indication that he's been sexing and sleeping, and even those make him look unbelievably hot. And not even a hint of morning breath.

Dorian shrugs his bare shoulders. "I don't know. Magic?" His blue eyes melt into my hazels. I know they must be wide with shock but I try to recover with a nervous giggle.

"I don't think so. You might just be lucky." I joke.

"I don't believe in luck." Dorian turns his body towards me, revealing his chiseled chest.

"But you believe in magic?" I ask with an arch of my eyebrow. I know I am in dangerous territory but it's just playful banter.

Dorian smirks and his eyes suddenly darken. "Don't you?"

We stare at each other, both with a question on our lips. What is he trying to tell me? That he knows my secret? He couldn't. No sane human being would believe that even if they read Natalia's journal for themselves. I don't know if even I can entirely believe it.

"I know there's magic in you. I've felt it. Right here," Dorian murmurs, reaching down to stir my swollen, damp sex. And with that, there's no more talking, just moaning, gasping and heavy breathing.

An hour later, we sit in the vast living room of the suite looking at the room service menu, my legs draped over his thighs. We have showered, together to my delight, and would have gone for round 4 if it weren't for my rumbling tummy. Luckily, the Walk of Shame Kit included a shirtdress, underwear and flip flops so I wouldn't appear as shameful in my tight backless dress and pumps. Dorian is barefoot, dressed in jeans and a simple black t-shirt. Even dressed down, he looks amazing.

"So what do you like? Eggs? Bacon? Pancakes?" he asks looking up from the extensive menu. He wears a boyish grin that makes his blue eyes twinkle.

"Isn't it kinda late for breakfast?"

Dorian looks down at the intricate titanium watch on his wrist. With its unique, almost robotic design, it's easily the coolest timepiece I've ever seen. And though it isn't covered in diamonds, I can tell it probably costs a fortune. Yup, the theory that Dorian is a rebellious trust fund baby seems pretty spot on.

"I suppose you're right. Burger and fries?"

"No onions and mayo on mine, please."

While he calls down to order our lunch, I get a better look at the suite. It's draped in black and gold filigree and animal prints. A little gaudy for my tastes. It's luxurious, that's for sure, and mirrors a high-end furniture showroom.

"A bit ostentatious, huh?" Dorian remarks pensively. He must've spied me checking out the room.

"You have to live here, not me."

"Yeah, but it's only temporary. Besides, this suite was the least extravagant of them all," he waves his hand around the room and rolls his eyes. "I prefer more understated elegance."

I think back to Luxe salon. He definitely put his stamp on that place, even if he is just an investor. Then there's me. I could say that I'm understated, in a way. I'm no model but I can hold my own. I'm curvy and soft yet toned. Not really glamorous, but I can clean up nicely when I want to. I'm ordinary, just like Natalia intended.

"I pegged you for the penthouse," I remark. It's obvious he can afford it.

"Why? All that space just for me? I'm not here much anyway. Plus imagine *that* magnitude of grandeur," he snickers, making a gagging gesture. I giggle at his playfulness, completely content in this moment.

Fifteen minutes later, we are sitting down at the extensive dining table with our elegant meal of burgers, fries and soda. We both chuckle at the irony before we dig in. I am ravenous, and barely come up for air until I'm halfway finished.

"Worked up quite an appetite, huh?" Dorian says observing my nearly empty plate. I finish chewing my bite of burger and grab my soda to wash it down before responding.

"Have to replenish after that workout you gave me last night. And this morning." My eyes narrow suggestively and I flash him a naughty smile. I slowly lick the tip of my straw before placing it back into my mouth. Dorian's eyes flash with blue fire.

"Looks like I should be thanking the editor at Cosmopolitan magazine," he says licking his lips.

Huh? Ok, what does Cosmo have to do with anything? Confusion is etched on my face.

"The magazine you were reading the first day I saw you at Starbucks. 'Top 12 Oral Tricks That Will Make Your Man Melt' was the title, I believe." Dorian chuckles and picks up a fry, placing it in his gorgeous mouth.

I feel my cheeks heat and cover my face with my hands. "Oh God! No, that wasn't mine! I swear, I didn't read it!" *Dammit!* Why did I have to pick up that freakin' magazine?

"Oh? You must have mastered the art all on your own," he replies, still smirking.

"Well actually . . . no." I look down at my plate awkwardly. "I've never done that before last night. Before you." I look back up to read his stunned expression.

"Never? So I was your first?" He looks amused. Maybe a little sentimental. "Wow. Well, thank you," he stammers. Not quite the response I was expecting. My revelation has caught him off guard.

"No need to thank me. I wanted to. I liked it," I say, looking him in the eye boldly. "With you, that is." I don't want him to think I've become some head-giving Jezebel.

Dorian furrows his brow in confusion. "But why . . . *me?*"

"I don't know," I shrug. "It just felt right, I guess."

"*Right,*" Dorian repeats, testing the word out on his tongue. He licks his lips and then gazes at me through dark lashes. "Hmmm, well I think it's time for dessert."

Dorian quickly grabs our plates and glasses and sets them on the buffet. He then sits back down in his chair, beckoning me to come to him with his finger. I do as he wishes and stand in front him. He slides his firm hands up the back of my thighs, massaging the base of my ass before suddenly lifting me up and setting me down on the edge of the table.

"Lie back," he commands, and I do as I'm told, trembling with anticipation.

Dorian spreads my legs apart and begins massaging my heated sex through the thin fabric of my panties. He reaches for its dainty waistband and begins to pull them downward. I flex my bottom up to aid him in his efforts and he lets them fall to the floor. He looks at my scorching heat like a hungry man in front of a feast. His breathing quickens and I can feel the cool air that escapes between his partially open lips. I give myself a mental pat on the back for grooming myself the morning before. Never did I expect Dorian to be this up close and personal and I'm nervous as hell. He can see everything, all of me. The look on his face as he studies every swell and crevice is of appreciation and wonder. My body screams for his touch, yet he tortures me under his gaze. *Damn, this is so kinky!*

Dorian takes a single index finger and gentle strokes my clit. I gasp at his touch, already throbbing and wet for him. He then moistens the tip of the same finger with his mouth and repeats, strumming a sweet song of pleasure. When I begin to arch my back and surrender to his teasing, he slips the finger inside of me and holds it still. My walls contract and grip the digit, holding it captive. He begins to inch it in and out, curving it upwards to meet my most sensitive spot. *Oh no, not yet!* The pressure is so intense, so blissfully exhilarating that I am in fear of losing myself already. Dorian can feel my quivering and responds by joining his index finger with his middle. I cry out and pulsate viciously against them both.

I look down at a stern faced Dorian. He's concentrating on the lustful task, biting his bottom lip. He looks so damn sexy; I just want to pull him on top of me. Dorian catches me eyeing him and locks his glistening baby blues on my blissfully tortured face. Slowly, he leans forward and licks my swollen clit with the tip of his tongue, still penetrating me with his long, searching fingers. He licks again, applying more pressure, letting his saliva meld with my essence. He continues his oral assault, licking, sucking, nibbling my delicate flesh until my moans and cries beg him to stop. I can't take anymore; the feeling is too strong, too good. I am at risk of completely losing control, something I'm struggling like hell to avoid.

Noticing my trembling knees, Dorian slides them onto his shoulders, pushing his tongue deeper into the soft, wet folds. He lets his fingers drop and replaces them with his tongue, greedily devouring me as if I am his last meal, hoarsely groaning his gratification. I am a mess of garbled screams, vulgarities and praise, unable to form an intelligible thought. In this moment, all I know is pleasure. And Dorian is giving me more than I can possibly take.

After another mind-numbing orgasm, I lie on the table breathless, squeezing my thighs together in an attempt to tame the endless ripples and rolls. Dorian reclines in his chair, watching the show as I writhe and convulse violently. He's an amused spectator, watching the poor, wrecked girl in front of him. I feel so exposed, so vulnerable, but I can't help it. He's done this to me. He's made me this jumbled mess of tangled tresses, piercing moans, and drenching wet sex. My body is his captive, his to torture and tease whenever he pleases.

"So is this what you meant when you said you wanted to ruin me?" I ask Dorian after I've found my breath after several minutes.

I sit up and smooth my dress over my legs. My panties lie rumpled on the floor yet I'm too embarrassed to reach down to retrieve them. Dorian follows my gaze and leans down to pick them up. He slowly pulls them over my bare feet, up my legs and to my thighs. I want to lift my butt up but I'm too spent, my muscles still quivering.

"That depends. Do you feel ruined?" he smiles, letting his hands rest on top of my thighs.

"Well, sorta. I don't know. I kinda feel the opposite." I give him a contemplative look, cocking my head to one side. "Spoiled, maybe."

"Spoiled?" he asks with a raised brow.

"Yes, spoiled. You've given me so much . . . ," I can't find the words to describe how incredible he just made me feel, *is* making me feel. Just the thought makes me giddy and I giggle involuntarily.

"What?" he asks, licking his lips. He leans his head down to nuzzle the entrance of my thighs. *Oh God, not again!*

I chew my bottom lip, urging myself to step up to the plate and tell Dorian how I really feel. "I feel like you're . . . doing something to me. Changing me, in a way. The day I met you, it's like, the earth shifted. Every bit of doubt and reluctance instantly dissolves whenever you're around me. Things make sense that ordinarily wouldn't. I don't fully understand it so it's incredibly difficult for me to even try to explain it to you. But I know something happened. I know what I felt."

Dorian's eyes darken a fraction, the makings of a dark storm brewing behind crystal blue. "You're overthinking it."

"Am I? Or am I not thinking about it enough?"

For several heated moments, we stare at each other, both our expressions guarded and defensive. He has secrets, just like I do. But while we may be hell bent on safeguarding the most secluded spaces of our psyches, the devastatingly strong attraction between us keeps penetrating the rouse. In our most intimate moments, he can't hide from me and I can't hide from him. And I don't want to, though I know it's extremely stupid of me to feel that way.

But looking at him now, seeing how distant and cold he has turned towards me makes me realize that I am just kidding myself. He's content with obscurity and omissions. He's content with not caring.

"Come on. Let's get you home," Dorian mutters.

Dorian stands and places his hands under my arms, lifting me off the table and onto my feet. I plaster on a fake smile and try to appear lighthearted. And just like that, my wall is back up. I'm back to impassive glares and pursed, tight lips–defensive tactics to protect my already fragile heart. The beautiful man in front of me doesn't truly want me, and as much as it pains me to my core, I know it's better this way. It has to be. And hopefully, if I keep telling myself just that, I could actually start to believe it.

FOURTEEN

"Let's pull over here," Dorian says, stopping a few houses down from my house. It's been a quiet, tense ride and I'm guessing he wants to clear the air before we say goodbye.

Goodbye. My heart constricts at the very word.

He turns the car off and we sit in silence for a beat. "Look, I'm not good with this." I know what he means–feelings, relationships . . . love.

"Neither am I," I say quietly. It's the truth. My longest relationship was two months and it only lasted that long because I was too lazy to break it off.

"I don't know what you expect of me. I don't want to sell you this dream then you realize it's really a nightmare. That *I'm* a nightmare." He exhales loudly and looks at me for a reaction. I give him nothing, my face stoic and unreadable. "You've made me . . . happy. I didn't expect you to, but you did." His brow furrows at his words and he shakes his head as if to dispel the possibility of true happiness.

Whoa. That was an odd turn. I turn my head abruptly to read his face. I don't know what to say; I can't find the words to tell him that I feel exactly the same way.

"I'm not sure what I should do with that," he continues. "I don't know what I *can* do with that." His expression is so pained. I just want to reach out to him and let him know that it's ok; he's not alone in this. But pride keeps my hands twisted in a knot in my lap.

"Don't do anything," I urge. "Let it happen naturally. What will be, will be."

Dorian looks so tortured in this moment. Part of him wanting to give into something he can't control, part of him wanting to reject it because it's all foreign to him. And just like that, the strange blue mist slowly enraptures him. He's covered by the dense fog and I see it. I see *him*. I know my eyes are not playing tricks on me.

I tentatively reach my hand towards him into the mist, stroking his cheek. He nuzzles against the contact, taking a deep breath and gently kissing my palm. I give him a smile of reassurance. We can take this journey together. We can write our own story.

Dorian leans over and plants a tender kiss on my lips. Within it holds possibility, fear, joy. Neither of us knows what the future holds but we choose to live for this moment. It's the only one that matters.

After a goodbye kiss that almost developed into something unsuitable for the wholesome Briargate community, I walk the few houses to my house. Dorian is still watching me until I make it inside, then he pulls off in haste.

"Gabriella? Is that you?" my mom calls from the kitchen.

"Yeah Mom, it's me," I call out. I scramble to my room to throw on some sweats and a tank top and stow the t-shirtdress and flip flops in the back of my closet. She never comes in here but better safe than sorry. Then I retreat to the bathroom to try to wash the '*Just Properly Fucked*' glow off my face. I skip down the hall to the kitchen to see Donna. *Yeah, dammit, I skipped.* Crap, what's gotten into me? *Dorian.*

"There you are!" my mom says, breaking me from my inner ramblings.

"Here I am," I respond.

"Did you have fun with Morgan?" She's rushing to whip up my smoothie since I missed it earlier this morning. I've got to make more of an effort to remember them now that I know their purpose.

"Sure did," is all I can say.

I let my mind drift to the night before. Showing up at Dorian's suite, letting him push me up against the wall to thrust his tongue into my mouth, tasting him, feeling him pulsate deep inside of me . . .

Donna clears her throat loudly, causing me to blink wildly and meet her eyes.

"Huh?" I say, a bit dazed from the memory of Dorian's tongue kneading the tenderness between my thighs.

"Um, honey, you know I don't like to pry, but I have to ask. Are you seeing someone?" Donna is beet red and clearly uncomfortable. I'm shocked that she would ask; there hasn't been any indication of me dating anyone.

"No," I say slowly, though it sounds more like a question. "Why do you ask?"

"Well, your aura is light red, almost pink," she states.

"And that means?" I should really do some research. Especially if I'm going to have to keep my emotions at bay.

"Well, um . . . passion. Romance. Love," she beams. Love? *Oh hell no*.

"Sorry to disappoint you, Mom, but I'm still pathetically single."

It's true. Dorian and I never defined our relationship and it was, in fact, just one night/morning of mind-blowing, uninhibited, scorching hot sex. Sure, it'd be nice to be able to get a repeat performance without the fear of appearing like a whore, but Dorian just isn't there yet. And I don't know if I can ever get there at all.

"But there is someone. It's more than just physical attraction too. Jared, maybe?" Geez, since when did my mom get psychic abilities? *Invasive much?*

"Jared is still in the friend zone. Or I should say, *I'm* still in the friend zone. I thought I wanted more." I shake my head. "No. I did want more, but it could never work. Not with what I am. What I'll become."

Saying it out loud stings. The realization that I will never have a normal relationship with anybody, Dorian included, tugs at my heartstrings. Maybe that's why I'm not so hard-pressed to venture that far beyond the bedroom.

Donna places her small hand on mine and looks at me regretfully. "I'm so sorry, honey. But you never know, there could be someone out there for you," she says wistfully.

"They'd have to be either very strong or very dumb, but hey, a girl can dream, right?" I down the rest of my smoothie and head to my room to call Morgan. She's been blowing up my cell since this morning and I know she'll want the scoop.

"*Oooh*, girl, tell me everything!" she shrieks. Usually she's the one with the wild, raucous stories to share, but now that I'm in the hot seat, it just doesn't feel right.

"Well, you know, I went over to his suite and knocked on the door. Luckily, he was alone. I was so worried Aurora would be there. She didn't mention being in a relationship or dating anyone?" The best place to get the latest gossip is a salon. Hairdressers and shrinks are pretty much one and the same.

"No, not really. She said there was a guy she was seeing. I'd see her texting all the time but I never read any. What did Dorian say?" Morgan asks, a hint of worry in her voice.

"He really didn't say anything. I didn't press the issue much." Crap. I went all the way there and didn't get the answers I was searching for. And I was so sure I'd get to the bottom of the things. But seeing him, feeling him, totally disarmed me. I could barely remember my own name, let alone what I went there for.

"What do you mean? You didn't ask him if he was dating Aurora?" she says incredulously.

"Uh, not really." I know I sound like an idiot for being so easily distracted. I just wish I could explain the uncanny magnetism between Dorian and me. Even if I wanted to, I couldn't begin to put that into words.

"Then what did you do?"

I know I have to throw her a bone. That'll get her off my back for not grilling Dorian about Aurora. "Stuff. Really good stuff," I reply, knowing this will only lead to a line of questioning that would put Detectives Perkins and Cole to shame.

"Stuff, huh? The kind of stuff that makes you wanna cry because it's so damn good? The kind of stuff that could get you locked up in some states?" Morgan and her colorful lingo–gotta love her.

"Oh yes. That and then some." I'm smiling so hard my face hurts.

"*Oh hell yes!* Tell me everything!"

After vaguely informing Morgan of my absolutely sinful yet exhilarating night with Dorian, I decide it's time to finish Natalia's book. I have been putting it off, not quite ready to let it end because it is my only connection to her. It's as if I feel her presence while reading it and once it is over, she will dissipate. I want to keep her memory alive for as long as I can. I need to feel like I'm not alone in this.

As I mentioned before, your delayed ascension was part of a spell to protect you and your new family. However, that is only part of it. All magic comes with a price. You will not have the ability to grow old after you ascend. You may age from the use of magic but you will never age naturally. Because of this, it may be impossible for you to lead a normal life. The Light was afraid that your unique mix could potentially create another enemy race if you were to consort with the wrong type of force. With the Dark. The law of the Light forbids this type of behavior, hence my harsh punishment for said transgression. I am so sorry.

So what is she trying to say? That I can never have children? Have a family?

I bound up from my bed and stick my head outside my bedroom

door. "Mom!" I call out.

Donna comes running just moments later. "What? Is everything ok? Are you alright?" She's frazzled and looking around wildly. I instantly regret alarming her.

"I can never get pregnant?" I ask with wide eyes.

Donna's shoulders immediately slump, both relieved that there seems to be no threat of imminent danger and remorseful of my discovery. It confirms my suspicions.

"So it's true. I'll never have a baby."

"Honey, I'm so sorry. But they were afraid of what you could create, what power you could hold with that ability." She's dancing around the truth. The Light didn't want me to procreate because my offspring, if mixed with more Dark blood, could destroy them. "How do you feel about that?"

I think about the question carefully. "I don't know. I've never thought about having children, really. I can't even wrap my head around my own life, let alone be solely responsible for someone else's," I shrug. It is peanuts compared to finding out that I'm some Light-Dark hybrid.

"Ok, honey. Do you want to talk more about it?" I shake my head and give my mom a reassuring smile. She lightly kisses my forehead and returns to her task.

Whew! Talk about dodging a bullet. I had been secretly chastising myself for having unprotected sex. What was I thinking? Yes, we all have those 'caught in the heat of the moment' incidents, but we didn't even use protection the second time around. Yet, I'm still not off the hook. STDs are a very real threat, and it'd be a shame if I, the abomination of Natalia and Alexander, were struck down by such a mortal hazard. I shake the thought from my head. Is that even possible?

Before I can harp on my impending immortality any more, my cell buzzes to life. To my surprise and delight, it's Jared. I had been worried that things would get weird between us and was furiously hoping we could go back to normal.

"Hey you!" I greet with genuine enthusiasm. Just the thought of him puts me in a jovial mood.

"Hey, Beautiful! Whatcha doing?" His deep voice is music to my ears.

"Nothin' much. A little reading. What's up?"

"So there's a rinky-dink fair in the parking lot of a strip mall with our names on it. *Whadayasay?* Funnel cakes? Cotton candy? Overpriced games? Ridiculously high Ferris wheel that can't possibly be safe?" he chuckles.

"Sounds great!" It actually does. The sun is shining and there's nothing like a greasy, fried funnel cake covered in powdered sugar to make you feel like a kid again.

"I'll be over in an hour. Tell my other girlfriend I miss her oatmeal chocolate chip cookies." He means Donna. Jared is such a charmer; he's always playfully flirty with my mom whenever he comes over.

"I'll tell her. You know she'll have a batch ready for you when you get here," I chuckle.

After we hang up, I jump in the shower, throwing on some feel-good music on my little iPod dock in the bathroom. I belt out my favorite tunes and let the hot water soothe and relax my muscles, which are a bit sore from the sexual acrobatics from the night before. *Dorian.*

I can't help but think about the odd moment we had in the car earlier. He seemed so puzzled, as if he couldn't figure out how someone like me could make someone like him happy. Or was it that he couldn't believe that he could even *be* happy at all? Why would he feel that way? Surely he's had relationships in the past. With his remarkable sexual abilities, I'd hate to think his experience was solely achieved through meaningless one-night stands. Oh crap. Could I have been just another one of those said meaningless one-night stands?

I decide to go casual, letting my feet recover from the previous night's platform-heeled tryst, and opt for Chucks, jeans, and a hooded sweatshirt. I tie my hair back in a ponytail and use just a little light makeup for a natural look. Jared has seen me at my very worst and he's one of the few people whom I can be totally comfortable with.

By the time the doorbell rings, Donna has wrapped up a plate of fresh, warm cookies for Jared and has even included a plastic container of extras for his mom and James. When their mom was at her worst, Donna would take over a weeks-worth of meals every Sunday so the boys would have home-cooked meals in light of all the distress they were enduring. Jared, James, and their mother, Tammy, were incredibly grateful, though my mom wished she could have done even more.

"Oh wow, Donna, is that a new haircut? If you get any prettier, I might have to steal you from Mr. Winters," Jared winks. Donna insists that Jared and the rest of my friends call her Donna. It makes her feel young. Chris prefers Mr. Winters. Always so formal, except when it comes to me.

"Why yes, it is, Jared! Thank you for noticing!" my mom blushes, batting her long lashes. *Geez, Mom, get a grip.* She cheeses at him as if he has '*Cougar Bait*' stamped onto his forehead.

"Ready to go?" Jared smiles down at me.

"Yup!" This is just what the doctor ordered. Time to get back to my regular, paranormal-free life.

The make-shift carnival off Powers Boulevard is everything Jared promised. Lots of yummy junk food, rides, games and booths to awaken my inner child. Jared is as buoyant as I am, grabbing my hand and pulling me to the first ride we see. He quickly pays for our tickets and we strap in tightly to the teacup style attraction. The ride is fast. *Really fast.* And if I weren't already a bit reckless and hell-bent on forgetting that I'm the Dark's #1 target, I would be worried.

As a result of the ride's speed, Jared and I are squished together in our compartment. I am wholly aware of our conjoined bodies in the small space, yet it doesn't bother me. It's strangely comforting. Jared adjusts his arm and swings it around me, enrapturing me in his massive bicep. My cheek presses against his hard chest, and I relish in his scent of Irish Spring soap and deodorant. The mix would be pedestrian to most, but to me it speaks of home.

Home.

I am at home in Jared, and as the saying goes, Home is where the Heart is. Is my heart really with Jared? Is that why I am willing to reject his offer of love and devotion for heart-stopping, mindless sex with Dorian with no strings attached?

The ride ends too abruptly, jolting me from my muddled thoughts. Jared takes my hand to help me out and I don't object when he doesn't release it as we stroll through the carnival.

"Thank you for bringing me. I really am having a great time," I say, stuffing the last puff of cotton candy into my mouth.

We've conquered just about every ride, sampled every carnival food from corndogs to deep-fried Twinkies, and spent a small fortune on carnival games. Two hours later, we're lugging around the giant-sized stuffed lion Jared won for me at the Strong Man game and walking off the massive amounts of trans fat.

"No problem. I knew you'd enjoy this. Remember when we used to skip school and burn our lunch money on Skee-ball and pizza at Chuck E. Cheese?" he laughs.

I recall the memory fondly. Every other week, I was in some kind of altercation with a random bitchy Queen Bee or massive douchebag that tried to get in my pants and couldn't take the rejection. Jared was my saving grace. Escaping with him was the only way I wasn't expelled for fighting. When things got to be too much for me to brush off, he'd insist we go buy our weight in tokens and rack up tickets until we couldn't hold anymore. We'd always give them away to youngsters as a way of restoring our good karma for ditching school. Just having that outlet was enough for me. *Jared* was enough for me.

"I miss those days," I say smiling up at him. "We should do it again." Lord knows I could use an escape.

A cold gust of wind runs through me and I shiver noticeably.

"Are you cold?" Jared asks. Before I can answer, he shrugs off his hoodie and places it over my shoulders, revealing his boulder-like arms and chest swathed tightly in a navy long-sleeve tee. The chill in the air kisses is nipples, and I can see them protrude through the thin fabric.

"No, I'm fine. Take it back before you get sick," I protest, but Jared hears none of it. I know better than to dispute his chivalry, and slide my arms in the giant sized sweater.

"Look! A fortune teller. Let's do it!"

Jared pulls me along and bounds up to the dark tent. It's absurdly cliché: burning candles, crystal ball on a small table, complete with an old woman draped in a flowing robe. I roll my eyes, and signal for Jared to go first. He hesitantly approaches the woman who appears to be meditating. She hasn't opened her eyes once since we entered and I instantly deem her a graduate of the Miss Cleo School for Psychics. It's all in good fun though.

"Put your money on the table and have a seat," she calls out dryly in a bad accent. Jared looks back at me and I shrug. He does as he's told and the woman holds out her hand, indicating that Jared should put his own hand in hers. Reluctantly, he does, and she gasps and begins to caress it animatedly. *Oh, come on!*

"You have a great heart," she begins in her corny accent, still with eyes closed. "A brave heart. You have love in it, and it is returned, though there is turmoil. You must be patient. It will come. However, tread lightly. Danger lurks nearby. Do not be fooled by those who try to lure you with worldly pleasures. It will only end in tragedy." Then she drops his hand, her blank, bored expression restored. Ok, that was a waste of five dollars. That could have applied to just about every guy in America!

Jared stands nervously and motions me to sit. I shake my head when the fortune teller calls out "Sit!" Her eyes are still closed; how could she have seen I was refusing? I sigh and pull a crumpled five dollar bill from my pocket and drop it on the table, flopping down with a huff. The woman extends her hand, and I shakily give her mine. When she encloses her hands on it, she gasps and her eyes fly open violently. Her pupils are clouded with a misty grey haze. She's blind. I mentally reprimand myself for pegging her as rude and melodramatic.

"I . . . I . . . am so sorry. I did . . . not realize," she sputters. She drops my hand as if I have snakes for fingers. *The fuck?* "I can leave. Tonight. I . . . I did not realize." She's really freaking me out. This has to be part of the act.

I look back at Jared who looks just as alarmed as I do. Shit. I've got to make this right. "No, please. I've paid my money. What do you see?"

The old woman swallows loudly, clearly afraid to speak. She shakes her head vehemently. "No. I cannot. I will leave now! I apologize! Please, spare me!" She's pleading.

"No, I don't want you to leave. I won't hurt you. Tell me what you see. Please!" She really is starting to scare me. I wish I could excuse Jared so I could be alone with the contrived soothsayer, but that would be too obvious. He would object anyway and the fortune teller may run away screaming.

The blind woman reaches for my hand, trembling furiously. She closes her eyes again reluctantly and loudly sucks in a large puff of air. "You are in great danger. Grave danger. Darkness approaches you from many angles. It eclipses the light around you, pulling you further and further into a world of great pain and tragedy. It seeps into you. Alters you. Soon it will consume you completely. Yet, you will allow it. You will welcome the darkness. Because you . . . " She hesitates.

"Go on," I urge. I need to hear this.

The blind woman painfully swallows as if she has razor blades in her throat. Her breathing is rapid and her dry lips tremble.

"You are the darkness."

And with that, she drops my hand and recoils.

I don't know what to say to that. What *can* I say to that? I slide the money closer to her but she shakes her head fiercely as if she can see what I am doing.

"I cannot take that. Forgive me. I am just an old woman. I meant no harm!" She is nearly shaking the table from her tremors. I grab the bill and crumple it in my palm tightly, afraid to face Jared's reaction to my bizarre fortune. He is stock-still, wide-eyed and pale. He, too, has been shaken by this woman's words.

"Come on," I mutter, pulling Jared out of the tent with me, abandoning my oversized stuffed animal.

I have to escape, and a few games of Skee-ball and pizza won't suppress the anxiety rising inside of me. This is beyond anything I could have ever expected. I have been so wrapped up in rejecting the Light and what they want from me that I couldn't see what I was actually doing in turn. The fortune teller has seen it, the darkness within me. I am not fighting it. I'm embracing it. I'm not running from the Dark.

I am the Dark.

FIFTEEN

"Holy shit, Gabs, did you know that lady?"

I am urgently pulling Jared away from the dark tent that houses the hauntingly perceptive fortune teller, no small feat considering he outweighs me by nearly 80 pounds.

"No," is all I can manage to choke out. My throat is tight with emotion and fear. How did she see that? *It can't be true!*

"Will you hold up a second? What is going on?" Jared shouts, refusing to walk any further so all I'm tugging on is his shirt. I have to get out of here. Far away from that woman and her lies.

Jared grasps me by the shoulders, holding me in place. I'm disoriented, lost. My eyes dart around violently, unable to bring anything into focus. Jared reads the anxiety etched on my face and instantly relaxes his stance. He's worried about me and reflexively pulls me into the warmth of his arms. I begin to resist his embrace but surrender after a moment. I feel defeated. There's no fight left in me.

"Just tell me what's wrong. Whatever is going on, we can fix it. Together. I'm here, Gabs," he whispers. His chin rests gently on the top of my head and I clutch his back as if he is my lifeline. My salvation, here to save me from myself.

Neither one of us speaks for what seems like several minutes. Here we stand, in the middle of a bustling carnival in the dark of night, holding each other as if our lives depend on it. The best thing about Jared is that he can be so silently strong; his arms are all I need to find solace. He knows when to press the issue and he knows when to be quiet and let me draw from his strength. He is my best friend, the love of my life, and my protector all in one. He is all I need.

"I feel like I'm losing myself," I finally croak. Jared remains quiet, letting me finish my thought. "I just don't know anymore. I just want to fast forward to when I know who the hell I am. I want to just get this shit over with already!" The tightness in my throat restricts any more words from escaping and I nuzzle my face into the comfort of Jared's firm chest.

"You'll get there, baby. There's no rush. You are perfect just like this." Jared dips his face down and places a gentle kiss on the crown of my head. "I wish you could see what I see. Just let me in. You don't always have to be so tough. It's ok to be vulnerable."

And with that, an aching sob escapes me, followed by a barrage of tears.

"You know, there's nothing you can't tell me," Jared remarks as we ride back to my house.

After I had finally calmed down, Jared insisted that we not let the fortune teller's unnerving vision ruin our evening. He wouldn't let me leave until we rode the bumper cars and split a ridiculously large candy apple. Then we rode the Ferris wheel, as promised, illuminated by the neon flashing lights under the clear night sky.

"I know," I say with a warm smile. *But in this case, the less you know, the better.*

We pull up to my house, neither one of us knowing how to cease the deafening silence. The tension suffocates us with every strained second and it's evident that there is something that we both want to say. Jared begins to open his mouth to speak when the double *Ding!* from my cell phone cuts him off.

From Dorian, 7:57 PM

– *I need you. Now.*

He needs me? Shit. Can't I deal with my mixed up emotions one guy at a time?

"Sorry about that," I say sheepishly, cramming my cell phone back in my sweatshirt pocket. I stow the rising excitement brought on by Dorian's text. So I guess it was more than just a one night stand for him. Though it *is* approaching booty call hours.

"No, it's fine," Jared says passively.

The moment has passed. Part of me is disappointed but the better part of me is relieved. Dorian's intrusion has reminded me of what just transpired not even 7 hours ago. I can't go there with Jared now; I'm tainted with Dorian's delectable essence. I can still taste him, can still feel the soreness between my thighs . . .

"Well, I better get inside," I say reaching for the door handle. Jared's large hand stops me in my tracks, pulling me back towards him. I look back at him puzzled, and read the ardor in his eyes. He gently tugs me to him, closing the distance between us inch by inch. I'm captivated by the sheer emotion emanating from him and it doesn't register that I should turn away. Jared dips his head forward, pressing his warm lips on mine. It's tender, heartfelt, and *real*. Like two teenagers experiencing their first kiss together. Uncharted territory full of promise and surprise.

We both pull away simultaneously, not sure of what to do or say next. Do I close with '*See ya later!*' or just leave? No, Jared deserves better than that.

"You know there's nothing I wouldn't do for you," I say softly. "You are so much to me. So much more than just a friend." I let out an uneasy sigh and look up at him through my dark eyelashes, unable to fully meet his eyes. "But it would be unfair of me to subject you to my bullshit right now. At this point in my life–"

"I've got it, Gabs, ok?" Jared says cutting me off. He isn't angry; he's resigned. Maybe more upset with himself for trying. I hate to see him tormented. I reach out to stroke his cheek but let my hand rest on his forearm instead. No need to throw salt in the wound. "I guess we both suck at timing, huh?" he chuckles.

I sigh with relief. "Yeah, we do. But maybe that's a sign that whatever is in store for us in the future will be epic." *Let's just hope it's not an epic fail.*

Jared nods. "Besides, we don't want to end up like Morgan and Miguel." My eyes grow wide with shock. Oh crap, he knows? Reading my surprised expression he continues, "Oh yeah. Miguel told me. What's funny is he actually likes the girl. But he knows she'd never consider him."

"You never know," I remark. "Stranger things have happened." Seems like *strange* has been a reoccurring theme lately.

"Well, I gotta get inside. Might be able to catch dessert with the parents."

"Dessert? Good God, girl, where do you pack all that food in with your figure?!" he laughs. I shrug my shoulders; what figure is he talking about?

"Growing girl," I smile. And with that, we hug goodbye before I skip to my front door.

When I enter the living room, Chris and Donna smile brightly at me, both surprised to see me home so early on a Saturday night. They're watching a college basketball game; well, Chris is watching and Donna is reading. I love seeing them like this–content, comfortable, normal. I would *kill* for normal right now. I fight the invasion of sorrow and self-pity creeping into my heart and give them each a kiss on the cheek. They've been so good to me, considering what I am. They've loved me unconditionally and have never tried to mold me into something they knew I couldn't be. They have always been, and always will be, my parents.

I pull my cell phone back out when I get to my room. I still haven't answered Dorian's text and I know I shouldn't be rude. But tonight, I need to take some time for myself. Some time to sort out my own shit before I bring somebody else into the fold.

Dorian has been amazing, a welcomed distraction. But is it fair of me to surrender my body to him and pray that my heart doesn't follow?

To Dorian, 8:47 PM

– Raincheck? I'll be in touch.

I turn my phone off and plug it in to charge. After a hot shower, I throw on a pair of comfy pajamas and settle in for the night. The past week and a half has been a whirlwind of emotion. I need time to process.

Ding! Ding! What the . . . ? I know I turned my cell phone off. I sigh and reach over to check my message. Probably a salacious text from Dorian. Oh well, his needs will have to wait for now.

Unknown, 9:35 PM

– *Align with the Dark or Die*

What. The. Fuck.

I look around my room wildly, not quite able to move my legs yet. How did someone get this number? How did they find me? Oh my God, have they been watching me all night?

As soon as I regain my faculties, I bound to my bedroom window, scared out of my mind at what I might find. There's nothing, no one in my backyard. The window is securely shut and locked. I scurry to the living room to my parents and they both jump at my alarmed expression. I don't know what to say to them, how to explain the terrifying messages I've been receiving. I can't do this on my own. I don't know what possessed me to think I could. Everyone needs help, myself included. It's obvious that I'm not as strong as I thought I was.

"Well, what is it, sweetheart?" Donna finally says. *How the hell do I explain?* I look down at my cell phone, still captive in my rigid hand. Reluctantly, I extend it towards them, holding my breath as they glance down at the message on the screen.

"What is it that you want us to see?" Chris asks after a few moments. They both look back up at me, clearly puzzled. I step forward and grab the phone, unsure of why they'd need further clarification. It's right there in black and white.

Unknown, 9:35 PM

It's blank. Completely-*freakin'*-blank.

What the hell just happened here? I want to tell them what I saw; want to prove to them that I'm not going crazy. The message on the windshield, the text, the ghostly assailant in the parking lot. They would believe me. But then what? What could they possibly do other than worry themselves to death to protect me? They are defenseless, just like me. And it is selfish of me to expect them to risk their lives when they've already done so much. They took me in. I can't repay them by involving them in this any further.

I shake my head fervently. "Nothing. I thought I saw something but it was nothing. Just been having trouble with my phone." I turn on my heel and retreat back to my bedroom, despite my parents' pleas to stay and talk.

If I am the Dark, maybe this is me creating this turmoil. What if this is all in my head? The parking lot phantom . . . what if that was just a manifestation of the evil inside me? What if it is calling out to me, urging me to embrace the darkness that already flows through my veins? I thought the messages were a demand. Could it actually be a proclamation?

And the most disturbing factor of all . . .

The string of dead innocent girls. Could I be that evil? That cold and calculated?

That Dark?

"Hey Kiddo, can I come in?" my dad calls out, rapping on my bedroom door.

It's well into the day and I haven't surfaced, missing both breakfast and lunch. I even called in sick for my shift at the mall. I haven't been able to face them since last night and I am genuinely afraid of what I could be capable of. If I ever hurt them, I could never live with myself.

Realizing that Chris won't let up until I let him in, I open the door then quickly turn to flop back onto my bed. He steps in tentatively, holding a plate holding a sandwich and a pickle, no doubt the work of my mom. The woman swears I'll starve to death if I go without food for a few hours. He has a bottle of water, which he tosses towards me unexpectedly. I catch it just before it smacks me in the face and see a ghost of a smile on Chris's lips. *What is that all about?*

"Geez, Dad, thanks a lot," I mutter sardonically. I open the plastic bottle and take a large swig, realizing how parched I am. Chris sets the plate on my dresser and takes a seat on my bed.

"Just making sure you're paying attention," he chuckles. He's dressed in blue jeans and a sweater, fitting for the day's chilly, rainy conditions. "What's going on, Kid? You've been hiding out in here all day."

"Just not feeling well, that's all," I lie, shrugging my shoulders.

Chris looks at me quizzically. "But you're not sick. You're never sick. So why don't you tell me what's really bothering you."

Huh? Never sick? It's true, come to think of it. I was never ill as a child, not even as much as a cold. But I just chalked it up as me having a healthy immune system.

I shake my head at Chris. "I don't know. I can't involve you and mom any more. I don't want anyone else to get hurt."

"What are you talking about? Who is getting hurt?"

"Those girls!" I shriek.

"That wasn't your fault, Gabi," my dad says exasperated. He

feels I'm being irrational and he despises self-loathing. Like me, usually, though lately I've been a major hypocrite.

"But what if it was? What if it was me?" I say barely above a whisper. "Dad, I think I'm more Dark than Light."

Chris lets his head drop, rubbing his eyes with his thumb and forefinger. He looks back up at me with assurance.

"Gabriella, you are not Dark. Yes, your biological father was a Dark One but that means nothing. There is a misconception that all Dark are absolutely evil. And that all Light are completely good. If that were true, how could they murder Natalia, a woman whose only crime was love, and force her to abandon her newborn child?

"There is good and evil in everyone, even we mere mortals," he winks. "Your father, Alex, was not all evil. He loved your mother. He loved you. They say the Dark are incapable of love. Maybe he was an exception to the rule. Maybe not."

My dad reaches over and places a gentle hand on my shoulder. "You're good, Kid. Yeah, you've been known to crack a few skulls-," he chuckles.

"Hey!" I protest playfully.

"But you're good. Don't forget that. And when you ascend, no matter which side you choose, you'll still be good."

Chris leans over to give me a reassuring kiss on my forehead but before he can pull away, I wrap my arms around him. He slowly embraces me into a big bear hug. I feel like a little girl again, afraid of the boogie man. But in this case, I'm afraid of *being* the boogie man.

We finally pull away from our embrace, both of us feeling renewed. Chris ruffles the top of my head as if I'm an 8 year old boy. I believe he always pictured me as the son he never had. He stands and makes his way towards the door.

"Before you go, can I ask you a question?" I say. It's always been in the back of my mind but I never thought it was appropriate to ask. But now I'm wondering if it had something to do with me. "Why didn't you and Mom ever have kids of your own? Was it because you were afraid I'd be a danger to them?"

Chris looks at me sullenly. *Oh no*, it was just as I thought. He then shakes his head as if reading my mind, dispelling my doubts. "No, of course it wasn't because of you. You've never been a danger." Chris takes a deep breath and drops his head a bit, unable to make eye contact. His hands turn into hard fists, the stretched skin over his knuckles turning white, almost translucent. "The Warlock, who attacked your mother . . . *did* things to her. Horrible, disgusting things. She isn't able to conceive children. Natalia healed her the best she could but the damage was too severe."

"Oh," is all I can choke out.

I can tell the thought of someone so brutally violating his wife still enrages him. He nods just a fraction and exits without saying another word, and I regret conjuring that horrible memory.

I glance over at my haunted cell phone. There's no point in hiding out in my room. If I am a threat, four walls won't be able to hold me. I have to believe in what my dad says. He knows me better than some cheap carnival fortune teller with an overactive imagination. I've never been a threat to anyone who didn't deserve it. And even then I was never capable of murder. That whole scene last night must've been an orchestrated coincidence. I tentatively pick up my cell and begin to tap rapidly on the keypad.

To Dorian, 3:18 PM

– How about that raincheck?

I've got to start somewhere. And no one makes me forget my unease better than Dorian.

Ding! Ding!

– *I'll be home around 5.*

– See you then ;)

Yes! What is it about that man that instantly brings a smile to my face? I still hardly know him yet his presence is oddly soothing. He has such an effect on me–on my body, more specifically. Every touch is like a shock to my system. And his ability to make me explode with just his piercing blue eyes . . . how the hell does he do that? Some Tantric sex technique? The man has talent, that's for sure.

I devour the pastrami on rye with haste and then jump in the shower, ensuring that I am groomed to perfection. Noticing that my hair smells like a mixture of hot grease and peanuts, I give it a quick wash. Once I'm clean, dry, moisturized and blow dried, I head to my room to pick out my outfit for the evening.

Knowing that what's under my clothes will be more awe-inspiring, I choose a super skimpy, see-through mesh bra and panty set that I bought while lingerie shopping with Morgan. It's black with pale pink trim and little ruffles on the butt. I haven't had a chance or a reason to wear it before now. It looks pretty hot on me, and I'm tempted to show up to Dorian's suite wearing only the sexy undergarments, a trench coat and high heels. *Yeah right*, Chris would wring my neck! I opt for a charcoal grey sweaterdress and knee-high boots as an alternative.

I make the trip across town listening to some sultry R&B tunes to get me in the mood. It reminds me of the first ride I took with Dorian, and the memory makes me smile instinctively. Dorian really does make me happy. I want to keep this casual, maybe even a little superficial, but something within me wants a little more. It's selfish of me, I know, because I could never ever give him all of me. But is it wrong of me to want all of him? Can I try to have something substantial with him while hiding such a crucial secret about who and what I am?

I pull up to the Broadmoor and marvel at its splendor. It's even more expansive than I thought now that I see it in the daylight. I notice the vast green golf course and even what looks to be a large body of water. Wow, impressive. For a moment, I wonder if Dorian golfs though he looks more biker boy than preppy golfer. After I let valet take my little hatchback, I square my shoulders with confidence and gracefully saunter through the extravagant entranceway.

As I make my way to the building that houses Dorian's suite, I get a better look at the lake conjoined with a huge pool. It's gorgeous and I imagine strolling along the little bridge with Dorian. The thought makes my heart flutter with hope and anticipation. I approach the doorman with a broad grin and bound up to the elevator, anxiety and excitement building with the rise of each floor. Soon I am face to face with the elaborate double doors of Dorian's suite. I take a deep breath and knock three times before exhaling. Here goes. Time to finally get a sense of peace. *And a night of illicit pleasure.*

As the door swings open I am met with a pair of familiar blue eyes shrouded in glossy dark hair. A devilish smirk displayed on perfect full lips slowly evolves into a look of shock and disdain. The gorgeous face, evidently not pleased to see me, causes my heart to sink into the plush carpeting, though I plaster on a cold, dismissive guise. Animosity and friction heats the small space between us. This is not the welcome I so wistfully imagined and now I am relieved that I scrapped my trench coat plan. However, the person staring back at me with contempt is not Dorian this time.

It's Aurora.

$\mathscr{S}IXTEEN$

"Oh, Gabriella, right?" Aurora recovers, quickly replacing her scowl with a fake smile. "This is a surprise. We weren't expecting anybody."

We? "Really? Dorian invited me," I say with a twinge of viciousness, bathing every syllable of Dorian's name with my tongue.

"Is that right?" she remarks doubtfully. She openly analyzes my appearance with a sweep of her eyes. "Oh well, please come in," she says holding the door open. I step in, my chin high, ready to get to the bottom of this. "Dorian is in the bedroom. He should be out shortly." Bedroom? *Oh, hell no!*

Aurora and I stand silently looking at each other for several long seconds. Thankfully, before either one of us has to exchange any more false pleasantries, Dorian emerges, his expression initially surprised then contented. He's wearing a light grey suit and no tie, the top couple buttons of his shirt undone. He looks so handsome and refined in his work attire and it causes my heat below to stir. He strolls over to me without hesitance and places a soft kiss on my forehead before turning to Aurora.

"Here, this should be good," he says handing her the papers in his hand.

Aurora's mouth is hanging wide open with utter disbelief. She grabs the paperwork weakly and tries to shake off her staggered expression.

"Are you sure this is all? I should go over this with you first because I'd hate for there to be a mistake and have to come back. Again." What the hell was the point in her adding *'Again'*? Was she implying that she comes here often? I feel my blood start to boil, and not in a hot and steamy kind of way.

"That's all, Aurora," Dorian states dismissively.

Aurora picks up her broken ego and pulls her shoulders back with a pretentious air. She walks over to the dining table to retrieve her purse and briefcase. Little does she know that just a day ago, my wetness covered that very same table as Dorian greedily consumed me. I try to stifle a laugh at the irony causing Dorian to peer down at me with a smirk. He licks his lips instinctively. *Yes, he must be thinking about it too.*

As soon as the door clicks behind a humiliated and fuming Aurora, Dorian shrugs out of his jacket, exposing a crisp white shirt. He then turns to me and pulls me to him by my hips. He places a gentle kiss on my lips, one full of peace and contentment. He's relaxed dramatically since Aurora's exit and I chalk it up to their having an uncomfortable past that Dorian doesn't want me to know about.

"She doesn't care for me much, does she?" I remark, looking towards the door.

Dorian releases my hips and takes a seat on the couch, patting the seat for me to join him. He extends his arm around me, though it feels the movement is strained for him. It's as if he's a 13 year old boy, putting his arm around his young date at the movies. I remain still rather than snuggling against him. It's odd; he's been so sure of himself and confident since the day I met him.

"Aurora doesn't like most girls that aren't her," he says nonchalantly with a shrug of his shoulders.

So he knows her well. *How well?* I suppress the urge to ask more about her. It's not my place to question him; I'm not his girlfriend. Besides, he made it blatantly clear that he preferred my company over hers.

I give Dorian a playful smile. "So do you always bring your work home with you?"

"That all depends. I brought you home, didn't I?" He replies with a sly smile.

I feign shock and offense. "First of all, you didn't bring me home. I came on my own accord. And secondly, I highly doubt sex was a matter of business!"

Dorian pulls his head down towards mine, his lips brushing my earlobe. I gasp at the contact. He begins to leave soft, delicate kisses on the sensitive skin of my neck.

"Au contraire, Gabriella. That's where you're wrong. It is business. Very hard,"–*kiss*–"back-breaking,"–*kiss*–"labor intensive,"–*kiss*–"business."

Before I can even form a response, Dorian hurriedly eases me down on my back, positioning himself between my legs with ease. Our mouths and tongues unite hungrily while I grab ahold of his soft hair. His hands roam my bare thighs as my knee length dress bunches at my hips, exposing my see-through ruffled panties. I can feel the growing bulge in his slacks against the ultrathin fabric. He begins a slow grind, circulating his hardness at a torturous pace. I breathe heavily against his lips, trying to conceal my mounting moans. I lift my hips to meet his stiff middle and the encouragement causes him to speed up the tempo. We are both nearly breathless when his hands move upwards to relinquish me of my panties, breaking us from our impassioned lip-lock. My pelvis is already so elevated that he is able to slide them off easily. Dorian then rapidly unfastens his slacks as I look on in awe. He unleashes his hard length, taking in my fascinated expression. He knows what he's doing to me. He knows how much he affects me. He's making a game of this; he wants to toy with me. And I am more than willing to let him.

I expect him to lie back down on top of me, yet Dorian easily flips me over onto my stomach. He scoots me forward, his hands guiding me to take hold of the arm of the couch. He begins to knead my backside, firmly massaging while propping it upward. I brace myself for his entry when I feel his erection lightly slapping the insides of my thighs. Dorian is feeling my wetness, stroking my heat with his long agile fingers. I hear sounds of his smacking lips and know he has sampled me. The eroticism brings on a fresh wave of dampness as I imagine him savoring my nectar. Inside, I'm begging for him to put it in to relieve me of my yearning but he prolongs it, electing to tease me instead. My whimpers grow stronger and with a hard thrust, Dorian puts me out of my misery. I cry out in sweet agony.

Dorian buries himself deep inside of me. *So very deep.* He pulls out inch by inch until I fear he will leave me, but then slams back into me. The pain is so amazingly pleasurable. A series of throaty groans escapes Dorian's mouth with each thrust, harmonizing with my shrill carnal cries. His fingers dig into my ass with desperation as he plunges himself in and out of my dripping wetness in an unhurried pace. I can't believe how good this feels. He is filling me up, stretching my walls, losing himself in my secret place. No one has gone here before, not this deep. Yet Dorian is at home inside of me, and I want him to stay forever.

Just as I feel myself climbing higher, reaching for release, Dorian grabs the base of my neck, pulling me up fiercely. The sweet, tender Dorian is gone and the animal inside him takes the reins. He is still pumping furiously inside me when his mouth finds my shoulder, his hand still tightly gripping my throat. *Oh God.* His sudden change is frightening me and the physical strain is bringing a new element of pain. Yet his aggression arouses me even more, my moans becoming louder, harsh vulgarities spilling from my lips.

Dorian's hand moves from my neck just so he can take a handful of my long tresses. He pulls down on my hair hard forcing my head backwards and leaving my entire throat open and exposed. *Shit.* He could slit my neck right now and I would die in sweet ecstasy. He keeps his grasp on my hair, using it to level himself as he continues to punish me viciously. His other hand frees my ass and finds its way to my neck. He holds on tightly and I feel his lips on my ear.

"IS. THIS. WHAT. YOU. WANT?!" he grunts through clenched teeth. When I don't answer he pulls my hair harder, pushing himself even deeper. I didn't think it was possible.

"YES!" I scream.

He lets his hand leave my throat and rewards me by finding his way up my dress and to my breasts. He begins to fondle my erect nipples through the thin mesh fabric.

"IS. THIS. WHAT. YOU. WANT?!" His voice is so severe, almost menacing. There's a dark element to it. I do not dare to hesitate this time.

"YES!"

Again he rewards me, this time by moving south to my clit, stirring its swell. He releases my hair from its captivity and moves back to my throat, this time gripping it tightly. The sensation is . . . pleasurable, and it scares me.

My senses are on overdrive. The room is spinning and I feel dizzy from my rapid breathing. My neck is strained so rigidly, I can barely make a sound. The intense tingle from my hypersensitive clit, the throbbing penetration that Dorian delivers, his firm hold on my neck–it is too much for me to endure. I can't hold on any longer. The feeling is drowning me, taking me under. I have to climb higher. I have to escape this delicious misery and find release.

Dorian's breathing is rougher; he is searching for freedom of this torment as well, though he is the vicious tormenter. I feel him swell inside of me as he slows his pace and tightens his grip around my neck. I try to cry out but only a hoarse garbled stream of praise escapes. His growth is my defeat and I violently release a flood of intense passion, shuddering wildly. He loosens his grip and wraps his arms tightly around me, steadying himself in anticipation of his undoing. I am nearly limp in his arms when he finds his own sweet surrender, drawing me into him and gently leaving a trail of kisses on my neck and shoulders.

SEVENTEEN

"How do you feel?" Dorian asks me after several minutes of listening to the sounds of our own ragged breaths. We've collapsed on the couch and he's still positioned behind me.

I think about my answer for a beat then smile. "Ruined." I can feel Dorian's lips spread slightly at my ear. "And *hot!*" I still have on my sweaterdress and boots and the fabric is beginning to itch against my dampened skin. Dorian reaches down and pulls my dress up over my head, and I instantly feel cooler. He strokes my scanty bra.

"*Mmmm*, nice," he murmurs at the romantic detailing. He kisses where my bra strap meets my shoulder then slides it to the side, leaving another kiss on the indention left behind on my skin. It's sweet, tender. A total 180 from the Dorian that just choked me while pounding me hard from behind. He really is an enigma.

"Tell me something about yourself," I say after a long minute passes. I really know very little about him and if we're going to make this a regular thing, I should probably confirm that he isn't an ax murderer.

"What do you want to know?" Dorian replies, playing with a tendril of my hair.

I take a deep breath. Ok, here goes. "About your family. What are they like?"

Dorian instantly goes rigid and releases my lock of hair coiled around his finger. I hear him take in a sharp breath and know that I've hit a sore spot. "What about them?" he says flatly.

I'm torn. On one hand, I want to press for information now that I know the subject affects him so much. On the other, I want to forget I ever asked him about his family and laugh it off in an attempt to keep this light and casual. I go with my gut. And my heart.

"Are you close with them?" I ask timidly. I stow my brazen nature for his sake and pray that my reticence puts him at ease.

Dorian takes a thoughtful moment to ponder his response. "I used to be," Dorian mutters.

I hear a hint of emotion in his voice. He abruptly clears his throat as if reading my thoughts. "My parents had high hopes for me. I was bright and strong-willed," he laughs stiffly. "But I was stubborn. I rebelled and chose not to follow the path they had chosen for me. Didn't want to enter the family business, so to speak. Being the eldest son, that was a huge scandal." He recalls the memory as if it were decades ago, the nostalgia in his voice resonating through his words. This recollection is *real.*

"So I take it they're very old fashioned. What was the family business?" I am genuinely interested.

"Politics." Dorian says amusingly. I'm intrigued as to why that would be humorous. Must be a family inside joke.

"So you rebelled, and they what? Disowned you?"

"More or less. I was sent away for some years, cut off from everyone and everything I knew," Dorian replies. "Hence the career change. We take tradition very seriously. In order for me to reclaim my place as their son, I have to become what they want me to be." His voice is filled with pain, though I know he is trying to make light of the conversation.

A piece of me hurts for Dorian. No child, no matter what path they may have chosen, should be abandoned by the people who should love them the most. When two people come together and make the conscious decision to create a life, they have an obligation to protect and love that child until death. Like Alexander and Natalia did for me. Tradition or not, there is nothing that Dorian could have done to be undeserving of the love and support of his parents. In an attempt to soothe his forlorn thoughts, I turn around to face him, letting his light blue eyes meld into mine. I just want to be his comfort in this moment. I just want to take away his pain. I only wish I knew how to.

I let my hand stroke Dorian's cheek. It's smooth with the prickly threat of stubble, leaving tiny tickles on my fingertips. Dorian closes his eyes and nuzzles his face into the touch as if it is his source of sustenance. He inhales the scent of my skin and lets out a serene sigh. He automatically unwinds and looks back up at me with grateful eyes. It's odd, how I can bring him peace with such a modest gesture. I don't question it though. I know he needs this; he needs this contact.

"If you could, would you have done things differently?" I ask, unable to come up with anything better. I just want to keep him talking.

Dorian's mouth twists as if he is thinking. The gesture is adorable and makes him seem youthful and playful. "Yes. No. I can't say." He then looks at me, all humor gone from his eyes. "If I did things differently, you would not be here now."

"Why do you say that?" I whisper. Something about the coldness in his tone stops me up short.

Dorian closes his eyes and shakes his head lightly. When he reopens them, his eyes are no longer icy and grim. "I wouldn't have come here. We would not have met," he states simply with a shrug of his shoulders. The man is seriously complex. In the span of this short conversation, he has probably had 10 different mood swings. It's hard to keep up.

"You never know. It's a small world," I say optimistically. I have to believe that everything happens for a reason. If Dorian and I were meant to be here, to share this moment, our paths would have crossed sooner or later.

"Not as small as you think," he mutters. "Enough. I need you to put your dress back on," Dorian says sitting up. He reaches for his pants and begins to slide them on.

The fuck? Is he really kicking me out like some cheap hooker? My face heats with rising fury. I sit up straight and snatch my sweaterdress from off of the floor and put it over my head in a huff, visibly annoyed. When I look back up, Dorian is smirking at me as if he is on the verge of laughing.

"What?" I snap coldly, standing up to face him.

"Just wondering what got into you. Besides me of course," he chuckles though I don't return his amusement. "Seriously, you have something against dinner?"

Shit. Me and my quick temper. I smooth my dress over my hips, taking extra time to avoid eye contact and try to appear impassive. Here I was, thinking Dorian was dismissing me after sex, and all he wanted to do was take me to dinner. *Stupid, stupid, stupid.*

"Sorry," I mutter.

"For what?" Dorian asks quizzically, a ghost of a smile on his lips. He knows why I am apologizing yet he wants to hear me say it. He wants me to admit my weakness.

"I thought . . . ," I begin timidly. I clear my cracking voice and pull my shoulders back, looking Dorian straight in the eye. "I thought you wanted me to leave. I was just having a *girl* moment," I say shaking my head, as if to reject the notion.

"Well you *are* a girl, correct?" Dorian looks amused at my guffaw and my carnal instinct is telling me to smack that smug look right off his beautiful face. I opt to tease him instead.

"Oh, that and so much more," I say seductively, with hooded eyes, channeling my inner sex kitten. Dorian instinctively licks his lips. I expect him to push me back down on the couch but instead he grabs my hand, leading me out of his suite and to the elevator.

The sounds of live music lure us to the Tavern and we are instantly greeted by a friendly hostess. She greets Dorian by his first name casually, even asking him a few questions about the opening of the salon as she leads us to our cozy, intimate table. *Hmmmm.* So Dorian has been friendly with her. *How* friendly, is the question. I quickly dismiss the thought, reminding myself that I, in fact, am not his girlfriend and have no right to ask him. Once we're seated, the hostess, who Dorian calls Tiffany, hands us our menus and leaves us with a warm smile.

"How very informal of you . . . seems like you're pretty casual with the staff here," I smirk. Dorian raises a curious eyebrow at me and I realize that my comment has come out much more snarky than I intended. He looks a bit offended. I perk up into a smile and decide to change my tactics. "So you must eat here often. Is the food as good as the music?" A band is playing the smooth sounds of a jazz piece, emitting a sultry, sexy vibe.

"Eating in the suite gets old, so when I do get a chance to enjoy a meal, I like to come here. Much more *informal* than some of the other restaurants."

Crap. So I have offended him. I engross myself in the menu to avoid eye contact. Let's hope I'm able to eat anything seeing as I keep putting my foot in my mouth.

Dorian and I spend a few quiet minutes scanning the menu though I am mentally cursing myself the entire time. Maybe he'll see I really am too crass and immature to deal with and he'll dump me before I embarrass him further. The thought causes a clenching ache in my chest and I stifle an uneasy gasp. By the time our waiter arrives for our drink orders, I'm unprepared and stammering.

"Oh hi, uh . . . I'll, um . . . ," I begin.

Luckily Dorian swoops in and saves me, ordering bottles of wine and sparkling water before I really make a fool of myself. I am red-faced and mortified once the waiter leaves to retrieve our beverages.

"Thanks," I mutter. Shit. I've got to get it together. I'm not used to caring this much about what someone, especially a guy, thinks of me. It makes me feel weak, and I don't like it one bit.

"This place has excellent steak and seafood. Would you like me to order for you?" Dorian asks, a reassuring smile lighting his gentle eyes. He knows he's totally unraveled me and now he pities me. *Ha!*

"Please," is all I can seem to choke out.

When our server returns with the wine and water, Dorian turns to him and orders our entrees. I'm so preoccupied with my own conflicted feelings that I can hardly make out what he's saying, not that I have much of an appetite anymore.

"Something wrong?" Dorian asks after a few strained moments of silence.

"No. Yes. I don't know." So *am* I being honest with him? Yes. What else do I have to lose? "I just don't like feeling so self-conscious. You make me so . . . uneasy." I take a hearty sip of wine to reduce my anxiety.

"I do?" He sounds surprised.

"Not intentionally, at least I don't think so," I shrug. "I, uh, care too much. About what you think of me." There. The cards are on the table. He knows that my affections go beyond just mind-numbing sex. *I care.* The exact thing I swore I wouldn't–I couldn't–do. I can't afford to.

"So because you care, it makes you uneasy?" I can see the makings of a smirk creeping onto his lips. Great, he finds me amusing.

"More or less." I sigh and shake my head.

"Why does that bother you?" Dorian looks at me inquiringly as if I am some rare breed of girl.

"Because it's not a feeling I'm used to. Feeling so . . . vulnerable," I cringe.

"And that's a bad thing?" He folds his hands in front of him and rests his chin on them, gazing at me intently.

"Yes," I nod. "Especially when you don't have much experience with . . . *feeling.*"

"How is that possible? Surely you've opened up with boyfriends in the past," he says incredulously.

"You'd think so, but no. There were a few but nothing serious."

The reality that I've never had a serious relationship or whirlwind romance hits me and I have to swallow my forlorn thoughts before they consume me.

"So you've never been in love?" Dorian looks a bit sad for me, the exact reaction I was trying to avoid.

The question is a complicated one for me. I have been in love.

With Jared. At least I think I was. But so much as changed since meeting Dorian and finding out that I am some Dark-Light crossbreed. *Am* I still in love with Jared?

"Let's just say I was never in love with someone who was in love with me." I try to tack on a bit of buoyancy at the end but I know Dorian sees right through me. *Oh great, he surely thinks I'm pathetic now!*

Before we can delve deeper into my lack of relationship experience, our waiter returns with a large bowl of clams and mussels in a tomato sauce and Shrimp Cocktail with possibly the largest shrimp I have ever seen.

Dorian looks at me sheepishly. "I didn't know what you would want." I smile and put a little of each on my plate.

The clams and mussels are amazing, though I prefer them in the white wine sauce like we had at the bistro. The shrimp is plump and juicy and I dip it generously in Remoulade sauce. Obviously my appetite has returned.

"So how about you? Any past great love affairs?" I ask after I've had my fill.

Dorian takes a lengthy sip of wine to mull over my question. "Great love affairs? No. I haven't really had time. Just casual relationships here and there. No-frills, no strings attached arrangements that fit . . . both our needs."

I bite the bullet, and swallow my pride with a laborious gulp. "So, I'm assuming that I would be considered one of those arrangements." Geez, I don't know how this evening took such a serious turn but I guess it's best to get this conversation over with.

"Do you want to be?" Dorian asks smoothly. He refills each of our wine glasses then takes a sip of his own. I follow suit.

"I don't know. Honestly, I thought that's exactly what I wanted. But like I said, something shifted the day I met you. Believe whatever you want, but it's true. I honestly have never met anyone like you. And I have a feeling that it was meant to happen . . . that we were destined to cross paths.

"You make me frustrated. Not with you, but with myself. When I'm not with you, I have all these questions, these doubts. But when we're together, I feel oddly at ease. The doubt, the apprehension disappears. And I can't even remember why they even inhabited my mind. Does that make sense?" The wine has obviously taken its effect and I can't seem to shut up. I reach for my glass of water and down half of it.

I really hope he can decipher what I'm trying to say to him, though I'm not entirely sure what I'm trying to convey. Before Dorian can respond to my jumbled rant, our server arrives with our entrees; New York Strip steaks, steamed broccolini, and loaded baked potatoes.

"Oh my God, Dorian, you're going to make me fat!" I exclaim with wide eyes.

"I'm sure that's the least of your worries. Besides, you only live once, right?" he says with a devilish grin. He's right. *Even if you can live forever.*

The steak melts in my mouth like butter and is accompanied with some kind of peppercorn sauce. The combination is perfection and the meat is cooked just how I like it. It's as if Dorian already knows me inside and out. No one has ever been so in tuned to my likes and dislikes, especially considering we hardly know each other.

"I hope you like everything. I wasn't sure what you'd want. Would you rather have something else?" Dorian seems oddly tentative, and I can't help but blame my previous rant for the awkwardness.

"Everything is great, Dorian." I look at him with question in my eyes. "How about you?"

Dorian gently chews his bottom lip, contemplating my question. He knows I'm not asking him about his food. He looks up at me intensely through his long dark lashes, and I have a feeling he's trying to distract me. A familiar tingle slowly crawls up my thighs, meeting my heated apex. His tactics are working and I instinctively squeeze my thighs together and shake my head. He will not divert me until he tells me how he feels.

"Seriously, Dorian. I told you how I felt, and as confusing as that may have been to understand, I need to know that we're on the same page." I've never felt so much like an annoying, nagging girl in my life. This conversation is just as tedious for me as it is for him but I need to know if I'm alone in this.

Dorian sighs heavily, and I know he's grown tired with the questioning. He looks as if he's aged in the past 5 minutes. "Gabriella, you can be whatever you want to be to me. If you want to be with me, be with me. If you want to keep this light and casual, we can do that. If you want me to just keep fucking you senseless every chance I get, I'll be more than happy to oblige." His words are so vulgar and provocative. I feel heat flood my cheeks and my already moistened sex.

"Now I've had about enough of this food and this conversation. I want dessert." Dorian stands and pushes his chair in. He gazes down at me sternly and my heart stops. He's so cold, so menacing. I know I should be frightened but instead all I can think about is how he had that same look as he took me from behind while choking me just a couple hours earlier. That thought carries a wave of shame but I ignore it. *Dammit*, I like this side of Dorian and I won't apologize for it.

Dorian extends his arm, inviting me to intertwine mine with his. I slowly stand on shaky legs and do as he wishes, letting him lead me out of the restaurant. Dorian has had the last word, and though I would never take this from any other guy, I willingly let Dorian have full control in this moment. He's already fully controlled my body, it's only fitting that my mind follow suit. We walk in silence until we reach his suite and I hold my breath in expectation as the door clicks behind us.

Dorian shrugs out of his pale grey suit jacket and drapes it over the arm of the couch. The recollection of clutching that very same armrest causes my breathing to shallow as the heat between my legs becomes damp and humid. It's amazing how just a memory can cause such a reaction. Dorian notices the change in my once composed stance and gracefully strolls over to me, closing the distance between us in three easy strides. Without hesitation, he takes my hand and pulls me towards the bedroom. Words still have not passed between us yet communication is seamless. He wants me. And I want him too.

Before I can take in the black and gold room, Dorian bends down to grab the hem of my dress, relieving me of it in one swift movement. I stand before him, stripped and vulnerable, as his baby blues molest my scantily clad frame. He reaches to touch my see-through bra. His touch is so gentle as if I am made of delicate porcelain. His expression is . . . torn. It's as if the contact physically hurts him yet he can't help himself. He relishes the anguish. He's teetering on the line between pleasure and pain, and I want to nudge him into my pleasure. Yet, part of me yearns for that pain. The notion is maddening, sickening even. How can I expect Dorian to define his feelings for me if I can't even admit what I really want in all this? Our tryst on the couch has brought it all to the surface for me.

I just need Dorian to fuck me good enough to make me forget.

As if reading my mind, Dorian covers my mouth with his, letting his hands palm the soft flesh peeking out the back of my ruffled panties. He grips my ass and lifts me high enough for me to wrap my legs around his waist. He's already begun to harden and I welcome it by squeezing my legs even tighter. Dorian breaks our kiss to look at me. His eyes are earnestly searching for something, seeking understanding in all the confusion that I've inspired this evening. I say that I have feelings for him but on the other hand I don't want to care. Just another layer to the indecisive complexity that is me.

Before I let myself overthink this moment, Dorian carries me over to the bed, gently laying me down. I hurriedly kick off my boots and scoot myself up onto my elbows as I watch him undress before me. One by one, Dorian undoes each of the buttons on his crisp white shirt, locking his eyes onto mine. The anticipation is torture. He reaches for the zipper on his pants but hesitates, instead kneeling at the foot of the bed and taking hold of my hips. He pulls me to the edge of the bed until he's eye level with my sex. It's still silent except for the sounds of my labored breathing. I can't quite see Dorian and the mystery of the unknown is killing me.

Before I give into my curiosity and push myself onto my elbows, I feel the warm softness of Dorian's lips on the inside of my thigh. I shudder at the unexpected contact and my back arches a bit. The way my body reacts to his touch instantaneously is uncanny. I've never been with someone so in tuned to my every desire. It's as if our bodies were designed especially for each other.

Dorian leaves a trail of soft kisses on each of my thighs, anticipation and wanting building with each caress. His hands find the waist of my panties and he eases them down easily, letting them drop to the floor. I'm on the verge of begging him to continue down this path of my destruction when Dorian's tongue finds the wetness between my legs. It teases and twirls as the sounds of my agonized moans fill the silence. I'm surprised at my brazen display, letting Dorian have his way with my body as I twist and writhe under the torment of his tongue. As much I want to pull away and cover myself, this unimaginable pleasure holds me captive.

Dorian pauses long enough to insert a finger inside me before continuing to lick my softness with deliberate control. He thrusts it in and out, going a bit deeper each time, my cries matching the intensity. He speeds up, adding a second finger and sucking me hungrily. I know that the end is near; it has to be. It is impossible to endure much more. I want to feel him; I want him inside of me. Though the feeling of his tongue is indescribable, I need to be one with him right now. My hands reach out for him but he is out of my grasp. I pull at the comforter in desperation, begging him in my harsh whimpers. He ignores my pleas and continues to thrust and lick determinedly.

I know what he's doing. He's giving me exactly what I need,

not what I think I want. He knows I could never fully give myself to him, and he's making it known that he doesn't even care. My body is enough. I can give him that entirely and withhold the part of me that guards centuries of secrets, lies, and deceit. My Dark side.

As if realizing that my thoughts have wandered into unknown territory, Dorian sucks my flesh *hard*. I yelp from the pleasurable sting and come back to him. I can let go with Dorian, and right on cue, I do. I give him all of me in the waves of my severe orgasm as I hoarsely cry out his name. My back arches off the bed and my legs quiver uncontrollably, causing them to collapse awkwardly. My eyes are closed tightly but I can feel Dorian rise and lie next to me on the bed. I'm reluctant to open them and face him so I focus on controlling my ragged breathing. I can only imagine what he's thinking right now, after seeing me so exposed and vulnerable but I can't hide from him. It's too late.

"Sorry," I mumble quietly, opening my eyes after a minute or two. Dorian is propped up on his elbow, watching me intently. He looks amused at my chaotic climax.

"For what?" he smiles.

"For . . . that. Being so dramatic, I guess." I gaze into the light blue depths of Dorian's sparkling eyes. He's so strikingly gorgeous; it literally causes all intelligent thought to abandon me.

"Don't be. I like it." Whoa.

"You do? Why?"

"You're uninhibited. You're raw. You're always so guarded, Gabriella, it's hard to get you that vulnerable. It really is beautiful. You should let people see that side of you more often." Dorian twirls a lock of my hair between his fingers and then brings it to his lips, kissing it gently. "Minus the orgasm, that is," he chuckles. Dorian's laughter is infectious, and I join him.

"You think I'm guarded?" I ask.

"Very." He focuses on the task of running his fingers through my hair from root to tip. I've noticed that he plays with it often. Could the elusive Dorian Skotos have a thing for hair?

"So many secrets, little girl," he mumbles barely above a whisper. His voice sounds so old, almost ancient, and there's a hint of an accent. It's so alarming that I can't find the words to question him about it.

Suddenly, Dorian's eyes are on my subtly shocked expression. He gives me a quick half smile to mask the mystery that lies in his words. I want to ask him what he means; what does he know of my secrets? I've been as open and honest with Dorian as I could be, more so than with any other guy, outside of Jared. How can he make that assessment?

"Turn over," Dorian commands. I roll over onto my stomach hesitantly and look back at him. "I'm going to massage you. I don't want your neck to be sore." Dorian shuffles off of the bed and goes into the bedroom's adjoining bathroom. He emerges seconds later with a small bottle of scented oil. "I'm going to straddle your back."

"No," I say abruptly as Dorian kneels on the bed. He instantly looks perplexed and stands up straight. I can see a storm brewing behind his crystal blues. "Not unless you get undressed," I add with a sly smile.

Dorian exhales lightly and nods, visibly unwound. He unzips his slacks and lets them drop to the floor, standing before me in black boxer briefs. I take in the magnificent sight of his chiseled, cut body. His olive complexion glimmers under the dim light flooding from the bathroom vanity. I lick my lips wickedly. "Now the rest."

Dorian eases down his boxer briefs and then removes his dress socks. My eyes widen with appreciation at his soft yet substantial member hanging between his legs. Slowly he advances to the bed, straddling the backs of my thighs. I can feel him lightly pulsating on my ass and I know our skin to skin contact is causing him to swell. Dorian undoes my bra and eases the straps off of my shoulders. He then picks up the small bottle and squeezes a bit in his hands, rubbing them together before gently grasping my shoulders. I instantly relax under his touch and lay my head flat onto the comforter to allow him to knead and caress. It feels heavenly, and I catch myself before letting a soft moan escape.

"*Ooooh*, Dorian, your fingers are magical," I murmur into the comforter.

Dorian chuckles a bit. "You have no idea," he says slyly, no doubt a smile on his lips.

"You think I have secrets," I say as Dorian lets his fingers rub the soreness from my neck and shoulders. It's not a question.

"Oh, I know you do."

"I could say the same about you." Dorian knows more about me than I do about him. Who's really the one with secrets here?

"I am an open book, Gabriella. If you want to know something, all you have to do is ask." Dorian gently gathers my hair into one thick handful and lays it to one side to allow access to my entire bare back. Such a contrast to the tight grip he had on it just hours ago.

"Ok," I respond reflectively. "Your relationship with Aurora . . . how far does it go? Don't tell me there's nothing to it because it is obvious that you two share history."

Dorian sighs, I'm sure expecting the question sooner or later. "Our families have been involved in business together for many years. We've known each other for a long time. Though Aurora has tried, I was just never interested in a long term, serious relationship with her or anyone else for that matter. When I moved away, she tracked me down, thought she could help me rebuild. She's the one who actually brought the Luxe opportunity to me."

Ok, that makes sense. It doesn't ease my anxiety about her advances and also tells me that Aurora won't back off, but it makes sense. Aurora has staked her claim and I am an intruder in her grand scheme to be Dorian's angel in his time of need.

"So you are both from the same place. And that is?" I have no idea where he is from. *Good going, Gabs.*

"Originally we're from Greece."

Ok, had I let Morgan do a background check on Dorian like she offered, I would have known that. Explains the exotic good looks, the hint of an accent, and his last name.

"Hmmm, that makes sense. So your family is wealthy? You've mentioned the family business. Politics, right?"

"That amongst other things. Nothing that is of great interest." Dorian moves down to the base of my shoulder blades. A low groan leaves my lips.

"But you want to gain your family's approval. That's why you came here, right? What is it that you hope to achieve in this little town?" A salon is great but I'm pretty sure his family is not in the cosmetology market. And Colorado Springs is not exactly a mecca of industrialism.

Dorian takes a moment to ponder my question before answering. "I must acquire something that could prove very valuable to my people. It's here. We would amass a great deal of power."

"Sounds really important. And they trust you with such a crucial task; they must have a lot of faith in you. Especially to be so young."

"I am only young to you. I've experienced enough for a dozen lifetimes." The weary, ancient tone to Dorian's voice has returned. It is so full of sadness and turmoil. I turn my head a fraction to gauge his reaction but he begins to knead the sides of my neck.

Something within me sympathizes with Dorian and his predicament. All he wants is his family's approval and love. I want the same, but I want it from Dorian, though I would never, ever admit it. As much as I want to keep this as superficial as possible, the more I get to know about him, the more I want him. And not just his body. I want his heart as well. I'm no better than Aurora; I want to be his savior too. Dorian is far from helpless yet I sense sadness within him that I just want to ease. There's a piece of him still hiding in the shadows, the part that never fully recovered from being disowned by his own family. Can I be what he needs? Will he be able to bare his soul to me though I could never bare mine entirely to him?

There is something that I *can* do for Dorian that Aurora can't. I can soothe him the only way I know how to. I reach my hand back and find his hardening penis resting on the middle of my backside. I stroke it gently, awakening it immediately. I can hear Dorian's breathing turn ragged and he kneads my shoulders a bit deeper. I guide his stiff rod towards my wetness and Dorian shifts to eagerly meet it. I spread my legs a bit, inviting him into my heat, and he thrusts forward, plunging deep within my warm comfort. We gasp simultaneously, appreciating the depth this new position brings. Dorian continues to massage my neck and shoulders, while thrusting into me slowly. I praise him with soft whimpers and sighs.

"So no more questions?" Dorian breathes raggedly, filling and stretching me to my limits.

"No, Dorian," I murmur between gasps of air. He feels so good here. This is where he belongs. This is where *I* belong.

Dorian lowers himself onto my back, his lips finding my ear and he continues his measured strokes. Grabbing each of my hands, he pins them down above my head, using the leverage to push himself even deeper. He gently takes my earlobe between his teeth to nibble and suck. Feeling his labored breath on the back of my neck, the heat of his body melding into mine, sends me over the edge. My moans intensify with every stroke, and Dorian feeds my hunger by delivering them faster and harder.

He begins to mutter something in my ear, so low I can't even make out what he's saying over the noise of my own harsh breaths. It's foreign, and I assume he's saying something in Greek. *Oh my God!* It's incredibly erotic. He continues the chant in my ear, now rapidly pounding into me. One hand finds my hair, and he pulls, causing my head to bend back to him. His murmurs grow louder and harsher, as if he is urgently trying to convey something to me, and I know his own orgasm is on its way. I feel the familiar building inside of me, and I know this one will do me in for sure.

Dorian delivers one hard, deep thrust and then holds himself stiffly inside of me. He's touching every pleasure point, pushing every one of my buttons. I can't hold it any longer; I let myself explode and contract around him, crying out my intense satisfaction. Dorian pushes deeper still, emptying the contents of his lust into me, colliding with mine.

"*Shit!*" I exclaim, still lying flat on my stomach. Dorian has eased off of me and is resting beside me, trying to find his breath.

"What's wrong?" he breathes, sounding a bit alarmed though his voice is sluggish and sated.

"Dorian, we really need to use protection." I am cursing myself for being so stupid yet again.

"I can't impregnate you, if that's what you're worried about," he says simply.

"I'm not. But there's other stuff, you know." I can't even bring myself to say STDs. And what does Dorian mean he can't impregnate me? Is he sterile?

"Top drawer of the nightstand to the right. There's a piece of paper with a recent blood test. I knew I wanted to be with you without worry or barriers. I had it done last week. It's yours." Wow, he really thinks of everything. Not to mention, extremely confident in his methods of seduction.

"And what about me?"

"I'm not worried about you. I trust you. But if you want to have a test done as well, I can arrange it."

"Thanks, but I can manage that myself." I make a mental note to go to the clinic as soon as I get out of class tomorrow afternoon.

"How do you know you can trust me?" I say with a smirk. Oh, if Dorian only knew how untrustworthy I really am. I'm endangering his life every second I am here with him. Why can't I just walk away and save us both the inevitable heartache and regret?

"Good judge of character," Dorian says with a sexy half smile. It's the last thing I see before I succumb to the sudden heaviness plaguing my tired eyelids.

I jerk awake in pitch dark, my eyes darting around fiercely, looking for any sign of familiarity. *Dorian's bedroom.* I'm alone and the room is completely silent and still. I sit up and feel around for my clothes. My foot hits a pile of crumpled linen. Dorian's shirt. I slide it on and wrap it around my naked breasts before heading out of the room in search of my missing lover.

Dorian is standing at the grandiose glass doors that lead out to the large balcony. He's wearing only his slacks, no underwear. I can tell they're not fastened by the way his pants hang around the cut of his hips and the slope leading to his tight, hard backside. He's holding a crystal glass containing a light brown liquid. He takes a sip and then leans his forearm against the pane of glass, looking out into the dark stillness of the night. I hold my breath, and tiptoe silently towards him. I don't want to disturb him during his private moment but I am curious as to what has called him from the warmth of the bed and my arms.

"You should be asleep," Dorian says aloud. *Shit.* I was sure to be quiet. I give up on tiptoeing and walk towards him.

"So should you," I reply quietly, standing beside him.

I look up at Dorian's weary, guarded eyes. Even in the dark, they sparkle. He gives me a rueful grin, unsuccessfully trying to mask whatever troubles him tonight. I want to reach out to him and comfort him but something is telling me not to.

"What do you see?" Dorian asks, nodding towards the window. He takes another swig of his drink and then offers me the glass. I take it in my hands and take a small sip. The strong liquid burns my throat, generating heat as it makes its way down. I hand it back to Dorian and he smirks arrogantly.

I look out into the night, and see the faint glistening of the lake and the shapes of tall swaying trees. "Nothing. Darkness," I respond just above a whisper.

"You think darkness is nothing? So much, more than you could ever imagine, is shrouded in darkness. As we stand here, looking out into nothingness, as you say, we are witnessing life.

"A man is secretly meeting with a woman whom is not his wife. He tells her that he will leave his wife but he truly has no intention of doing so.

"Two young men, workers at the hotel, disappear into the woods, engaging in sexual intercourse. No one knows of their relationship or their sexuality. Or the fact that they have HIV. They both have girlfriends.

"A night guard has been stealing the valuables of hotel guests when they stay out late. He's carrying the jewels and money to a secret place in the pool house so he can pick them up after his shift.

"A woman is on her balcony, whispering into her cell phone as her husband is asleep in bed. He believes they are here on vacation but she is plotting to empty out their accounts and run away with her lover.

"A businessman is stumbling back to his hotel room with a prostitute. Little does he know that his guest for the evening is not a woman. He won't care either way. It won't be the first time."

I look up at Dorian, slightly bewildered. "So many secrets and deceit in the darkness, it seems," I remark quietly. How does he know all this? Or are his ramblings a result of the potent alcohol?

"You would think so. The world thinks that darkness is synonymous for deception. Evil. But look again." Dorian nods his head towards the night once again.

"An elderly man and his wife stroll along the lake, hand in hand. It's their 50th anniversary and they've just come from a grand celebration in one of the resort's banquet halls, thrown by their 5 children and their families and friends.

"A young man is proposing to his longtime girlfriend over by the bridge. He's shipping off to basic training soon and he wants to marry her when he returns. They've been dating since high school.

"A new dad is frantically calling the airlines after finding out his baby has been born unexpectedly. He's here on a business trip with very important clients but he is sacrificing it all to be with his family.

"Another night guard has been suspecting his coworker and

friend has been stealing to help his family during hard times. He is looking for him in hopes to talk him into returning the items and is willing to help him get back on his feet."

Dorian looks down at me to gauge my dumbfounded expression. He gives me a reassuring grin and strokes my cheek with his hand. "You see, Gabriella. Darkness is not always what it seems. It can appear frightening at first but there is truly nothing to fear. Sometimes the light can blind us from the truth."

Ok, now he's officially freaked me out. Does he even know what he's saying? The thought that Dorian could possibly know about me passes through my mind. But that's impossible. And if he did, he would not be so comfortable standing here with me now. *Either that or I would be dead.*

Dorian bends forward and plants a deep, tender kiss on my lips, erasing the feelings of unease and disbelief. He tastes and smells of the sweet, strong liquor.

"Come on, we both need to get some sleep."

Dorian downs the last of his drink and then takes my hand, leading me to the bedroom. He turns down the comforter before I climb in. After he steps out of his pants, he climbs in behind me completely naked. He pushes his white shirt off my shoulders and I awkwardly maneuver my body so he can remove it completely. Then he pulls my head down to his hard, smooth chest and I nestle into him comfortably, intertwining my leg between his. This feels so good, yet I know it will only cause confusion in the future.

"You're not, Gabriella," Dorian says suddenly.

"Huh?"

"You're not just one of those casual arrangements. I felt it too."

I don't know what to say to that. Part of me is elated at the revelation because I, too, see Dorian as so much more than just a fling. But another part of me–the logical, shrewd part–is cringing at his admission. Because nothing good can come of this. I can't give him any more of me than I already have, and it's not fair to sell him the illusion of an ordinary, carefree young woman. Less than a year stands between us and my ascension. *And then what?* What if I don't even make it until then? He could be hurt in the crossfire.

Instead of responding to Dorian's declaration, I plant a soft kiss on his chest, and try my hardest to fall asleep to the rhythm of his beating heart. I will give him this moment. I will let myself enjoy his warmth and security. It may be the last bit of bliss I get to experience.

EIGHTEEN

Bright sunlight creeps through the dark curtains and caresses my sleepy eyelids, beckoning them to open. Reluctantly I oblige, knowing it's earlier than I'm used to.

"Morning, Sleepyhead," a silky deep voice greets me. Dorian.

I blink rapidly, remembering where I am and feeling intensely self-conscious. My eyes focus on his gorgeous smiling face looking down at me. He's freshly groomed and dressed in a dark suit and tie.

"Oh shit, Dorian, what time is it?" I struggle to sit up, wrapping the sheet around my naked breasts. Every muscle in my body feels like lead and I haven't gotten nearly enough sleep.

"7:30. I've got a meeting soon but I ordered you some breakfast. Go ahead and take your time and eat. Leave whenever you want." Dorian leans down and kisses my forehead tenderly. He flashes me a crooked smile before walking out of the bedroom and exiting the suite.

Once alone, I scramble out of bed and head straight to the bathroom. Fifteen minutes later, I am showered and sitting down at the dining room table where Dorian has left silver covered platters of eggs, bacon, pancakes and sausage. I take some of each, realizing that I am famished after not finishing my steak dinner and receiving yet another workout from Dorian. I splatter syrup on all of it, thankful he isn't here to be repulsed by my goopy breakfast. After I've sated my appetite, I grab my purse and head home.

I get to Briargate in record time, rushing to the bathroom to quickly brush my teeth and wash my face. My mom is right on my heels, no doubt looking for an explanation for my absence.

"Sorry, Mom, fell asleep at Morgan's last night. I would have called but I really didn't expect to sleep all the way until morning," I lie. I hate lying but there's no way I could tell her about Dorian. She surely would not approve in light of everything else going on in my life.

"Well, I'm glad you're safe. Please don't scare us like that!" she says, clutching her chest. I feel bad for worrying them but right now is not a good time to bring home a guy for them to meet. "What would you like for breakfast?"

"I already ate. I'm good," I say, smattering on some mascara and lipgloss. I throw my hair back into a ponytail. This is all the primping I have time to achieve before my morning class starts.

Donna follows me into my room where I pull out a pair of jeans and a t-shirt. "Well, make sure you take your smoothie. I'll put it in a travel cup for you."

"Thanks, Mom!" I call out, as she turns to leave, closing my bedroom door behind her.

I change out of my skimpy undergarments, and put on something more practical before getting dressed. Then I step into my white sneakers and grab a hoodie before scampering to the kitchen for my smoothie. Chris has already left for work and I know I'm in for a stern look of disapproval this evening at dinner. Maybe I'll eat at the mall to avoid the whole scene.

I pull up to the PPCC Rampart Range campus, and scramble out of my little Honda, walking briskly to my Art Appreciation class. It's an easy enough class and honestly just an elective I chose for filler, but the instructor is overly strict about tardiness in her class. I walk in just as she's closing the door and grab the first seat I see. Whew, that was close. I really don't want to deal with her condescending attitude or the repercussions of my smart mouth.

After my mundane morning classes, I head out to the atrium to meet up with Jared. His handsome, smiling face instantly puts me at ease when I approach our usual café table. I feel the tension of quizzes, homework, and mid-term papers evaporate when in his presence.

"Hey there, Handsome. How was the rest of your weekend?"

It's amazing that things are this seamless even after the awkward kiss Saturday night. It seems like such a distant memory.

"It was cool. Hit the gym, played a little football with the guys. You?" Jared looks just as beautiful as always–dazzling green eyes, chestnut hair and bright pearly white teeth. He's wearing a heather grey V-neck tee with a hoodie and jeans. Even in his plain, everyday clothes, he looks more like a model than a college sophomore.

"You know me, just hung out. I was pretty freaked out about Saturday but I'm fine now. Thanks for being there."

Jared is most definitely the first part of my coping mechanism. He helps to soothe my anxiety, while Dorian distracts me enough to put it out of my head. I hate to admit it, but it really seems like I'm using them both. *That's because you are, asshole.* Wow, some friend I am.

"Of course, don't worry about it. Hell, I was freaked out for you."

Jared runs his hair through his tousled locks. Just as I'm thinking how sexy he looks when he does that, I realize why it turns me on so much. *Dorian does it.* His intrusion into my thoughts carries a fresh wave of guilt.

"Yeah, crazy shit. Obviously that so-called fortune teller was a fraud," I murmur.

"Did you say fortune teller?" a strange guy from a nearby table chimes in. I've seen him before but we've never spoken, and we're definitely not familiar enough for him to be listening to our conversation. I give him a sharp look.

"Sorry to interrupt, but I couldn't help but wonder if this is the same woman." Mr. Nosy hands us today's newspaper. Jared and I both zero in on the front page story.

Ice pick Murderer Still At Large

Latest victim local carnival fortune teller

Jared and I look at each other with shock and horror etched on our faces. The fortune teller was killed and I know that I had something to do with it. I can't help but feel responsible for her death. She knew what I was, she could tell. She was genuinely scared of me and had every right to be. Her involvement with me pretty much put the nail in her coffin.

"Says here she died sometime last night. Maybe she played that prank on the wrong person? Poor old woman," Jared mutters, but I can hardly make sense of what he's saying.

"Jared, I've gotta go," I say gathering my books and purse.

I've got to get away from here; no one is safe with me around. First Summer and now the fortune teller. Seems like anyone I have an issue with ends up dead. Great, the detectives will surely have a field day with this.

"What? What about class?" Jared is confused at my reaction. He is still thinking this is just a coincidence, not quite adding up all the facts.

"Take notes for me. I have to get home."

I dart out of the building and don't stop until I am safely in my car. I look around me cautiously as I pull out of the parking lot, making sure that I'm not being followed. When I pull up to my house, I'm panting rapidly as if I've run the entire way.

"*Fuck!*" I scream, slapping my palms against the steering wheel. How could I have been so stupid? How could I let this happen? People are dying because of me and all I can think about is my insignificant-ass love life. This has to end *now*.

I run into the kitchen hoping that Donna skipped her 11:30 class but come up disappointed. Could my parents be next? Oh no, my friends! They would be so caught off guard they wouldn't even have a chance to defend themselves. And Dorian. *Oh God, not Dorian.* I pull out my cell phone and begin keying a mass text message to my friends.

To Morgan, Jared, James, Miguel, 11:46 AM

– Are you all ok? Please respond ASAP.

I receive a chorus of chimes a moment later.

From James, 11:47 AM

– *All good here. You?*

From Morgan, 11:47 AM

– *Headed to work. Later, bitch ;)*

From Miguel, 11:48 AM

– *Some of us do have class to attend, Gabs. LOL*

From Jared, 11:49 AM

– *What's going on, Gabs? You've really got me worried about you. Call me later, ok?*

Good. They're all safe and sound for now.

To Morgan, Jared, James, Miguel, 11:50 AM

– Just be careful, guys.

I look back down at my cell phone. Chris can't keep his cell on him at work and I know Donna keeps hers in a locker at the gym. Now Dorian. But how do I do that without making him feel like I'm checking on him? Yes, he said I wasn't just some casual fling but he also didn't say what I am to him. I could very well be just some chick he's banging for the time being. I bite the bullet and begin to construct a text message.

To Dorian, 11:53 AM

— Thank you for breakfast. And dinner. And dessert :) Hope you have a great day.

There. I know I shouldn't be worried about morning-after text etiquette during a time like this, but there's something about Dorian that makes me overly aware and self-conscious.

Ding! Ding!

From Dorian, 11:55 AM

— *How about lunch? I'm sure dessert is appropriate then too.*

Oh, what I wouldn't give to let Dorian make me forget the knowledge of the fortune teller's death. But now more than ever, I have to be cautious about our encounters. Maybe I should warn him so he can be aware and make the decision to stick around for himself.

To Dorian, 11:57 AM

— Gotta work in a couple hours. Maybe meet me at Starbucks later so we can talk?

— *Sure. Dumping me already?*

Dorian's playfulness makes a smile spread across my face. Even his texted words work magic on my mood.

To Dorian, 11:59 AM

– You couldn't get rid of me even if you tried. See you around 6.

Knowing that all my friends are safe for now fractionally eases my mind. I know I can't keep tabs on them throughout the day and I'm just as defenseless as they are, but I would never forgive myself if something happened to them. And I would definitely be out for blood as soon as I ascend.

When I arrive at the mall a few hours later, I'm determined to put the day's disclosures behind me. I smile and greet my coworkers then head to the back stockroom to stow my belongings and put on my nametag.

"Feeling better, Gabi-girl?" Felicia beams. *Sheesh, does this chick have an OFF switch?*

"Yes, thanks. Hope it wasn't too busy."

"Oh, it was fine. Nothing we couldn't handle. Pretty dull actually. I bet people are scared to go out with that killer on the loose."

The reminder brings it all back to the surface. Knowing that a Dark One is killing innocents because of me is just too hard to forget. I nod at Felicia politely then head to straighten some clothing racks. So much for my positive outlook.

By 5:50 PM, I am practically running out of the store. If I fold another pair of jeans or hang another shirt without caffeine, I will surely strangle someone. I head to the stockroom bathroom to check my hair and apply a fresh coat of lipgloss. I've upgraded my outfit from this morning with a knit top and my favorite boots and curled the ends of my long ponytail with the prospect of seeing Dorian. Satisfied with my appearance, I head down to Starbucks, almost skipping with each step.

Dorian is sitting at our usual table and I smile at the magnificent sight of him. He's still dressed in his dark suit, though he's ditched his tie and has unfastened the top buttons of his white dress shirt.

He's has two disposable cups again and I resist the urge to grab him by the face and plant a wet kiss on his lips.

"Hey," I smile ruefully sitting in the chair across from him. He still makes me so anxious; it's as if I can't gather the right words when he's around.

"Hey yourself," Dorian jibes, sliding one of the cups towards me.

"Thanks," I say, taking a sip of the hot latte. *Mmmmm.*

"So you wanted to talk?" he says with a raised eyebrow. *God, he's sexy when he does that.*

"Try not to look so damn hot and maybe I'll be able to get my head together," I say before I can stop myself. The remark causes Dorian's eyes to flash momentarily, obviously taken aback. He must've been prepared for one of *those* talks. "It's nothing bad, Dorian. Well, not for you, I hope. I don't really know how to explain it."

"Oh? How about from the beginning?" His shoulders have obviously relaxed and he sips his own beverage.

The beginning? Absolutely not. But I have to tell him *something.* I sigh heavily and let my shoulders slump. Just having to say it out loud makes my stomach snarl with worry.

"I think someone is trying to hurt me. And I'm afraid they'll go after my friends to get to me," I say lowly. I can't even bring my eyes up to meet his in fear that he'll laugh in my face at the outrageous claim.

"I see," Dorian says stiffly. "Have you told anyone else?" The question causes my eyes to dart to his. He's serious. He believes me without question.

"No," I shake my head. "I just thought you should know. Being around me could put you in danger. And I wanted you to be able to make the decision whether or not I'm worth the trouble." I can feel a lump forming in my throat at the thought of losing Dorian and I take a sip of hot coffee in an attempt to wash it down.

"Don't worry about me. You're going to have to scare me off

some other way," he smirks. I am genuinely relieved and overjoyed that Dorian is willing to stick around, though I wish he'd take heed. "Do you have any idea who might want to hurt you?"

"Not really. And I don't know how I can keep my friends out of the crosshairs without revealing too much."

"Don't worry about them," Dorian shakes his head. "I'll take care of it. And don't let this get to you. No one is going to hurt you while I'm around."

His bravery is endearing, though I know he doesn't stand a chance against the Dark force that is hunting me. I wish I could warn him but I know it would mean trouble for us both. And I refuse to bring that to his doorstep.

"Thanks, Dorian. But I don't know what you could really do in this situation. Let's just say it goes beyond anything I could ever fathom. Beyond our worst fears, our worst nightmares." I know I need to shut up right now before Dorian starts to probe for more information.

Dorian nods, slightly smirking. Does he think I'm joking? I begin to feel my face heat from his lack of confidence in my admonition.

He runs his hand through his black locks, disturbing them from their once neat style. I like it better like this anyway. Makes him look like the bad boy Dorian that likes to give it to me rough and hard. The heat that began to flush my face makes its way down south.

"I had been living my nightmares, Gabriella. Finding you has freed me from them. No one is going to take you from me." His words are so earnest and unexpected; I can't stop my hand from reaching out and touching his. He turns his hand and lets his thumb caress the inside of my palm. "And your friends will be safe. I'll see to it personally."

I really don't know how to respond to Dorian's admission. He seems so confident and protective, I don't have the heart to tell him that he doesn't stand a chance against my supernatural assailant. I need to just let him believe that he can help and try to keep him as far away from my secret life as possible.

"Thank you for the massage. It was the best one I've ever had. My neck isn't sore at all," I say slyly, hoping to steer the conversation into less somber territory.

"What a pity. I like to make you sore," Dorian remarks. His blue eyes smolder under his dark lashes, and I feel the familiar throbbing down below. The way my body reacts to him always surprises me.

"I like it too," I murmur. Wow, I'm getting pretty bold. And what's even more shocking, I really do like it when Dorian gets aggressive with me sexually. I've never been into that kind of thing with anyone else, but with Dorian it just seems so damn erotic.

"Careful, little girl. I might take you right here on this table if you keep this up. And I won't care who watches."

"Don't threaten me with a good time," I giggle. Giggle? *Geez, get a grip, Gabs.* "As much as I'd love to stay here and talk dirty with you, I do have a job I have to get back to."

"Will I see you later?" Knowing that Dorian wants to be with me as much as I want to be with him brings an involuntary smile to my face.

"I wish I could. But I probably should go home tonight. Actually, for now, let's just shoot for Thursday night. I don't want my parents to start asking questions." *Plus I have to try to keep my distance for your own safety and my heart's sake.* Not to mention Morgan is not too pleased with me always being unavailable.

Dorian nods with understanding. "Good idea. It's nearly impossible to focus on handling the task I was sent here for when all I can think about is bedding you."

Good, at least I'm not the only one getting distracted. "So how's that coming anyway? Any closer to achieving what you'd hoped for?"

"Oh, Gabriella, closer than you could imagine," he replies icily.

His moods are an anomaly; one minute he's joking and the next he's so cold it's alarming. I sip the last of my coffee, unable to come up with something to say in response. Maybe that's a sore subject for him and something I should steer clear from in the future.

"Well, I better get back to work. So Thursday, right?" I say gathering my purse and empty cup.

"Sure I can't persuade you to come see me sooner?" Dorian asks. His tongue skims his bottom lip suggestively and I have to fight the urge to suck that very same lip. He's so damn sexy; no one has ever aroused me with just a look. Sex appeal like that should be bottled and sold.

"You're dangerous, you know that?" I snicker, shaking my head. "You're making me rethink all my decisions and do things I swore I'd never do."

"Dangerous? Me?" Dorian feigns offense. "Well, that makes two of us. Just think about it. If you feel like you want to see me, don't fight it. Don't fight what your body needs."

Dorian's words hit me like a ton of bricks. I know he's right; I shouldn't fight what I feel. But then again, is this only physical for him? Does he want to keep this strictly about sex? I know I told myself that this was how it should be. It's the only logical way we could have any type of relationship. And this is the time to be logical. I have to be smart about this and stick to the game plan. Throwing feelings into the mix will only blur the line between sexual and emotional.

"I'll think about it, Dorian. Thanks for the coffee."

Dorian stands as I do, like the perfect gentleman that he is. I think to step forward and stand on my tiptoes to plant a kiss on his lips, but that would be leading with my heart. Before I can overthink it anymore, Dorian gently cradles my face and brings it up to his. He pauses just as our mouths are centimeters apart and lets his blue eyes melt into mine. They are burning white hot, becoming the lightest, iciest blue I've ever seen. A surge of invisible electricity radiates from them and sends tiny shockwaves throughout my body. They kiss every nerve ending, leaving a prickly trail of pleasure that leads to my own pulsing current down below.

Just as quickly as he grabbed me, Dorian releases my face and takes a cautionary step back. I'm panting, tingling, disoriented. My hunger for him is suddenly raging like a wildfire and only he can extinguish it. I will writhe and burn until he puts it out. I look up at Dorian with bewildered eyes.

"Go to work," Dorian commands. His voice is aged, archaic again.

I can't find my own voice. I can't even form an intelligible response. I simply turn in a robotic fashion and walk out of the coffee shop, not stopping until I reach my store. It's as if I am having an out of body experience. I can see myself; I can comprehend my actions. But I have no control. And I don't want it. I've relinquished it all to Dorian.

Only when I've entered the stuffy stockroom do I begin to feel like myself again. I retreat to the tiny bathroom to assess my appearance. I look the same, though my eyes are wild with confusion. I splash some water on my face and finger-comb my hair, in hopes of bringing back some normalcy. When I step back onto the sales floor, the tingles have subsided and I feel coherent again. *What the hell was that?*

The evening drones on in slow motion. I can't quite seem to wrap my head around what happened with Dorian. Every one of his touches is like a shock to my system. But he didn't even touch me; what could have caused that rush of intense energy? All I know is that my body is craving him. I need release and no one can deliver that better than Dorian. He knows what he's doing. This was no accident. I told him I couldn't see him and he somehow awakened a beast within me, making it so I can't *not* stay away. I can't let him win. If I give in this time, he'll know he can manipulate me whenever he wants. But would that be the worst thing in the world? Being manipulated by Dorian when the payoff is so damn good? I can live with being used for sex by him, can't I?

No. This is what he wants. He wants me to crave him. He wants to constantly be on my mind so I give into my carnal desires. This is all part of his game; unraveling me to the point where I need him to stay sane. He wants me totally dependent on him. I wasn't lying–he really is dangerous. If I'm going to maintain control of my faculties, I need to be able to fight fire with fire. I pull out my cell phone and head back to the stockroom.

To Dorian, 8:26 PM

— Nice try. See you Thursday.

To Morgan, 8:26 PM

— Can you meet me tomorrow at the mall? Taking my break around 6.

— *Sure. I'll be there.*

Great, now I can put my plan into action. No one does hot and sexy like Morgan.
Ding! Ding!

From Dorian, 8:27 PM

— *Nice try? What do you mean?*

I decide not to play into Dorian's text, though my fingers are itching to key in a response. I won't give him the satisfaction of knowing that he's ruffled me once again. Instead, I busy my hands by folding a new shipment of denim until it's time to go home. Only a few more days and then it's time to show Dorian the magic in *me*.

NINETEEN

These past couple of days will go down in history as the hardest, most emotional, sexually frustrating days ever. Every night, another vivid, sensual dream that leaves me throbbing and wet by morning. The days are no better–walking around like a zombie, feeling so sluggish and lethargic as if I haven't slept in weeks. I can't concentrate in class, no matter how hard I try and have even been caught zoning out by my instructors when called upon to answer questions.

"Damn, Gabs, are you sure you're ok? You haven't been yourself all week," Jared asks, obviously exasperated by my dispirited state. It's Thursday. Finally. And he's had to deal with my dejected disposition long enough.

"I'll be fine by tonight." I know exactly what's wrong. *I need Dorian.* This goes so far beyond wanting him. My body literally *needs* him.

"Good. I'm getting tired of seeing you moping around like this. It's downright depressing to watch," Jared chuckles. "Hey, I know what'll cheer you up. There's an open air concert this weekend. Over at Palmer Park. Bunch of different bands, food, drinks. Come with me."

"Oh Jared, I'd love to but I think I have to work," I lie. I've never purposely lied to Jared but I can't tell him about Dorian. He'd flip, especially since I turned him down. That would surely put the nail in the coffin of our friendship.

"That sucks. Oh well, maybe next time."

Work is like being stuck in quicksand and I have half a mind to tell Felicia that I'm sick just so I can go home early. But since I changed my schedule to free up my weekends, I just have to suck it up and try to get through the long, torturous hours until closing time. All is prepped at home and I just have to shower and leave. I've even prepared a story for my parents about a weekend trip to Denver with Morgan just in case I stay the entire weekend at the Broadmoor. I'm getting ahead of myself. Dorian and I agreed on Thursday. Who's to say he won't kick me out Friday morning?

"Hey, Kiddo, can I talk to you for a second?" my dad calls out as I pass his office, rushing to my room to get ready. I reluctantly turn on my heel and walk into the study to face him.

"Everything ok? You've been kind of down and out lately and I just want to make sure nothing else happened." I can tell Chris has wanted to broach the subject all week but let me have time to work it out myself. That's what he'd want for himself–space and time to deal.

"I'm ok, Dad. Just been a rough week. But I've got a fun-filled weekend with Morgan planned that'll pull me outta my funk," I smile.

"Speaking of Morgan . . . I think it's important that you know who she is." Chris takes off his reading glasses and motions for me to sit down. I do as he wishes and wait for him to continue. What could *he* possibly tell me about *my* best friend? "I know you two are very close and Morgan is a wonderful young woman. But Morgan is a little something extra, if you know what I mean."

"What are you talking about? What do you mean, '*extra*'?" I'm on the edge of my seat.

Chris sighs and rubs his tired eyes like he usually does when he has to talk about something uncomfortable. "Morgan's grandmother was a very powerful Haitian Vodou priestess. That same black magic runs through her veins, though it's quite possible that Morgan has no idea. But because of it, she is naturally drawn to you. She can't help it. You are a source of power. Being in your proximity is like sustenance for her."

The news is beyond anything I could ever comprehend. I seriously thought Chris was going to inform me that she was involved in some type of scandal with a powerful government official. Okay, *that* I could believe. But Morgan has black magic in her lineage? How does that fit into the fiasco that is my life? Is she really even my friend or is she drawn to me by some inner influence?

"You have to understand just what you are, Gabriella. You will soon be the single most powerful magical force. Ever. There will be others that will draw from your power. Be wary of people around you, especially those who want to constantly be in your presence. They are trying to harness your energy, and it will only get worse once you ascend."

The first person that pops into my mind is Dorian. He came into my life so unexpectedly, and has been persistent in staying there. But I feel like I need to be around him. He has been a source of energy for me. Every time we are together I feel so anxious yet *good*. He makes me forget about the burden of my birthright. With him, I am free of those worries. All I feel is pleasure.

"Can I draw energy from others?" I don't know how Chris knows all this but he seems to have all the answers.

"I suppose so but I'm not entirely sure. Did Natalia say anything about it in the book?" *Of course.* The book.

"I haven't finished it yet. Just haven't been able to bring myself to read any more bad news." After learning that I will never have children of my own, I couldn't put myself through anymore disappointment. Not until I was strong enough to deal with it.

"Well, it's certainly possible. Although I'm not sure how Morgan's bit of power would be enough to sustain you. I'm assuming it'd have to be a very powerful force of Light." Chris sighs and rubs his eyes again. "Or Dark," he mutters.

"Good thing we don't have to worry about that right now," I say, standing. I give my dad a smile and kiss him on the cheek. "I gotta go, Dad. I'll check in later."

Chris's words haunt me as I mindlessly shower. I've been feeling crappy for days, ever since the strange encounter with Dorian in the coffee shop. And I know I need him to feel better. My body literally craves him. And not just in the sexual sense either. I just need to feel his presence. Even the thought of him momentarily clears my troubled mind. *Could he be . . . ?*

No. That's impossible. I've entertained that possibility before and concluded that I'd be dead by now if that were true. Maybe all that Dorian is to me is a mystery that I can't solve, a challenge I can't conquer. Maybe what draws me to him is his unattainability.

After I am sparkling clean and meticulously groomed, I look down on the skimpy lingerie I purchased from Frederick's of Hollywood, or as Morgan calls it, Victoria's slutty younger sister. The piece is completely see-through, black, and has light blue detailing on the bodice. It comes with a matching thong that looks more like a piece of black dental floss than underwear. Morgan insisted that Dorian would love it and chose it for me after we had looked at several risqué pieces on Tuesday night. I moisturize with the shimmery scented body butter we also purchased before slipping on the short chemise. It hugs every curve in the right place and the stitching at the bust is the only thing obscuring my nipples. Satisfied and praising Morgan for her impeccable taste in lingerie, no matter what may run in her bloodline, I finish dressing and grab my small overnight bag.

The ride to the Broadmoor seems like hours instead of a mere 15 minutes. I let valet take my little hatchback and pull my coat tightly around me as I make my way to the Lakeside building of the resort. My anxious stride takes me to the elevator and to my dismay it's occupied by a man and woman who are passionately kissing. I think they are going to step off, being that it's the ground floor but they stay on and squeeze their panting bodies into a corner. I try to stay towards the front to give them privacy but I can't help but catch their hushed conversation.

"How long do we have until you have to go back to her?" the woman whines. She sounds desperate and saddened at the prospect of losing her lover.

"A couple hours. Whitney is starting to really get suspicious." It sounds like the man is planting kisses on his forlorn companion.

"You said you would leave her last week. What happened? You said we would be together."

"Look, Rebecca, it's just not that easy. You know I love you. It's just complicated. She will take everything if I'm not careful. Just give me more time."

I bite my lip in an attempt to stifle a snicker. That man is not leaving his wife. He's scum, and I fight the urge to turn around and tell him and his mistress so. The memory of Dorian's late night narrative enters my mind. He did say that there's a man and woman here having an affair and that he would never leave his wife. *Lucky guess, Dorian.*

I stow away the information I've gained on the heated elevator ride, and step off eagerly when I reach the top floor. Only a few yards separate me from him at this point. Finally I'll be free from this hell I've been experiencing for the past few days. I know that he is the cure. All I need is right behind that door.

I finger comb my long, dark hair, take a deep breath and undo the waist tie of my long coat before knocking. Seconds tick by and there is no answer. No sound from the other side of the door. *Shit.* I knock again, this time a bit harder. Still no activity or noise. *Shit!* I begin to panic, my chest rising and falling dramatically with my rapid breaths. I lift my fist to knock one last time before retreating back to my car humiliated and frustrated when the door suddenly opens, startling me.

Dorian stands before me wearing a stoic expression, his bare arms glistening with tiny droplets of water. He's wearing only a low-hanging pair of grey sweatpants, a white tank top, and nothing else. It's amazing how such pedestrian attire can look so damn good draped on his luscious body. His dark hair is damp, reminding me of slick black oil. I am momentarily stunned by his disheveled yet sumptuous appearance and nearly forget my own plan of action. I tear my eyes away long enough to open my long trench coat, exposing the see-through chemise and thong. I'm wearing my spangled platform heels accompanied by silk black thigh-high stockings and soft ringlets cascade down my back and shoulders. I've applied more eye liner and mascara than I'm used to wearing and my lips are perfectly glossed and pouty. I place my hands on my hips for added effect and take in Dorian's hungry, appreciative expression.

"Get in here. *Now*," Dorian growls between gritted teeth before grabbing me by the arm and pulling me inside his suite.

He slams the door behind him. For a second I think he's angry at my brazen display until his firm, eager lips find mine. His kiss is deep and desperate, like he has just sought nourishment after days of famine. He's missed me. Just like I've missed him.

Dorian reluctantly breaks our impassioned lip-lock and leads me to the living room. He leaves me in front of the couch and goes over to the bar, pouring amber liquor into two crystal glasses. He takes a sip from one of the glasses and then walks over and hands it to me. I take a small sip and let the silky liquid make its way down my parched throat. It doesn't burn as bad this time and I welcome its warmth after being outside nearly naked. Dorian picks up a small remote and presses a button. Racy, provocative music resounds through an unseen sound system, filling the dimly lit room with hypnotic melodies. I instantly raise my eyebrows in recognizance.

"Interesting choice in music. I never would have pegged you as a Prince fan," I remark.

Dorian smirks. "You know of him," he observes. "I'm surprised. A bit before your time."

"Morgan is obsessed with him. She's made me watch Purple Rain with her at least twenty times." I take a sip of my liquor and stifle a gasp at the burn sliding down my chest. Then I turn to Dorian with a questioning narrow of my hazel eyes. "Uh, before your time, too."

Dorian nearly snorts with amusement then shakes his head. "I told you, Gabriella. I listen to whatever moves me. And it is very fitting for what I have planned for you."

I place a hand on my curvy, lace-covered hip. "And that is?"

Dorian takes a seat in the middle of the very same sofa that he violently sexed me on. The memory is harsh, vulgar. It instantly makes me wet with anticipation.

"Dance," he commands.

I look at him incredulously as if he's just instructed me to bark like a dog. "Dance? I don't dance." At least not the kind of dancing Dorian has in mind. I'm tempted to wrap my coat around me and hightail it out of there.

"If you can fuck, you can dance. Drink."

I do as he commands like a good little girl and am instantly repulsed by my submissiveness.

Dorian takes a sip of his own poison. "You've come all this way dressed like that. I want to enjoy you, savor you. Imagine what I see right now. How sexy you are. I want you to be as aroused by your body as I am." Dorian takes the small remote and turns it up a bit and then walks over to me, standing at my backside. He places his hands on my hips and presses himself against my ass. Slowly he sways my hips side to side in rhythm with the music, grinding against me with the stiffened bulge constricted in grey cotton. I stifle a low groan at its pulsing hardness.

Never in my life have I had a guy make me want to abandon all my morals and boundaries. Here I am, standing in lingerie, a trench coat and heels in the middle of a man's hotel room, seriously considering doing a striptease for him. *And why shouldn't I?* He wants me; he thinks I'm sexy. Why can't I be as confident and uninhibited as Morgan, who can nab any man she pleases? I should own my sex appeal, and flaunt it heartily in front of Dorian. This gorgeous, drop-dead sexy man wants me. I arouse him and he only wants to take me to new heights. I've never backed down from a challenge and I shouldn't start now.

"Sit," I demand, taking Dorian's hands and gently pulling him back toward the couch. He smirks and licks his lips, taking his front row seat.

The song ends and another sexually-charged tune takes its place. I take a gulp of the burning liquid courage and set the glass down, ready to show Dorian that he isn't the only one with methods of seduction. *Here goes.*

From right to left I sway my hips, riding the beat of the music, running my hands over the soft lace of my lingerie. I keep my hooded eyes locked on Dorian's fervent expression, biting my bottom lip a little. I decide to switch it up a little and start to roll my hips, definitely feeling the effects of the alcohol. It makes me feel free and sexy. The move is not lost on Dorian and he responds with a lick of his succulent lips. I begin to slowly slide the coat off my shoulders, never breaking eye contact or halting my sinful dance. The sight of my bare, creamy skin causes Dorian to gasp. The gesture is appreciated and motivates me to continue. The trench coat is only covering the lower half of my arms. Instead of letting it drop to the floor, I use it to entice Dorian, letting it slide down inch by inch until it hangs around my waist. Dorian's mouth is partially opened and I can tell his breathing is deep and labored. *Time to go in for the kill.*

I let the coat drop to the floor, exposing my curvy frame draped in see-through mesh and lace. I saunter over to Dorian with catlike grace, putting a little extra *oomph* into each sway of my hips. When I am standing directly in front of him, I nestle between his parted legs, inviting him to touch me. His eyes are aflame with blue fire, burning pure lust and desire. I up the ante by propping my stiletto-heeled foot beside him on the couch, giving Dorian a full view of my shapely thighs and lace covered sex. His breathing is ragged and shallow. He swallows loudly and looks like a thirsty man at a well. He's affected, and I mentally relish in my victory. I've done it; I've won. Dorian isn't the only one who can play this game.

With a tentative hand, Dorian finally reaches out to caress my extended leg. His fingertips dance over the sheer stocking, making its way up to my thigh. I think he's about to take it off but instead he runs his hand up towards my bare backside. He slides it up under the flimsy material and gently grasps my cheek. A low moan makes its way from my lips as Dorian continues up my other leg, again clutching my behind. He leans forward and grazes my now damp panties with his nose. It teases the swell behind the skimpy fabric and I can't contain my raspy sighs. My knees are beginning to shake and I'm in fear of losing control. No. This is my show.

"Sit back," I command.

Dorian looks up at me quizzically and does as he's told, leaning back on the couch. I place my foot back on the floor and take an admiring glance at the bulge under Dorian's sweatpants. I lean forward and place a single finger under his waistband, grazing his firm, defined abdominal muscles. *Geez, he must work out like a madman.* I pull the waistband a bit and bite my lip hungrily at the sight of the trail of fine, dark hair leading to his generous erection. I want it. *Right now.* I yank down his sweats, allowing his hardness to spring to freedom. I kneel down on the plush carpeting and let my carnal instincts take the driver's seat as I greedily take Dorian deep into my mouth. He sucks in a large gulp of air in surprise, followed by a chorus of deep groans, harmonizing with the slow, seductive music, as I feed the Dark beast raging within me.

TWENTY

"I've created a monster," Dorian says between rapid breaths.

He's completely naked, still sitting upright on the couch with me straddled on his lap, resting my head wearily on his bare shoulder. My sheer nighty is still intact except for my scanty thong that Dorian eagerly ripped right off of me so I could mount him with haste.

"Have you?" I breathe. I feel lightheaded, almost intoxicated, though I know I'm only slightly buzzed from the alcohol.

"That was . . . incredible." Dorian sounds bewildered, as if he can't understand how someone like me could unravel him. "Sure you don't have some salacious past I don't know about?"

"Hey!" I say, playfully slapping his shoulder. "I guess we all have our talents. Some are just a bit more depraved than others," I giggle. I groggily lift my head to look in his glossy, drowsy eyes. "Honestly, I've never been like this with anyone else. I know you don't want to hear that or you don't believe it, but there's something about you. When I'm with you . . . ," I explain. I can't find the words though they're right on the tip of my tongue. I search Dorian's crystal blues for understanding.

"I know," is all he says in response. What does *that* mean? He knows how I feel because he feels the same way? Or he gets what I'm trying to convey? "Looks like I owe you a pair of panties," Dorian chuckles, changing the subject.

"I've got another pair in my car. No worries."

"And how do you expect to go out and get them? Dressed like that?" Dorian's lips turn up into an amused smirk. My mouth forms into an 'O,' causing him to look even more tickled. He shakes his head. "Don't worry about it."

Dorian gently tries to lift me off of him and I reluctantly dismount him. He grabs his rumpled sweats from off the floor and pulls them on, while I watch him from the couch. My legs are still shaky from the overwhelming orgasm I suffered minutes ago.

Dorian makes his way to a phone and punches in a number. He's calling room service. He orders a variety of dishes, and even loads up on desserts. I shake my head at him when he hangs up and looks my way.

"What?" he asks with shrugged shoulders. He looks so young right now, and I remember that he actually *is* young. He's still a kid in most people's eyes.

"Think you ordered enough? Geez, how much do you think I eat?" I giggle. I mentally scold myself. I'm always extra giggly around Dorian. *So* not me.

"I need to ensure you're replenished. I highly doubt you ate before you came here. Besides, I'm famished. Haven't been eating much these past few days." His expression is troubled as if he's recalling an unpleasant memory.

"You too?" I say quietly.

Dorian's head snaps up and his eyes meet mine. He knows what I mean. He's been as tormented as I have since Monday evening. He caused the turmoil yet he's had to suffer through it as well. No further explanation is needed. We both feel the inexplicable need for each other.

I shakily make my way to my feet and retreat to the bathroom in the bedroom. Hanging on the hook is one of Dorian's white dress shirts, probably the one he wore today. I slip it on over my lucent slip and button it halfway up. It smells like him, like pure sin and heaven. *What a combination.* I let his scent envelop me, trying to record it to memory. I want it all over me.

When I step back into the living room area, Dorian is looking out through the glass doors again. Into the darkness. The music has changed and I recognize it as the band he introduced me to that evening in his car. I downloaded their album soon after he played it for me. I take a deep breath and walk up behind him, wrapping my arms around the front of his waist. It's a risky move, something I would never do. But it feels so good, holding him. Dorian pulls me tighter around him, obviously appreciative of the contact. I exhale in relief.

"What do you see tonight, Dorian?" I murmur, eyes closed, resting my head against his bare broad back.

"The usual. Depravity, pain, lust, deceit," he answers matter-of-factly.

"No happiness and love?" I take a deep whiff of his warm skin. *Ahhhh.*

"Oh, there is." He turns to face me, still holding my arms around him. His expression is so content, so tender. I can't bear to tear my eyes from his. It's the first time I've ever seen him so vulnerable.

Three quick raps on the door interrupt our intense moment. We both look towards the door defensively with stern expressions. When a voice on the other side of the door announces the arrival of room service, we both relax our tense stances. Dorian walks over to the door to let in the concierge with our feast on his wheeled cart. Once he's gone, Dorian leads me to the dining table where a huge spread of Italian antipasti, oysters on a half-shell, stuffed mushrooms, and fresh fruit await us. He's also taken the liberty of ordering more decadent desserts than appropriate.

"I like dessert," he shrugs, smiling. His smile makes me smile, seeing him so carefree and unburdened. His positivity is infectious, and all the worries of my world are a distant memory.

"Well then," I say picking up a slice of cheesecake with some type of fresh berry compote on top, "we should start there."

I take a fork and scoop up a bit, walking over to Dorian and offering it to him. He keeps his eyes on mine as he opens his mouth and receives the smooth, creamy bite. Then in a swift movement, he picks me up with ease, setting me down on the edge of the table where I once was his dessert. He grabs another dessert plate–I'm guessing Crème Brulee–and sits in the chair facing me. He scoots himself forward so that he is right between my thigh-high clad legs, obtaining a full view of my naked sex.

"Open up," he says, and for a moment I think he means my legs. I open my mouth instead and welcome the sweet, sugary custard.

We continue like this for a while, sampling each dessert, laughing, flirting. Once we've each satisfied our sweet tooth, I scoot off the table and sit beside him at the table.

"Can I ask you a question?" I say reaching for a raw oyster. I suck down the slippery shellfish and wipe my hands and lips on a napkin.

"Shoot." Dorian says, going for an oyster as well.

"What do you think about this Ice pick Murderer?" Dorian seems to know a bit about everything, and while I have my secret suspicions, I really do feel more comfortable talking to him.

Dorian takes a moment as he swallows his oyster. He takes a long sip of the wine he's poured for us, mulling over my question. "I think it's someone who is desperate, unaware, and ignorant of the consequences he faces for such savagery."

Dorian's words catch me off guard. I expected him to describe the killer as ruthless and vile, but yet he's somewhat explaining the reasons behind his actions. *Unbelievable!*

"Do you have an idea of who it might be?" I have to ask. Dorian is talking about this person, this Dark murderer, as if he knows him. *Does he?*

"Why would you think I'd know something like that?" Dorian asks, quizzically. He isn't upset. He's curious. I shrug my shoulders and go back to eating silently. Now is not the time to let my imagination run away with my rationality.

After a few quiet moments, I open up the conversation to something a bit more light and casual. "So have you thought about Morgan working at your salon?" The question has been gnawing at me and I didn't want to bring it up right away in fear that he'd feel I was owed a favor after sleeping with him.

"I have actually. I think you were right; she'd offer a fresh, young perspective to our more mature, youth-seeking clientele. As soon as she's licensed, she will have a job at Luxe, if that is what she desires."

I flash Dorian a bright smile and don't stop myself from jumping up and planting a quick peck on his lips. Morgan will be thrilled.

"Thank you, Dorian," I say sitting back down and collecting myself. "She will be so excited. We're hoping to get a nice place together with the extra money I'm sure she'll get from those big tippers."

"About that . . . What kind of place are you two looking to rent?" Dorian says with a raised eyebrow.

"Just something nice enough, a couple of bedrooms, bathrooms. Oh, and pet-friendly. Morgan has her little rat, Dolce," I chuckle. Dorian looks bemused. "Oh, not a real rat. A Chihuahua. Morgan is crazy about that thing. She dresses him up and everything. That dog has a better wardrobe than most people."

"I see. Not an animal lover, Gabriella?"

"I guess I like animals alright. Not overly crazy about them, especially pretentious little lapdogs."

Dorian looks oddly interested in the news. Maybe he pegged me for some zealous tree-hugger since I told him I like being outdoors. Oh God, I hope he doesn't think I like camping or stuff like that. Sunshine, I like. Bugs, rodents, and no indoor plumbing? Not so much.

"Well, if you're interested, I happen to own an apartment complex. Have you heard of Paralia?" My wide eyes and dropped jaw answer his question. "If you would like to live there, I can offer you and Morgan a place that should suit your needs."

"Geez, Dorian! You own that place? Since when?" The questions roll out a bit more excitedly than I intend.

"A little while now. An investment that fell into my lap unexpectedly." Dorian shrugs as if it's no big deal to own a luxury apartment complex.

"If you own Paralia, why do you live here?"

Again, he shrugs. "Convenience." He looks back down at his food. "Think about it and let me know."

"Dorian, I really appreciate it, I do. But I don't think we could afford to live there. But thank you for the offer. I know the waiting list must be really long." I give him a warm smile.

"Gabriella, are you trying to insult me?" Dorian's expression is dark and serious. Shit.

"No, of course not!" I say fervently, shaking my head. But Dorian's face is frozen with ire. "With me working at the mall part-time and no real plan after graduation, I wouldn't be able to carry my weight. I can't expect Morgan to foot the bill."

"There would be no bill, Gabriella. Don't you understand that?" Dorian's icy expression thaws a bit but he is still obviously annoyed.

"No. How could I?" I'm floored by Dorian's offer. Even a bit offended that he would assume I'd expect that. Now it's my turn to look irritated. "You know I would never accept that. That's ridiculous."

"How so?" He's genuinely curious.

"For starters, we are still getting to know each other. What if you decide I'm really not worth your time? Morgan and I would be out on the street. And secondly, Morgan wouldn't feel comfortable working for you *and* living in your apartment. And lastly, I'm not that kind of girl. I don't know what kind of women you've dealt with in the past, but I can assure you, I'm not like them. I don't look at you and see dollar signs. That's not what I'm about." I am fuming; Dorian really pushed the wrong button.

"Calm down, Gabriella. I wasn't trying to offend you. Honestly. All of my full-time employees have the opportunity to live at Paralia. It's part of the package." He looks like he is on the verge of laughter, only making me more angry and humiliated.

"Oh," is all I can choke out. My face is red with embarrassment.

"And for the record, there's absolutely no chance I would ever think you weren't worth my time. You are of great importance to me, Gabriella. You will see that soon enough. The closer you are to me, the better."

"Seriously?" He's always catching me off guard with these grand declarations. It's hard to determine if he's for real or just blowing smoke up my ass.

"I never lie. Ever. That is the one thing you must remember about me. I will always tell you the truth." Dorian looks deep into my eyes, letting his words sink in.

I think about each encounter I've had with Dorian since I've met him. I think about the difficult questions I've asked him about Aurora, the Ice pick Killer, his feelings for me. He's always given me a logical answer, even if he simply answered with a question of his own. No, I don't think Dorian has ever lied to me. He's always been painstakingly honest. But can I be honest enough about my own suspicions about Dorian and work up the courage to ask him? He would tell me. I know he would.

Just do it, Gabs. Put on your big girl panties and ask him already.

"Something you want to know, Gabriella?" I look up to meet his eyes, unaware that I've been looking down at my hands.

I could ask him. I could ask what he was. I could ask if he knows who and what I am. I could ask him why someone is out to kill me. And he would answer every one of my questions. But then what? This would all end. Dorian would no longer be mine. Though he's far from being mine now. Shit. How did we even get to this?

"Yes," I say, confidently. Dorian's expression darkens and he gazes at me through dark, full lashes. "What does your tattoo say?" I give him a sly smile. No, I'm not ready to let go of this beautiful illusion.

Dorian lifts his right arm, exposing the foreign characters inked on the side of his torso. I had gotten a glimpse of it before but we were always too 'occupied' for me to ask. Now that I see it in the light, I realize that it is a series of what I'm assuming is Greek lettering.

"Skotos," Dorian answers flatly. He looks puzzled. This must be the most perplexing dinner in history. "You can see it." It's not a question, but not necessarily an astute observation either.

"Uh, yeah. It's right there on your right side. Were you trying to hide it?" I say cynically.

"Most don't see it. Special ink, you could say." Dorian gives me a smug crooked smirk.

"Don't know how special it is. Looks like every tattoo I've ever seen. I actually love tattoos, so I don't understand why there's any reason you'd want to hide it."

The look that Dorian is giving me can only be best described as incredulous. It's as if I'm not getting the punch line to a very obvious joke and he can't believe how dim I am. Am I missing something? Maybe tattoos are frowned upon in his culture and he doesn't understand how I can be so casual about them. Hell, I'd have a few myself if Donna hadn't been so against them. Getting some body art is one of the first things I plan to achieve once I move out.

"You really have no idea, do you?" Dorian mutters, shaking his head.

Ok, time to quit with all the serious talk. It's becoming exhausting and life is too short to worry about trivial things. At least mine is.

"Well, how about you enlighten me, *old wise one.*"

And with that, I scoop a bit of whipped cream from one of the partially eaten desserts and lean over to place the small dollop on Dorian's perfect nose. I suck the remaining cream off my finger and burst into a fit of hysterics. Dorian looks bewildered, and for a split second, I think he's angry. But before I can think too much into it, he scoops me into his arms playfully and swings me over his shoulder, exposing my bare ass.

"Oh you think that's funny, do you?" he chuckles.

Dorian carries me to the bedroom and flops me down onto the bed. He still has the whipped cream on his nose and begins to rub it all over my face. I am squealing and laughing like a child as he continues to spread the white froth then launches into tickling me.

"*Dorian! Ahhh! Stop!*" I squeal.

He's absolutely thrilled making me surrender to him in such an innocent way. I try to fight back and begin to tickle his ribs. He is wildly ticklish and soon, I gain the upper hand. He falls flat on the bed while I straddle him, continuing to playfully torture him with my fingers.

"*Ok, ok, ok! I give up! I surrender!*" Dorian hoots.

He's trying unsuccessfully to buck me off of him. I put my hands up, indicating that I acknowledge his white flag, and we both take a moment to catch our breaths.

"I win again," I say proudly. "Who knew that the elusive, powerful, intimidating Dorian Skotos is ticklish?" I chuckle looking down at his dazzling face.

"What do you mean, '*You win again*'?" Dorian asks with a raised eyebrow. He extends his finger up to my cheek, scooping up a smidgen of whipped cream before putting it in his mouth.

"You know what I mean. You thought I would come crawling back here after your little eye-fuck stunt at Starbucks. Like I said, *nice try*."

"I underestimated you. Seems as if you have a few tricks up your sleeve." Dorian licks his lips in the sexy way that I like. I feel a stir between my legs.

I bite my bottom lip. "Stick around. You might learn something," I say with bold seduction.

I take it a step farther and begin to grind my naked flesh onto the growing bulge under me. Dorian pulls his knees up, giving me a better feel of every inch of his stiffness. He starts to unbutton the white dress shirt I'm wearing as I continue my slow dance on his lap. Once the shirt is completely unfastened, he pushes it off my shoulders, exposing my sheer chemise.

"Take this shit off," Dorian mutters between gritted teeth.

He grabs it by the bottom hem and pulls it over my head in a swift movement. Then he yanks at my stockings, indicating that he wants them off as well. I happily oblige. He's eager; our flirtatious game has aroused him.

I'm naked, and Dorian is eyeing my body enthusiastically. He caresses my skin as if I am a rare gem, admiring each line and curve. His fingertips brush the roundness of my breasts, the dip of my hips, the hollow of my navel. It's like he's never touched a woman before, and I feel cherished.

"You are the most beautiful creature I have ever seen. I never could have imagined this," he whispers.

I want to freeze this very moment. I want to be trapped in time just like this. With Dorian. I know that we will never be; we could never have a real future together. But for the time being I can pretend that he is mine, and I am his.

I lean forward and place my wanting lips on his, letting our tongues unite while our hands roam each other's bodies. Being here with him is the only thing that matters. I'm not what I am. I'm not Light, I'm not Dark. *I'm his*. And the honest part of me wants to truly be his forever. This goes so far beyond sex and passion. Dorian has penetrated my heart.

As if reading my mind and hearing my secret admission, Dorian gently pulls my face from his, breaking our kiss. His blue eyes are a gleaming pool of crystal and his expression is tormented, yet wistful. But the most shocking discovery is the sheer layer of dense pink fog that surrounds him. *I see him.* I try to ignore it, not wanting to spoil this moment with my bizarre omissions. Right on cue, Dorian's lips curl into a sexy half-smile. He's telling me to let go; feel what I want to feel. I don't have to be afraid of what my heart wants, no matter the ominous consequences.

"It's ok," Dorian whispers. "It's ok." He pulls my lips back down to his and we greedily devour each other.

Maybe it's admitting my true feelings for Dorian to myself or his reassurance, but I have never felt so free and so comfortable in my own skin. As our kiss grows with fervor, my hands move down to his sweatpants to liberate the rest of his beautiful body. He maneuvers himself so I can pull them down without letting his lips leave mine. Slowly, I mount him, letting him fill me inch by glorious inch. We both gasp in unison with amazement. How can something we both know will only amount to pain feel so *good*?

For a moment I am still, savoring the feeling of Dorian inside of me, stretching me, filling me to capacity. I look down at him, the most gorgeous man I have ever seen. All I want to do is please him. And I do. Rocking back and forth, slowly at first, Dorian lightly moans my praises. I roll my hips, let him feel me contract around him, squeezing him. I'm careful to keep an even pace, not wanting this to end too soon. Dorian bites his bottom lip, concentrating on my languid movements. I can feel him building inside me, can feel him pulsing within my walls. He's on the edge, just like me.

For some unknown reason, I am compelled to lean forward and let my hazel eyes burn into his blue, just he has done with me. I channel all the passion, ecstasy and bliss he gives to me and pour it all back into him. Dorian's pupils dilate and his face reflects utter contentment when I pull away. He is high–intoxicated from the pleasure I give him. The exchange is euphoric and our moans increase with ardor. I can't hold on much longer. The edge is so close, and I want to let myself fall. I want to fall with Dorian.

My movements grow with intensity, and Dorian grips my behind to level the rise and fall of my hips. We both know that we can't hold on forever; we have to let go. I begin to quiver, feeling the force tugging at me, beckoning me to give into this pleasure. Dorian feels it as well and the strained look on his face is telling me that he, too, must submit. I gyrate my hips forward and feel his unbelievable growth, telling me that it's time for our sweet surrender. And with a final cry of passion, we fall, hand in hand into our own piece of paradise.

TWENTY-ONE

"Forget about it, Dorian!"

We are at a boutique in downtown Colorado Springs after Dorian insisted he replace my torn panties. I tried to assure him that it wasn't necessary, especially after waking up this morning and finding that my overnight bag had somehow ended up in his suite. Dorian wouldn't take no for an answer, plus he thought it'd be a good idea to get out and explore the charming little shops together. I was happy with spending the entire day in bed, especially with these dark, cloudy skies indicating imminent rainfall.

"What? These are for me, not you!" Dorian chuckles holding up a skimpy lace thong. I shake my head at him, smiling. A sense of humor is the last thing I'd expect Dorian to possess. But I'm not even surprised; he is perfect after all.

"Sure, buddy. They'd match perfectly with your feather boa," I laugh. Even with this dreary weather, it's hard for me to be in a sour mood when I'm with Dorian especially when he's being so playful.

"What about these?" I ask him, picking up a practical pair of lace-trimmed cotton boyshorts. Everything in here is so expensive; it was the first pair of underwear I spotted with a semi-reasonable price tag.

"Well, not really my color. I need something to bring out my eyes," he winks.

"Not for you! Me, silly!"

Dorian strolls over and takes the pair of panties from me. He rubs the modest fabric between his fingers and inspects the delicate stitching. "Nope," he shakes his head.

"Why not?" Dorian ignores my question and motions towards the sales clerk.

"Yes, Mr. Skotos?" the beautiful blonde asks, batting her eyelashes. Her blouse is unbuttoned dangerously low at the top and she is very obviously trying to poke out her perky breasts. *Skanky much?*

I can't help but grow annoyed at the rising suspicions in my head. How the hell does she know his name? *It's a women's clothing boutique for crying out loud!* How often could he come in here? Does he frequently bring other women here to shop? After he's ripped their panties? I can feel my face heat with jealous rage.

"Allison, I need you to pull some intimate pieces for Ms. Winters. Only the best. I want her to look more dazzling than she already is," he beams down at me. When I don't return his smile, his eyes narrow with question.

"Yes, Mr. Skotos," Allison purrs, and she scurries to do as she's instructed.

"What?" he asks, once she's out of earshot.

I shake my head, trying not to feel so irrational. Who he's dated and who he chooses to spend his money on is none of my business. But I can't help it; the girl in me just won't let it go.

"Just wondering how many other women's panties you've had to replace. Seems like you come here a lot," I say coolly.

"I come here enough. But only when I have to." Dorian pauses to take in my disgusted expression. Then he has the audacity to chuckle. "I own it, Gabriella. Well, most of it."

Once again, my size 7 foot has found its way to my big mouth. I sigh and look at Dorian's amused face. He likes it when I embarrass myself. "Sorry. I have a habit of jumping to conclusions."

"I see. You really have nothing to worry about. How many times do I have to tell you? No one is as important to me as you. I don't want anyone else," he says stroking the line of my jaw with a single finger. The sincerity in his eyes enraptures me for a moment, and I yearn to touch my lips to his. But before I can, Allison interrupts us.

"I have a room ready for Ms. Winters, Mr. Skotos," she says.

"Great," Dorian replies as he ushers me towards the dressing area. Allison has filled it with an array of lingerie, from white frilly pieces to dark shiny PVC. I step in and look back at Dorian who is wearing a naughty grin. "I'll be right out here," he says, closing the door.

I begin to peel off my jeans, ribbed tank and cardigan when I hear whispering on the other side of the door.

"Mr. Skotos, Ms. Órexis came by for you. She wanted you to have this." I hear the rustling of paper.

"Thank you, Allison," Dorian replies with a hushed voice.

"You're very welcome, Mr. Skotos. If there's anything you ever need, I'd be more than happy to oblige," she breathes seductively.

Oh hell no! I'm two seconds from pulling my jeans back on and kicking that *slore* of a sales clerk's ass when a light tap on the door stops me in my tracks.

"I'm out here waiting to see you. Don't be shy; come model for me," Dorian says softly.

I try to stow my temper, deciding not to reveal what I heard in fear of appearing like a jealous nag.

"Are you crazy? I'm not coming out there dressed like this!"

"Well I'll just have to come in there then."

With that, Dorian cracks the door open, leaving just enough space for him to squeeze through. His eyes dance with delight at the sight of me in a pearl pink satin slip with black lace cutouts on the sides. It hugs my frame perfectly and stops halfway up my thigh.

"Do you like it?" I ask meekly. I feel so exposed being on display for him. I can't even look him in the eye.

"Do I? I love it." Even the word '*love*' falling from his lips gives me a flutter in my stomach. *Sigh, wishful thinking.*

"I don't know how this ended up in here being that we came here to shop for panties," I say uncomfortably.

Dorian is still sizing up my body appreciatively and I'm starting to feel like a raw steak in front of a hungry lion. "I'm sure glad it did, though." He takes a step forward then stops, visibly battling something in his head from the slightly perplexed look on his face. He sighs. "You shall have this. And everything else in here. As much as I want to see you try on each piece, I'm already two seconds away from taking you right here and right now."

Dorian licks his lips, taking another eyeful before shaking his head. "Go ahead and get dressed. I'll wait for you out here." He leans forward and plants a tender kiss on my forehead before tearing himself from the dressing room.

When I emerge, I am nearly floored by Allison standing at the door, waiting to collect the lingerie. She gives me a phony smile before brushing past me and I am tempted to turn around and snatch the pretty blonde hair right off her head. Not out of jealousy though–for the simple fact that she blatantly disrespected me by hitting on Dorian when I was only a few feet away. And who the hell is Ms. Órexis? Another shameless admirer?

Chill out, Gabs.

I need to stop getting ahead of myself. Dorian isn't officially mine and he didn't introduce me as anything more than Ms. Winters. I could be his cousin for all she knows. Allison's locks are safe for now, but if she crosses me again, I can't make that same promise.

After shopping, Dorian stows my bags in his car and insists we walk down to one of the nearby restaurants, even though it's drizzling. I don't complain; he's in such a jovial mood, there's no way I'd risk ruining it with my superficial concerns. We stroll into a little Italian restaurant, complete with red checkered table cloths and candles propped in empty wine bottles. A little cliché but the charm is not lost on me.

"You heard what Allison said to me," Dorian says once we've settled in with glasses of wine.

"I did. Not my business," I say simply, looking at the menu. I avoid eye contact to purposely show Dorian that I am not ruffled by the encounter, though it is far from the truth. *Ugh!* Why does it even matter to me?

"It is. I don't want you to feel like I'm hiding something from you. Like I said, I will always be honest. Plus, I have a proposition for you."

"Oh?" I say with a raised eyebrow, looking up at his beautiful face. Even dressed in simple jeans and a lightweight sweater, Dorian takes my breath away. How can I *not* be mesmerized by him?

"As I said, I'm only part owner of the boutique. The person who actually runs the day to day stuff may be gone for a while. I wanted to see if you'd be interested in running the store. And if you like it, maybe making it a permanent thing. In that case, I would purchase the boutique in full."

"You're kidding," I say, clearly stunned.

"No, I'm not," Dorian responds, folding his hands in front of him and then resting his chin on them. "I need someone I can trust, and I got the idea that you weren't interested in working at the mall for much longer. You still haven't told me what you plan to do after graduation."

"Because I don't know myself," I say with a hint of shame. Truthfully there aren't many things I am certain about. And with the recent revelation of my identity, my ambiguity is at an all-time high. I take a hefty sip of wine in hopes of swallowing my insecurity. "So this offer isn't out of pity, right? You just need someone for the job that you can trust?"

"Correct," Dorian nods.

"Ok, well in that case, I'll think about it. Thank you for considering me," I say a bit more formally than I intend. "Are you sure you don't have another friend better suited to run a high-end boutique?" The opportunity would be great and would definitely provide me with the funds to move out. I just want to be sure.

"No, I don't," Dorian states stiffly.

I give him a cynical look. "You don't trust anyone or you don't have a friend?"

"Both." Dorian's breezy mood has dissipated and his icy façade has rolled in with the dark storm clouds that threaten to drench us after lunch. But behind his cold demeanor I get a glimpse of something else. *Sorrow*.

"Dorian, everyone has friends. That can't be true. Look at how open you were with getting to know me. And if you can trust me, I'm sure there are other people you trust." I regret bringing it up but if I bite my tongue every time I hit a nerve, I'll never get to know him.

"No. There's not." Dorian reaches over and takes a sip of his red wine. Then his eyes burn deep into mine. "I had a friend once. My best friend. More like a brother. But his weakness and self-loathing led to his death. I could have stopped him; I should have. But I didn't. I wasn't a very good friend to him," Dorian says quietly.

I'm taken aback by his sad account. His best friend died and he feels somewhat responsible. How do I respond to that? I reach a tentative hand towards him and let it rest gently on his.

"I'm sorry," is all I can say. The fact that Dorian has chosen to open up to me warms my heart. He really does trust me. *Why?*

"I had a feeling you'd say that," he smirks, shaking his head. "Nothing you or anyone else could have done. He made his choice. I remember how incredibly stubborn he was." Dorian chuckles at the recollection. He looks so thoughtful and nostalgic; I just wish I could share this memory with him.

"Scusami Signor, Signora," the friendly, rotund Italian gentleman, who I'm guessing owns the restaurant, interjects. "Are we ready to order?"

I quickly pull my hand away from Dorian's. He slightly flinches in response and nods to the older man, then gestures for me to begin with my order. I opt for something simple: Tortellini alla Panna while Dorian goes for oven baked rigatoni.

"Why did you do that?" Dorian asks after the man has retreated to the kitchen.

"Do what?" I ask, perplexed.

"Pull your hand away from mine."

I shrug. "Oh. I don't know. Reflexes, I guess."

"Does touching me bother you?" Dorian asks simply. He isn't

upset or offended; he's curious.

"No. Not at all. It makes me feel . . . good. I'm just not used to public displays of affection, I guess." I hadn't realized it before this moment. And I surely never meant for Dorian to feel it had anything to do with him.

"It makes me feel good, too. To touch you," Dorian murmurs thoughtfully.

"Why do you think that is?"

"Honestly?" Dorian asks, reaching out to grab both my hands. His thumbs caress my knuckles, sending tiny tingles throughout my entire body.

"Of course." My voice sounds so different. It's high-pitched, almost squeaky. A ringing soprano. I clear my throat.

Dorian smirks as if he hears the difference too. "I think we are like two separate powerful surges of energy, and when we collide, we ignite, creating fireworks. Chemistry, my dear Gabriella. Our chemistry is explosive," he states as if the answer was right in front of my face the whole time.

"You think that's all it is?"

"Maybe, maybe not. Maybe a bit of fate. Maybe a bit of magic." Dorian's lips turn into a devilish grin and I know he's toying with me.

"That's right, because you believe in magic." I'm on dangerous ground. My head is screaming '*Abort! Abort!*' but my mouth keeps on freaking moving. "And your explanation for that is?"

"How can you not believe in magic? Science and logic can't explain everything. You've heard of those people that can move objects with their minds? Or can see things that others can't because they have unlocked a dormant part of their brain, right?"

"Yes," I say cautiously. Where is he going with this?

"What if I told you that it had nothing to do with their brain function? That they were simply destined to do those miraculous things?" Dorian's eyes are wild with excitement. He brings my hands up to his mouth to gently kiss my knuckles. "Magic brought us together. Can you explain it any other way?"

I'm baffled. This is the most impulsive, illogical, and animated I have ever seen Dorian. But I know what he's saying is true, as ridiculous and far-fetched as it sounds. I shake my head nervously, knowing I should shut this down right now. This conversation has gone far enough. Talking like this will only get us both killed. But I can't help myself; I need answers. And Dorian appears only too forthcoming at the present time.

"Dorian, what do you know about Haitian Vodou?"

Dorian furrows his brow and cocks his head to one side. He shrugs. "It was birthed by Africans enslaved by the French. They worship different deities, one in particular though. Mostly it's a bunch of chanting and dancing, though it got a bad reputation by some more extreme followers. It's pesky; I've known some that have pissed off the wrong Vodouists and had a real headache on their hands," Dorian chuckles. This is the most lighthearted I have seen him, even considering the serious nature of our conversation. "Best to avoid them at all costs. They're not worth the trouble. That kind of magic is unnatural."

"How do you know all this, Dorian?" I ask suspiciously.

He shrugs with nonchalance. "Common knowledge."

Our entrees arrive before I can ask any more questions, though my appetite has dissipated. All I can think about is the mass of information I have learned over red wine and breadsticks. Dorian is saying so much yet it can be misconstrued as casual conversation. Should I look at it as such? Is he just making small talk? Surely, if he was affiliated with either the Light or the Dark, he would not provoke me. He would be aggressive, murderous even. Dorian wants me to trust him. He wants me to know him. He wants me to love him.

"Since you brought it up, tell me about your friends, Gabriella." Dorian says with a smile.

Geez, he's in a good mood today. I don't see why; the light drizzle has transformed into a torrential downpour. There goes my perfectly flat ironed hair.

I perk up into a cheerful grin. Finally, something I can comfortably discuss. "Well you've met Morgan. She's fabulous. Poised, beautiful, loyal to a fault. A bit of a spoiled princess but I can handle that. She's dramatic, pretentious, loud, and sometimes as shallow as a kiddie pool." I smile genuinely. "Her brutal honesty makes up for it. I like someone who can give it to me straight, no chaser. Makes me respect them more."

"She sounds like a handful," Dorian observes, taking a bit of pasta on his fork.

"Oh, that and then some. We've been best friends for a few years. An odd couple to most outsiders but we seem to work. We balance each other out. Any time with Morgan is sure to be a blast."

"And the boy?" Dorian asks. His solemn expression tells me who he means. *Jared.*

I reach for my wine glass and finish its contents in one large gulp. Dorian has promised me honesty. I owe him the same respect.

"Jared." I nod my head, confirming Dorian's thoughts. My eyes stay down on my plate as I recall my most intimate friend. "Jared is probably the one person who knows me best. He's caring, funny, easy to talk to. I never have to hide who I am with him. Being around him is soothing. He has one of those spirits, you know? It's like, when I'm with him, it's easy to breathe." I look back up reluctantly to meet Dorian's eyes. He's thoughtful, as if trying to make sense of what I'm saying.

"And you love him," he says simply.

"Huh?" Whoa. How the hell did he come up with that?

"You love him," he repeats. He isn't angry; he's simply stating a fact. A fact that I've tried like hell to keep concealed.

In the spirit of honesty, I nod my head slightly. "I thought I did. But he didn't return those feelings. Not when I needed him to."

I'm ashamed. I feel like such a whore, admitting my feelings for another man to the man that I'm sleeping with. *Awkward* doesn't even begin to sum it up.

"He loves you too," Dorian says taking another forkful of his food. He's still lighthearted, not at all disconcerted. "And you're wrong; you do hide who you are with him."

Ok, that's it. There's no way I can eat after that. What does he know about my relationship with Jared? And who is he to tell me I'm not being myself with him?

"And you know this, how?" I say with a layer of attitude. There are subjects that are just off limits. Jared is one of them.

"I've seen how he looks at you. I've seen how you look at him. And how you've just described him . . . It's not hard to interpret," Dorian smiles, in spite of my serious glare. "And if you were truly yourself with him, you would have disclosed how you really feel. You wouldn't be here with me. Yet, here you sit. Because it's easier to pretend with someone who hardly knows you than to be yourself with someone who loves you for all that you are."

I stare at Dorian in disbelief, totally thrown by what he's said. He's so right. Yet I hate him for bringing my biggest fears and regrets to light. John Mayer plays on repeat in my head, begging for someone to stop this train of life, to slow down so he can return to how things once were. To simpler days of youth and oblivion. It's all moving too fast for me. I'm not ready to admit who and what I am to anybody. Especially not Jared. His opinion of me is the one that counts the most.

"Don't worry, your secret's safe with me," Dorian murmurs. *Seriously?* Is he fucking with me?

"Dorian, I don't know what you *think* you may know about me, but let's get one thing straight." I push my plate forward, indicating that I'm done with my food and Dorian's snide remarks. "I am who I am. And what I choose to disclose to *my* friends is *my* business. And if and when I withhold information, it has nothing to do with my comfort. It's for their protection.

"The people in my life are not disposable, Dorian; they are everything to me. And like it or not, you're one of those people. I'm not here with you because I am running from my feelings for Jared.

If I wanted to be with him, I'd be with him. I'm here with you because I want to be. I actually have feelings for you. Sorry but sometimes my vagina and my heart meet on common ground. But don't worry; I'm used to disappointment. I get that this is just about sex. Just two consensual adults having fun, right?"

Dorian gently pats his mouth with his napkin and sets it on the table. He puts down his silverware and pushes his plate away as well. "Gabriella, you think I feel you view me as some consolation prize? Like an alternative to what could have been with your childhood crush? It's completely the opposite. You are just now living. And you are experiencing this new life with me. I could not be more honored.

"I see you for *who* and *what* you are, Gabriella. And what I see is truly *beautiful*. You try like hell to mask the truth with this asinine tough girl act but I see right through you. *Dammit! I see you.* You can't fool me. I know I could never compete with what you have with Jared and I don't want to. I just want *you*. I just want to be here. I just want to be where ever you are. Why can't you see that? Why are you so afraid to *feel*?"

Dorian looks to me for reaction, and all I can think about is how the hell I am going to swallow down the massive knot in my throat. My eyes are wide and unblinking, because if I blink, fat, salty tears will roll down my flush cheeks. The rapid rise and fall of my chest does nothing to conceal the wave of emotion that threatens to drown me here at this table.

"Um, Dorian, um, I'm sorry, I have to go," I croak, scurrying out of my seat just as the first tear escapes from my eye. I can vaguely hear him calling my name as I make my way to the door, throwing myself into the pouring rain.

I dive under the restaurant's awning in an attempt to stay somewhat dry as tears stream down my face. Seconds later, Dorian appears, furiously searching for me, expecting me to have run away in the torrential downpour. He's instantly relieved when he sees me leaning against the storefront window, a bumbling mess of sobs.

Dorian hurries to my side, ignoring the rain, and wraps his arms around me tightly. He pulls my face into his chest with no regard for my tear-streaked mascara. He comforts me. After I basically told him to stay out of my business and that I was in love with another man, *he* comforts *me*.

"I'm so sorry, Dorian," I sob heavily. I try to get myself under control but my efforts are futile. "I am such a fucking mess! I don't know what's wrong with me! I'm so sorry!"

"Shhhh. Hush, little girl. It's ok, baby," Dorian whispers into my hair. "Let me make you better."

I lift my tear-stained face to meet his, trying to understand exactly what he means. Dorian nods reassuringly and kisses my forehead chastely. He then cradles my face and his azure irises transform into ice blue, almost clear, as he lets them fuse into my hazel eyes. The familiar tingles begin and soon I feel nothing. I hear nothing. I see nothing. But darkness.

TWENTY–TWO

It's pitch-black and I am unsure of where I am. My body is stiff as if I have been lying in the same position for hours. I sit up and try to feel around. The familiar satin comforter indicates that I am in Dorian's bed. But where is he? And how did I get here?

Light floods the room and I am momentarily blinded. I raise my hands to shield my eyes, letting them adjust. Once they've adapted, I see that Dorian is there with a glass of water.

"Sorry," he says, walking towards me. "I knew you'd be up soon." He sets the glass of water on the nightstand and sits on the bed next to me.

"How long have I been asleep?" I ask groggily. I reach for the glass of water and take a long sip. "And how did I get here?" The last thing I remember is crying outside of the restaurant in the rain and Dorian comforting me. Crap.

"You were exhausted so I brought you here and put you to bed. You slept for a few hours," He strokes my wild hair and gives me a cautious grin.

"You're wet," I say observing Dorian's damp shirt and slick, dripping hair.

"I went for a walk while you were asleep."

"In the freezing rain?" I ask skeptically.

Dorian shrugs. "Doesn't bother me." He strokes my cheek admiringly and I notice how weary he looks. It appears as if he's aged while I was sleeping. "Are you hungry? You didn't eat much at lunch."

The somber memory causes a dull ache in my chest. "No, I'm fine. Dorian, please don't tell me you've been sitting around here waiting for me to wake up." I look out through the bedroom's window, out into the darkness. I've slept the entire day away.

Dorian shrugs. "It's ok. I got some work done. Seeing as I played hooky today. And like I said, I went for a walk."

It's hard not to feel responsible for Dorian's dreary appearance. Just hours before he was so vital, so carefree, even in spite of my less than gracious attitude. And now he sits before me, apprehension etched into his hallow eyes. They still sparkle yet they've dulled in intensity. His skin looks pale and ashen.

"Come," I say, pulling him down into the bed with me. "You look like you could rest. I think walking outside in the rain has made you sick."

Dorian shakes his head but doesn't resist when I pull him under the covers and into my arms. He rests his head on my breast, nestling his nose into me and inhaling deeply. Tension rolls off his shoulders when he releases the breath.

"I'll be ok soon," he murmurs with closed eyes.

I feel horrible for my outburst. I must've wounded Dorian, leaving him to wallow for hours while I slept it off. How could I be so callous when all he gave me was complete honesty? I asked for it. Knowing that I am so transparent is unsettling, but that's not his fault. He could have abandoned me today, yet he brought me here to care for me. What kind of man would do that after learning that my heart is torn between him and another guy?

"Dorian, I'm so sorry about earlier. You have been so good to me. You didn't deserve that." I stroke his cold, damp hair. I wish I could just pour all my warmth into him and heat him from the inside out.

"Are you feeling better?" he mutters into the fabric of my shirt.

"I am. Thank you. I'm more worried about you though," I say soothingly. My voice comes out in a silky soprano, nothing like my usual raspy tone.

"Don't be. Being here with you is enough," Dorian breathes.

"Why do you say that? Why do you think so much of me?"

Dorian lifts his head to meet my questioning gaze. The dark

circles around his eyes have begun to fade and his beautiful olive complexion is returning. His crystal blues twinkle brightly.

"Why wouldn't I? You are unlike anyone, any woman, I have ever met. And sorry to say, I've met a lot of women," he snickers. Good to see his sense of humor has been restored as well. I smile back at him. "No one has ever moved me like you, Gabriella. I've never been so affected."

"I could say the same about you," I whisper.

"That's why I want you around at all times. I like the way you make me feel. I need it." His words are desperate yet I understand that type of desperation. I feel it too–the magnetic pull to him. It's so much more than sexual attraction. It is what sustains us.

I am suddenly filled with restless energy, and get the urge to care for Dorian as he has done for me. He deserves that much. "Come on. Let's get you out of those wet clothes."

I flip the comforter off of us and shimmy out from under him. Then I leap off the bed and bound to the bathroom. The giant garden tub looks as if Dorian has never used it, opting for the large standing shower instead. The complimentary gift basket still sits by the faucet, filled with an assortment of bath time goodies. After choosing a combination of lavender oil, chamomile scented bath salts and floral scented bubble bath, I begin to fill the tub with hot water. When I turn back around, Dorian is standing in the doorway, stock-still, watching me intently.

I jump in surprise, clutching my chest. "Geez, Dorian, you scared me!"

"Did I?" he smirks. He enjoys seeing me ruffled. He looks like his old self again–magnificently beautiful and composed.

I close the few feet between us and run my hands up his hard chest. "Here, let me."

I grab the bottom hem of his long sleeve shirt and pull it up. Dorian lifts his arms to aid my efforts. His chest is splendid–hard, defined cuts of muscle under smooth tan skin. The only mark is the tattoo on his side. I lean forward and place a gentle kiss on his chest.

He feels so warm under my lips. I continue with a trail from his soft nipples to the ink etched into his flesh. He gasps in surprise and I look up to meet his stunned eyes then give him a sly smile. I let my hands roam the taut mounds of his shoulders and down his arms. I intertwine my fingers with his and search his face for a sign of acceptance. Holding his hand–such a simple gesture that holds so much weight. Dorian lightly squeezes my fingers between his own in response.

Reluctantly, I pull my hands from his to turn the water off before it overflows. I return to Dorian eagerly, reaching for the fly of his jeans. Once they're undone, they crumple to the ground, exposing his black fitted boxer briefs. I see the large swell in the front of them and caress it with the feather-light tips of my fingernails. I can feel it pulsing subtly with vigor and strength. Dorian's breathing is shallow and ragged. The gentle touches are arousing him, and when I push down his underwear, his manhood springs to life. Dorian takes the liberty of stepping out of his jeans and removing his socks while I admire his impressive length.

"Like what you see?" Dorian smirks.

I smile and shake my head. "You are so crass, you know that?"

Dorian chuckles and runs his hand through his damp, tousled hair. "Guess you're rubbing off on me." He reaches for the hem of my shirt and gently yanks it over my head. "My turn," he teases.

Dorian's eyes dance with excitement at the sight of my modest white lace bra. It's such a contrast from the black see-through chemise I donned just last night. Instead of unfastening it, his hands move down to the button of my jeans, which he slides down with ease. I stand before him, clad in my angelic white panties and bra letting Dorian absorb the sight.

He swallows hard. "You look so . . . pure. And *good*. So beautiful," he mutters caressing the soft lace of the bodice.

"Don't like the racy black number?" I ask with a raised eyebrow.

"Oh, I like it. Very much. But I like this too. Reminds me of the good girl I wanted to ruin when I first saw you." Dorian licks his lips at the memory.

"What makes you think I was a good girl?" I run my hands up and down his bare chest. His hardness rubs against my stomach.

"Well, you aren't a bad one." His hands cup the full roundness of my breasts. My nipples throb with delight.

"Can't I be a little of both?" I say sweetly. I bite my bottom lip, my eyes the color of hot liquid amber.

Dorian's ice blue eyes meet mine. There's wonder and anxiety behind them. He blinks it away quickly, breaking eye contact and reaching around to undo the clasp of my bra. Once my breasts are free from their lacey imprisonment, he bends down to bathe them with his tongue. I moan gratefully. He flicks one nipple with the tip of his tongue before moving to the other to do the same. My nerve endings sing with sheer glee.

"If you're not careful, our water will get cold," I say breathlessly. Dorian brings his head up reluctantly and then reaches down to relinquish me of my panties. I step out of them and grab his hand, leading him into the grand bathtub.

We sit facing each other, suds enrapturing us in white froth. So many unspoken words between us, yet neither of us can articulate what is on our minds. The questions are rhetorical; we know the answers in our hearts. But this dream, where we are just an ordinary couple in an ordinary world is so much better than our reality. We're not ready to wake up. Though we know this dream will eventually manifest into a nightmare.

"You don't look 25," I say thoughtfully.

"Oh? How old do I look?" Dorian is humoring me, a willing participant in my dangerous game.

"Maybe 28. No older than 30. You're too mature, too certain of yourself for 25."

"Is that right?" Dorian takes a handful of warm water and lets it trickle down onto my shoulder.

"And you're way too successful. Do you even know any 25 year olds? Most of them don't own salons and luxury apartment complexes."

"But 28 year olds do?" Dorian says with a sexy half-smile.

"I don't know," I shrug. Keep him talking, I think to myself. I bite the bullet and formulate my next question. "The eye thing . . . What is that? Hypnotism?"

Dorian strokes my erect nipples with his thumbs. I sigh at the contact. He leans forward and kisses the base of my throat. "Something like that," he murmurs into my neck.

"And you can do that to me whenever you want?" I close my eyes and enjoy the sensation of his lips and fingers.

"As long as you're open to me. Which can be difficult when you're being so guarded." Dorian's lips travel to my jaw. He pulls me towards him, sloshing water onto the bathroom floor. I place my legs around his hips.

"Must be pretty tricky stuff. How could one learn something like that? Is there an online class? A manual? Eye-fuckery for Dummies?" I chuckle. I lean forward and let my lips taste his chest once again. His skin smells fresh and exotic. Like crystal clear waters off a tropical island.

"Nothing to learn. You're already a natural." Dorian pulls me closer into him, grasping my ass and scooting me to meet his hardness. I wrap my legs around his waist.

"How do you know that?" I ask nuzzling his neck. My submerged lower half begins a slow grind.

"Because you've done it to me. Last night," Dorian states plainly as if we're discussing the weather. He gently sucks my earlobe, gripping my behind and following my rhythm.

"I did?" I ask, shock resonating in my voice but not halting my carnal dance. It feels too good.

"Yes. It was the most intense pleasure I've ever experienced. But as much as I enjoyed it, you shouldn't do it again." Dorian's own hips rise and fall, causing incredible friction. "You're not ready. It takes too much out of you. Hence, your breakdown earlier."

"But you fixed me."

I tangle my fingers in his hair, pulling a bit. Dorian gasps as I tug his disheveled locks. "I did. But not without consequence. You drain me." He nibbles my neck, letting his teeth graze it. Then he gently bites down.

"*Mmmm*, Dorian," I breathe. "Let me make you better then."

"You do, baby. Just touching you. Smelling you. Kissing you."

Dorian then lifts me and eases me onto his hard thickness. I gasp at the feeling of absolute, perfect fullness. "Feeling you," he breathes.

For the next thirty minutes, Dorian and I fix each other. All the shattered pieces of our charades scattered on the bathroom floor, creating a mosaic of pain, lust, deceit, passion, fear. And love. Piece by piece we pick up the shards, trying to recover just a fragment of who we once were. But what is broken can never be as it was; it will never be the same. So we create a new portrait of ourselves and let our secrets become the glue that holds us together. Because if we admit the depths of our depravity, we can never turn back. We won't be able to pretend anymore. He will know me, and I will know him. And that's just a risk neither of us are willing to take.

Twenty-Three

"So you're really not going to tell me where we're going?"

We're riding in Dorian's lavish Mercedes, windows down, music blasting from the speakers. It's a gorgeous day–a total 180 from yesterday's depressing dreariness. We were even able to enjoy our breakfast of waffles topped with fresh berries out on the balcony, letting the sunshine kiss the tops of our heads.

"Nope," Dorian says from the driver's seat. His dark shades and black V-neck tee make him look every bit like the sexy bad boy I imagined him to be. All that's missing is a Harley. "You'll have to wait and see." He smirks, obviously pleased with himself for making me squirm with excitement.

"Oh, come on! I'm curious!" I giggle. I'm in high spirits today. How can I not be? After our little game in the bathtub followed by mind-blowing water sex, I got to wake up to the most fascinating, gorgeous man alive. I'd be a fool to take that for granted.

"Careful, little girl. Curiosity killed the cat." Dorian looks over and flashes his devilish grin.

"Oh, it'll take a whole lot more to kill me," I say darkly, biting my bottom lip.

Dorian smiles and shakes his head, returning his eyes to the road. "Is that a challenge?"

"Nope. It's a fact," I say simply.

"Well in that case, I better hurry up and get you to our destination."

With that, Dorian hits the gas, causing the car to lurch forward. He weaves in and out of traffic with incredible ease with no regard for speed limits or fear of traffic cops. Every light turns green as we approach and I look on with astonished wide eyes. I know I should be afraid but the speed is absolutely exhilarating. Before I know it, we are whipping into the parking lot of Palmer Park, already crowded with cars and people.

"Palmer Park?" I say looking at Dorian questioningly.

"There's a music festival going on. Thought you might like it."

Dorian pulls into a parking spot and turns to take in my somber expression. "What's wrong?"

"Oh, nothing. Just surprised." I try to shake the creeping anxiety from my head and plaster on a smile. "I heard about this."

Dorian leans over to plant a soft kiss on my forehead before exiting the car and coming over to open my door. Always the perfect gentleman. He grabs my hand and leads me into the park, and for a moment I feel like we are just a normal couple, doing what normal couples do. We stroll along the park grounds for the better part of the day, listening to the various live bands, eating junk food and drinking beer. I've brought my little digital camera, and we take turns snapping candid shots, even taking a few silly ones of ourselves. It's nice. I feel safe and carefree with Dorian, and it seems he has let himself unwind and relax too.

"Gabs?" a familiar voice calls out to me as Dorian and I are making our way back to his car hand in hand. Shit.

I quickly drop Dorian's hand and turn around to face my dearest friend. "Jared. Hey. Um, what's up?" I stammer.

"Looks like you didn't have to work after all," Jared remarks stiffly. He looks to Dorian and gives him a nod. "Hey, man. Jared," he says extending his hand.

Dorian receives Jared's outstretched palm and shakes. I feel my stomach tie itself into a thousand knots. "Nice to meet you. Dorian."

"So this," Jared says gesturing between Dorian and me, "is a thing? You didn't tell me you were dating somebody."

"Hey, baby, I'm going to get the car. You two catch up," Dorian murmurs to me. "Jared. Good to meet you." Then he leaves me alone to face my friend and former love interest.

"Wow, Gabs. You work fast. And here I thought things were too complicated in your life for you to get involved with anybody. Must've gotten them straightened out," Jared smirks.

"Look, Jared, it's not like that," I try to explain.

"Really? Because it sure as hell looks like that." Jared shakes his head and grits his teeth with contempt. "The creepy guy from the club, Gabs? *Really?* So how long has this been going on? For the past few weeks? And you let me play myself like a fucking fool?"

"Calm down. Like I said, it's not even like that. And he's not creepy. We're just hanging out, that's all." I know if I explained everything to Jared, he'd understand. But this situation has totally caught me off guard. I can't get my thoughts together and seeing Jared so angry at me doesn't make it any better.

"It's cool, Gabs. Whatever. Do what you have to do. I guess that night in my car didn't mean shit to you. That the past 6 years didn't mean enough for you to be honest with me."

Jared looks away, trying to reel in his anger, his jaw tight with ire. "But just tell me, did you ever really care for me? Or was I just convenient at the time?" A mixture of pain and rejection washes over his face and my heart aches for him. I reach my hand out for him but he instantly recoils, taking a step back. "Just answer my fucking question!"

"Yes, Jared. I did. I do. But it's complicated." *Shit!* This would be so much easier if I could just be honest with him!

"Complicated." Jared again looks away then brings his green eyes back to me. "Do you love him?" he asks quietly.

"What?" I try to swallow down the regret and remorse clutching my chest. I need to be honest with him. I need to be honest with myself. "I don't know. Maybe."

"So I guess it's not too complicated, then, huh? You know what, it's fine, Gabs. You go be happy with him. Let him pick up the pieces the next time you fall apart. It's fine. I don't need you."

Jared turns and stalks away angrily. Only then do I notice Miguel, James, and few other guys watching the scene a few yards away. I can't bring myself to chase after or even call out to him.

Humiliation has consumed me. I simply turn and seek the refuge of Dorian's waiting Mercedes.

"Are you ok?" Dorian finally asks after several minutes of silence. We're on our way back to the Broadmoor, the sun setting on the horizon, casting gorgeous pinks and oranges across the sky. Unfortunately, I'm too rattled to enjoy it.

"I will be. Just a bad situation. Something I'll have to get used to." I look out the window, too ashamed to meet his gaze.

"I'm sorry," Dorian mutters.

I whip my head around to look at Dorian incredulously. What could he possibly be sorry about? "Are you?"

Dorian slowly nods. "I am."

"Does it get any easier?" I whisper softly, though I know Dorian will hear me.

His hands tighten on the steering wheel, as if his own painful memory has come to haunt him. "No," he replies, tight-lipped. I don't dare to ask him anymore. I don't want to hear any more truths.

Once we are in the comfort of Dorian's luxurious suite, I head straight to the bar. I take two crystal glasses and fill them halfway with the brown liquor in the decanter. I'm guessing it's scotch but at this point, I'm not picky. I take a sip from one of the glasses and then hand it to Dorian, as he did with me before my little striptease.

"Let's get drunk," I state, clinking my glass with his.

"Sure you want to do that?" Dorian says with a raised eyebrow. He gives me that look a lot, probably because of all my questionable behavior.

"I'm not sure of anything anymore," I say with a cynical chuckle. "But I know I'm tired of disappointment. And I'm tired of keeping secrets. *And I'm tired of fucking things up!*"

Dorian nods, understanding my frustration. "Do you want me to help you?" he asks quietly. I know what he means. Dorian is offering to *fix* me like he did the day before.

"No," I shake my head. "I want you to drink with me. Then I want you to do things to me that are as dirty and immoral as I already feel." I take another hefty gulp and let the searing burn strip away the guilt and shame in my chest.

"Ok, let's get drunk." And with that Dorian downs the entire contents of his glass and turns on the music.

It's late, and Dorian and I have finished the scotch and have decided to order up a few beers. I've accomplished my mission; I am completely wasted and dancing on the coffee table. I've scrapped my jeans and am gyrating my hips in only a snug tee and my new teal lace hip-hugging panties. Dorian is seated on the couch, bare-chested, watching the show with sinister, hooded eyes.

"Come join me," I slur, beckoning Dorian with my index finger.

"Why don't you come down here?" he says licking his lips.

"*Mmmm*, I think I will." I clumsily jump off the coffee table and stumble onto Dorian's lap, laughing hysterically.

"I think it's safe to say you are drunk, little girl," he snickers.

"*Mmmm hmmm*." My head is rolling around as if my neck can't support it. Dorian moves my tousled hair out of my face. "Why do you call me that, Dorian? Why do you call me a little girl?" My eyes are barely open and I'm wearing a lazy grin.

"Because you are," he states simply.

"No, I'm not! Little girls are babies. They're delicate and helpless."

"So are you." Dorian places my head on his chest. The rhythm of his beating heart is so soothing, almost melodic.

"I'm not helpless! You can't hurt me!" I laugh.

"Yes, I can." Dorian's fingers gently stroke my mussed waves.

"Are you going to hurt me?" I ask meekly. Something in his tone sobers me a fraction.

Dorian looks down at me with cold, menacing eyes. "Yes."

"Can you do it right now? Can you hurt me?" I challenge him.

"Is that what you want?"

I muster the last bits of my coherency and meet Dorian's solemn gaze. "*Yes*," I breathe earnestly without hesitation.

Before I can utter another slurred word, Dorian lifts me up and slings me over his shoulder like a rag doll. Once my lace clad bottom is in the air, he smacks it. *Hard.* I gasp at the sting. He's walking swiftly, making my dizzy head spin even faster. When I see we are in the master bedroom, Dorian literally throws me onto the bed. He snatches my panties off, effortlessly ripping them to shreds and my thin t-shirt is the next to go. His face is ferocious, calculated and menacing as he fingers my floral satin bra.

"Do it," I urge, panting wildly.

I look up at Dorian's smoldering expression. His eyes burn blue fire, full of darkness, rage, and desire. He moves his fingers to the front clasp, brushing it gently. Then in one quick movement, faster than I can see, he pops it, yanking it off me fiercely.

"You want me to hurt you?" he hisses between gritted teeth.

"Yes," I beg, my chest heaving wildly with labored breaths. I want this. I *need* this.

Dorian grips my ankle and suddenly flips me over onto my stomach. I hear the familiar sounds of his zipper and the crumpling of his pants. Then a sharp pain rips through my scalp. I cry out in surprise. Dorian has gripped my hair and is pulling my head back, causing me to get on my knees to ease the strain. He positions my ass so it's aligned with his rock hard erection, giving it another hard smack. I cry out once more, this time letting it develop into a throaty groan. There is pleasure in this pain.

Dorian yanks my hair again, and my head bucks back, exposing my throat. I can't move my head; his hold is so tight. Before I can dwell on it any further, he plunges into me without warning. He's buried himself all the way in, not even giving me a chance to adjust to the fullness. My garbled cry is futile; he begins to relentlessly pound into me without an ounce of mercy. I yelp with every hard thrust, unable to move my neck to look back at him. I try to reach my hands back for him, but he quickly stops my pursuit with another stinging slap on my behind.

Over and over he slams himself into me viciously. There is nothing tender or remorseful in him. The darkness in Dorian has returned and he is giving me just what I asked for. He is giving me pain. I hear a low groan escape his lips, almost like a growl. I know he is close, and he will have to take pity on me and end his assault. Somehow I feel it too–the familiar surge building inside me. My cries are not of agony. They are of pure ecstasy. I can't stop it; I can't not enjoy this. And before I can stop or even fight it, I give into it and let it drown me in deep, dark waters.

The intensity of my downfall is enough to unravel Dorian. He deeply thrusts into me once more, and an angered, frustrated groan seeps between gritted teeth. He is pouring all the hurt and regret deep-seated within him into me. He is giving me all his pain. He is as tortured and fucked up as I am; he's just mastered the art of disguising it.

Dorian collapses on top of me, releasing my hair and allowing my knees to buckle under me. Our heavy labored breaths are the only sounds in the entire suite. Even the music has ended.

Here we lay, two people so full of anger and grief that we are somehow anchored to one another. We need each other just so we can feel somewhat normal in a world that is not meant for us. Whether or not we can coexist is the question plaguing my foggy mind. I know I can ask him. I know I *should* ask him. But I also know that he'll tell me the truth; he'll tell me exactly who and what he is. He'll no longer be the mystery I can't solve. He'll no longer be *my* Dorian. And now that Jared is out of my life, I need Dorian more than ever. And a part of me–the honest, vulnerable part that was once reserved only for Jared–is desperately hoping that Dorian needs me too. At least enough to ignore the growing suspicions, double entendres, and questioning glances.

Sleep envelops me, halting the seeds of doubt and insecurity from growing in my inebriated mind. I dream in high definition. I'm tied between two sides. On one side is all that I love in this world: my parents, Morgan and Jared. They are the people that mean the most to me, the people I would gladly die for. I feel like all they do is give and give and all I do in return is disappoint them. Being tied to someone like me is not fair to them. I owe them everything–my love, devotion and protection. I just want to give them *forever*.

The other side is shrouded in darkness. The cold vacant space is filled with a dense eerie fog. It's difficult to see any sign of life in the icy mist. Yet, obscured within the shadows, I can make out familiar shapes. There is life lurking in the darkness. I don't know what but I know it's there. And then I see them.

Eyes.

Cold, desolate ice blue eyes. I only see one pair at first, but then there's another. And another. Until it appears that dozens of menacing blue eyes are staring back at me, floating within the fog. Yet I am not afraid; I am intrigued.

I see the makings of a tall masculine figure. He is surrounded by the ominous eyes, drowning in a sea of azure. *Dorian.* I want to call out to him. I want to save him from this dark isolation. But I cannot find my voice. I open my mouth to scream his name but no sound escapes me. So I go towards him slowly. I am unsure of this foreign territory but I must go to him. I must save him. His arms are outstretched; he needs me. I need him too. But my arms cannot reach him. The farther I go into the darkness, the farther he is from me. Soon I am consumed by it. I can no longer see my loved ones on the other side; can no longer hear their pleas to return to them. But I can't turn back now; I need to get to Dorian. I must save him from this dark place.

"Gabriella? Gabriella?" a cool voice whispers in my ear. I feel someone gently shaking me. I begin to stir, struggling to open my heavy eyelids. The light is too bright and I squint against it. "Gabriella, wake up, baby." *It's Dorian!* I have brought him back from the darkness!

"Dorian," I croak. My mouth is parched and feels grainy. It tastes terrible.

"I'm here. Wake up, little girl," he breathes into my ear. My eyes flutter open and I realize that it was only a dream. Dorian was never in the darkness, luring me from my family and friends. He was right here next to me.

I try to sit up but my aching head feels like a ton of lead. Dorian eases me up by my shoulders and props me against a mound of fluffy pillows. "Here take these." He hands me what looks to be pain medication and a glass of water. The cold liquid feels like heaven in my dry, cottony mouth. I down it all and lay back on the pillows.

"What time is it?" The bright sunshine indicates that it's at least late morning. Dorian is freshly showered and groomed, looking handsome as always in a cerulean blue tee and jeans. I must look like death.

"About noon. I would have let you sleep longer but it sounded like you were having a nightmare."

"I'm ok." I muster up the strength to sit up and swing my legs to the edge of the bed. I need to use the bathroom and wash this nasty taste out of my mouth. I shouldn't subject Dorian to my ghastly breath any longer. The walk across the room to the bathroom is torture with every step but I suck it in. It's self-inflicted; I wanted to get drunk and I got my wish. Now I must pay the piper.

When I emerge from the bathroom, looking ten times better than when I entered, the aroma of fried food hits me, causing my queasy stomach to churn. I know I should eat since I didn't have anything last night, but the threat of vomit makes me reluctant.

"You need to eat something fatty and greasy. I know it doesn't seem like it, but it'll make you feel a lot better," Dorian says, taking in my repulsed expression. "I know from experience."

Dorian looks glorious. The beautiful cerulean blue of his shirt brings out his eyes even more. The effect is hypnotizing. I realize it's the first time I've ever seen him wear a bit of color. He's always dressed in dark tones, and while they look incredibly sexy on him, the bright hue makes him seem youthful and vibrant.

"You know, you should wear that color more often," I remark, sitting down at the dining room table.

Dorian has taken the liberty of ordering every hangover food possible from French fries to pepperoni pizza. I take a small slice and a bit of Lo Mein noodles. I don't know how he managed to get Chinese food at the Broadmoor but he's pulled it off.

Dorian looks down at his shirt and shrugs. "You think so?"

"I do. Makes you look younger. And I like it when you haven't shaved in a few days." Dorian has let the bristly black stubble grow over the weekend, making him look like the bad boy I've always imagined him to be.

"Well sorry to disappoint, but it'll be gone in the morning," he says rubbing the tiny hairs on his chin with his hand. The reminder leaves an ache in my chest. Tomorrow I'll go back to my normal mundane life. School, work, and the threat of a Dark One trying to kill me. No big deal.

"So as a last hoorah before graduation, my friends and I are planning to go to Breckinridge for the final weekend of ski season so the guys can get in some snowboarding. I'd like to extend the invitation to you, though I'm not sure I'm still welcomed to go with them," I chuckle weakly, trying to mask my unease.

"I'm sure you'll patch things up with Jared. Actually I have to leave for a while. I have to go back to Greece and will be gone until around that time."

Dorian takes in my forlorn expression, though I'm trying hard to mask it. Spring Break is coming up and I was hoping to spend the entire time in his arms. What the hell keeps calling him to Greece so often?

"How about I meet you there?" he suggests. My face instantly transforms and a hopeful smile plays on my lips. "Take these next couple weeks to make things right with all of them and then I'll join you there. Enjoy the first day or so with them, ensure them that nothing has changed. Then you and I can have our time together."

Dorian's plan is genius. I need to give my friends my undivided attention so I can prove to them that I am the same old Gabs. God only knows how much time I have left with them. I give Dorian a genuine smile and take a bite of my noodles. He really does have the answer for everything. I'm even starting to feel better just being in his presence. It's as if he knows what I need before I even know I need it. Yes, a little distance will be good for us so I can fix things with Jared without the distraction of Dorian. I just hope I'm not writhing with emotional and sexual turmoil the entire time he's gone. Or that the Dark doesn't get to me before I get to say goodbye.

"Will it be difficult this time? Like it was last week?" I ask meekly.

The ghost of a smile plays on Dorian's delicious lips. "Not as bad; no," he shakes his head. "I will miss you though and I hope you will miss me as well."

"I will," I respond too quickly. Gone are the days of playing it cool.

"Good," he says, licking his lips.

"And my friends . . . they'll be safe?" I doubted Dorian before, not knowing all that he's capable of. After this weekend, I won't doubt him again.

"Yes. I've already taken care of it. I told you not to worry about them. Just focus on keeping yourself out of trouble. I'd hate to have to come back and commit murder," he says with a dark smirk. I laugh it off uncomfortably, his words gnawing at the back of my mind. He can't be serious . . . *right?*

I finish my food in silence, stealing admiring glances at Dorian whenever I can. It's happened; he's opened my heart. The man in front of me has done the impossible. He's gone to a place that I've withheld from the world, a place that even Jared has failed to penetrate. And while my heart still holds a place for him, there's space for Dorian too. I know that we both have secrets that we will probably die trying to protect, but for right now, I can live with that. I don't need to know everything about him. Because what I do know about him–his strength, his compassion, his incredible mind, his sense of humor–is enough for me. Dorian, shrouded in all his mystery, is enough for me. More than enough. I just pray that one day I can be enough for him. Or that I live long enough to get the chance to try.

TWENTY-FOUR

It's hard enough trying to get through my classes without falling asleep or daydreaming, but it's downright impossible without Jared. He's avoided me all week–sitting across the room during classes we share, ignoring me in the atrium. It's been days of this treatment and at this point, I can't take it anymore. I sit at our usual small round table like I do every day, the hood of my sweatshirt hanging low over my brow. I haven't been sleeping well, and I take the liberty of resting my eyes between classes.

"Hey," a low voice murmurs.

I snap my head up to meet a familiar pair of green eyes. *Jared.* It's already Thursday and he's finally decided to speak to me.

"Jared." I quickly drop my feet from the adjacent chair and sit up. Then I slide the hood off my long dark hair and try to plaster on a solemn grin.

Jared sits down cautiously and returns my remorseful look. Neither one of us knows what to say so we just sit in silence for a little while, enjoying each other's proximity. How did it get like this? How did being friends become so complicated, such a change from our once seamless companionship? Jared used to be the one person I could bare my soul to. He's seen me at my worst and he's seen me at my best. I need him now. Things in my life are growing to be so difficult. I need him with me, not against me.

"I want you to know that I'm sorry for the way I reacted on Saturday. That was stupid of me. I had a few too many and I was just caught off guard when I saw you with that guy," Jared finally says.

"No, I'm sorry for not telling you about him." I've wanted to say that to him for days. I should've been honest with him from the beginning and avoided this whole mess.

"I want you to be happy. Really. And if this guy is what makes you happy, you should be with him. I'm sure he's got to be a good guy for you to like him." Jared tries to give me a reassuring smile but there is pain behind his fabricated guise. "I'm happy for you."

"Thank you," I grin warmly. "I think he and I just have a lot in common. Both kinda been through similar situations. Maybe it's just a comfort thing for right now. I don't know. But I do care about him. A lot. And I hope he feels the same about me." It feels so good to talk to someone about my feelings for Dorian, even if it is Jared.

"Well, he better not step outta line or he'll have me to deal with," he chuckles.

I exhale, relieved at the sight of Jared's boyish grin. "Thanks, but you know I am more than equipped to kick his ass if he does," I laugh heartily.

After work that evening, I stop in to talk to my parents before heading to my room. I'm exhausted. Being at odds with Jared has taken a lot out of me and not being able to talk to Dorian while he's in Greece hasn't made it any easier. I know Chris and Donna had grown weary with my ever changing moods so I wanted to make it a point to show them that all is well.

"Feeling better?" my mom asks as I flop onto the couch in the living room. Chris is watching the evening news and Donna is flipping through a book.

"Yeah. Me and Jared were kinda having a spat but we made up." That's the condensed version.

"Good. You know that boy is crazy about you. He can't stay away," she smiles. Chris shakes his head at our silly girl talk.

"So I wanted to talk to you guys. I'll be graduating soon and Morgan will be getting licensed. She was offered a job at a really prestigious salon. I actually was offered a job as well."

"Oh, that's great, honey!" Donna beams.

"Good, Kiddo. What's the job?" Chris adds.

"Um, at a boutique downtown. Managing it actually," I say sheepishly.

"Sounds good. So what's the problem?" Of course, Chris would want to cut to the chase.

I take a deep breath and square my shoulders. "We want to get an apartment together. Actually, part of Morgan's benefits package is an apartment in a really nice complex. And her boss said he would upgrade the apartment so I could live there as well. I would just pay the difference." I add the last bit to dispel any concerns about our living arrangements. And let's just leave out the tiny detail that I'm sleeping with said boss.

Chris's brown eyes meet mine. "Absolutely not," he says sternly.

"Why not?" I reply incredulously. I thought Morgan would have an issue living in a place Dorian owned but she was thrilled. Getting her on board was a lot less stressful than I thought. Plus we could never afford to live at Paralia on our own.

"*Why not?*" Chris asks with wild eyes. "Because you won't be safe there. We won't be able to protect you. And I told you about Morgan."

"Yes, and you also told me she might not even know! Morgan is my friend and she has been for a long time." I can feel my face heat with anger. How dare Chris insinuate that Morgan is only my friend because of her ancient Vodou heritage. "And do I need to remind you that I am 20 years old? And will have graduated?"

"I don't care how old you are! The answer is no!" Chris shouts. He has really lost it; he hardly ever raises his voice.

"I don't care what your answer is!" I shout back. "And I wasn't asking your permission! I was just giving you the courtesy of knowing what my plans are!" Unfortunately, another trait Chris and I share is our hot tempers, and stubborn tendency to never back down.

"Calm down you two!" Donna chimes in. She looks at me with pleading eyes. "Honey, your father is just worried about you. If you leave, we can't keep you safe. The wards are only for the perimeter of the house. We can't watch you if you're not here."

I stand to my feet and move towards the hall before looking back. "No offense, but there's nothing you can do to protect me now. I'm not going to be a prisoner here. I can't live here with you guys forever. I may have a very short time left on this Earth and I want to spend it living. Not hiding out. This is beyond you. There's nothing you can do." And with that, I stalk to my bedroom and slam the door.

This is not how I imagined this conversation going. Sure, I thought they'd have reservations, but I never thought it would come to that. Too upset to do any reading from Natalia's book as I planned, I put on my pajamas and go to bed, hoping that sleep overcomes me soon to ease my troubled mind.

"So we'll get there Friday afternoon, drop off our stuff, grab a bite, and then Cecilia's right afterwards," Morgan says over her chicken Caesar salad.

It's Friday afternoon, and we are having lunch at a local restaurant to go over final details for our Breckenridge trip. Morgan and I used to do this at least once a week but we hadn't been spending as much time together since Dorian came into my life. I have to admit, I've missed her. She is in fierce Fashionista mode this afternoon in a leopard print mini skirt, a white tank and a pale pink blazer. I am much tamer in jeans, a black tank, and my leather jacket, topped off with a printed silk scarf.

"So your friend Bobby is spinning that night and can get us in?"

I ask. Leave it up to Morgan to have connections in all the hot nightclubs.

"Yup. He even told me about this event at the brewery there. Super exclusive, meaning only the hot, young and rich are getting in. So bring you're A-game!"

"I don't know, Morg. You know, Dorian is meeting us up there. I thought it'd be a good chance for you guys to really get to know him. He's really cool and laid back. Not '*creepy*', as Jared likes to think." Inviting Dorian was a risky move. My friends could disapprove of him and then what? Would I stop seeing him? Probably not.

"Yeah, yeah, I know. Kinda freaked out that I'll be partying with my future boss, but hey, if he can roll with you, he can't be all that bad," she winks. Her approval means a lot to me and having her on my side eases some of my anxiety.

"Thanks," I smile. "I just hope Jared isn't too freaked out about it."

"Oh, I highly doubt that," Morgan says mindlessly.

I give her a raised eyebrow, like Dorian usually gives me. "Why do you say that?" Not that I want Jared to be freaked out, of course.

"Well, I was going to wait and tell you after we had eaten and all sharp utensils had been removed from the table," she snickers. I put down the half of club sandwich on my hand and give her my undivided attention.

"So of course after the big blow up at Palmer Park, I hear about it . . . from Miguel but that's a different story. Anyway, I call Jared to check on him because Miguel said he was really broken up about it. He was pretty pissed, Gabs. You really broke his heart."

"I know," I say solemnly. The memory of his pained face that evening flashes in my mind. Then I get a glimpse of my salacious coping mechanism later that night with Dorian. I feel a flame ignite down below at the thought of him. God, I miss him.

"So anyway, I thought it'd be a good idea to fix him up on a blind date to get his mind off of it. You know, give him someone so he won't be so upset about losing you."

"You did what?" My jaw drops in shock. This was the last thing I expected Morgan to say.

"Well, um, that's not the worst part," Morgan says, pausing for my reaction. I urge her to continue with a nod of my head. She inhales deeply. "I fixed him up with Aurora."

"*You did what?!*" I repeat more loudly. Some nearby diners turn to stare at us. I can't even return their glares; Morgan has just hit me with a ton of bricks.

"Just hear me out! My intentions were good, I swear!" she says holding her palms in front of her defensively, trying to calm me. "I figured if she was occupied with someone else, she wouldn't be so hard-pressed for Dorian. I mean, she was pretty pissed about him blowing her off for you."

The news of Aurora being upset because of my relationship with Dorian brings a tiny smile to my face. But Morgan is not off the hook for involving Jared. *The slore in designer shoes? Anyone* but *her!*

"So what happened?" I ask stiffly.

"They went out on Wednesday just for dinner or something. Jared wasn't into it at first; I had to practically drag him there. Even had to make a deal with him to cut his hair for free for the next 3 months."

"So? They didn't hit it off?" *Whew.* Disaster averted.

"At first, no. But I guess they kinda liked each other. Neither one of them was psyched about being set up, but I guess they had a lot in common. Jared said they've been talking ever since."

So Jared and Aurora. *How could this happen?* The woman I can't stand, with her gorgeous model body and exotic features, dating the guy I've loved since the 9th grade. Jared is too good for her, no matter how beautiful she is. Well, that explains why Jared was all of a sudden so remorseful. He had been momentarily stupefied from his date with Aurora the night before. No, I can't approve of this. There's no way I'm letting that catty bitch sink her claws into my Jared.

"I can't believe you did that," I say shaking my head.

"What do you mean? I thought I was doing you a favor," Morgan replies dubiously.

I feel bad; she really was trying to help rectify a situation that I had created. Her plan was logical, being that I hadn't informed her of what had gone on with Jared or my heated run-in with Aurora.

"You were. I'm just being overly sensitive," I sigh. "I just miss Dorian, I guess." It's true; I miss him terribly. And not being able to at least text him has been killing me, though this separation is not nearly as bad as last week's. That was incomprehensible.

"Still no word from him yet?" Morgan picks her fork back up and resumes eating.

"No," I frown. "I know it's family stuff so I'm not tripping. I just wish I could hear his voice."

"So what . . . they don't have phones in Greece?" Morgan asks.

"Of course, they do. But I don't have his family's number." *Not that I'd call even if I did.* I shrug and pick up a fry, swirling it in ketchup.

"Well, as long as you have his last name, you can find it. Google it! I mean, unless his family is poor or something and they really don't have a phone," she says.

"No, that's not the case. He's rich, actually," I remark quietly. "His whole family is very wealthy."

"Even better!" Morgan squeals. "It should be easy enough to find where his family lives with a little snooping. Geez, Gabs, you sure know how to pick 'em!"

"Well, of course I didn't know that when I met him! But I guess it doesn't hurt. At least *we'll* be living in luxury," I grin.

When I shared Dorian's job offer with Morgan, she was ecstatic. Luxe and the boutique, Cashmere, are within a block of each other, and Paralia is only a three minute drive as well. We already mapped out our carpooling route to work and toyed with the prospect of walking during sunny weather. I secretly relished the fact that

Paralia is so close to the Broadmoor, though I had hoped that Dorian would just move into his apartment complex so we could be neighbors. I have no desire to live with him though; I need my space. Weekend sleepovers are enough for me right now.

"Oh! So you talked to your parents?"

"I did, and unfortunately, it didn't go as well as I thought. But hey, they'll have to deal with it. I'm an adult and they can't keep me locked up forever." Or away from my best friend, for that matter.

"Well, they'll get used to it. Besides, you'll be rooming with me. And have I ever steered you wrong?" Morgan sneers.

"Oh hell, too many times to count," I say shaking my head, and we erupt into a fit of girlish giggles.

Late that evening, after downing a bottle of cheap wine in the privacy of my bedroom, I am mindlessly tapping away on my laptop. I've been avoiding my parents all day, and though I know I'll have to face them eventually, I'm just not over our argument. After checking the usual social networking sites and growing tired of the many self-absorbed, idiotic posts and pictures, I pull up a search engine and type in a telephone directory in Greece. I know I shouldn't, and even feel ashamed for trying but I look up Dorian's last name. Zero records are found. Shit. Well, that was a waste of 60 seconds.

Still not satisfied and a little influenced by Morgan, I decide to Google '*Skotos Greece*' instead. A page full of definitions and religious depictions pop up. I click on the first one and read the meaning and origin of the name with shocked, horrified eyes. My heart is racing and I can hear it pounding loudly in my head. It's as if time has stopped around me. I no longer hear my iPod playing in the background. I don't hear the ticking of my alarm clock. I don't even see the images flashing on my muted television. All I can see are the words printed in black and white in front of me on my laptop computer.

The definition of Skotos is Darkness.

Terms such as '*immoral*,' '*ungodliness*,' and '*evil*' accompany it. I quickly hit the back button and click on another link, certain that I have stumbled upon a hoax. I open the next webpage and read on about Greek mythology and the origins of Skotos. Still the same theme–sin, shadiness, obscurity, the absence of light. The absence of *Light*.

Could I be reading this correctly? Am I looking too far into this? Dorian's name would be translated as Dorian Darkness. Dorian of the Dark. That can't be true. Dorian is anything but Dark. He's helped me, soothed me in my times of need. If I'm really being honest with myself, I know he's something but not Dark. Anything but Dark. If he were, I would be dead by now. He wouldn't have helped me when I was troubled and weakened. He wouldn't be so gentle and caring. Yes, there may be a dark element to him, especially in the bedroom, but I asked him for that. That was *my* darkness beckoning him. It needed to be fed; I had been stifling that side of me for too long. If anyone is Dark, it's me. Not Dorian. Not *my* Dorian. If he was Dark, I wouldn't need him like I do.

Right?

In an effort to convince myself that this is all bullshit and nothing more than a cheap Merlot-induced mind-fuck, I power down my computer and close it shut. No random webpage is going to sway my opinion of Dorian. He is good and kind and thoughtful, the opposite of everything the Dark stand for. There are other supernatural forces out there. He must be something else. But definitely not Dark.

I lie back on my bed and try to wrap my head around everything that's happened in the past few weeks. They have been more eventful than the past 20 years of my existence. I've found out that I am the product of a Light-Dark love affair that killed my parents and made me the target of a sadistic killer. Jared confessed his love for me after knowing how I've felt all these years. I met Dorian, the man who has opened my heart to more emotions than I've ever felt and given me more pleasure than I ever imagined. I have to ignore the warning bells sounding wildly in my head and lead with my heart. Dorian is not Dark. He would never hurt me. He cares for me, just like I care for him. I have to believe that. I have to hold onto it. Because whatever he may be, whatever paranormal blood runs through his veins, I love him.

There are things that you will experience over the months preluding your ascension. You will begin to feel things, see things. You are becoming who you were meant to be. There are no spells to learn, though Donna may ask that you study certain herbal combinations to help keep you safe until you receive your power. The power is in you. YOU, my child, are the magic.

Because your Light is so bright, you will notice the people around you may begin to change. They will become drawn to you, almost pulled to you in a way that you haven't experienced before. It's as if you are a warm fire in frigid cold weather. They need you to be comforted. Your proximity is mollifying for both humans and magical forces. However, be careful of those who seek your presence at all times. Your power is euphoric to them; it intoxicates them and makes them stronger and more powerful. It will become a source of sustenance for them, and they will stop at nothing to feed their need. If they pull too much from you, it can kill you. Until you ascend and can defend yourself, stay away from all sources of magic–Light, Dark or other. They can, and will, take your life. And if you lose your power, you will die.

I wish there was someone there for you to help you through your transition, but other than Chris and Donna, I trust no one. Neither should you. While I would prefer you pledge your allegiance to the Light, be careful of them. There may be radical followers that feel you are a threat to them and their way of life. They may wish to do you harm. Keep your eyes and ears open for any sign of danger. You will know when it is near; the Dark Hunter in you will sense it. Though powers of the Light and Dark will not be able to sense your power, there is a way that your secret will become unveiled. If they touch you, they will know what you are. They will feel your power. They may not know exactly what you are, but they will know you are something special. My sweet child, take heed of this warning. Do not let any strange persons make physical contact with you. Once they touch your skin, you will be exposed and your life will be in jeopardy.

My dear Gabriella, I must go now. My heart aches with great regret, though I do not regret creating you. You will be my greatest victory, and my love and devotion will live on in you. You will achieve so many wonderful things. You will bring peace and prosperity to our people. You will help spread the Light.

Your father and I are so proud of you and the person you will become. He loves you so much already. He would even sing to my belly every night. He said music was the language of the soul, and any message could be conveyed through song. His wish for you was that you would grow to be immensely happy, and find love even in adversity, like we had. You are so special to us. We will love you forever, in this world and the next.

Natalia

I close the book, and will myself to hold in the tears that are beginning to pool in my tired eyes. I told myself I could do this; I could finally end my mother's journal and move forward. I had been holding onto the last pages for so long, fearing that her memory would die once I was finished reading. She has given me so much to think about, so much to ponder and yet, all I feel is longing for her warmth and embrace. I wish I could've known my parents. I wish I could have felt their love, could have seen their undying devotion for each other. I can only imagine how gloriously beautiful they were. Even their beauty shines through on the pages of the aged journal.

My father loved music, just like I do. He sang to me when I was still in my mother's womb. I wish I could have heard his voice, wish I could have curled up in his lap and let him sing me a lullaby as a little girl. Wish he could have been there to hold me when I experienced my first heartbreak or take me to my first Father-Daughter dance. I'll never have that. I'll never know him. Never have I felt so alone, so incredibly abandoned. For the first time ever, I truly feel like an orphan.

I blink away the tears and then look over at the clock, realizing the late hour. Since it is Spring Break, I've taken on some extra hours at the mall to distract my mind and heart from missing Dorian so much. Plus I've wanted to stay away from my parents, our argument still fresh in my head. I love them; they have been so good to me. But every bit of knowledge I gain about who and what I am pushes me farther away from them. There's no way they could possibly understand the confusion I am dealing with, and while it isn't their fault in any way, I can't help but feel like an outsider. Or better yet, an inherited obligation.

"So what's been up, Gabs?" Jared says settling into our booth at our favorite restaurant. He mindlessly flips through the menu though we always order the same thing: Italian Nachos and deep-dish meat lover's pizza.

I've invited him here to find out first-hand what's really been going on between him and Aurora. It's been damn near a week since we've seen each other which is rare for us. I know I have contributed to the distance but I can't help but feel slighted at Jared's nonchalance. It's like he doesn't even notice the awkwardness between us.

"I don't know, you tell me. Busy Spring Break thus far?" I ask quizzically. Translation: Has *Aurora* been keeping you busy?

"Not busy, but eventful," he replies casually. He takes a sip of his soda.

"Is that right? What'd you do?" I can't believe Jared is playing coy with me. Why doesn't he just come out and say it?

"Well Friday, hung out over at UCCS, picked up a game or two. Then there was a dorm party. Saturday I worked most of the day. And Sunday, just hung out, helped Mom around the house, did some yard work. Monday I worked most of the day and today pretty much the same."

"And that's all you did?" I ask with an edge of skepticism.

Jared shrugs nonchalantly. "Pretty much."

Argh! He can be so frustrating! "Jared," I say flatly. "*Really?* Are you really playing like I don't know? Is this some ploy to get back at me?"

Jared has the nerve to shrug again. "I don't know. Didn't realize we were back to sharing."

"Jared, I can't believe you can say that! Yes, I made a mistake, and I'm sorry. But our friendship hasn't changed. At least for me, it hasn't."

Jared sets his menu down and folds his hands in front of him, resting his chin on them. "You're right. I'm sorry," he finally says. "So what do you want to know?"

"Well, for starters, do you actually like Aurora?"

Jared ponders my question for a beat, moving his head from side to side as if trying to sift out the right answer. "You know, at first, I really didn't. I thought she was a lot older and one of those hoity-toity types. I just figured we'd have nothing in common and she'd be too prissy to even be into the same stuff as me. But she was totally different from what I expected. Super cool, down to earth. And *hot! Holy shit!* I never thought girls that pretty even existed outside of magazines and TV!"

I can't help but feel jealous and hurt over Jared's depiction of Aurora. Can't believe she exists? But my mediocre, ordinary existence is totally believable, of course. Jared doesn't know what he's up against. There's something very strange about Aurora and I have a feeling that she's dangerous. I don't want Jared caught in her web.

"Jared, you can't really expect to like her after just one date, can you? You hardly know her." I try to take the snarky undertone out of my voice but it's hard to hide.

"I know that, Gabriella," Jared replies stiffly. "That's why I've seen her just about every night since our first date. And we've been texting and talking every day. She's a great girl, Gabs. Funny, easy to talk to, really smart and cultured. And gorgeous, of course. Unlike anyone I've ever met." *Ouch.*

"Of course, she seems like that now. But something about her just doesn't sit well with me."

"And you know this because . . . ? What, you've seen her like two times?" Jared says cynically. "What's the problem, Gabs? I thought you'd be happy for me. Like I said I was for you. Finally a totally amazing girl is into me and she's got to have something wrong with her? She can't just genuinely like me too?"

My shoulders slump with resignation, and I shake my head. The last thing I need is for Jared to be at odds with me again. "No, no. Nothing like that. She's lucky to have you and I'm sure she is great for you. I wish you two the best. Of course I want nothing but good to come of this," I say with an apologetic grin. Until I find confirmation of who and what Aurora is, I have to play nice.

"Thank you, Gabs. I really think this could go somewhere with Aurora. I even invited her on our trip this weekend. So I'd really like it if you could make her feel welcomed."

Oh hell no! I agreed to feign friendliness whenever our paths may cross, but I wasn't planning on vacationing with her. Well, this is as good a time as any to inform Jared of Dorian's presence in Breckenridge.

"And I hope you'll do the same when Dorian arrives. I asked him to come too. You don't mind, do you?"

Jared's expression becomes rigid. "No. I don't. But I'm sure you're aware of Aurora and Dorian's past, right? That won't be awkward for you, will it?"

Past? Other than them knowing each other since childhood and their families doing business together, what kind of past could they have?

"I don't know what past Aurora told you about but there's nothing to feel awkward about. Unless she tries to make a move on him again," I say tersely.

"Um, Gabs, Dorian didn't tell you? About them?" Jared almost seems amused as if he knows something that I don't.

"Tell me what?" I ask annoyed.

"When they were younger, before Dorian got himself into trouble, I guess, they used to be together. Like *really* together. They were each other's first love. She thought she could help him get on his feet after he came back. She admitted that she was a little hurt that he had just pretty much forgotten about what they had when he was gone, but people change I guess. He obviously has some commitment issues."

The fuck?

Rage heats my face instantly, and I fight the urge to scream and accuse Jared of lying just to hurt me. But I know he would never do that. He is just reciting what Aurora told him. Could she be lying? Of course she could. But why? Why risk telling lies and looking like a fool to both Jared and Dorian? She surely wouldn't go that far just to get under my skin. I can't be that important to her. But Dorian said he would always tell me the truth. I asked him what was going on between he and Aurora and he told me nothing.

Of course. Nothing is going on right now so he didn't lie. He did tell me that they have known each other a long time and that Aurora wanted more. He didn't want the same. So he wasn't completely dishonest, just not 100% forthcoming. Now I really want to see Dorian, and not to sate my sexual appetite.

"Look, Jared, not everything is always what it seems," I try to say with a level voice, masking my seething anger. "Just be careful, ok."

"You too, Gabs," he replies, nodding. "You too."

The following days drag on, and I struggle to digest the news of Jared and Aurora's newfound romance. His cheerfulness is sickening because I know that Aurora and her lies have created that illusion for him. He even started dressing differently, exchanging his t-shirts and athletic shoes for button-ups and oxfords. She's trying to change him, and it's only making me despise her even more. It's like she wants to sink her teeth into him and make her place in his life as quickly as possible. Probably so I'll eventually become obsolete.

"Don't let it bother you, Gabs," Morgan says as we're shopping during my break at the mall. She insists we need new outfits for our trip. We leave tomorrow, and I can hardly wait, though I'm not thrilled about having to spend three days with Aurora.

"Don't you think it's kinda soon for Jared to be inviting her on trips? I mean, damn! They just met a week ago." I pick up a blue dress that reminds me of the hue that Dorian wore before he left for Greece. The image of him in that beautiful color makes my heart skip a beat.

"Well, yeah," Morgan begins thoughtfully. "But how long did you know Dorian before you spent the night with him?" *Touché.*

"I just don't see how that relationship makes any sense whatsoever. Yes, they may be physically attracted to one another . . . " I say, feeling my stomach churn at the thought of them being intimate. "But what else could they really talk about?"

"Look, Gabs, I love you, girl. You know I do. But you have to let this go and focus on your own relationship. Who cares what the hell they're doing. You're happy with Dorian, right?"

"Yes," I reply simply.

"Well then, worry about that," Morgan says brusquely. My complaining has gotten to her and I don't blame her for being snippy. All I've talked about is Jared and Aurora.

"You're right," I say somberly. "So, anything new going on with Miguel? Or was that DOA?"

"Girl, that boy has been blowing up my phone since I gave him a taste of this cookie!" she laughs. "The sex is good, great even. And we get along. I actually like him as a person. I don't know though. He graduates next month and then he's supposed to be getting some job at Lockheed Martin."

"That's a really good job, Morgan. What's the problem?" Chris even had a hand in helping Miguel land the job after learning he was majoring in Aerospace Engineering.

"I don't know. It has nothing to do with money or status. I just don't want things to get weird, ya know? I'm keeping an open mind about it. Who knows what will happen on this trip. We may realize that we can't stand to be around each other for more than a few hours." Morgan shrugs but I can tell she really likes Miguel. This is the most thoughtful she's ever been when referring to a guy. I like this more sensitive side of her.

"It's ok if you like him. Miguel is a great guy." Secretly I am rooting for him; he's one of the few men that have earned the right to be in Morgan's life. He's ambitious, loyal, and fun to be around. In a nutshell, Miguel is a catch.

"Of course, I like him. I wouldn't have slept with him if I didn't. But whether or not it goes beyond that is the question." We both shrug simultaneously and go back to rummaging the racks.

Morgan and I continue our hunt for clubbing outfits for Breckenridge. I've purchased the blue dress and a few practical pieces, while she's snagged a few sexy numbers that are out of my price range. While we're browsing in another store, I get the keen feeling that we're being watched. It's as if all my senses have been heightened and they're picking up some unknown signal, telling me to turn around. I spin on my heel and scan the store floor, my eyes darting around rapidly. Nothing appears to be out of place yet I know something isn't right. I extend my arm out in front of me. The soft thin hairs on the back of it stick straight up. The air in front of us has a shimmery effect to it, like the hot sun beating down on asphalt. I can actually *see* the air. I can hear a familiar murmuring in my ears yet I can't place where I've heard it before. All I know is we better get out of here. *Now*. Something is terribly wrong.

I turn to Morgan, alarm etched in my face. "We better go," I say with a hushed, urgent voice. "I just have an eerie feeling something bad is going to happen. I know it sounds crazy, but just trust me."

Morgan takes in my anxious expression, my hazel eyes devoid of all humor, and nods. She knows I'm not kidding around and this is not the time for questions. She casually yet hurriedly puts the dress she's holding back on the rack and follows me out of the store. We're trying our best to keep calm, not wanting to bring any attention to our exit. If someone is looking to hurt us, they would surely zero in on two girls running for their lives. We try to remain as collected as possible until we've walked far enough away that I no longer feel the strange sensation. Once we have taken a seat in a quiet corner in the food court, I turn to face Morgan's worried eyes.

"What was that?" she asks.

"I don't know. I just got a really bad feeling something horrible was going to happen. Call it intuition; I just didn't want to stick around to find out. Would you think I was crazy if I told you I could just sense stuff? Like dangerous stuff?"

"Yeah, I heard of things like that," she whispers. She looks up to meet my eyes when reluctance and doubt wash over her face. "My dad used to tell me stories about my grandmother. I guess she was some weird Vodou priestess who used to deal in black magic. You know, my dad was raised by his aunt so he wasn't around all that mess. But he used to see things, really scary things that would haunt him at night. His mother was known for . . . ," she trails off. I can see this subject makes her uneasy, and I know now that she isn't aware

272

of what she is. "She conjured the dead."

"Holy crap, Morgan! Are you serious?" I say, playing it up a bit. Nothing really surprises me anymore.

"Yeah. Really freaky shit. And once you open some doors, they can't be closed. Before my dad was sent to live with his aunt, those spirits would visit him."

"And after he left? He never saw them again?" I really am intrigued. Could Mr. Pierre be some kind of Medium?

"I don't know. He never talks about it. After his mother died, he just acted as if she never existed."

Before I can delve any further into Morgan's past, a chorus of horrified cries rings out, echoing through the mall. Then right on cue, a stampede of screaming shoppers begins to rush towards the exits, many falling down the escalators and stairs, causing some to be trampled. Morgan and I both stand simultaneously, eyes wide with alarm. Something has happened. Several security guards and mall police officers rush towards whatever dread the shoppers are running from. It is just as I feared.

Morgan and I cautiously make our way towards the scene, maneuvering around petrified patrons so we can get a better look. We both know we should be running away from the terror, but curiosity has taken its hold on us. We look down the long corridor, assessing the scene.

"The cops are going towards the store we just left," Morgan says mindlessly. Her unblinking eyes are dazed with fright.

"I know."

A police officer steps out among the crowd and waves his hands wildly. "I need everyone to back up! No one beyond this point!" he shouts, trying to block off the perimeter of the store from onlookers.

I spot a young looking security guard who looks almost green with disgust. His face is familiar and I realize that we graduated together.

"Hey, what happened here?" I ask him as he shakily sets up plastic cone barriers several storefronts down from the scene. His horrified eyes fall on Morgan and me, registering familiarity.

"Someone was killed in the dressing room," he says with a quivering voice. "More like slaughtered. I've never seen that much blood in my life! It's like someone ripped her fucking neck out!" he cries. Tears stream down his face and he's hyperventilating. The poor guy is in shock.

Though there are paramedics on the scene, a frantic security guard is the least of their worries. Morgan and I usher the young man to a nearby bench. I take one of the smaller bags I'm holding and combine its contents with another purchase.

"Here, breathe deep and slow," I say handing him the bag.

The guard, whose nametag says Paul, takes the thin paper bag with a shaky hand and begins to breathe in and out in it. After a few moments, he begins to calm down, and the shudders have ceased.

"Paul, can you tell us what happened?" Morgan says with a calm voice once he begins to get his breathing under control.

"I . . . I . . . I don't think I should be talking to you two," he stutters.

I reach my hand out and rest it on Paul's bare forearm, and give him a reassuring pat. Instantly, almost *magically*, Paul begins to relax. Apprehension and fear roll right off his shoulders and his breathing has returned to normal. *Holy shit!*

"It's ok," I coo. "You can trust us."

Paul's once terror-stricken brown eyes meet mine and he nods his head robotically. "Yes. I can."

"Now why don't you tell us what you saw," I say with a level, soothing voice. Morgan is looking on questioningly, unsure of what to make of this odd exchange and the sudden shift in Paul's resolve.

"I heard the screams as I was patrolling. I was the first one there. Screaming girls were running around everywhere, crying that someone was hurt. They were pointing towards the dressing room. I hurried, expecting to find a minor injury. But what I saw was . . . .inhumane." Paul swallows loudly but remains calm. "Someone ripped her neck right out. There was a big hole where her throat used to be. And her eyes . . . They were so big and wide open."

Hearing enough, I release my hold on Paul's arm. He is still relaxed, though his eyes dance wildly, unsure of what just occurred. Even I don't know what happened.

"I better get back to work, ladies. Thanks," he says rising and jogging towards the other security officers.

"I think it's safe to say you're off early," Morgan remarks as we make our way back to the quiet corner of the food court. "I've parked right out here. Walk me to my car and I'll drive you to yours?" I can tell this whole ordeal has really shaken Morgan, as it should. I have to admit that even I'm freaked out.

"At least tomorrow we'll be gone and will get a break from all this," I mutter, as we make our way to the other side of the mall complex. Emergency response vehicles, police checkpoints and frantic onlookers have made it a time consuming feat. I would just leave my Honda here if it weren't for us leaving in the morning.

"Yeah. That was insane." Morgan looks at me with fear and question in her big brown eyes. I can tell she wants to ask me what happened between Paul and I but just can't find the words. How would I even explain it to her? How *could* I?

Once we've made it to my car, we say our uneasy goodbyes, confirming our plans for the morning. Morgan looks as if she's on the brink of tears, and I reach over to hug my forlorn friend before exiting her Mustang. This incident will forever change her, and my heart aches at the thought of knowing that her once carefree spirit will be hindered.

"Oh goodness, Gabriella, I'm so glad you're home! Are you ok?" my mom cries when I enter our home. Chris is right by her side and it looks as if he has been out.

"Yes, I'm fine," I say nodding frantically to assure her. It's late and I'm sure they've heard about what happened at the mall.

"Oh thank goodness! We thought . . . ," she sobs, holding me tight. Chris ushers us to the kitchen and puts on a pot of water to boil for tea.

"What happened over there, Kiddo? I went by to search for you but there were police barriers everywhere," my dad says from the stove. He's calm yet the sweat on his brow tells me that he was really ruffled. Donna gets up to help him with the tea, breaking out her container of secret herbs.

"Someone was murdered. In a dressing room." I look up to meet their eyes, fear and exhaustion washing over me. "I felt it. Like someone was there. It's like an alarm went off in my head and I got us out of there."

"Us?" Chris asks, distributing mugs.

"Me and Morgan. We were shopping in this store and then I felt it. I don't know what it was, but I just got this feeling that something was about to happen. I told her we should leave. Once we were away, and I didn't feel it anymore, we heard screaming and people were running everywhere." I turn to Chris. "She doesn't know, by the way. She shared what she knows about her family, and she doesn't know what's inside of her."

Chris nods, understanding what I mean. My best friend isn't an immediate threat. "How did the girl die?"

"They said it looked like her throat was ripped out. I heard it was gruesome," I cringe.

"Oh no!" Donna gasps, shakily pouring tea into each of our mugs.

"Someone was there for me. I know it! And Morgan could have been hurt!" Now it's my turn to freak out.

"But they couldn't track you. That's a good thing. Must've been someone else there that you either came in contact with or had a little something in them already." Chris takes a sip of his tea.

"So what are you saying? That they are tracking people's

powers? Or that they can pick up my scent if I touch them or something?"

"Yes, dear," Donna chimes in. "That's why the herbs are so important! You need to have them twice a day now. The smoothie in the morning and tea at night," she says pointing to my mug. I take a small sip in response and nod. She gets up from the table and pulls a small plastic container from the cabinet. "Here. Take this with you on your trip, if you still feel the need to go. I really wish you wouldn't. But if you insist, make sure you consume these twice a day. No exceptions."

"Yes, Mom." Combining it with hot water and drinking it as a tea should be easy enough to handle.

"Look, I'm exhausted. Don't worry about me. I'll be fine this weekend. The worst thing I could do is start acting strange and draw attention to myself. I'll be safe, I swear. We'll talk later, ok."

Fatigue suddenly has hit me and I chalk it up to the trauma at the mall and my contact with Paul. Once my skin touched his, he was instantly soothed and cooperative. I'm reminded of the time Dorian helped me after my meltdown outside the Italian restaurant. He was so drained and visibly rundown, it was as if the process aged him. Could I be experiencing the same thing?

After a quick shower to wash away the day's horror, I lie in bed, trying to piece together a reasonable explanation for the senseless murders. Someone obviously knows who I am. I've received messages, demanding that I pledge my allegiance to the Dark. So why is someone brutally murdering random women? Why not come straight to me and finish the job quietly? Why draw so much attention from the police and FBI, and risk exposing themselves? It just doesn't add up. Even Dorian said that he thought it was someone ignorant, someone that didn't realize what he was getting himself into.

The only logical explanation would be that there is more than one Warlock after me. One trying to intimidate me into ascending into the Dark, the other trying to silence me altogether.

TWENTY-SIX

Honk! Honk!

"Come on, Bitch, let's go!"

There should be a rule against calling someone a bitch so early in the day. But try telling Morgan that. The only thing worse than Whiney Morgan is Excited Morgan and right now, Excited Morgan is in full swing. I shake my head at her sitting in the passenger seat of our rented van, clad in a fur vest and dark oversized shades. Miguel is in the driver's seat and he jumps out to help stow my suitcase in the trunk as I approach. Usually it would have been Jared helping me but I discover that he's a bit occupied in the backseat when I climb into the 9-passenger van.

"Oh hey, Gabs," he says pensively as I take my seat next to James.

I look back and flash a lukewarm smile. "Hey Jared. Aurora." *Ugh.* This is so not how I pictured our ride up to Breckenridge. Thank God it's only a few hours.

"Hello, Gabriella. Oh, I just love your sweater. It's so cute!" Aurora says with artificial kindness. I just want to punch her in her perfect little pink pout.

I look down at my V-neck black sweater and shrug. "Thanks," I mutter, sliding on my own sunglasses and sitting back in my seat. This is going to be a long ride.

"Ok, ladies and gents! Our badass weekend getaway has officially begun!" Miguel announces, pulling away from the curb. The car erupts into cheers and applause.

About an hour into our trip, I get a nudge from James sitting a seat over. I've had my headphones in listening to my iPod to drown out Aurora's singsong soprano as she giggles and flirts with Jared.

Ugh, gag me. I remove one of my earbuds and look over at him.

"So I heard you've been holding out on us. A boyfriend, young lady?" James jokes.

I smile shyly at James and shrug. "Oh, it's not what you think. But yes, I am seeing someone."

I feel bad for not telling James the whole truth about Dorian. He's a couple years older and I've always seen him as a big brother. Next month, he'll graduate from UCCS along with Miguel and is planning on heading out to Denver to spread his wings in a bigger city. It's hard to believe that our little group will get smaller. But then again, most of us are paired up now. Everything is changing, and though I love having Dorian in my life, I miss the old days.

"Well, I hear we'll get a chance to finally meet this mystery man. Don't worry, we won't embarrass you *too* much," James laughs.

"Oh, yes, James, since Gabriella here has been hiding Dorian from you all. I wonder why," Aurora chimes in from behind us. I roll my eyes from behind my shades and purse my lips, refusing to even acknowledge her comment.

"Yeah, Gabs, are you ashamed of us or something?" Miguel calls out from the driver's seat. I see Morgan jab a knuckle into his side, hinting for him to shut up.

"No one is ashamed of you guys. You know that. I'm just a private person. And you know how it is . . . when people feel the need to flaunt it, it's usually because things are really not as great as they pretend they are," I say sweetly, though from James's sly grin and slight head nod towards the back, I know my comment is not lost on him. My statement closes the conversation and we all go back to our individual activities.

After another 20 minutes, we stop for a bathroom break at a rest stop when Jared approaches me. I try to smile warmly at my friend but after witnessing him and Aurora canoodling in the backseat for the last hour and a half, I can barely look at him without gagging.

"So Dorian is supposed to come up tomorrow?" he asks

nervously, obviously trying to feel me out. When did things get so weird?

"Yeah. He's coming in from Greece then meeting us there. Where'd your date go?" *Hopefully back to where ever the hell she came from.*

"Oh, she's in the bathroom with Morgan. Freshening up, doing girl stuff, getting pretty, I guess." He smiles then cringes, clearly worried about offending me. I wave it off.

"Seems like you two are pretty hot and heavy," I remark.

Jared shrugs. "Well, you know how it is."

I can't argue with that. I know what it's like to be totally consumed with someone. To want to feel them all over you. To feel physically sick and weakened when they're not around. I've felt like that with Dorian. I still do, though this time is different. This time, I can breathe. I can actually function when he's not around though I miss him terribly. This time I am anchored only by my love for him.

"There you are!" Aurora squeals, wrapping her arms around Jared's waist. She stands on her tiptoes to give Jared a peck on the lips before turning to acknowledge my presence.

"Do you ski, Gabriella?" she asks in her sickly sweet voice.

"No," I reply curtly.

"Well, that's too bad. I would have loved to get you out there on those slopes." *Sure you would . . . so you can kill me and bury my body beneath the snow.*

"Maybe next time," I respond. *Or just wait 11 more months then give me your best shot, sweetie.*

Aurora smiles, showing her dazzling white teeth, and turns around with Jared to head back to the van.

"Just breathe, Gabs. It's only the weekend," Morgan mutters, standing behind me. Both of us are gazing at the lovebirds, strolling hand in hand.

"Let's just hope she lives that long," I say under my breath. Morgan chuckles and ushers me towards the parking lot.

An hour later, we pull up to the grand cabin-style property and scramble out of the van anxiously. Morgan's parents have been generous enough to let us stay here at their time-share property, saving us starving college kids a ton. The décor is rustic but the amenities are modern and up to date. We set off through the vast house, claiming our bedrooms. The place is huge, boasting 4 bedrooms and 4.5 bathrooms. Morgan and I claim the only rooms with conjoining bathrooms while Miguel and James agree to sleep in the room with two twin beds. Leaving Jared and Aurora in the room with a queen size bed. I'm no fool; I know they've been intimate. Even a blind man could see that. But it just sickens me that they're so open about it. As if it wouldn't hurt me.

"So I was thinking us girls would head to the market, maybe do a little shopping if you guys wanted to hit the slopes for a few hours," Morgan says as we all gather around the charming breakfast nook. Everyone nods in approval, while I internally cringe.

"Sounds like a great idea," Jared remarks. "Give you girls a chance to gab about us."

"Well, we sure wouldn't have much to say then," I retort coolly.

"Burn!" James laughs. "Guess she told you!" The rest of the gang chuckles along.

"Alright, alright, throw in your share for groceries and booze so we can get going," Morgan says with an open palm. The guys fish out their wallets and pull out twenty dollar bills.

"Oh, it's ok, honey. I've got it," Aurora says to Jared. They engage in a whispered conversation, Jared ensuring her that he can pay. Finally he gives in with a shrug and stuffs the bills back into his pocket.

We drop the guys off with their snowboards and gear and head into town. It feels odd being able to wear our winter coats and snow boots in April but I don't mind. The air is crisp and fresh and the sun is bright and warm. Being this high up on the mountain makes it feel like July in wintertime.

"Those boots are hot, Aurora!" Morgan gushes. We're strolling along the supermarket aisles, grabbing all the essentials.

Aurora extends her leg, giving us a better view of her burgundy and leopard print fur ankle-length heeled boot. I have to admit, they are pretty cute. *The slore does have good taste.*

"Oh these old things? Just my friend Alexander McQueen," she winks. "But you are workin' those Michael Kors boots, Morgan. Very nice on you." Aurora then turns to me. "So who are you wearing, Gabriella?"

I shrug and give Aurora an easy smile. "Timberland," I say flatly, extending my own leg to show off the tall tan lace up wedge boot.

"Humph, well . . . they're cute on you," Aurora says, struggling to recover. Her hope was to embarrass me. Little does she know, I'm fluent in Asshole.

After grabbing enough food and alcohol to sustain us for the weekend, we decide to check out some of the high end boutiques. The price tags are outrageous, and I scan the sales racks in hopes of something in my modest price range.

"Oooh, Gabs, this would look hot on you!" Morgan squeals holding up a white long sleeve mini dress. Black piping creates a keyhole design in the front and the sleeves are see-through mesh. I check the price tag. It's nearly $500. I give Morgan an alarmed look, not wanting to disclose my money woes with Aurora lurking nearby.

"Don't worry about it," she whispers. "I'll charge it and then you can just pay me back whenever you start making those big bucks at your new job." She gives me a wink and I respond with a grateful smile.

"Oh wow, Morgan! Where did you find that beauty?" Aurora says approaching us, pointing at the dress.

"It's for Gabs, actually. She's getting it." Morgan looks to me and beams. "Girl, Dorian is going to eat you alive once he sees you in this!"

The look on Aurora's face is priceless, and I have half as mind to point and laugh. But that would be too much like something she would do. I follow Morgan to the shoe section where she finds the perfect pair of pumps to go with the dress, insisting that I can't live without them. Once she's found a few items for herself, we head to the register. Aurora is sure to grab just about every sexy dress in the store, and isn't shy about whipping out her platinum credit card. I refuse to give her the response she seeks for her pretentiousness. I guess it's true that money can't buy class.

"So we have an hour before we have to leave for Cecilia's. We have reservations so don't be late!"

We've gathered the guys, all in one piece to our surprise, and are back at the house. Morgan has again coordinated our events for the evening. We all quickly disperse to shower and dress for dinner and dancing. I'm excited to get out though my heart is heavy that Dorian isn't here.

In honor of him, I opt to wear the blue dress I bought at the mall before all hell broke loose. He said that my friends would be safe. He told me not to worry about the killer. What happened was too close for comfort. The Warlock was right there in that store with us. If it weren't for my uncanny sense to detect the threat, Morgan and I would have been slaughtered.

A tap on the door breaks me from my deliberations, and Jared enters cautiously. It's odd, feeling so disconnected from him. We've hardly spoken the entire trip and just weeks ago we were planning to spend just about every waking moment together. It's hard to believe I used to consider him my closest, most intimate friend. Now it's like I'm looking at stranger, standing before me in designer jeans, a crisp white shirt, dark blazer, and Italian leather shoes. *What happened to my Jared?*

"You look nice," Jared comments, gesturing towards me in my tight blue bandage dress and embellished nude platform pumps. I guess my wardrobe got a bit of a makeover too.

"You too. Wow, did you hit the lottery and not tell me? Those shoes are sick!" I remark. He actually does look great. The update makes him look older and more mature.

"Yeah, uh. Gifts from Aurora. She likes me to dress this way."

Jared shrugs.

"Yeah, but do *you* like it?"

"I guess it's not bad. The jeans will take some getting used to though. A bit tighter than I like," he says scrunching up his nose, making him look boyish and cute. It's the first glimpse of the old Jared I've seen all day. "Hey, I just wanted to say thanks. For trying with Aurora. I know she can be a bit much. And you don't really like girls like that."

"I don't have any problem with girls like Aurora. I just don't like silly, slutty girls. Aurora is . . . fine. Maybe I'm a bit biased but if she's what you choose, then all I can do is be happy for you," I smile. I mean it; Jared's happiness means the world to me. "Now let's go before Morgan loses her shit with us for being late."

Jared extends a crooked arm towards me so I can link mine with is. I do and smile up at him brightly as we exit the room and join our friends in the living room. Everyone is dressed and ready, including Aurora who looks like she is about to have an aneurism. As much as I enjoy her discomfort, I try to make good on my promise to play nice and casually untangle my arm from Jared's. He acts as if he doesn't even notice her brooding stare. After we've all taken a shot of tequila, toasting to our first night in Breckenridge, we pile into the taxi van that has just arrived. Nothing like alcohol mixed with contempt to fuel the fire.

The taxi drops us off in the heart of the historic district and the partygoers are already in full swing. We step into Cecilia's, supposedly one of the hottest places to be on Friday nights. A hostess leads us to our section which is a bit smaller than we anticipate. It's just a couple of round tables with some bar stools, not at all what I'd expect from one of Morgan's hook ups.

"Excuse me, Miss, but I think you may have mixed up our reservation with someone else's," Morgan says to our hostess as we observe the cramped space.

"Nope, I don't think I did. This is what was set aside for you and your party," she replies snippily. This chick is obviously not happy with her job.

"Look at the reservation again," Aurora commands. The hostess fixes her lips to say something indignant when she looks up to meet Aurora's icy glare. A visible shiver runs down her spine and she quickly looks back down at her tablet.

"Oh, yes, I apologize. Right this way please," the hostess mutters, clearly shaken. She leads us to spacious private section with modern white couches and low tables with a view of the dance floor and DJ. Now this is more like it! However, the hostess's reaction to Aurora does not go unnoticed by me.

"Wow, thanks, Aurora! How did you do that?" Morgan gushes after the hostess has left us with our menus. Trembling bass lines vibrate us in our plush seats.

"Oh, I've been here a few times. She must've recognized who I am." Aurora turns to meet my gaze. It seems like her iciness was not only reserved for the hostess.

"Well, whatever you did, thanks!" Miguel says.

"Yeah, babe, that was awesome." Jared cozies up to Aurora and kisses her on the cheek. She giggles like a schoolgirl.

We order an array of appetizers and drinks and dance around our little section. After several overpriced, pretentious cocktails, we're all feeling pretty spirited. Jared and Aurora are dancing closely in a corner while Morgan and Miguel flirt and chat on the couch. James has made friends with a group of girls here for a bachelorette party. Which leaves me–pitiful, lonely Gabriella.

I decide to venture out to the main dance floor to get away from the PDA. The party is lively and infectious, and I quickly ease into the crowd. My head is a bit foggy, though I feel totally coherent as I feel someone come up from behind me and begin to sway with me. At first I think it's just James playing around, but then I feel warm lips on my ear and cool breath on my neck. My body begins to tingle from head to toe, and not in a good way. The hairs on the back of my arm stand to attention and my body feels heavy as if it has been submerged in quicksand.

"Align with the Dark or die," a voice whispers. Even with the music pounding loudly in my ears, I hear it clearly.

I quickly spin around but no one is directly behind me. My eyes dart around frantically at the sea of tipsy party goers. No one seems to be paying me any attention. The tingling sensation has ceased and I go into survival mode, crouching into a defensive stance, my fists hard and tight. Someone from the Dark is here. They've followed me. My thoughts are racing a mile a minute and I can't seem to line them up with my actions.

My friends. I quickly weave through the crowd and make my way back to our private section. Jared, Aurora, Miguel and Morgan are still there, totally oblivious to my alarmed expression. James. I have to find him. I make my way back out to the main bar area. I don't see him anywhere and the giddy women he was sitting with are all still seated in their booth. Shit. James is gone.

Fear snarls in my belly, blood pounding in my ears as my eyes dart around frantically. This isn't supposed to happen. My friends are supposed to be safe! And here I am, half-drunk and unable to even defend them or myself! An involuntary whimper at my pathetic vulnerability escapes my lips, followed by a choking sob.

"Gabs?" I spin around to face a familiar pair of green eyes. *Thank God!*

"Holy crap, James, where were you?" I crush my body against his, genuinely happy to see him.

"The bathroom. What's wrong?" James embraces me hesitantly, puzzled by my sudden anxiety.

"Nothing. Just got scared when I didn't see you," I mumble with a shaky voice.

"Come on, I think you've had one too many martinis," he chuckles.

I let James lead me back to our friends. Miguel and Morgan are dancing to a slow song and Aurora and Jared are making out on the couch, her body draped over his lap. I'm too shaken to care and turn my body away to ignore them.

"How about we head back to the house and jump in that hot tub!" James shouts over the slow, sensual music. He gives me a little wink, indicating that is motive is to get me home to sober up. At this point, I feel completely coherent but I play along.

After we've closed out our tab, we grab a taxi and make our way back to our vacation home. My friends are still rowdy and restless with intoxicated energy and we all disperse to put on our bathing suits. I'm more thoughtful and cautious than anything else but reluctantly change out of my dress into my swimsuit. I'd rather stay indoors than venture out next to naked in the frigid air but I don't dare let my friends go out there alone. Who knows what could have followed us home.

"Come on, girls! We're waiting!" Jared catcalls from the hot tub. He, James and Miguel are already there with a bottle of tequila and shot glasses.

Morgan sashays out first, flaunting her fuchsia sequined bandeau bikini as if she is a runway model, despite the freezing temperatures. The guys erupt into playful hoots and hollers. I follow, a towel wrapped around my black monokini, ignoring the requests to reveal what's underneath. Aurora is last, of course, strutting with catlike grace in a bejeweled teal string bikini that leaves little to the imagination. The guys nearly burst with hormone-charged glee. I don't resist the urge to roll my eyes, and grab a shot and down it before anyone else. The conversation is casual, consisting mostly of Aurora telling us about her travels around the world. A few more shots later, she straddles Jared and I take that as my cue to go to bed. James, Miguel, and Morgan soon follow.

After a hot shower, sleep comes surprisingly easy. Again, my dreams are vivid yet distorted. Just flashes of different scenes, like frames from a camera. A picture of all of my friends together, laughing, happy, united. Then in the next flash of light, they all begin to fade away, each one by one. Darkness swallows the frame, and there's . . . nothing. The dream shifts again, manifesting into a horrid nightmare. My friends, shown sprawled out in different locations, their necks ripped wide open, blood sprayed on every surface. Their eyes are open, cold and vacant. They were living witnesses to their own deaths. But there's something else. Their eyes are now blue. Bright, glowing, icy blue.

I jerk awake in the dark room, my eyes wide and searching for some sign of familiarity. It's suddenly become very cold and I shiver violently. I sense movement at my bedside and reflexively turn to look. Someone is here. A shadowy figure stands but a few feet away from me. I can hear my heart beating like a drum in my ears, and I can't will myself to breathe. My chest aches, gripped by the unleashed scream caught in my throat. I am frozen with immense fear.

This is it. He's found me. The Dark One is here with me, alone in this room.

TWENTY-SEVEN

My trembling hand mindlessly reaches to flick on the bedside lamp. If this is my demise, I want to look at death in the face. I want to stare into the eyes of this Dark Warlock as he massacres me. Light floods the room with bright intensity, revealing that no one is there. I am alone. But I know I saw someone. Someone was definitely here hidden in the shadows. I sit up and rub my eyes, scanning the room for any sign of movement or disruption. Just seconds ago I was dreading death, and now I am searching for it.

The faint sounds of raucous lovemaking interrupt my search for my would-be assassin. The moans are melodic and high-pitched. The soprano voice sings praises to her lover, climbing higher and higher in ecstasy. Aurora. Aurora's cries of pleasure are for Jared. Tightness again grips my chest, causing me to gasp for air. I can hardly breathe; the air in the room has become extremely dense. I pull on my robe and slippers and pad out of the bedroom, desperately trying to escape this reality.

"Can't sleep either?" Morgan whispers as I enter the kitchen. She's dressed in a colorful kimono with a silk scarf wrapped around her hair.

"How can I?" I say nodding my head towards the bedroom shared by Jared and Aurora.

"I know, right? Damn! You'd think Jared's dick was made of gold," Morgan shakes her head. Leave it up to her to say what I was thinking. "You ok?" She stirs a cup of what looks like tea. It reminds me that I haven't had my second dose of herbs. Crap.

"I'm alright. It's just weird between us. And seeing Jared like this with some girl we hardly know . . . " I shrug and walk over to my purse to retrieve the little container housing Donna's secret herbal mixture. I place a scoop in a coffee cup and add some of the hot water that Morgan has heated. I'm not sure what it could possibly do. They already know who I am.

"Yeah, I don't know how you're doing it. I don't think I could be ok with this." She takes a sip of her tea. "When does Dorian get here anyway?"

"He told me Saturday. So later, I assume. I gave him the address before he left so I guess he'll just show up whenever."

"Well, at least we'll have some time to relax. Though I highly doubt I'll be able to look Aurora or Jared in the eye ever again. *Ewwww*," she cringes. "They've been going at it for over an hour now! I mean, damn!"

I chuckle and shake my head. There's not much I can say to that. I'm no prude but witnessing proof of their sexual activities is a bit much for me to stomach. I drink down the bitter herbs and turn to Morgan's solemn expression. Something else is bugging her.

"You ok, Morgan?"

Morgan looks around, as if someone else is here. "I had a dream. It scared the shit out of me." Morgan swallows hard before looking down nervously at her teacup.

"Ok, what happened? What was it about?" Whatever it was, it has clearly shaken my usually poised friend.

"There was an old lady in it. She told me darkness is coming. She said it will kill us all." Morgan closes her eyes, as if to erase the image from her sight. "It was my grandmother. I know it was; I could *feel* it. I swear, Gabs, it was like she was right next to me!"

I walk towards Morgan and wrap my arms around her. She is panting wildly, clearly petrified and disturbed. I don't know what to tell her. I, too, know that darkness is coming. It was already here.

"Hey, how about we head to your room and have a sleepover like we used to do? Isn't there a TV in there? I bet we could find some old cheesy reruns to fall asleep to."

I give Morgan a reassuring smile and she eventually nods. After placing our empty cups in the sink, I usher her to the master bedroom, thankful that it's farther from Jared and Aurora's love nest. We put on an old black and white sitcom and make idle chitchat until we eventually fall asleep, both trying to clear our minds from the ghosts that haunt our dreams and realities.

"Breakfast is ready!" James calls from the other side of the door. He knocks again before opening the bedroom door, finding Morgan and I slowly stirring awake. "Oh, if I would have known it was *that* kinda party, and would have asked to join!"

"Shut up, James!" We shout in unison.

"Ok, ok, just letting you girls know that Aurora made breakfast." He closes the door, leaving us to slink out of bed.

"I bet she did," I mumble.

"Especially after the hurtin' Jared put on her last night. Bitch probably woke up singing," Morgan adds. She groggily makes her way to the bathroom while I slip on my robe and retreat to mine.

Ten minutes later, I make my way to the kitchen in sweats and a t-shirt. I have on no makeup, my hair is pulled back in a ponytail and I honestly don't care. I've gotten very little sleep and Aurora and Jared's sexcapades didn't make it any easier. If anyone should be embarrassed, it should be them. Yet, they are laughing and smiling as if the entire house didn't bear witness to their most intimate sounds. It's as if I have just stepped into the Twilight Zone.

"How do you like your eggs, Gabriella?" Aurora beams from behind the stove. Oh God. It seems as if sex has made her even more chipper.

"Whatever everyone else is eating is fine with me," I respond munching on a piece of bacon. I go to prepare my herbal tea when I notice the container isn't where I left it. "Hey, has anyone seen a little plastic container with some tea leaves in it?" I call out.

"Oh that?" Aurora says. "I didn't realize that was yours. It didn't smell fresh so I assumed it was left here. I poured them down the disposal, thinking it could possibly be drugs or something. Sorry!"

There are no words. I just see red. Bright, blood red.

I nod slowly and turn on my heel to head back to my room. Hushed voices behind me question what my problem could be. Before I let my temper get the best of me, I click the door shut and block out the world. If Aurora knows what's good for her, she will stay the hell away from me.

"So do you think she did it on purpose?" Morgan whispers. We're at a spa on Main Street, and while I was hoping for a relaxing afternoon, Jared insisted Aurora join us for some girl time.

"I don't know. I wouldn't put it past her," I whisper back.

Aurora is in one of the treatment rooms getting a body scrub. *Too bad they can't scrub that fake smile off her face.* Ugh, I really wish I could stop harping on her and just enjoy my massage.

"Feeling any better?" I ask, trying to change the subject.

"A little. Thanks for that last night. I really did not want to go back to sleep." I wish I could tell Morgan that I felt the same way after my own nightmare, and then waking up to find someone in my room. But that would only scare her more than she already is.

After our massages, pedicures, manicures and facials, I feel a lot better, though Aurora's presence keeps me from relaxing completely. She insists on treating us to lunch as an apology for discarding my herbs and I reluctantly agree.

"Ms. Winters, your visit today has been taken care of," the front desk receptionist responds handing me back my debit card. I had been internally cringing in expectation of the damage displayed at the register.

"Huh?" I reply dumbfounded.

"Your treatments have already been paid for," she clarifies.

"By whom?" There must be some mistake.

"Mr. Dorian Skotos, ma'am."

My eyes widen with shock but it pales in comparison to Aurora's look of sheer disbelief. I don't dwell on it though; I'm too excited at the prospect of seeing Dorian.

"He came here?" I ask the receptionist, barely containing my joy.

"No ma'am. He called with his information."

I try to mask my disappointment with a shrug and a smile, thanking the receptionist before exiting. Aurora leads us to a popular sushi bar nearby. She is just bursting with glee at the fact that she gets to order in Japanese for us. If it weren't for the fact that we're sitting close enough to see the chef preparing our maki and sashimi, I'd think she would have instructed him to poison me.

"So I'm assuming you and Dorian are doing well, Gabriella?" Aurora asks as the waitress brings us our sake.

"We're fine," I respond.

"Oh, Dorian . . . So restless. It's so hard for him to settle down with anyone. I'm sure Jared told you about our history, that is if Dorian hadn't informed you already," she smiles sweetly.

I pick up my little cup of sake and down it. I'm going to need more if I am to get through this lunch with Aurora without bloodshed. "Yes, I know about that." I'm not sure what else I should say to her. Dorian hasn't exactly been as forthcoming when it comes to that or any other part of his past.

"So you know that we practically grew up together. Shared many firsts together." The waitress has arrived with our large platter of sushi and Aurora helps herself to a piece of spicy tuna roll. "I just want you to know that what we had is all in the past. I am with Jared now and I really care for him. I know it hasn't been long but I truly feel like he and I have something special."

Is this bitch serious?

I look over at Morgan who shrugs her shoulders as if she could hear my unspoken question and continues to enjoy her salmon sashimi. Then I gaze back at Aurora, who is still smiling like an idiot, oblivious of the storm already brewing behind my hazel eyes.

"Aurora, whatever is going on with you and Jared is your business. His happiness is all I care about. And if it's you that makes him happy, so be it. As far as Dorian goes, I would hope you would show us the same courtesy." I flash her a sweet smile of my own and take another drink of sake.

Aurora finishes chewing her sushi roll slowly. "Oh, I didn't mean it like that. I just thought I could warn you about him. He's never going to commit. I didn't want you to get hurt like I did," she says meekly.

"You really shouldn't concern yourself with that. I'm a big girl. And besides, how do you think Dorian would react to what you are saying right now? Or what Jared would think about you trying to get back with Dorian right before dating him?" I casually pick up a Caterpillar roll with my chopsticks and pop it in my mouth with ease. Morgan signals for more sake, seeing exactly where this heated exchange is heading.

"I've underestimated you, Gabriella," Aurora says darkly. The sweet and innocent act has dissipated. Miss Prim and Proper has an ugly side. "I apologize. No hard feelings?"

"None at all," I reply, matching her ominous expression.

When we have arrived back at the house, I am in desperate need of some alone time. The guys are still out snowboarding and Aurora and Morgan have decided to watch a movie in the living room. I grab my iPod and one of the extra blankets and head outside. The sun's warmth is infectious, and I instantly feel better. I sit on the wooden porch swing, wrap the blanket around me then let the music envelop me.

The sunshine feels so good and comforting; I allow my eyes to close and my mind to wander. I think of the days when the most exciting events were ones spent with my closest friends, going out and causing havoc. I think about how close I was with my parents. There was nothing I withheld from them. And I think of Jared–how much he once meant to me. How I would do anything for him, be anything for him. *Oh, how times have changed.*

Suddenly a gust of cold wind blows past me, causing me to shiver. It's no longer bright; something has eclipsed the sunshine beaming down on me. Light has abandoned me. My eyes pop open with alarm only to be met by the bluest irises I have ever seen.

Dorian. He's here.

I quickly sit up and spin around to meet him. He is just as gorgeous as I remember him–smooth olive skin, black hair, perfectly full lips, long, dark lashes. I am instantly elated and soothed by his presence.

"You're here," I smile, pulling out my earphones. I realize it's the first genuine one I've had for days, weeks even.

"I am. I missed you." Dorian leans forward and presses his lips against mine. He pulls away too soon for my satisfaction.

"I missed you too," I breathe. "So much." Having him here now makes me realize just how much I have craved Dorian. Feeling the tension and fear literally melt away, I realize how miserable I have been since the last time we were together. My need for him is evolving into an addiction.

"Mmmm. Well, you'll have to show me just how much that was," he says wickedly. *Oh hell yes; my Dorian is back.*

"I can't wait," I say biting my bottom lip in anticipation.

Dorian holds out his hand to help me up. I eagerly place mine in his and stand. Feeling his skin on mine sends the familiar shockwaves throughout my entire body. The sensation causes my heart to sputter and ignites a flame down in my belly. Every nerve ending feels as if it being kissed with electricity. *Fireworks.*

"I have something for you," he murmurs as we enter the house.

We walk towards the living room and I brace myself for the staggered expression that is sure to be etched on Aurora's face. Of course, she doesn't disappoint.

"Dorian! Uh, I didn't know you were here," she stammers. Morgan simply beams at the both of us.

"That's because I just arrived. Now if you'll excuse me, Gabriella and I have some catching up to do."

With that, Dorian escorts me to my room and closes the door. He knows exactly where it is without me having to tell him and his carry-on bag is already there. I know it's odd, considering Morgan and Aurora didn't see him come in, but I don't question it. I'm just happy he's here. Nothing else matters.

"I got this for you while I was away."

Dorian removes a gift bag and hands it to me. I receive it tentatively and peek inside, pulling out a cerulean blue lace negligee. It's the same color blue he wore the Sunday before he left for Greece, and it's gorgeous. I look up and smile brightly at him. Before I can show him just how thankful I am, he pulls out another gift. This time a little box.

"And this. It reminded me of you."

I open the box and gaze upon the beautiful pendent attached to a white gold chain. A single cultured pearl cradled by dazzling white diamonds, and then those diamonds are surrounded by black diamonds. So simple and understated, yet complex. Like me. It's incredible and I am struck speechless.

"Do you like it?" Dorian asks after a few moments of me staring at it in awe.

"Oh my God, Dorian. I love it. It's gorgeous." I look up at him with grateful eyes. He's so in tuned to what I want before I even know I want it. "It's perfect."

Dorian reaches over and removes the necklace from its box. He stands behind me, taking my hair into his hands and gently sliding it over my shoulder. His soft lips graze my neck before he places the necklace around it. I turn and look up at him lovingly.

"I want you to keep this on, always. And think of me. I want to always be on your mind," he says tenderly. "As you are always on mine."

I take the opportunity to wrap my arms around Dorian's neck, my fingers tangling in his hair furiously as I press my lips to his. He welcomes it, allowing our tongues to slowly dance to the rhythm of our panting breaths. Dorian grips my lower back, crushing my body against his. His hands move down to palm my ass, kneading the soft flesh to the tempo of our intense lip-lock.

Swiftly, he lifts me up, turning and walking towards the bed effortlessly without breaking our kiss. He lies me down gently on my back, and I open my legs wider to welcome his body on top of mine. Fire erupts between us, our friction causing the flames to rage out of control. I clutch his back in desperation, pulling his shirt up over his head. I want to feel his skin on mine. As if reading my mind, Dorian moves his hands up my sweater, quickly relinquishing me of it. He eyes the black floral lace bra he purchased for me from Cashmere. The contrast of the dark fabric against my creamy beige skin causes him to take in a sharp breath. He gently caresses the tops of my cleavage appreciatively, his long fingers stroking each curve and mound. His touch is so erotic and deliberate; my nerve endings come to life with every stroke. God, I've missed him.

Dorian's index finger moves under the front clasp of my bra. But before he can undo it, we hear the booming sounds of laughter from the living room. The guys are back, and their liveliness has intruded on our intimate moment. Dorian slowly closes his eyes to compose himself then sits up to my dismay.

"We better save this for later," he mutters, offering his hand to help me up. I sigh heavily and reluctantly take it.

We search for our shirts and slide them on, though I can't mask my irritated expression. I've been waiting to be with Dorian for two weeks. Not only feel him inside of me but just to have him near me. His proximity makes me feel whole, complete. It soothes me and I feel secure and safe with him. I've concluded that whatever he is, his powers have healing and comforting properties, not unlike the gifts of the Light. Dorian is too good to be anything less.

Dorian and I begrudgingly leave the sanctuary of the bedroom. He grabs my hand, our fingers intertwining like old lovers, and leads me out to my rowdy crowd of friends. And Aurora. Conversation ceases as we approach and I smile nervously to break the tension. Jared looks uncomfortable with Dorian's presence, and I can't help but feel glad that he's affected. Having Aurora here hasn't exactly been a cakewalk, especially with them being so openly affectionate. Though I would never flaunt my relationship with Dorian to prove a point, it feels good to know that Jared's getting just a tiny taste of his own medicine.

"Hey guys," Morgan says to break the ice. "We were just talking about our plans for this evening. Since the guys really don't want to go to the event I had set up, any thoughts?"

"I may have a suggestion," Dorian says. "There's a place that just opened up here. I think you all may like it. My treat, of course. And I just so happen to know the owner." I look up to give Dorian a curious smirk, and he returns it with a wink. Something tells me that I know the owner too.

"Sounds great!" Morgan says. Everyone else nods approvingly, even Jared, to my surprise.

After we've all been dismissed to get dressed, Dorian and I are back in the confines of the bedroom. There's only one thing on my mind, and dinner is not it. I want to show him just how much I've missed him, just how much I need him. I want to show him how much I love him.

"I'm so glad you're here," I breathe once I've clicked the door closed. My body is craving him like never before.

"Come here."

Dorian pulls his shirt over his head, exposing his tan, chiseled chest, his tattoo peeking out from under his arm. His blue eyes are alight with desire, beckoning me to come to him. I saunter my way to him, offering my body. He strokes my cheek with the back of his hand adoringly and gives me a half-smile, as if I am a child. A little girl, as he likes to call me. Being in his presence, in all his glorious beauty and domineering power, I feel like one. Not because he makes me feel inferior but because I want to relinquish myself to him. I want to be his sacrificial little lamb.

Dorian grabs the hem of my sweater and slowly pulls it over my head. His eyes never leave mine, yet his hands caress my smooth skin with precision. It's as if he is studying every curve, rise and line. A blind man who is committing my body to memory.

I gasp at the feel of his strong yet gentle fingertips. They roam to the button of my jeans, unfastening them without pause. They slide off my hips slowly and I step out of them, gazing back up to Dorian to ensure that the gesture pleases him. The blue fire in his eyes tells me that it does. I tentatively reach to undo the button of his slacks, being sure not to break eye contact in the process. I fumble a bit but soon they fall from the severe cuts of his hips. I let my fingertips explore the hard defined muscle and resist the urge to run my tongue along them. Every bit of him is mouthwatering; how can I *not* want him?

We stand face to face, next to naked, unable to tear our eyes away from each other. Dorian lets his finger slide under the clasp of my bra, this time unfastening it quickly. My perky breasts are grateful for the release and throb under his appreciative gaze. He cups them gently, tenderly, grazing his thumbs along my nipples. My body trembles in response and a soft moan falls from my lips before Dorian swallows it, covering my mouth with his. Our kiss is deep, passionate, and urgent. Desperation drips from our lips, tongues tangled in a sensual tug of war. He lays me down on the bed, climbing on top of me and scooting me upwards, never breaking our kiss. His hand slides under the waistband of my panties and he easily slides them off. I reach to remove his boxers, and he aids me in my efforts, kicking them off eagerly. This is it–what I have been waiting for, yearning for.

Dorian guides himself into my warmth, easing himself in inch by inch. He is so careful and gentle, leaving soft kisses on my neck and shoulders before finding my lips again. He stretches me, fills me, lives in me. With slow, measured strokes, Dorian loves me from the inside out. I am covered by him, totally consumed by him in every way.

This time is different. Admitting to myself that I love him has made this act so much more meaningful. It's as if Dorian has heard my secret admission and is feeding my love for him. Once again, he is giving me what I want, what I need, without my asking. He knows my heart just as well as he knows my body. The two have become one and the same.

Together we climb, seeking the warmth and solitude of our twin peaks. I flex my hips against him and wrap my legs around his waist. This new layer of depth excites him and he plunges even deeper. My fingers grab handfuls of his soft tresses, pulling gently as he sinks inside of me faster and faster. A low guttural groan erupts from his throat; he's almost there. I, too, feel it surging from every limb, traveling swiftly to my burning heat. I can taste it; sweet release is so close.

Then in an intense wave of passion, it drowns me. I can no longer see or hear or even breathe. Dorian has taken me under with him, and we are lost at sea. There's no use in fighting against the current, because it has already won. Dorian has already won. I wholeheartedly surrender to him, mind, body and soul.

"We should get ready," Dorian pants after several minutes. He is still on top of me, still inside me. I sluggishly nod, unable to speak. My devastating orgasm has relinquished me of all my faculties.

Dorian pulls out of me to my disappointment, and grabs my hands to lift me up. My limbs are like Jell-O and my head rolls around on my neck like a newborn.

"Come on, little girl. We need to shower," he chuckles. Seeing me so undone is amusing for him. Proof of his victory over me.

"Nooo," I groan begrudgingly. All I want to do is sleep. How can he expect me to function after *ruining* me like that?

Dorian lifts me onto my feet despite my protest and leads me to the bathroom. He turns on the shower and ushers me inside, as if I am helpless. In this moment, I am. He has created this convalescent.

"I would take you right here in this shower, but I'm afraid you wouldn't make it," he smirks. He's right. Instead, he washes my body meticulously and tenderly. He even washes my hair, his long magical fingers massaging my scalp.

"That feels so good," I finally say when I've regained my sense of speech. I suddenly remember his first gift of the day. "Thank you for the spa treatments. It was so surprising; how did you know? You didn't have to do that."

"I know, but I wanted to. Since I couldn't be here with you." He rinses the shampoo from my hair with the detachable shower head. "And I assume Aurora wasn't easy to stomach. You surely needed to unwind," he adds with a chuckle.

"Holy crap. I don't see how you stayed with her for so long," I say shaking my head. There. That got his attention.

Dorian furrows his brow, realizing what I'm trying to get at. I know about his past with Aurora. "Is that what she told you?" He begins to wash his own body. I would like to do it for him but right now, I want to get to the bottom of this. And touching him will only distract me.

"Between what she told Jared, and then told me earlier today at lunch, I could say I have a pretty good idea of what you two shared," I reply stiffly.

"Aurora and I were children then. Like I said, she wanted more. More than I was willing to give her or anybody else. I thought you understood." Dorian puts his head back in the stream of water, looking every bit like a model for some fancy shampoo ad. It's hard for me to be irritated or even questioning when he looks so sexy.

"I'm not really worried about it or jealous of something that happened long before me. I was just caught off guard, you know. I didn't like feeling like Jared had information that wasn't shared with me," I say meekly. His beauty has taken all the fight out of me.

"Maybe she thought there was more to it than there really was. I don't know. But I do know that there has been nothing between us romantically for many years."

Dorian leans forward to plant a kiss on my pout before turning off the water. He then steps out, naked and glistening to retrieve our towels. After wrapping one around me, he takes one for himself. So thoughtful and caring; how can I even think of being angry?

"I believe you. Now get out so I can get pretty," I smile playfully, easing him out of the bathroom.

Forty-five minutes of primping later, I am dressed in my new sexy white dress and heels. Soft dark curls cascade down my back, and I've expertly applied my makeup for a smoky, sultry effect. The necklace Dorian gave me goes with it perfectly, and the pendant peeks out from the keyhole opening in the front. Dorian has gone out into the living room so I can get ready, armed with a bottle of Ouzo from Greece for my friends. He's making an effort with them and it sounds as if they are all warming up to him nicely.

I emerge from the bedroom, and all heads turn to me and gasp. But the only reaction I care about in this moment is Dorian's. He gazes at me in awe and my cheeks heat under his display of approval. I step tentatively towards my friends and Dorian, genuinely happy that for once, almost everyone that I love is all under one roof. Even Aurora's scowl couldn't ruin this for me. I look at Jared standing beside her, his eyes full of admiration and uncertainty. Just weeks ago, his attention was the only I sought. Now a Greek god stands before me, and I am his choice. *He chose me.*

Dorian approaches me eagerly, bathing my neck and ear with praise and kisses. The public display of affection is uncomfortable at first, with having such an audience, but I let myself enjoy the attention. He wants to show me just how much I mean to him, and why should I stop him?

"Ok, ok, lovebirds! Are we all ready to go?" Morgan says over the roar of chatter. We all nod and head out to the van.

James has offered to chauffeur us in the van tonight. However, when we step outside, we are all floored by the sight of an SUV limousine. I immediately look at Dorian, who nonchalantly shrugs his shoulders. He is just full of surprises today.

"Whoa! Now this is how you party in style!" Miguel exclaims checking out the exterior. I've gathered that it's a stretch Hummer but that's as far as my car expertise goes.

After a barrage of enthusiastic gratitude, which Dorian humbly accepts, we all clamber in excitedly. The interior is incredibly plush, stocked with champagne and enough room for a party of 20. I've only been in a limo once, and that was sharing it with 12 other rowdy teens at prom. Half of them I either didn't know or didn't care for but it was an experience nonetheless.

Morgan pops the champagne with ease and lets it bubble and flow into the flutes. I go to assist her and we giggle like schoolgirls, attempting to fill each glass without spilling a drop. Out of the corner of my eye, I notice Aurora slide next to Dorian while the guys play with all the limo's gadgets and secret compartments. She is whispering to him, something in Greek it sounds, and I will myself to play it cool. *Just two old friends catching up*, I tell myself.

Then her speech changes, as if speaking in a different dialect. Maybe a different language altogether. However, this language I can understand. At least bits and pieces. I have never known any language other than English so I am secretly floored by this revelation.

Unfortunately, that is not the most surprising factor. What she murmurs to him–the scattered words I am able to make out–*that* is what leaves me breathless.

"Safe . . . the Dark Light . . . Kill her."

Then Dorian coolly turns to his old flame and companion and utters in this unnamed tongue, *"Yes."*

TWENTY-EIGHT

My head is dizzy with horror and confusion. Morgan's mouth is moving but I hear nothing. Just muffled noises over the rapid pounding of my heart roaring in my head. I concentrate on controlling the furious heaving of my chest, yet my breaths are shallow and labored. I grab a glass of champagne and down it, attempting to wash away the bitter taste of shock and betrayal. It does nothing to ease the ache in my heart.

What. The. Fuck.

Dorian knows about me. Worst of all, he's teamed up with Aurora, and it sounds as if they're planning my demise. How did this happen? Just over an hour ago, Dorian made tender, passionate love to me. He's been so attentive and generous, not at all like someone who wishes me dead. Why would he? What would he have to gain from my death? I must have heard wrong. Obviously, I do not understand whatever language they were murmuring. I am mistaken. Maybe a little bit drunk from the champagne. And even if I think I heard correctly, I could just ask him. He told me he would always be forthcoming. But am I ready for that dose of honesty? And if they find out that I do, in fact, understand their secret language, could that put me in even more danger?

What am I thinking? This is Dorian. In all the compromising positions he's had me in, if he wanted me dead, I'd be dead. All those times he's had me bent over, naked, his hand clutching my neck, pulling my hair . . . He could have easily ended me then when I was exposed and vulnerable. Why put it off? I am defenseless and he has already proven to be a much more powerful force than me. Dorian wouldn't do that. He cares about me; he told me that no one is more important to him than me. He said he didn't want anyone else. I have to believe that's true. I *need* to believe it.

"You ok, Gabs?" Morgan eyes me suspiciously. She refills the empty flute in my shaking hand.

I plaster on a strained smile. "Yeah, just thinking I should have eaten more at lunch. Feeling a little lightheaded. Probably just from the motion of the limo."

"*Mmm hmm*, that or the motion of that bed Dorian had rockin'!" she giggles. I give her a sharp look. "Oh, relax. No one heard. But I'm sure we could all imagine. *Ooooh*, look at that ice on your neck! Don't tell me, another gift from Dorian?" she squeals, taking the intricate pendent in her palm. "It's gorgeous!"

"Yes, it is. Thanks," I say quietly.

Morgan looks back at Dorian, who is gazing out the dark tinted window thoughtfully. "Hey Dorian, you don't have any brothers, do you?" Morgan says with a sly wink. Miguel's eyes flash with jealousy.

"Actually I do. Not sure he'd be your type though," he replies.

Morgan smiles slyly, "Honey, hot, rich and sexy is always my type. And if he's anything like you, we'll get along just fine."

I honestly think Miguel's head will explode if she keeps this up. She's toying with him, trying to see what he's made of. Morgan is a master manipulator of men, and her fun with Miguel is a welcomed distraction from my dilemma.

Dorian notices the heated glances between Miguel and Morgan and doesn't take the bait. Instead he fixes his intense gaze on me. Under his stare, the feelings of doubt and betrayal from minutes ago begin to abandon me. I almost can't remember what instilled my confusion. I grab two glasses of champagne and carefully make my way to him, desperately trying to salvage the evening and my jovial mood.

I take a sip of champagne from one glass and then hand it to him with a sultry smile. He looks at me musingly with a raised eyebrow and receives it, taking a sip of his own where my lipgloss has left a shimmery print. I'm doing my best to remain cool and guarded, as he calls me, in an attempt to keep him out of my head. How did I get myself into this? How did I get involved with a man so extraordinarily intuitive to my thoughts and feelings? But considering what I am, is there really any other choice?

"Something on your mind, baby?" Dorian murmurs to me silkily. His voice is like melted hot caramel; it simply oozes off the tongue.

"Just . . . thoughtful. Glad you're here. Happy," I say meekly.

And I mean it. Dorian has made this shell of what I thought was life worth living. Losing him would mean returning to mediocrity, always yearning for something more. I can't go back to that. Ever.

Dorian gives me a sexy half-smile. "That's all I want–to make you happy. Always." He twists his finger around one of my coiled tendrils.

"Do you mean that? Do you honestly want to be here with me for no other reason?" I ask him with pleading eyes. They are willing him to tell me the truth.

He furrows his brow and cocks his head to one side quizzically. "Yes. I mean that. I want to be here because I have feelings for you. Deep feelings. Feelings that scare me yet excite me. Feelings that I have tried to avoid for many, many years. Feelings I thought I'd never have the ability to feel."

Dorian's explanation floors me, and I know without a shadow of doubt that he is here for me. I have no reason to distrust him; he's shown me nothing but gentleness and generosity. I can't be sure of what I heard, but I do know that Dorian cares for me. He's shown me in more ways than one. I'd be a fool to discount his actions and ignore what's in my heart, right?

"I feel the exact same way for you," I breathe. "That and more."

Dorian plants a kiss on my lips and I instantly feel the doubt and apprehension fall away from me upon contact. The unknown language, he and Aurora's staggering conversation–it all suddenly seems like a distant memory.

His lips are forced to abandon mine when the limo comes to an abrupt halt. We're here. I can make out the bright marquee, a black and white sign simply stating Shade. It's very chic and modern, much like the Luxe salon in Colorado Springs. Yes, Dorian has his stamp all over this. The first thing I notice upon exiting is the sound of saxophones, drums, piano, and guitar. There's a live band playing. Then the sumptuous aroma of food causes my stomach to growl, confirming my hunger. Dorian grabs my hand and leads our party inside, breezing past security and the crowd of freezing people huddled around outdoor heaters awaiting entrance.

A handsome young man dressed in a black suit approaches our group, shaking Dorian's hand enthusiastically. He introduces himself as Brian and tells us that he, along with the attentive staff at Shade, will be taking care of anything we need this evening. As we hand over our coats for hanging, I get an opportunity to marvel at the impressive interior. The place is amazing; with its dark cushioned walls, contemporary furniture and metallic hued tapestries, it could easily rival any hot NYC lounge. I've personally never seen anything like it and I instantly smell the eroticism, mixed with delectable gourmet fare, wafting throughout the swanky building.

Brian leads us to a table that I'm assuming is reserved for us, being that it is intricately set with seven table settings. Dorian sits at the head of the table, of course, while I take the seat to his right, Morgan grabbing the spot next to me. We can see the band playing from where we sit, and the tunes are intoxicating, putting us all in the mood for good food, libations, and conversation.

"I hope you all don't mind, but I have arranged a special tasting menu so we could try a little bit of everything. But if there's anything you don't eat or are allergic to, please let Brian know immediately." Then he turns to me, winks, and quietly murmurs, "I know you're hungry. It won't be long, little girl." *Geez, is there anything he doesn't know?*

Moments later, servers bring us course after course of Mediterranean and Asian-fusion cuisine. Everything is ridiculously delicious, and I relish in the fact that I get to experience just a little piece of Dorian and his culture. A variety of wines are served to accent each dish and by the fourth course, showcasing an array of Greek meat and seafood dishes, I'm convinced that I'll burst. But of course, there's dessert, and my Dorian loves dessert. He doesn't go easy on us either. While the boys are loving the endless stream of food, I am secretly praying that my stomach isn't protruding. Morgan and Aurora have slowed down as well.

"Dorian, I can't eat this!" I say, my eyes taking in the individual dessert platters of several miniature confections. His love for sweets makes him seem so young and incredibly cute, and I think about the time we had a tickling war with whipped cream. Then my mind wanders to when *I* was his dessert and heat quickly floods my cheeks and the apex of my thighs.

Dorian gives me a wicked smile as if he's recalling the same memory, and licks his lips. He scoops up a tiny bit of his chocolate mousse and holds it out to my lips. I roll my eyes playfully and take it into my mouth slowly, making sure to flick my tongue out onto the spoon first. He likes this; something about feeding me clearly arouses him. I don't deny trying to make a show of it either.

After we are all sated and clearly a bit tipsy from the wine, Brian leads us to an upstairs area, equally chic and alluring. Something about its dark walls and furniture accented with just a hint of metallic color gives it a sultry, sexy feel. A DJ is spinning all the latest hits and sharply dressed men and women are on the dance floor. Again, we walk to a special section reserved for us, and Dorian does not fail to impress. Leather sofas, oversized plush pillows, teakwood accent tables, luminous candles and many bottles of chilled champagne and spirits await us. Now this is a VIP section!

I barely have a chance to sip my glass of bubbly before Morgan grabs my hand, leading me to the dance floor with Aurora in tow. We're all feeling good, and I am even being friendly with Aurora as if we're old girlfriends. We giggle and dance to several songs as the men look on and chat idly. I can see they're all getting along, Dorian and Jared included. This is how it should be. I should be able to have all my friends together, having a great time, doing what normal young adults do. Last month, I couldn't stand being so normal. As the saying goes, be careful what you wish for.

By 2 AM my feet are aching, I'm beyond tipsy, Morgan is flat out drunk and stumbling and James has made a new friend. After collecting our coats, we head back to the limo, conveniently waiting on the curb in the front. James invites his new Ms. Right Now back to the house and she joins us on our ride home, clearly awestruck. I secretly hope she's not feigning interest in James because she thinks he's wealthy judging by tonight's overflow of champagne and the limo. She will be sadly disappointed when she realizes he's a broke, soon-to-be recent college grad. But it'll serve her right if she sleeps with him with hopes of monetary gain.

When we get home, Miguel helps a giggling Morgan to her room and shuts the door behind them. Looks like James won't be the only one getting lucky. Aurora and Jared had been making out the entire ride home and they continue their uncomfortable display all the way to their room. Which leaves Dorian and me.

"Zip me down?" I say innocently once we're in the confines of our room. *Our* room–I like the sound of that.

Dorian licks his lips and coolly walks towards me. He positions himself behind me and zips down my dress slowly, leaving soft kisses on my shoulders and back once they're exposed. I shiver at the feel of his caress.

"How about a dip?" he whispers in my ear.

I turn my head to eye him suspiciously. "Did you bring your swim trunks?"

Dorian gives me his devilish grin and bites his bottom lip. "No."

"Then absolutely."

We strip out of our clothing excitedly, cackling like naughty teenagers. Once we've wrapped ourselves in towels and Dorian has grabbed a chilled bottle from the fridge along with two glasses, we race to the hot tub outside. This is risqué behavior for me; I've never been one to be outwardly affectionate or sexual with anybody. But I can't deny that I'm aroused at the prospect of getting caught skinny-dipping.

Dorian sets down the bottle of champagne and glasses then lets his towel drop to the ground, exposing his beautifully chiseled body. I gawk in amazement at how comfortable he is stark naked, especially outdoors in the freezing cold. He climbs into the Jacuzzi gracefully then turns to face me with a beckoning hand. I stand nervously clutching my towel around me, suddenly feeling shy.

"Come on, you'll warm up as soon as you get in the water," Dorian says soothingly. Reluctantly, I let my towel fall and take his hand, letting him pull me in. God, I hope none of my friends are looking out the window! They'd get a glimpse of more than just one full moon.

The water feels great, and the bubbly jets cause my sensitive areas to tingle out of control. Dorian fills our champagne glasses, and I gladly sip mine to ease my apprehension. After playful banter and flirting, Dorian takes the glass from my hand and sets it down with his. He positions my body onto one of the powerful jets and the water shoots up fiercely, making me squirm. I gasp at the sensation as Dorian looks on with hooded eyes. He stands between my open thighs, massaging them slowly. His hands find their way to my slippery wetness, causing a jolt of electricity to shoot through my body. His eyes stay on mine, like always, burning deep with desire. He's lips are moving as if he's murmuring something, but I can't hear it over the rapidly bubbling water and the sounds of my own pleasure.

Then it begins–the prickling little shockwaves coursing through every inch of my body. It's as if Dorian has a hundred magical fingers and they are stimulating me all at once. I try to hold my breath in fear that my moans will alert our occupied friends but I can't help myself. I'm moaning wildly, panting, writhing. I can't stop it, I have to let go. Yet when I do, ecstasy continues to overcome me in intense, violent waves. A never-ending orgasm. Only when I squeeze my eyes shut and let my head roll back do the sensations finally cease.

Once coherent thought has returned to me, I lift my head up and look at a smirking Dorian. He seems satisfied with himself, cocky even. I think to say something smart to him but before I can, he spreads my legs wider and enters me with a swift thrust. I cry out his praises as he begins his slow assault. The combination of the hot water and the streaming jets adds a new level of pleasure. I link my ankles together around his waist to pull him deeper into me, and he groans his approval. My hands clutch his back and shoulders ferociously as Dorian's measured deep strokes grow faster and harder. Water sloshes all around us, causing my wet tresses to stick to my face and neck. I'm bucking against him, pulling his hair, moaning, savoring his tongue on my neck and shoulders. I feel his fingers dig into my flesh as he pumps himself in and out of me and the sting only heightens my arousal. I like the pain; I need it. This pain that Dorian gives me makes me feel so alive, so vital.

As if reading my thoughts, Dorian digs himself deeper into me, and I can feel the strain in his body as he tries to fight against his own orgasm. He doesn't want to stop but it's pulling him under. He bites down onto my shoulder, his teeth leaving little indentions in my skin. It's so intensely erotic, I don't even try to stifle my carnal cries. I couldn't even if I wanted to. I know that they make it harder for him to resist; my arousal provokes him more than anything else. Seeing him so undone does the same for me, and I will myself to slow down. But it's too late. The telltale sign of his climax, the substantial swelling inside of me, pushes me over the edge, and we both plunge into dangerously thrashing dark waters.

I gasp Dorian's name, followed by a series of hoarse expletives, resting my head on his hard shoulder. His face is buried in my neck, trying to regain his own breath through gritted teeth. I secretly relish his vulnerability in this moment, and the pinkish haze of our combined auras makes this scene so serene. I've tried to ignore them, and honestly, it freaked me out when I first saw it. But now it's simply become another nuisance of my new life. The upside of it is that I can read people's moods and proceed with them accordingly. Almost like reading their minds. I wonder if Dorian has the same ability, being that he always seems to know my thoughts. I store the question away for later, not wanting to spoil the tender moment.

"Will it always be like this?" I murmur, still cradled in his arms.

"Like what?" Dorian replies. I feel his cool breath on my throat and get a little chill, despite the hot water and our vigorous activity. Dorian holds me tighter.

"This . . . good?" I sigh. "Does it ever get bad with you? Or even mediocre? Will you always make me feel so amazing?" I chuckle at my ridiculous questions.

Dorian lifts his head and looks at me quizzically. "Is it that good to you?" He's being coy; he knows exactly what he does to my body.

"Crazy good," I say, lifting my eyebrows for dramatic effect. Dorian looks down for a beat, and when he returns his gaze to me, it's thoughtful and serious. *Oh no, did I say something wrong?*

"It's good for me too, you know. Inexplicable." He swallows to give himself a moment to align his thoughts with his words. "No one has ever moved me like you. Ever. The feeling you give me is insane. It's unnatural. You intoxicate me."

Whoa. That was unexpected. I look at Dorian in awe, totally beguiled by his sudden intimate confession. So maybe he feels it too–the incredible need that draws me to him. Maybe he feels the tiny prickles that flow through my body whenever we touch. Maybe, just maybe, his feelings for me could go deeper than the physical. Maybe he could love me too.

"Have you ever been with someone . . . like me?" I ask meekly. He knows what I mean but we haven't gone into that territory yet. We are both stuck somewhere between denial and obscurity.

Dorian shakes his head a bit. "No. No one like you."

I lay my head back down on his shoulder, exhaustion washing over me from the intense orgasms, alcohol, and late hour. I close my eyes just for a moment, and inhale deeply, breathing in Dorian's fresh, cool aroma. He always smells so crisp and clean, reminding me of the scent of fresh linen or island air, though I've never seen him wear cologne. Yet another mystery that makes Dorian so damn irresistible.

"Come, little girl. Let's get you to bed."

Dorian lifts me up, cradling me so my cheek rests on his chest. My eyes are still closed but I feel him maneuver easily out of the hot tub and then feel the softness of a towel draped over me. I can tell he's walking into the house, and I should really tell him to put me down so I can walk the rest of the way, but my eyelids are so heavy. And his arms feel so good wrapped around me, the soothing rhythm of his heart my own personal lullaby. Through the tiny slits of my eyes, I see that we've entered the bedroom. Dorian sets me down gently on the bed and puts the comforter over me before walking to the other side to climb in. We lie facing each other, naked under the thick blanket. It's dark but I can still see his eyes twinkling brightly.

"I've never been with someone like you either," I whisper.

"I know," Dorian replies. "And you never will be." Then sleep envelops me, filling my head with vivid images of Dorian, Aurora, and piercing blue eyes.

Twenty-Nine

The next morning, I awaken to the soft thudding of Dorian's beating heart. My head rests on his smooth, bare chest and his arms are wrapped tightly around me. This feels so good, so right. I want to pretend to still be asleep but judging by the sounds resonating from the kitchen, everyone is already up and at 'em. Plus the bathroom is calling my name. I try to ease out from under his embrace when he begins to stir.

"No. No. I'm sorry," he murmurs.

I look up, expecting to see him peering at me but his eyes are still shut tightly, his brow furrowed with angst. Again, he mutters something but it's in Greek, I believe. However, the anguish in his voice tells me that he is urgently pleading. The tone of his voice changes, and so does the language. It is the unnamed language from last night, the one he spoke with Aurora. I can pick up a few words but they are so random that they don't make much sense to me.

"No . . . Mine . . . Don't . . . Please."

I reach out to stroke his cheek to comfort him, and he jerks awake. His eyes are wild, searching, disoriented. He then crushes my body to his, holding me tightly in his arms for several silent seconds. I don't dare utter a word; who knows what has caused him such distress. When he finally loosens his grip, I look up to give to him a reassuring, yet weak, smile before retreating to the bathroom, leaving him confused and disheveled.

As I brush my teeth, I can't help but wonder if I handled the situation correctly. Did he expect me to say something to soothe him? Should I have stayed and asked him what he was dreaming about? No. If he wanted to tell me, he would have. I could never reveal the content of my nightmares; why should I expect him to?

After we're all dressed and packed, we begrudgingly say goodbye to our vacation home. We pile into the van and head into town to have brunch before hitting the road. Dorian didn't drive his car here so I assume he hired a car service to bring him. I don't question him, just like I don't question the heated glances between him and Aurora over waffles, bacon, and eggs. They are not passionate or longing stares. They are . . . odd, to say the least. Their expressions reflect those of an intense, serious conversation, yet neither one of them says a word.

"So Miguel, what are your sister's plans after high school? She graduates in a few weeks, right?" I ask, trying to distract my overactive imagination.

"Yeah, she does, but I have no idea what her plans could be. Carmen is adamant about not going to a traditional university. She's really into fashion design and wants to attend some fashion and art institute. The problem is my parents just can't afford it. I wouldn't have been able to go to college if it weren't for my scholarship. So she's looking for a job to help her get into that industry. And we all know the Springs isn't that cutting edge when it comes to stuff like that."

"What? Not into Mountain Chic?" Morgan chuckles. She gives Miguel a flirtatious smile and I notice him stroking her back. They definitely hooked up last night.

"Well, let me know if she doesn't find anything she really likes. I might be able to help her," I say.

I look over at Dorian, who has returned his attention to me, and give him a wink. I told him I'd accept his job offer only if I could do the hiring. And firing. Meaning Little Miss Allison will have to flaunt her perky breasts elsewhere. Not being that fashion savvy myself, Carmen could be just what I need to help me run Cashmere. Plus, I know she's trustworthy and hardworking. I'd be helping out a friend and helping myself as well.

Once we've gotten on the road, I rest my head on Dorian's shoulder and fold my feet into the seat. We've claimed the back row while James, Miguel and Morgan sit in front of us. Jared has offered to drive this time so he and Aurora sit in the front seats. This time the trip is different. Everyone is engaging in lighthearted conversation and getting along. It gives me hope that there will be many more trips together as a group.

"Hey, before I forget, I wanted to invite you to Morgan's house this weekend," I whisper to Dorian. "Her parents are throwing her a little get together in honor of her getting her license and landing a great job at such a fabulous salon."

Dorian instantly becomes rigid. "When is it?"

"This Saturday. And of course, my parents would be there. That is, if you want to meet them." Yikes. I literally hold my breath until he answers.

"Yeah, you see, I would but I don't think that's such a good idea. With me technically being Morgan's boss, I don't want it to look like I'm showing her any favoritism. I'm sure other employees of the salon will be there." Dorian toys with a lock of my hair and twirls it around his finger. "Don't want to give them the wrong impression." He plants a kiss on my pouting lips to silence any questioning. He knows the affect he has on me and he's taking full advantage of my weakness.

"You look younger," I murmur quietly, once he pulls away.

"Do I?" he asks in an equally hushed voice. I notice Aurora's head turns just a fraction from the front seat. She must be able to hear our whispers, though I'm positive no one else can.

"You do. Successful trip, I assume?" I cock my head to one side and give him a pointed stare.

"I guess you could say that. Just took care of some things. And conveyed a status report. Not very eventful."

"Will that happen often? You running off to Greece?" My tone is desperate, almost pained. Feelings that startle me.

Dorian looks at me intensely, his eyes searching mine for the reason behind my sudden show of emotion. "Yes."

I feel my face drop so I quickly turn my head to look at the blur of passing trees out the window. I hate myself for feeling like this, feeling so vulnerable and needy. I told myself I wouldn't get emotionally involved, that I could separate my body from my heart. Who was I kidding? That could have never happened. Dorian is the most sensual, intense, mesmerizing man I have ever met. He has made love to every single part of me, inside and out. I set myself up for failure from the start.

Dorian leaves me with my tortured thoughts and doesn't attempt to question me. He's giving me space, exactly what I need in this moment. It's crazy how well he knows me and how little I know about him. I don't know what awaits him in Greece. He could have a wife and kids there, and live some salacious double life. As gorgeous, successful, and, well, perfect as he is, it is certainly possible. Why *wouldn't* he be attached?

"Don't think too much," Dorian whispers, his lips suddenly at my ear.

I look at him skeptically. "How do you do that?"

"Do what?" he answers with a raised eyebrow.

"Say things to me as if you know what I'm thinking." I'm a bit annoyed at the possibility that he could be invading on my private thoughts. My pathetic ramblings are for me and only me.

"I don't know what you're thinking," Dorian chuckles. "I'm not a mind reader. Just perceptive, which isn't difficult considering my . . . background. And yours too."

"What do you mean, '*your background*'? And mine? What are you talking about?" I scoot closer to him and look at him anxiously.

"Your aura, Gabriella. I can see it. Just like you can see mine." Dorian assesses my shocked, mortified expression. "It's ok, you know. All kinds of average, ordinary people can see auras, too. It's really no big deal."

Whoa. So Dorian definitely knows that I'm different. But how different? And why is he just now divulging that he knows about my abnormality? All this time trying to ignore the vivid colors that halo his magnificence, and all the while he can see it too. In some odd way, I feel comforted with this revelation. Less alone in my new life. Though it is impossible for Dorian to be exactly like me, he's *something.* He can relate, sympathize. But that's as far as it goes.

I give Dorian a weak grin and shake my head. "You're not like me. No one is."

His finger captures my chin and he turns it to face him, his eyes wild with intense emotion. "I'm more like you than you think."

"Ok, bathroom break!" Jared calls from the driver's seat, pulling into the parking lot of a gas station. I hadn't even noticed we were slowing down.

Dorian and I stare at each other intently, neither of us wanting to look away, yet we don't want to delve any deeper. He's like me? That's preposterous. The Light vowed to remain out of my life until I pledged my allegiance to them. And he can't be Dark. He just can't. There's no way that someone so kind, generous, loving and passionate could be Dark. I may not know him as well as I'd like, but I know that Dorian doesn't have an evil bone in his body. He is the best kind of good that there is. I could never be that blind, that stupid. *Right?*

Reluctantly, I break his hold on my gaze to look towards the front of the van just as James hops out. Refusing to acknowledge the static between Dorian and me, I maneuver myself out of my seat and exit the van. I consciously walk ahead to catch up with Morgan, though I can hear Dorian's footsteps behind me. I need to put some space between us; I need to escape the magnetism that draws me to him like a moth to a flame and renders me completely foolish. He makes me forget all caution and sensibility, allowing me to abandon my usual skeptical, distrusting nature. I need some normalcy. I need my best friend.

Unfortunately, when we enter the ladies room, Aurora is there in all her grand perfection, looking anything but normal. Looks like my pow-wow with Morgan will have to wait, though I have no clue what I would tell her. It's not like I could be honest with her. And what would honesty entail? I am not even sure I could even explain my suspicions about Dorian to her without her laughing in my face or running for the hills. No. I can't confide in Morgan with this.

I spend the remainder of the ride into the Springs with a pleasant smile plastered on my face. Dorian has also abandoned his natural smoldering intensity and is engaging in casual conversation with the rest of the guys about random sporting events, or something equally monotonous. They could honestly be talking about killing puppies and the same dumb grin would be plastered on my face. My head is elsewhere. Dorian keeps dropping these bombs of truth on me, totally making me question my own judgment, which up until now was one of my most redeeming qualities. *Unless tequila is involved, of course.* But why would he do that? If he is truly Dark, wouldn't he want to conceal his identity in order to deceive, and then eventually, kill me?

"Would you like to come up?" Dorian asks as we pull up to the main building at the Broadmoor. We have already taken Aurora to her posh downtown apartment which, to my dismay, is not too far away.

"I better get home. Parents will be expecting me." It's the truth; I haven't sent more than a couple text messages to confirm my safety the entire weekend.

Dorian slightly nods then leans forward to plant a gentle kiss on my lips. "You know where to find me," he murmurs before exiting the van.

As we pull away from the Broadmoor, away from Dorian, anxiety and sorrow creep into my chest. The farther we travel, the more distance wedged between Dorian and I, the worse I feel. I want to tell Jared to turn back around, to take me back to the man that I love. I want run back into his arms where safety and security live but I know I have to go home. The thought of being miles away from him unsettles me. I can literally feel the dull ache gripping my heart. I don't understand it, and frankly, it scares me.

By the time we pull up to Briargate, I am barely holding onto my sanity. Pain is etched in my face, though I ignore the questioning glances from my friends. They don't understand. They never could. This goes so far beyond being in love with Dorian. *I need him.* He's ensured that. This is exactly what he wants. He wants me so dependent on him that I can't say no. I have to fight the crippling urge to run back to him. If I do, then he will own me completely. I struggle to gulp down the rising taste of melancholy in my tight throat and flash a weak smile goodbye. Chris and Donna can't see me like this. They will surely know that something is wrong.

"Gabriella! Oh thank goodness you are home!" my mom says rushing to me as soon as I open the door. *Sheesh.*

"It's only been a couple days, Mom. Nice to see you too," I murmur as she squeezes me in an urgent embrace. Chris is right behind her, a somber look on his face. *Shit.* Something is wrong. "What's up? Everything ok?"

Chris takes my bag from me and quickly closes the door, locking it. He ushers us to the living room where I flop down on the couch. Mugs of tea and papers litter the coffee table, an unusual sight in the ordinarily pristine room.

"This came for you, Kiddo," Chris says sliding one of the papers towards me. His disturbed expression alerts me and I automatically think it's a letter from my school. Crap. Am I failing a class? Does it say I won't graduate in a couple weeks?

I take the white sheet in my hands and hold my breath as I look at the words scrawled in black ink. It's worse than I initially thought. So much worse. Yet fear does not greet me. Only rage. Extreme rage that causes my face to heat and my knuckles to turn white over my fists. I'm shaking with violent anger and my jaw is tightly clenched, causing my gums to hurt from the pressure.

Dark Light,

We know who you are. And we are watching.

Eleven months.

Align with the Dark or Die.

It's the last thing I see before every light bulb in the living room grows blindingly bright, then pops and shatters instantaneously, leaving us all shrouded in complete darkness.

THIRTY

We all spring to our feet—my parents in alarm, me in anger. Though only a trickle of sunlight illuminates the room from between the curtains, I can clearly see the worry etched in their faces. They do not fear that someone has come here to hurt us, immobilizing us by breaking the bulbs. They are afraid of me. I caused the sudden darkness. The violent ripples of rage rolling off of me have caused the light bulbs to explode right before us. I try to loosen my tight fists and control the tremors ripping through me. I don't mean to frighten them. I didn't even know I was capable of this.

"I . . . I'm sorry. I didn't . . . mean to," I stammer between clenched teeth, shaking my head stiffly. I try to take deep breaths in order to calm myself. I begin to feel the tension dissipate from my shoulders as I will myself to relax.

"I know, honey," Donna replies meekly. She understands what has happened here though I'm not entirely sure myself.

Though fear has momentarily gripped her, my mom cautiously advances towards me and slowly places her hand on my shoulder. Chris is more hesitant and has not dropped his defensive stance, though his startled expression has grown softer. He approaches inch by inch with measured steps. My parents are afraid of me and what I will do. It's as if I am a wild animal—unpredictable, vicious, dangerous. The revelation stops me up short and I completely release the fury that has resulted in their trepidation.

I swallow loudly, though my mouth is dry. "I don't know what just happened. I don't know how I did that." My head drops to the floor in shame.

"I know. I know, dear," my mom repeats, patting my back. She's trying to comfort me but I know she is uncomfortable just touching me. It pains me to know that I am solely responsible for her terror.

"Have a seat, Kiddo. Let's just try to calm down and talk about this," Chris says, ushering his wife to the love seat, away from me. He is protecting her from me just in case I lose it again, as he should.

I take the seat farthest from them, tucking my hands between my knees. "I'm sorry," I repeat. "I just got so angry. How did this get here?" I say nodding towards the letter still lying on the coffee table. Donna stands to open the curtains to let the sunlight brighten the room and the mood.

"It was in our mailbox yesterday morning. It wasn't addressed or anything, just in a blank envelope. We tried to call you; didn't you get any of our messages or texts?" Chris asks.

I shake my head, not recalling any missed calls or voicemail, though I haven't actually been paying much attention to my cell phone. I know I looked at it earlier that morning and it didn't indicate any messages.

"Humph. That's strange," he murmurs, rubbing his temples. He looks like he's aged within the past 5 minutes.

"I didn't mean for this to happen, you know," I say quietly. "I tried to keep this under control, tried to handle this stuff on my own. I never thought they'd send something here."

"What do you mean?" Chris questions. "You've received other notes? And didn't tell us?"

"Yeah," I nod. "I started getting random messages a few weeks ago. My car, my phone." I leave out the mysterious voice in the Breckenridge nightclub. They would lock me up and never let me leave the house for sure.

"Why didn't you tell us?" Donna chimes in. She comes to sit beside me, despite Chris's rigid posture and flexed jaw. He's still on edge.

"And then what? What could you possibly do?" I ask incredulously, looking between the both of them. "Besides worry yourselves to death about something or someone we couldn't possibly fight?" I feel a wave of fresh anger begin to wash over me and I immediately start a series of deep breaths.

"We could've been there for you. You're a strong girl; we know that. But you can't keep taking things on alone. Everyone needs support." My mom wraps a warm arm around me and squeezes gently. Chris nods in agreement.

I shake my head in exasperation and shrug out of my mom's embrace, standing to my feet. "I wish that were true, but I won't put you two in danger. Not after all you have already risked in order to keep me safe. It's final; I'm moving out in a couple weeks. I'll stay through graduation but that's it."

I begin to make my way to my room when Chris's voice stops me up short. "Is there anything we can do to change your mind?"

I turn to look at him through watery eyes. He looks so solemn, so weary. Because of me. I shake my head. "Just be here."

I grab my bag and retreat to the solace of my childhood bedroom. Now I wish I would have just gone to the Broadmoor with Dorian to escape this fiasco. It's bad enough that the Dark have resorted to delivering threats to our home, but the fact that I've frightened my parents is unforgivable. I can't even begin to comprehend how I caused those bulbs to break. Could I be a danger to them? And to other innocent people? Is anyone truly safe around me?

Under normal circumstances, I would call Jared and drown my sorrows in cold beer and curly fries, but now that our friendship has done a complete 180, there's no one I would rather see than Dorian. I pick up my cell phone and scroll down to retrieve his number. No. I shouldn't. While he may be an effective distraction, things have been getting a bit too precarious between us. I'm in love with him, I can't deny that. But can I trust him? And even if I can't, can I really turn away from him after falling for him so hard?

I toss my phone onto my bed and sigh loudly. Until I know for sure that Dorian has my best interests at heart, I have to be smart. I have to ask him. Time to put my big girl panties on and face the giant elephant that's been suffocating me with its annoying presence. This is a conversation that can't be had over the phone. No, I have to look him in his mesmerizing ice blue eyes when I ask him to tell me what he is. And whatever that truth may be, I have to either deal with it and accept him wholeheartedly, or I have to walk away from the one man who has shown me more passion than I could ever imagine. The outcome may crush my heart and kill my spirit completely but continuing down this path of denial could very well get us both murdered.

As the week drones on, I engulf myself with studying for finals and tying up loose ends at work before resigning. My parents are more attentive than ever, calling and checking up on me every other hour. Lucky for them, I'm taking the threats more seriously now that it has literally hit home. Plus I want to ensure them that I am still the same old Gabs, and have been making more of an effort to spend time with them. Seeing them so afraid of me was eye-opening. I never want them to experience that type of fear again.

The bright spot of the past few days was seeing Dorian each evening during my break at work. He'd meet me at our little table at Starbucks, his sexy smirk, my favorite latte, and an espresso brownie in tow. Knowing that a mall coffee shop is the last place to have such a crucial, delicate conversation, I've planned to broach the subject Saturday night after Morgan's party. I still don't know how to even word it and couldn't imagine just simply asking him out of the blue. And what if my suspicions are wrong? What if he laughs in my face? Not to mention, it would surely indicate my true identity. I only have two days to figure it out, and though I've been racking my brain, there just doesn't seem to be a tactful way to present such a sensitive subject.

Since it's Thursday night and I usually head over to Dorian's suite after work, I feel oddly out of place sitting on the couch watching television with my parents. It used to be a nightly ritual for us, yet now I feel like an outsider, an intruder in their home. I could have gone to Dorian's place but then I would have to explain where I was and who I was with, and being that they will see Morgan's parents this weekend, I can't risk any holes in my alibi. No, the comfort and safety of Dorian's arms will have to wait another 48 hours. *Sigh.*

"That is a beautiful necklace, Gabi," my mom remarks during a commercial break.

My eyes shift down. Shit. I must've been unconsciously fiddling with it while thinking about Dorian. I had been making an effort to keep it tucked away in my shirt while at home to avoid questioning.

"Thanks," I smile. "Got it up at Breckenridge." At least I didn't have to lie. "Hey, guys, I'm beat. I think I'm going to call it a night," I say to evade any further inspection.

"Ok, dear. You get some rest," my mom smiles at me. I can tell she's more relaxed since I've been spending more evenings at home.

"Goodnight, Kiddo," Chris adds. I hate disappointing him and I can tell that he sees me in a different light since Sunday's incident. Just another indication that it's time to move out.

After a quick shower, I realize that I really am exhausted. Actually giving a damn about my GPA and worrying about Dorian's admission has really taken a toll on me. I brush my teeth and throw on my favorite flannel pajamas, a welcomed change from the lace and satin numbers Dorian purchased for me. Sneaking the lingerie into my parent's house would have proven to be a feat so I opted to just keep them at the Broadmoor where Dorian could enjoy ripping the scanty pieces off me at his leisure. I just hope he still wants to after I reveal what I am. Trying to shake the creeping feelings of doubt and anxiety in my head, I climb into bed, turn on some soothing, soft music, and quickly fall into a dreamless slumber.

THIRTY-ONE

I awake to the smell of bacon and freshly brewed coffee, and for the first time in a week, I feel home. Trickles of warm sunlight filter through my bedroom blinds beckoning me to wake and greet the day. I stretch my stiff limbs and yawn loudly. I feel good. *Great, actually.* Sleep hasn't exactly come easy since discovering that the Dark knew our address. Though I know they couldn't penetrate the wards around the house, somehow they got to our mailbox. The question has been gnawing at me incessantly, among the other numerous worries.

"Good morning, dear!" Donna exclaims as I enter the kitchen.

"Hey, Mom. Something smells good," I say grabbing a mug for coffee.

She doesn't touch the stuff, and Chris left hours ago for work. She must've made a fresh pot just for me. After I've doused my serving with a substantial amount of flavored creamer, I take a seat at our little breakfast table and enjoy the piping hot brew.

"You're just in time. Breakfast is served!" She places a huge plate of pancakes, scrambled eggs and crisp bacon in front of me.

My eyes grow wide at the mountain of food staring back at me. "Wow. This is great, but you know you didn't have to do this. I could have just had a bowl of cereal. Besides, won't you be late for your class?"

"I'm not going today. I got someone to fill in for me," she says proudly. "I thought we could chat. Catch up. I feel like we hardly get a chance to talk anymore."

I take the opportunity to drown my food in maple syrup before answering my mom. "I know. Just been really busy, you know. But once I graduate, I should have a little more free time."

"Really? Even with the new job? Running a store is a pretty big responsibility. Very time consuming, I'd assume." Donna digs into her bowl of yogurt and fresh berries.

"Yeah, but I'll have help. I plan to choose a reliable staff that will be able to handle things efficiently even when I'm not there." *Too bad Allison, the inappropriately flirtatious sales slore, won't be included in that bunch.*

"Sounds like you've put some thought into this. I'm proud of you. I didn't know you were interested in fashion. I mean, you've been working at the mall, but I thought you hated retail."

I munch my syrup-dipped bacon and shake my head. "I don't exactly hate it. I just don't particularly like hounding people to buy stuff. I hope to make it a comfortable experience for both the buyer and the seller. People are more likely to spend money when they feel at ease and welcomed. No one wants a pushy shadow following them around while they shop for undergarments," I chuckle.

Donna gives me a weak grin, though I can tell it's forced. "What?" I ask with a furrowed brow.

"Oh, nothing," she shrugs. "I just always flinch a bit when I hear the word 'shadow,'" she explains.

Of course, *the* Shadow. The organization of the Dark implemented to uphold their laws. And execute their punishments. My father, Alexander, was a decorated member of the Shadow. And when he broke their most sacred cardinal rule, he was put to death at the hands of his beloved brotherhood.

"Did he try to fight them? Alexander? When they took him?" I ask meekly.

"I don't think he did," Donna says shaking her head. "He knew it would just be worse for your mother. He didn't want her to get involved and fight on his behalf. He wouldn't risk either of your lives." Donna looks up and gives me a warm, comforting grin. "He really did love you. I remember how excited he was when he learned that he would have a daughter. You are like him in a lot of ways."

My face instantly brightens with the thought that I could

resemble my father, the skilled, cunning tracker that fell deeply in love with my mother, his mortal enemy. "How so?"

"You're brave like him. I mean, Natalia was incredibly brave, but he had this silent courage about him. You never really saw him ruffled. He didn't wear his heart on his sleeve, you could say. Natalia was quick to react. Alexander was calculated, always in control."

Calculated. Controlled. I don't think I've ever considered myself as either of those. Maybe Donna sees something in me that I don't remotely recognize in myself. But I have seen those traits. In Dorian. He is always so measured. Cool, calm, and collected.

"Really? Humph. How else?" Now I'm intrigued.

"Your love for your friends and family. You are protective like him. You don't want people to be hurt or uncomfortable. He was like that. He always wanted to take away your mother's anxiety when things got difficult. He hated seeing her so distressed."

I could see that. I do feel the need to protect my loved ones. But who wouldn't? I am reminded of the time when I had the meltdown in front of the Italian restaurant downtown. How Dorian took away my stress and pain. He was so caring, so loving. *He fixed me.* He protected me from myself.

"Believe it or not, you have his sense of humor!" Donna continues. "Unless you knew Alex, you couldn't tell if he was joking or not. He was wickedly sarcastic. I found him hilarious, and you wouldn't expect that from someone like him." I can tell this trip down memory lane has put her in good spirits. I smile at my mom brightly, encouraging her to keep going. "And he loved music. He had the most beautiful voice too. Would sing to Nat's belly, to his baby girl, every night."

To hear Donna affectionately call my mom Nat warms me thoroughly. They were close, all of them. Love was there. I wasn't the only one who lost when my parents were slaughtered. Donna lost her closest friends. She has suffered so much in the name of love.

"You knew him well. Alexander. Wasn't that difficult,

considering?" I don't dare elaborate.

"Extremely, at first. But I couldn't deny the immense love he had for Natalia. No one could. It literally radiated from him. Both of them, actually. By then, your dad, Chris was in my life. He persuaded me to give Alex a chance. Told me I couldn't hold an entire species accountable for the act of one cruel, disgusting being. He was right. Alex was a good one," she smiles and nods.

I imagine the four of them, laughing, talking, joking, being happy. Not unlike the bond my friends and I share. Though I can't picture my parents' faces, I can only imagine how gloriously beautiful they were. What I wouldn't give just to get a glimpse of them.

"Who do you think I look like?"

Donna narrows her eyes as if she's deep in thought. "I'd say Nat. You have her eyes, her beautiful hair. And her smile. She had the most dazzling smile. It could literally light a dreary day. You have Alex's nose though, and some of his expressions. It's funny; I see so much of them in you. They truly live on through you."

I can't deny the fresh emotion that pools in my excited eyes. To know that I have a piece of them with me, that I even remotely resemble their greatness, fills me with joy and hope. Maybe I can survive this. Maybe I can persevere with their strength, courage and tenacity coursing through me. They sacrificed so much for love. Maybe I can too.

I glance down at my half eaten breakfast and try to blink away tears. When I look back up at my mom, I can see that she is fighting with her own moist eyes. A smile stretches across my lips.

"Thank you for this. Really."

She knew I needed this pep talk. She knew I needed to know that I was created out of love and courage and goodness. I had been walking on eggshells, afraid of what I could be capable of, and she is telling me that it's okay. *I* am okay.

I rise to my feet and clear my plate. "I'm gonna grab a shower and get some studying done. Thanks for the talk, Mom." I mean it.

Though my apprehensions have not completely dissipated, Donna has made them easier to face. She's made me realize that I owe it to her, Chris, Natalia, and Alex to survive.

The hours tick by seamlessly with the help of the Dorian-inspired playlist on my iPod. When I look up, it's already 4 PM. Humph. Usually studying is like pulling teeth for me, yet it's been oddly painless this time around. I close my Astronomy textbook, and stretch my stiffened limbs. My growling stomach leads me to the kitchen, where I find Chris, surprisingly. He usually doesn't get home until 6 PM or later.

"Hey, Kiddo," he greets me from the refrigerator. He is still dressed in his smart navy suit and tie.

"Hey, Dad. You're home early." I grab the loaf of bread from the bread basket and search the cabinet for the jar of peanut butter.

"Yeah, thought we could all use a nice dinner out. Whadayasay?" He decides on a can of ginger ale and an apple, and looks up to smile at me, awaiting my reaction. It's a welcomed sight, considering how tense things have been between the two of us.

"Sure, sounds good." I opt for just a single slice of bread with peanut butter in an attempt to save my appetite.

"Great. Your mom ran out to the store. She should be back shortly. We'll leave in a couple hours, ok?" Chris is really trying to regain the seamless ease we once shared. His efforts don't go unappreciated and I smile back at him warmly.

"I'll be ready! Thanks, Dad," I say before heading back to my room.

My family and friends are all I have. I have to fix the fissures that threaten to tear us apart while I still have the chance. I grab my cell phone and scroll down for Jared's number. After a few rings, it goes straight to voicemail but I hang up before it prompts me to leave a message.

Since I have a couple hours to spare and couldn't possibly read another word about globular clusters or moon phases, I decide to turn up the music and start organizing the things I'd like to take to the new apartment. I grew up in this room; it's been my sanctuary since I was 14 years old. Six years of bittersweet memories. I couldn't possibly strip it bare of all the joy, pain, frustration, laughter, fear, and love that fill it. It's not like I will be gone forever, and it would destroy Donna if I emptied it and didn't leave at least an inkling of her daughter in here.

Assessing my closet, I realize that I need to go through it and discard old, outdated clothing. Many items are from high school, and though it was only a couple years ago, I'm not exactly going to be reverting to my old Goth days or the skater look complete with huge, wide-leg jeans. I begin to get nostalgic pulling the items from the hangers and tossing them into a pile for Goodwill.

High school wasn't exactly pleasant for me, but it was a necessary experience that helped shape who I am today. I can't believe I wore most of the apparel, and have a good laugh at my lack of fashion sense. I can only imagine what Morgan would say if she saw me in the tasteless frocks. She didn't move to the Springs until right before Senior year when I had finally found my fashion footing. If she had met me just a year earlier, we probably would not have been friends, supernatural bond or not.

After I deplete almost half of my wardrobe, I get to work on my childhood collection of stuffed animals propped up on a little wooden bench. These will not be thrown away. At least Donna can come in here and reminisce on the days when I was a normal, non-threatening little girl. However, I do want to take a few to the new apartment, just to feel some kind of connection to my old life.

I pick up an old rust-colored teddy bear. Jared gave it to me after winning it at one of the county fairs some years back. He was always so skilled at carnival games. He could knock down empty tin cans with rubber balls and pop balloons with darts like nobody's business. And I was always there cheering him on. I wonder if we'll ever be like that again. Chances are Aurora now occupies that place in his life, though I doubt she'd be caught dead at one of our usual haunts.

I notice what appears to be a slip of paper hidden behind my little display of furry friends. I knock a few stuffed animals out of the way, and reach my hand behind the bench to fetch it. I can tell from the thickness of the paper that it's actually a photograph. Once recovered, I look down at it cheerfully, expecting it to be an old picture of me and my friends. However, five totally different faces stare back at me from the aged photograph. They are all gloriously youthful, jovial and beautiful.

To the far left, I recognize what looks to be a young Chris. He looked so handsome, strong and carefree. Even back then his brown hair was clean cut, yet I can see a hint of boyish charm in his gleaming smile. His face is turned towards a slim, gorgeous blonde. Donna. It's strange how much she hasn't changed over the years. In the photo her hair is longer, and her skin is luminescent, almost like porcelain. Chris is looking at her lovingly and it appears that she is laughing, her eyes closed and head tilted back just a bit. She's happy, and I can almost feel her loving spirit exuding from the picture.

Next to Donna is the most stunning woman I've ever seen. Her long chocolate brown hair falls in deep waves down her back and her skin is the color of fresh cream. She is smiling brightly and her startling golden eyes hold immense ardor as she cradles her round, bulging belly. A large, masculine hand also embraces her pregnant stomach, the hand of the striking, caramel-colored man standing next to her. He, too, is smiling, and I can't help but be in awe at his exquisite beauty. His thick, black hair stands in tiny coils and his full lips are fenced by a neat goatee. His most attractive feature is the contrast of his hauntingly light eyes against his copper skin. I've never seen the combination before and it's breathtaking. The dazzling couple is obviously in love. And they seem overjoyed at the prospect of welcoming a new baby into their lives.

Their faces remind me of someone. They remind me of myself. The almond shape of the woman's golden eyes. Her heart-shaped face. Her long wavy tresses. The man's button nose. His dark hair.

This is Natalia and Alexander. My parents–the Dark Hunter of the Light Enchanters and the Dark One from the Shadow. It's hard for me to believe that I was conceived by such amazingly beautiful people. Their looks are otherworldly, astonishing, causing me to gasp in admiration.

I wish I could cherish this moment and enjoy seeing the faces of my birth parents for the first time. But their overwhelming beauty and their obvious affection for each other and their unborn daughter is overshadowed by another staggering discovery in the picture. Standing next to my father, Alex, stands a tall, sculpted figure displaying a seductive half-smile. Olive skin, hair.the color of onyx, and smoldering ice blue irises. He appears to be in his mid-twenties, full of youthful exuberance and delicious danger. Seeing him here makes my heart pound with alarming fervor, and my breathing becomes ragged and shallow.

The alluring man in the photograph is no stranger to me. I know him well, just as he knows every inch of me inside and out.

Dorian.

My Dorian.

And it all becomes crystal clear. What Dorian has been trying to relay to me all along. What I have been trying like hell to run from since my twentieth birthday, still trying to hold on to just a shred of normalcy. He knows who I am. He knows I'm the Dark Light. And the beautiful dream boasting colorful images of love, contentment and a future with the alluring man I so desperately love disintegrates right before my eyes, morphing into a horrifying, bloodcurdling nightmare.

GABRIELLA AND DORIAN'S

SPELLBINDING STORY CONTINUES IN THE
INTENSELY THRILLING SECOND NOVEL OF

THE DARK LIGHT SERIES

THE DARK PRINCE

MARCH 2013

SHOUT OUTS, THANK YOUS & IOUS

Deciding to write a full length novel was probably the craziest decision I've ever made. And while I'd like to believe I am somewhat put together, I know I've had my fair share of harebrained schemes and spontaneous ventures. However, creating The Dark Light series was probably the first thing that ever made sense. And there were a few influential people that stuck it out with me that never gave up no matter how ridiculous I sounded. And without these amazing people Dark Light would still be stuck in my crazy head and keeping me up at night.

My husband has been my rock. Through late nights, endless ramblings and countless glasses of wine, he has always been my biggest supporter. Thank you for letting me be who I am, though it has taken a few years to figure that out. And holding my hand throughout my journey.

I have some ridiculously amazing friends who let me talk incessantly about Gabriella and Dorian, as if they were real people. Because they knew that they were real to me. Thank you, ladies, for your constant support, patience, and genuine friendship. Extra special thanks to Daniela Taylor of Daniela Taylor Photography for all your motivation, dedication and hard work. Not to mention amazing talent. There's no way I could have done this without you. Shout out to Jessica Clark, the first cover model for Dark Light for being so gorgeous, inside and out.

Thank you to Stephanie White of Steph's Cover Design for creating a spectacular cover for Dark Light.

Thank you to my awesome team of beta readers who provided me with great feedback, advice, and lots of encouragement. You made me believe that I could actually do this. Your belief in this project means the world. Special thanks to Shenae Pruitt for all the inspiring chats and helping me weave through all the ins and outs of the literary world.

Shout out to Jess Afshar at Mimi and Chichi for all the style inspiration and promotion, as well as Chris Newberry at The Sweeter the Juice for his wonderful friendship and support.

Immense thanks to all the fans and readers that took a chance on a literary unknown. Your support is so awesome.

Most importantly, thank you God, for giving me an overactive imagination, an insane passion for writing, and the ability to share my story with the world.

And to all my friends, family members, and supporters that I may have missed, know that you were all instrumental in the development of Dark Light. Thank you for being an inspiration.

xoxo,

S.

ABOUT THE AUTHOR

S.L. Jennings is a wife and mother of three. Her husband is a member of the United States Air Force and they currently live overseas in Germany. While *Dark Light* is her very first full-length novel, she has always had an unshakeable love for writing short stories, poetry and music since childhood. She hopes to continue to share her passion for writing and entertaining with *The Dark Light series* and her contemporary romance novel, *Fear of Falling*.

For more info, visit:

http://www.facebook.com/authorsljennings

http://www.facebook.com/darklightseries

http://www.goodreads.com/SLJennings

Twitter: MrsSLJ

Made in the USA
Lexington, KY
05 May 2013